FLYWATER

AN M.D. BONNER NOVEL

FLYWATER

AN M.D. BONNER NOVEL

MARK LEE STOIA

FLYWATER
AN M.D. BONNER NOVEL

iUniverse books may be ordered through booksellers or by contacting:

iUniverse
1663 Liberty Drive
Bloomington, IN 47403
www.iuniverse.com
1-800-Authors (1-800-288-4677)

ISBN: 978-1-4917-9767-9 (sc)
ISBN: 978-1-4917-9768-6 (e)

Library of Congress Control Number: 2016910096

Print information available on the last page.

iUniverse rev. date: 06/17/2016

In loving memory of Katy Lee and Mark Dylan who left this world early, but they will never be forgotten and remain in my heart forever.

Special thanks to: Susan Edlinger, Jack Stevens, Donna Thompson, Karla Vento, and Kristie Hazelwood for reading the manuscript during its development, and Mitchell LaFrance for his work on the front cover. I am most grateful to Vivian Leigh Hamilton for her friendship and encouragement after the devastating loss of my children.

FOLLOW THE LEADER

ONE

T he rogue military trained assassin understood the importance of sleep to detoxify his body and rested on the day of a mission. Usually, the confidence that came from having an airtight plan was enough for him to rest with minimal pre-mission anxiety. However, this assignment was personal and tainted with a decades-old obsession for revenge.

The army's training taught him, an exhausted mind could be as lethal as a fatigued body, but he couldn't stop the obsessive thoughts that consumed him from the day he heard the identity of his next target. Against his better judgment and out of desperation, he reluctantly took a sleeping pill and began to pace while he waited for it to kick in. He was so weak, that even walking was an arduous task. His arms hung heavy, and after a few steps, he collapsed face-first onto a giant ball of bedding, ripped from the mattress during his previous attempt at sleep. He rolled onto his back, closed his puffy red eyes, and tried to concentrate on the only positive thought he could muster, the time had finally come for the vengeance he wanted and the retribution he needed.

The professional killer known only as "Just Carl" replayed the major events that shaped his life. The recurring memories were always the same; they began in his college days and ended in the jungles of Vietnam.

While attending the University of Oklahoma in the late 1960's, Carl and his closest friend Julio, were political activists, a rarity in the Bible belt at the time. Before enrolling at the politically naive college in the

"Sooner" state, they had been members of the SDS, a Berkeley-based student organization that trained them in the art of political unrest. Over the two years Carl and Julio were in training, the Students for a Democratic Society suffered many beat downs by overzealous police and National Guard troops at what were supposed to be nonviolent student protests. Disillusioned, they left the SDS to join the more radical, and often violent, spin-off group known as the Weather Underground and called, *Weathermen*. When the violence increased, and many of their leaders were under federal investigation, the group changed to a more appropriate name, the Underground. As the investigations turned to incarcerations, Carl convinced Julio it was time to leave California or face an eventual arrest.

Both young men were specialists at instigating violent chaos in the name of political change. Julio served as a logistics man in the protest planning, while Carl earned a reputation as the preeminent bomb builder.

Several days after a peaceful student sit-in turned violent, a brash young female FBI agent conducted a raid on a house used by Underground members and arrested Carl. She showed him a photo, taken with a zoom lens, of two men on the university's library roof. The picture revealed their identity and location adjacent to the National Guard Armory when it exploded in flames. Written beneath the photo were the names, Carl A. Perkins, AKA "Cap", and a local homegrown activist, M.D. Bonner, AKA "Bonn."

The morning of the FBI's raid, an unsuspecting Julio lay asleep in his bedroom, unaware of what his roommate had done. Even though Julio denied culpability in the bombing, he was guilty by association. Unable to find any warrants for young Julio, the overzealous female rookie trumped up a "harboring a fugitive" charge on him since his name was on the lease. The judge offered Carl and Julio the same option, prison time or join the army.

They decided to roll the dice and see if they could get a military job that would keep them off the front lines. Unfortunately, like most of the young men who were entering under forced enlistment, they ended up serving in the jungles and rice paddies of Vietnam. However, Bonn was able to avoid arrest and leave the state. At the time of his arrest and incarceration, Julio was engaged to his high school sweetheart, and unknown to either of them, a son would be born eight months later while he served his country.

At the start of the Tet Offensive, the largest North Vietnamese offensive of the war, Corporal C. Perkins was the only member of an already depleted squadron who had cross-trained as a weapons *and* munitions specialist. The death of two ranking officers left him in command; his first mission required someone with his training as an explosives expert.

On an oppressively humid and moonlit night, he chose his friend Julio to assist him in setting charges of TNT on a bridge used by the North Vietnamese to cross into South Vietnam. After rigging the explosives, they hunkered down in a makeshift foxhole and listened to the low rumble of tanks coming from the advancing communist troops.

"This is perfect, just perfect," Carl said. "I'm going to blow the bridge, and when the gooks who are waiting their turn to cross, take off runnin', set off all those surprises you planted around the staging area."

Carl's eyes rolled white as he danced in a circle and clapped with the enthusiasm of a teenager until he heard the trembling voice of Julio praying.

"Julio, don't you worry, we're going to make it out of here, just like we did during those protests at OU when the 'pigs' were coming at us. This time, we get to fight back."

"Yeah, let's…uh…, kill…every one of those gooks," Julio said nervously, looking in all directions for an approaching enemy.

"Listen amigo, do you hear what I hear?" Carl whispered.

"Que? I don't hear nuthin'."

"Exactly, I don't hear anything either. It is too quiet, no birds, monkeys…, not a sound. They're close." Carl said.

Julio raised his rifle and searched through its scope until the barrel began to shake.

"Relax Julio. We're going to make it out of here. We need to make it back home so we can kill that traitor."

"What *choo* mean?"

"Bonn's the reason our asses are in this hellhole, that bastard narc'd us out to the Feds," Carl said, angrily. "The bitch that busted us had a picture of me and Bonn that they took right before the Armory blew up. She suckered me into thinking Bonn already confessed and he wasn't going to take the blame for the bomb."

"Choo did that to the Armory?" Julio asked, surprised.

"You're damn right I did! If…*when* we get out of here and back home, I'm going to hunt him down and make him pay for what he did to us," Carl spoke, furiously.

Julio never had the chance to respond, he collapsed from a direct hit to his spine. Through the mist, hundreds of Viet Cong soldiers swarmed out the jungle, unleashing a swath of bullets that decimated everything in their path.

Before the enemy overran them, Carl pulled Julio's limp body on top of his and played the opossum ruse. The North Vietnamese soldiers pushed past the piles of dead and dismembered American troops littering the landscape. Just when Carl thought he had successfully fooled the enemy, a Viet Cong regular, indiscriminately began shooting the wounded and dead. Julio awoke in time to place a dead center shot to the soldier's forehead, then blacked out again.

While cradling his friend, Carl blew the bridge, dozens of unsuspecting enemy soldiers fell to a watery grave. When the personnel that had congregated at the foot of the bridge, turned to escape en mass, Carl grabbed Julio's magneto detonator. He pushed the plunger and engulfed the enemy in a blazing inferno as lines of strategically placed charges ignited the surrounding jungle and blocked any possible retreat.

Carl carried his brother-in-arms over his shoulder to a pick-up zone for extraction, but he never shared the true story of what happened. Corporal Carl A. Perkins received a battlefield promotion to the rank of *Major* and awarded the Bronze Star. At the end of the war, Carl never made the transition to civilian life. Instead, he worked with the Army as a "specialist of acute action" in the world of paramilitary operatives.

Julio woke up in a field hospital paralyzed physically and emotionally when he heard that his condition was permanent. He didn't remember shooting the North Vietnamese soldier, especially with a dead center to the forehead; he was convinced Carl had saved *his* life. When he returned to the States and discovered his high school sweetheart had given birth to a son while he was in Vietnam, they married. Julio remained a paraplegic from the waist down and his physical disability got worse from the paralysis of alcoholism. As his disease worsened over the years, he would tell the story of his college days to anyone who would listen.

Unfortunately, his son was the only person who paid attention to his rants. Repeatedly, he made his son promise to one day "find that traitor Bonner…, and kill him."

Eventually, Julio's rage turn violent and his wife filed for divorce. After twenty-five years confined to a wheelchair, broken and despondent, Julio turned his service weapon on himself.

TWO

J ulio Diaz Jr. became a successful attorney and devoted his time to the advancement of the Latino community. Unlike his father's decision to fight the establishment, he hoped to evoke political change from within, and ran for mayor of Tallahassee.

After winning the mayoral seat, the State's GOP leaders recognized him as a viable minority candidate that would fast track to a higher office. Before the end of his first term as mayor, he won the republican nomination for United States Senator from Florida, by a landslide. The Latino community, active duty military personnel, veterans, and NRA members came out in droves to show their support. Pro-military businesses across NW Florida, not only encouraged their employees to vote for Diaz, they opened their pocketbooks to his campaign. However, the financial support of a major Defense Contractor, gave him the political war chest he needed to win. Julio understood, at some point, he would be asked to reimburse the contractor but he didn't hear from his backers during his entire first term as a United States Senator.

Senator Julio Diaz Jr. spent his first five years making friends in Congress and developing contacts among the elite defense contractors. His networking skills earned him the reputation as a rising star and helped him become the newest member of the Armed Services Committee; an honor usually reserved for well-established politicians. His selection put him in a position of power where his voice and vote could make a difference. But it was his vote that his major contributor expected in return for their support. The day after Senator Diaz received a call from his largest supporter, pledging their continued support for his re-election, he decided to kickoff his campaign in the Florida Panhandle, at Eglin AFB.

While cruising in his limo on Interstate 10 from Tallahassee to Fort Walton Beach, the home of Eglin, his campaign manager gave him the particulars of the day's agenda, "Senator, your day will begin at a Change of Command ceremony for Eglin's first female commander. It will be an event for the press to take pictures of you shaking hands with...Colonel Cari Bentow. I hear she's a real looker, but tough as nails."

"If I get the support of the women *and* the military, we both get to keep our jobs," Senator Diaz said. "You know how much I love women."

"Senator, you'll be going to a 'meet and greet' at the Officer's Club before your fundraising dinner. That will be a good time to spend some time with her. I don't need to tell you how important it will be to have a few photos taken with the new commander, and it will also be an opportunity to glad-hand the 'big wigs' representing the Defense Contractors."

Diaz confidently said, "I've already been called by one of them and I have a feeling the others will be seeking *me* out. When do I tell everyone how great they are and ask for their support?"

"You'll be able to say anything you want after we fatten them up with prime rib and loosen their checkbooks at the open bar," his campaign manager said. "Before you're introduced, you will have to listen to another one of those dreaded patriotic speeches; it will be given by a Major..., Major McCain."

"Who's introducing me?" Senator Diaz asked.

"Since Military Affairs is paying for the dinner...their Chairman, General Bonner is going to do the introductions. I hear, this guy is a big wig...I'm sure you'll meet him before dinner."

The moment Senator Diaz heard the name, a wave of nausea overcame him. After so many years wondering if he would be able to keep the promise he made to his father, the time had finally come to meet the man he believed responsible for his father's pain and eventual suicide.

"Senator, are you okay?" his assistant asked.

"What? Yes, I'm fine," Senator Diaz, said while shaking his head.

"Excuse me for saying; you look like you've just seen a ghost. If you're fine, why are you shaking your head? I've been with you for four and half years, and I can tell when there's something wrong. The moment I told you who would be introducing you, your color went from Latino brown to pearly white. Senator, is there a problem with General Bonner?"

"I'm not sure. Is he my age?"

"I don't think so; he's retired and from your father's generation. Sir, I haven't met him…, would prefer someone else?"

Although he vowed revenge, and knew his father's story by heart, Senator Diaz wanted to find Major Perkins first, and have him confirm that General Bonner was the traitor who went by the name "Bonn".

Special Agent Sienna Harris sat motionless in the front seat of Senator Diaz's limo and listened intently to the conversation. The tailored black suit she wore was the standard uniform preferred by the Agency. Traditionally, a black suit was the perfect camouflage, almost to the point of making agents invisible in the mass of business suits surrounding the politicians they protected.

Agent Harris never highlighted her petite, athletic build by wearing a skirt. If she did, it would show off her muscular legs and make her stand out. She also kept her long, strawberry blonde hair pulled back in a tight bun; it gave her the constant expression of a serious professional.

Senator Diaz spoke freely around her; she wouldn't have it any other way. After all, anything an agent overheard in a meeting or private conversation had to remain confidential. She used the gullibility of even the most hardened and experienced politicians to accumulate a wealth of information that she could use in the future.

Unexpectedly, Senator Diaz broke away from the conversation with his campaign manager and said, "Driver, take this exit and gas up. I would like to speak with Agent Harris, privately."

While the driver put fuel in the limo, Senator Diaz excused his manger to the limo's front seat and then put up the glass partition inside the vehicle. Confident they had complete privacy; the senator spoke reverently as he told her the story of his father's experiences in Vietnam.

"Sir, your story is touching, but I have to ask, why are you sharing this with me?" Agent Harris asked.

"I'm in need of your help. I need to locate the soldier who saved my father's life," Diaz said with a raised eyebrow. "I need to do it as discreetly as possible".

Agent Harris did an extensive search of classified military databases and found an Agency profile for an off-the-grid operative on the agency's computer. Surprisingly, the soldier lived in Florida and he still worked with the military. She bypassed his military handler and arranged a secret meeting between Major Perkins and the senator.

When they first met on an isolated beach, Senator Diaz was a little hesitant to believe anything coming from a longhaired, unshaven man, who reeked of marijuana. Diaz changed his opinion, when the soldier, who fought with his father in the jungles of Vietnam, revealed who the real hero was that fateful day.

The only person, not touched by the story was sunbathing and wearing the Agency's latest high-tech earphones that allowed her to hear the conversation from a considerable distance away.

"There's one more thing, this is for you," Carl said and presented the Senator with the Bronze Star he received decades ago.

"You're not what I envisioned," Senator Diaz said without trying to insult Carl.

"I'm not what a lot of people envision, that's the way I like it."

"When I was a boy, and heard you saved my father's life, I thought you would be eight feet tall with the physique of a bodybuilder."

Senator Diaz didn't get a read on Carl's silence. "I want to avenge my father's death. I know where the traitor he called 'Bonn' lives…"

Carl stepped close and quietly said, "Important people are very dangerous, and…quite expensive."

Senator Diaz went to one knee and wrote in the sand an amount that brought a nod instead of a handshake.

"Well, we have the most important detail worked out. I'll also need a clean passport and a place to lay low after the job is done."

"Walk with me, I've come prepared," Senator Diaz said, and then began walking down the beach. Quickly, the reception for the Agency's earphones diminished until there was only static, whatever the senator wrote in the sand, washed away by the waves.

Diaz handed Carl a small beach bag filled with bundles of hundred dollar bills and two clear plastic tubes that held a couple of dozen gold coins in each.

"That should be enough cash to live comfortably until you complete the job, the Krugerrands can be your international currency. I'll deposit the balance at completion."

"There's one more thing…, when I take out that bastard, I'll use the shot your father used to kill that Gook in Nam'."

"What do I call you?" Diaz asked.

"Cap, just…, Cap."

PART ONE

FAILURE IS NOT AN OPTION

CHAPTER 1

T he National Computer Security Center at the NSA headquarters stirred with excitement and speculation. The Director, who also served as Chief of the Central Security Service and the Commander of U S Cyber Command, had not come to the Agency Research and Development lab alone. An entourage of men dressed in the BDU's of their military branch, flanked him on both sides. The group of dignitaries marched in perfect military step into the massive room filled with televisions on the walls and a computer on every desk.

A lone female CIA agent stood on an elevated platform at the base of the main display wall. She wore the standard black suit of field agents and the intensity of a veteran. She wasn't intimidated by the military presence and kept her gaze straightforward as she stood in front of a massive wall-mounted flat screen television. With the tone of a drill sergeant, she began explaining the purpose of their unconventional meeting with the Director.

"Gentlemen, welcome," Agent Sienna Harris said to the stone-faced men without identifying herself. "As you know, one of the responsibilities of the CSS is to facilitate cryptanalysis components between the military and the National Security Agency. The subversive software we develop at Central Security Service has in the past, been primarily used to locate foreign targets for elimination."

The expressions on the men didn't change, and she knew they weren't going to anytime soon. "Officially, the tracking programs are *not* used domestically. However, whenever a new tool is developed in our intelligence community, we believe it's paramount to share that technology with all the branches of the Armed Forces. The Director will explain today's meeting further and answer questions."

The NSA Director stepped next to Agent Harris to address each military representative individually and collectively, then made eye contact with each one of them. Since he had never met them, he wanted to ensure he remembered each one; the visual connection helped him place a face with each name.

"We have a new war on what is becoming the world's new battlefield; I'm talking about the cyber war. In case you don't already know how serious the NSA takes the threats coming from the tech world, I want you to look around. We have the representatives from the Navy Fleet Cyber Command, the Army Intelligence and Security, our Marine Corps Director of Intel, the Air Force's Intel, Surveillance and Reconnaissance Agency, and lastly, the Coast Guard's newest Commandant. Your men and women are the frontline defense, and when necessary, the offense against all cyber attacks by any country or terrorist organization against the United States and out allies," When the Director finished his patriotic speech and took one-step back.

As each head nodded in agreement, Agent Harris stepped forward and signaled to a ponytailed young man in a white lab coat to join them. His name badge identified him as J.J., a civilian contractor with a top-level security clearance. At first glance, he had the appearance of the stereotypical computer nerd, but if he removed the thick black glasses sliding down his nose, some women might consider him handsome.

Although she only knew him by reputation, she said, "Gentlemen, I would like to introduce J.J., our resident IT genius."

J.J. raised a hand and waved a timid acknowledgement to the line of smirks prejudging him, then nonchalantly swiped a finger across a bling-covered cell phone and watched all five military skeptics flinch when their cell phones vibrated. While a few reached for their phones, the Coast Guard representative remained motionless, unfazed by the distraction.

J.J. let out a muted chuckle. "I'm pleased that each of you kept to regulations and put your cell phones on silent when you entered the building. Go ahead and look at them."

The military men, except for one, retrieved their phones and acted confused when they looked at the screen. The Coast Guard Commandant hit his mute button without taking it out of his pocket and pursed his lips in an obvious display of agitation.

"Admiral, you didn't answer or even look at your phone. Are you aware of the regulation requiring you to not only be in possession of your Government Issue cell phone, you're supposed to answer…" The Director appeared to be agitated as well.

"Sir, yes sir! I'll answer it right now."

"Before you do, may I ask why you chose not to see who's calling?"

"Sir, I hate to be controlled by phones and computers. I make a conscious effort *not* to instantly grab my cell when it rings."

"Admiral, I totally understand your frustration with all of the modern communication devices, but we need to come into this century and learn to accept, or at least cope with them," J.J. said. "My father taught me that knowledge is power, and power comes from information. If we collect the right data, we have influence over our enemies. Now if you would…"

A chorus of expletives interrupted J.J.'s lecture: "What the hell?", "Is this some kind of damn joke?", and "I thought these phones were secure." The room buzzed as the normally cool, calm, and reserved officers showed each other the screens of their cell phones and cussed the very technology they worked with every day.

J.J. removed his glasses quickly, reminiscent of Clark Kent becoming Superman, and asked, "Gentlemen, could I have your attention? Will each of you please tell me what is on your phone?"

"There's a photo of *Putin* riding a horse with his shirt off. I didn't need to see that!"

"*Obama* is on mine and he's smoking a cigarette or something."

"I don't have a picture, I have our slogans: 'Semper Fi.', 'The Few, The Proud.', and…what the hell…, '*Ooh Rah*'?"

The Air Force colonel held his phone out in front of him and showed his screen, just to make a point. "I have a photo of Sarah Palin in the nude! This is exactly what the Coast Guard commander talked about; no matter what we do, our phones and computers receive this kind of unwanted junk."

"Do you know who sent it to you?" J.J. asked, even though he knew the phones had same the sender, UNKNOWN.

While they shared the images on each other's screen, the messages began to fade; they looked to J.J. who was beaming with the pride of a new father in a maternity ward.

"Get ready to witness the newest 'App' in undetectable communication. Shortly, the pictures be completely gone and if you'll look at the 'leathernecks' phone, you'll see the captions disappear as well." J.J. knew instantly, that calling the Marine by the organization's old nickname came across as disrespectful and inappropriate.

Fortunately, there wasn't time for them to dwell on his tactless use of the Marine Corps' moniker. The captions on the Marine's screen started disappearing one letter at a time until they were also gone.

Before his "geek" could speak again, the NSA Director jumped in with an explanation. "The photos and captions aren't the only things that have disappeared. There is nothing in your phone's message history that shows the call ever took place. The encryption programming allows it to be undetected; you will actually be going dark. In addition, once it's answered, you'll have complete access to everything on that person's phone. You will own that phone and be able to listen to every call."

"He doesn't know the half of it," J.J. mumbled.

The Agent Harris grabbed J.J.'s elbow with a vise grip and growled a deep-throated question:

"What did you say?"

J.J. almost went to his knees. "I said he couldn't wait to *have* it.'"

"Our young and *disrespectful* computer whiz has developed a roaming and rotating algorithm like none we have ever seen before," Agent Harris said. "I've turned it over to our in-house think tank to come up with as many possible clandestine uses as they can."

The Director stopped and put his hands on his hips. He appeared to have transformed into a much larger person and imposing figure ready to make a point.

"The project has a Top Security clearance level and the existence of this app is for Domestic clearances only. It is paramount not to discuss this project with anyone who isn't directly involved with the program, especially not with anyone who works in our foreign operations. Can you imagine if it fell into the hands of a terrorist government?"

Agent Harris chimed in with the Agency's stance. "I can't begin to tell you how important it is for this software to remain with-in this group. It is code named **BYE BYE**. Officially, it's designated as a *need-to-know*, there are no exceptions. If anyone asks you about the program, you will deny any knowledge and report the incident directly to me. Are there any questions?"

After a grueling Q and A about the software's inception and reliability, J.J. digressed and went on a rant about how *his* program could change the balance of power. When he finished and waited for an affirmation of his work, he heard, "hippie nerd".

The mood in the room turned cold when J.J. tried to sell his cunning as intelligence when he said, "*My* program will let you communicate with your operatives and attack them without a trace. Since there isn't any digital imprint, trying to map where the call came from is impossible. If anyone tries to run a trace of the towers used, the results will show the signal bounced off multiple towers at the same time. Tracking will be impossible."

J.J. paused again for questions that never came and said,

"I want to elaborate. Once the person you're calling, answers their phone or opens a text message that you've sent, you'll have real-time access to: every call, text, email, web search, and social media activity that comes to and away from that phone. More importantly, their contact list becomes yours. If you use the app properly, your call or text message can be identified as anyone you choose from their contact list. I can teach *any* novice how to use the **BYE BYE** software, in ways you can't imagine." J.J.'s time ended the instant he qualified the level of their technical skills.

The mood in the room shifted as a few clenched their fists and a voice called out, "Son, you need a lesson in respect."

Although J.J. couldn't identify the speaker, it didn't matter, someone else said, "We've been able intercept every phone number, email account and text for years, there is nothing new here and this is a waste of my time. Our cyber weapons are already able to attack and shut down factories, power plants, and even the Arab pipelines. You're an amateur hacker and listening to you is a waste of time."

Before J.J. disclosed the newest function of his software, the men broke rank and started milling toward the door.

The Director whispered to AIC Harris, "I never want to see that arrogant, son-of-a-bitch again. I don't trust him and I want you to find out everything you can about that weirdo. If he sends or receives an email, track it. If he does an internet search, I need to know what he's researching, even if its porn. Make sure our metadata collection software gives me every bit of information about him that it can; something isn't right with him. Since you're the Agent in Charge, I expect results and I want it yesterday. Am I clear?"

J.J. heard the whispers and felt disrespected. Therefore, he made the decision not to reveal its most important capability and he sell the software to the highest bidder. J.J. returned to his office, and while sitting in front of the bank of flat screen televisions that served as computer monitors, he tapped in a series of numbers on his bling-covered cell phone. After repeating the process four more times, the current real-time activity of each military representative's phone appeared on the agency's screens. J.J. laughed aloud as he keyed-in on the conversation between the Coast Guard's Vice-Admiral and his mistress.

J.J. stood in front of the mounted TV and said, "All of you think there's 'something not right' with me? By the time I get through, you'll be working as janitors."

J.J. typed in a number and with-in seconds, a live video feed from the camera of the Director's phone appeared on the largest of the screens. He watched the NSA boss snap to full attention, answer his phone; "Mr. President." J.J. disconnected his call and watched his nemesis try to figure out why the President would call him and hang up.

"Can we talk or are you having an important conversation with yourself?" Agent Harris said, and watched all the screens go black, but not before she saw the live feed capability of J.J.'s software.

"Do all agents learn how to sidle up on people at Quantico? What can I do for you?" J.J. asked and unsuccessfully tried to slip his bedazzled phone in his pocket.

Agent Harris pretended she hadn't noticed J.J.'s shutdown.

"I would like to apologize for the comments. They are all pricks and anyone not in uniform are beneath them. That includes a man with a genius IQ, who I think is a visionary."

"You obviously want something. No one, especially an agent with the CIA, shovels outs compliments like that without an ulterior motive; what do you want?" he asked.

"J.J., my assessment of you is accurate and you know it. Yes, I do have an ulterior motive, but it's not what you think. I should have said, 'we' would like to apologize. I'm talking about the agency I work for, not the NSA; I'm referring to the Central Intelligence Agency."

"So what, you don't work for him. I don't care. Whatever it is you're selling, I don't want any," J.J. said and crossed his arms.

"I understand your skepticism, but I'm not selling anything. We believe the Director is wasting your talent, and since you are a contractor, and you don't officially work for the Agency, *we* are wondering if you would consider coming to work for us. I'm not talking about working as a contractor, I'm talking about as an agent," she said, and watched him twitch. "You would need training, but we can fast track most of it. I don't need an answer today. I want you to think about it. If you have an interest, give me a call."

When J.J. finished reading the information on the card and looked up, he was alone. Immediately, he went to the hallway and caught a glimpse of the female agent leaving the facility with her cell phone pressed against her ear.

J.J. regretted not including her phone during the software demonstration, if he had, he would have heard:

"Yes sir…He may be a computer whiz kid, but he's not very bright if he thinks his stupid app is revolutionary. Yes sir, as soon as its mine, it's yours," Agent Harris said while standing at attention.

"I'll make sure it gets used…yes sir; all available resources will be used to blame him…yes sir, 'misdirection'. No sir, it won't get into terrorist hands…, if he offers to sell, he will be eliminated," she said, checking her watch.

"Sir, I expect a call from him any minute. No sir, I'll have to call you from a new secure…roger that…, exactly 1200 hours, three rings, terminate, and call right back."

Agent Harris smiled when, as soon as she finished her call, her phone rang with an incoming call. The only person with her cell phone's number was the man she gave her custom-made business card to only minutes before. "J.J., I'm glad you called."

CHAPTER 2

etired General M.D. "Bonn" Bonner awoke seconds before his alarm clock started blaring heavy metal music in the very early, pre-dawn hours. Although he rarely needed an alarm, he had set the dial to *WDMM 99 Metal Mania* for a wakeup call that would hit him like an espresso jolt. The sporadic slumber came between exasperating glances at the clock's red LED numbers that glowed brightly as they advanced from minutes to hours at a snail's pace. In truth, he needed an alarm as much as a third wife; they were both rude awakenings he wanted to avoid. However, it was opening day of spring hunting season and his passion as a hunter bordered on being an obsession. Since childhood, the night before a hunting trip, sleep remained as elusive as the game he would be hunting.

The early wake time was necessary if he wanted to arrive at his favorite hunting spot in the pine forest, twenty-five miles north of his Florida beachfront home, before sunrise. The military taught him to be obsessed with time and preparedness. So, before he went to bed, he lined up his camo clothing, boots, and gear.

The kitchen counter had its own evidence of a timesaving ritual. The line started with his Air Force blue mug next to a full pot of coffee that had been set to begin brewing at the same time as his alarm. After pouring what Bonn considered the most important part of breakfast, he reached for the loaf of bread that leaned against the toaster, and lastly, the bowl next to a box of cereal.

This compulsive attention to detail had been essential in his military career and became part of his pre-hunt routine. Bonn insisted his ritual wasn't necessarily something he did to improve his chance to kill an animal. In his military career, Bonn had killed more times than he wanted to remember, his dreams never let him forget the devastating feeling that overcame him every time he took a life. This day, the tables were turned, and he would be the hunted.

The drowsiness brought on by the morning's warm rays and a sleepless night vanished when the vibration of his cell phone made him jump. The screen showed a *NEW MULTIMEDIA MESSAGE* and identified the caller as *UNKNOWN*. To his surprise, it included an attachment, which turned out to be a picture of a "friend" from his past and included the message, *Flywater*. Although they had been intimate, he hadn't seen her in many years. The last he heard, she worked for one of the government's intelligence agencies as a field agent. Bonn furrowed his brow at the ex-girlfriend's 'selfie' she captioned with his family's safe word and a code that would never have been shared with her.

While he remained transfixed, the photo began to shrink to a pinpoint and left the screen with a distinctive, *POP.* After the photo's disappearance, the message slowly started to leave, one letter at a time. Irritated by the possibility of having to buy another cell phone, he tapped the screen several times, and then slapped it on his palm. Not only had the entire message gone away, after he did an extensive search, the phone's message history didn't show any record of ever receiving the text.

Bonn perceived the bizarre event as an omen to end the morning's hunt. To ensure he had enough time for a quick stop to have his malfunctioning cell phone checked out and still make it to his daily briefing, he left. While walking in an open field, half way back to his vehicle, the rustling of leaves coming from the edge of the tree line caught his attention. Bonn instinctively froze mid step and turned his hearing up a notch. Instinctively, the survival technique he used in the rice paddies of Vietnam and the jungles of Central America kicked in. His training taught him to focus on the shadows when trying to detect movement of the enemy; the dark will turn to light. When he scanned the area, the only movement came from his eyes.

He needed to make a decision, if he had walked up on game unseen, he could either harvest it quickly or keep walking and hunt another day. The choice was simple; nothing had changed in his fifty-plus years. He wasn't out for a leisurely round of golf at the country club; the only birdies he ever shot were with a shotgun. After a quick glance at his watch, he whispered at an inaudible level, "Why not?"

As he started to leave, Bonn's eyes slashed to the snap of a twig and focused on the shadows. There, in a split second, and in contrast to the stationary forms marked by shadows, several glints of light appeared. The intuitive instincts that came with being a hunter allowed him to sense an animal before actually seeing it, a presence. As slowly as possible, he eased to one knee, shouldered his shotgun, and began the hunting process: Identify, focus, and shoot. Unfortunately, he never made it to identify.

CHAPTER 3

During the 1980's, when the DEA, Coast Guard and law enforcement concentrated their efforts at stopping the importation of drugs in south Florida, Carl took the Panhandle's northern route and amassed a small fortune. Drug cartels renamed the panhandle of Florida, the "Redneck Riviera". The illegal importation of drugs expanded from the coastal city of Jacksonville on the Atlantic Coast to New Orleans on the northern Gulf Coast; Interstate 10 served as a mainland transportation route.

When searching for illegal drug shipments coming in by water, law enforcement targeted the major ports of New Orleans, Mobile, and Jacksonville. Destin's East Pass, which sat in the middle of Florida's panhandle, was unguarded. The area, used by thousands of anglers and boating enthusiasts, became the perfect gateway for local drug smugglers to unload their shipments. However, as the cartels grew, and the locals were forced out, the Agency shifted its limited manpower to the secondary ports of Destin and Pensacola. By the time their dragnets were capable of intercepting the major cartel shipments into Destin, most of the local dealers had made their fortunes and disappeared into the city's growing economic explosion.

North Florida's Panhandle became the new destination for the Mexican Cartel's illicit drug trade operating in the Southeastern United States. By the time the cartels took control of the market, a select group of locals from Destin to Pensacola had already made their fortunes and reinvested their drug money in waterfront property, seafood restaurants, and nightclubs. Early on, Carl and few of his friends from his early days in the army posed as fishermen. They fished their way to Mexico where they unloaded their catch then filled their cargo holds with enough illicit drugs to make up for the shortage created by the drug busts in south Florida's *Miami Vice* scene.

The largest portion of Carl's drug money financed the construction of the building that became Niceville's newest business. The mayor welcomed Carl to the community during a ribbon cutting ceremony, sponsored by the Niceville Chamber of Commerce. During his speech, the mayor recognized the various business owners and members of his administration, including his selection for the new Chief of Police. Ironically, Chief Barnes used his introduction to lay out his plans for the community and included a spin on solving Niceville's criminal problems with a new Anti-Drug campaign. He made his promise to clean up the city's drug problem while standing above one of the largest marijuana growing facilities in the area.

The smartest *ex*-dealers became part of the political, business, and social community as well-respected citizens. Carl's persona as an upstanding business owner, disguised his illegal drug operation. His mother, wife, friends, and workers were oblivious to his real identity as a Paramilitary operative, who had been off the grid and called back into service.

Beachside Landscaping used a geographical liberty that's a common practice among Florida Panhandle businesses when they christened their ventures into American capitalism. The owners, Carl and Paula Perkins, didn't hesitate to imply their business was on the beach and not fifteen miles north of the actual coastline. The closest beach to their office encircled a muddy cattle pond across the highway from their building. The mansions built on the ten-mile sliver of sugar white sand beaches in the tourist town of Destin had their lavish lawns groomed by his workers every week, whether they needed it or not. The wealthy Florida homeowners didn't care what the "Mexican gardeners" called their company, as long as they kept their lawns manicured.

The headquarters for Beachside Landscaping was a whitewashed, one story and cinder block building with enough storage space for everything they needed to care for the lawns of the rich Floridians. The weathered and rust stained exterior stood in stark contrast to the Sunset Orange, Turquoise Blue, and Sea Foam Green stucco homes of their clients.

A concrete slab inside the building served as a parking lot for lawn equipment and other pieces of useless machinery in various stages of disarray. There were several riding mowers: a new John Deere EZ-Trek, a 23HP V-Twin Zero-Turn mower for Carl "Boss man" Perkins to ride, and a classic 1970 Simplicity Wonder Boy 600 that everyone simply wondered if it would even start. Parked along one wall was a line of lime-green Lawn Boy self-propelled mowers with stripped gears that needed pushing. Along the adjoining wall were several old Toro Big Wheels brush mowers known for their ability to mow grass or clear a small forest. Each mower had its own flora arraignment of dried palmetto leaves and various plants from the flowerbeds of their clients draped on the starter and throttle cables. Buried beneath a ball of extension cords and leaky hoses, an original Black and Decker electric mower collected dust. The mower's tangled orange power cord had so many rings of black electrical tape from repairs; it resembled a coiled coral snake ready to strike. Various weed eaters, leaf blowers, rakes, shovels, hedge trimmers and gardening tools hung like broken venetian blinds around the building.

Buckets of chemicals, bags of fertilizer, and expensive grass seed were visible through the chicken wire enclosure that surrounded the office. In the center of the caged office, a scarred and whittled wooden desk sat as a monolith from decades past. Its leather padded wooden chair groaned and squeaked whenever Carl's wife Paula, a part owner and manager, sat down.

Her office accessories included an antique pink princess telephone from her childhood, four *Beatles* bobble heads, a *Lava Lamp* filled with green goo, and a collection of framed pictures. In front of her desk, an overstuffed easy chair completed the ambiance she wanted to achieve. Carl's contribution to the décor was a small metal filing cabinet covered with dozens of refrigerator magnets that were pinning her collection of bills to be paid and a dozen lists of things to do.

Carl didn't build the 12'x24' framed wire cage to secure Paula's eclectic office furnishings; it also held the expensive chemicals he used to keep the lawns of his wealthy clients, insect and weed free. Everything looked innocent enough at first glance. Wooden pallets surrounded Paula's desk like the walls of a homemade fort, and bowed from the fifty-pound bags of top soil, manure, and five-gallon containers of herbicides and pesticides piled on them. The not so subtle fragrance coming from the stacks of bagged fertilizer clung to Paula's clothes and permeated the early morning meetings when she handed out the daily work assignments. More importantly to Carl, the scent concealed the unmistakable odor of his illegal marijuana greenhouse hidden below the building.

The throw rug under Paula's massive double wide, imitation leather, Lay-Z-Boy concealed a trap door that led into his sophisticated marijuana growing operation. Paula, also a massive double wide, had never been "down the hole" and claimed claustrophobia as the reason.

On the surface of their shallow relationship, she pretended to be oblivious to her husband's secret business venture. The amount of drug money he laundered through their legitimate business would have shocked her as well as law enforcement. Carl refused to tell Paula exactly how much capital his endeavor generated, if his "toys" were any indication, the amount greatly surpassed the level of income coming from the landscaping business.

The money coming in from the landscaping business paled in comparison to the cash flow from his hydroponic pot growing enterprise. To keep his name out of the I.R.S. computers, Carl put their assets in Paula's name, including the business's bank account and used that account to purchase the best grow lights and irrigation systems available. Equipped with the latest equipment, he maintained an underground forest of several hundred pot plants at various stages of growth.

CHAPTER 4

T he blast from the 12-gauge shotgun shattered the morning's
tranquility and hit the right side of General Bonner's head,
knocking him down like a duck at a shooting gallery. A
second blast shredded small holes through his lightweight cotton
camo jacket, as he lay motionless on the ground. Any hunter with-in
earshot would assume another outdoorsman had succeeded at
putting a wild turkey on the dinner table, and never would imagine
the carnage that had just taken place.

Sprawled out, face down in a field of dried grass, Bonn awoke,
and placed a cupped hand to his head's burning scalp. He managed
to roll over and let out a low moan as he lightly touched the hot
searing flesh of his peppered body. When he tried to open his eyes,
only one would respond. The blue Florida sky from his rapidly
swelling eye had a light crimson coating, and consciousness, disguised
as a peaceful sleep, became a losing battle. After several panicked
attempts to breath, his limited vision blurred to darkness before his
body went limp.

In one urgent gasp, his lungs devoured the crisp spring air that doused
the fire in his breath. A slight degree of consciousness returned long
enough to see strange, red-tinted, passing clouds in what should have
been crisp blue skies.

"What the hell is going on?" he asked aloud, unsure if had
actually spoken. It wouldn't be the last time he found it difficult to
differentiate his words from his thoughts.

Another cool, cleansing breath brought a distorted degree of reality, but any significant clarity of his predicament, remained nonexistent. After propping his body up to a sitting position, his chin dropped and he stared at the blood-soaked camouflage patterns emerging through his hunting clothes. Warm, wet drops of red sweat trickled off the tip of his nose and dotted the belly of his shirt. Puzzled by the crimson tint wherever he looked, he wiped his drenched brow with the back of his hand and discovered it was oozing red streams of blood, not sweat. The gravity of his situation became real as he attempted to stand. Akin to a drunken stumble, General Bonner hit the ground face first as his world went black.

Bonn awoke again, only this time, to the sight of two men dressed in street clothes, standing over him with a look of disbelief on their faces. The larger of the two strangers was as rigid as a cigar store Indian and cradled a shotgun in the crook of his crossed arms. His disheveled, shoulder length and greasy blond hair matched the three-day gray stubble covering his face. The bill of his green John Deere cap shielded and concealed his eyes from the brilliant morning sun but accentuated a strange crusty brown substance in the corners of a twisted smile. His tall and physically imposing presence dwarfed the short, dark-skinned Mexican companion standing next to him.

Although small in stature, his accomplice bore a malicious facade characterized by long, coal-black hair, slicked and tucked behind his ears. He wore beltless gray dress pants that hung precariously on his butt and a white wife-beater T-shirt that was drenched with sweat. The only clean parts of his wardrobe were the white Adidas tennis shoes that completed his wardrobe; both men were dressed in stark contrast to the camouflage clothing used by most hunters.

Bonn made a barely audible plea to who he thought were two Good Samaritans, "I've been shot. I need to get to a hospital."

That's when it happened, the dirty blonde spit a slimy stream of tobacco juice that moistened the brown crust rimming his mouth. He then forced a tobacco-stained smile before saying, "We'll take you." In that moment, Bonn noticed a slightest change of expression, a "tell" in poker. Instantly, the adrenaline pumping through his torn body accelerated and blasted back the pain long enough for him to grasp the reality of the situation, the men were not saviors, he was their prey. Instinctively, as consciousness approached critical mass, and while he lay face down in a coagulated puddle of sand, dirt, and blood, Bonn's fingers tightened to a death grip around his shotgun.

"Did you hear me?" The dirty blond shooter asked then nudged the General's motionless body with the toe of his boot.

When he felt the boot push on his ribs, Bonn rolled over on back and squeezed the vice lock grip on his shotgun so he could raise the barrel. "Drop your gun," Bonn said. "Do it now!"

The shooter raised his hands in surrender. "Whoa, buddy. You've got it all wrong; we're here to help you".

"I'm not your buddy. If you make any sudden moves, I…will… kill you," Bonn said with a weakening voice that trailed off as he struggled to remain conscious. Instead of trying to stand and risk falling again, he was able to kneel and single-handedly shoulder his weapon. Then, with his free hand, he reached for the shooter's gun and pawed at the grass. While patting the ground in a blind search, the sensation of cold steel hit his fingertips. Trying to hold two weapons of considerable weight wasn't an option, so he pitched the shotgun into a dense mass of Palmettos.

The bulbs were waning dim as shock continued to impede his ability to think clearly, he pulled out his cell phone to call 911 and discovered a shattered black screen. Bonn's inability to process rational thoughts kept him from taking the logical step and using one of the attacker's phones to call for help. As he fought off feelings of hopelessness, he was painfully aware of his rapidly depleting strength, the concept of surrender lingered as an option.

"Where's your vehicle?" Bonn asked.

When neither man responded, he wasn't sure if he had spoken loud enough, "Where…is…your vehicle?" The question sounded eerily similar to screaming.

As he struggled to separate the onslaught of cognitive messages, and while teetering on the edge of a dark abyss, Bonn painstakingly forced himself to stand. The persistent shouting intensified his headache to the point where his world began to spin into a retching nausea of coffee colored bile.

After wiping his mouth with an already bloodied sleeve, he simply asked, "Where's truck?"

They answered together by hitching their thumbs towards the woods behind them. When it became obvious, Bonn might be losing his fight with consciousness, they waited to see if he would drop. Through the silence, the unmistakable click of the safety mechanism on Bonn's gun convinced them, he wasn't going to pass out any time soon, and he would shoot if he felt the world going dark again.

"What's your name big man?" Bonn asked and pointed his shotgun at the shooter.

"You don't remember me...*Bonn?*" the shooter asked and spit another brown stream of tobacco juice that splashed on Bonn's boot.

Bonn stiffened and spoke with authority. "You called me 'Bonn'; I've never met you in my life. Who the hell are you?"

Then, as though a monumental reveal was about to take place, the stranger used his index finger to gradually push the bill of his hat up so the sunlight would illuminate his face.

"The name is Carl, just Carl," he said, then raised an eyebrow, smiled, and with the tip of his tongue, licked a crusty deposit of dried tobacco juice from the corner of his mouth.

"Okay, 'Just Carl', here's what's going to happen, both of you are going to walk in front of me with your hands and fingers locked behind your heads," Bonn said. "When we get to your vehicle, you're driving me to the black Explorer you passed driving in here."

The blank stares on their faces had Bonn wondering if he had been unconscious with his eyes open and only thought he had spoken, "Do you understand? Comprende?"

Simple nods sufficed for an answer. They walked single-file on a worn game trail through the palmetto and pine forest, hands and fingers loosely wrapped together behind their heads. Bonn, who was staggering a safe distance behind, stopped abruptly when he spotted two pickups less than fifty feet away.

One was an older model coated with a camo-green paint job; the other, new and bright and white with the name *Beachside Landscaping* printed on the passenger-side door. In the bed of the pickup, rolls of rubber tubing encircled various digging tools secured to built-in racks and poked the air like stretched out fingers. Strapped against the cab was a 55-gallon drum with a pump handle sticking out its top and *H2O* stenciled on the barrel's side.

"We'll take white truck…let's go," Bonn said.

While keeping his shotgun shouldered and pointed at 'Just Carl', Bonn dug into his pocket for his keys. The first thing he touched wasn't his keys; he distinctly felt three shotgun shells slide between his fingers. As comforting as the discovery should have been, learning he held an unloaded gun brought on panic. Bonn had followed safety protocol when he emptied his gun and dropped the shells into the pocket of his hunting pants.

Now, without enough time to reload and avoid being rushed, he reduced the odds. "Buenos noches, amigo," Bonn said, then smashed the butt of his gun to the Mexican accomplice's head and watched him crumble. One-on-one and holding an empty gun, Bonn continued with his ruse. "Get in the truck asshole, on this side. You're driving, and keep your hands on the steering wheel where I can see them."

"Reminds you of the old days, doesn't it?" Carl asked with an almost imperceptible smile that didn't go undetected.

"Move it," Bonn said and waved the barrel of his unloaded weapon towards the passenger's door.

Bonn gingerly crawled in and knelt on the floorboard with his shotgun resting on the center console, and pointed inches from Carl's head, "Quit calling me that and drive the damn truck!"

. The air in the cab reeked of soured beer, marijuana and tobacco and had Bonn swallowing repeatedly to keep from dry heaving.

"Drive slowly, I might *accidentally* blow your head off," Bonn said.

"That's what I'm afraid of…, why don't you take your finger off the trigger?" Carl asked then drove at a snail's pace and flinched with every bump in the road.

CHAPTER 5

Paula started each day with a joint, and then drank a 32 oz. coffee laced with five creams and six sugars from an insulated plastic mug. When it was time to open the office, she poured half of a Two-Liter *Diet* Coke into a 64-ounce plastic mug filled with ice; it never left her side throughout the day. She was always concerned with her weight and made sure at least part of her diet was healthy and stuffed an entire chocolate chip granola bar in her mouth, and in as few chews as possible, swallowed.

In their twelve months of marriage, Paula ballooned from a tolerable one hundred and sixty-five pounds to an ever-increasing obese woman. She justified her new two hundred pound figure by claiming problems with her Thyroid. Based on her self-diagnosis, he gave herself permission to enjoy any type of food without guilt.

Beachside's "lawn specialists" were always outside the office by 7:00 am, regardless of daylight savings time. When Paula opened her trailer door, there would be a dozen or more men of various ages standing around their trucks smoking weed or unfiltered cigarettes, drinking coffee, and eating sausage biscuits from the McDonald's dollar menu.

Although Paula complained about the occasional whistling and hushed comments made in Spanish, she secretly relished the attention from "her workers". The moment she stepped out and headed across the gravel parking lot to the office, all eyes were on her. She acted oblivious to their laughter when her polyester stretch pants rubbed together on the length of her ham-size thighs. *Crunch, Swisht. Crunch, Swisht.*

Although she referred to the men as her "Little Taco, Hot Tamale, and Burrito Boy" during the morning meetings, Paula didn't mean to be disrespectful, she always wore a friendly smile when referring to them by their nicknames.

"Arnie", the lone bilingual worker with a green card, received a promotion to foreman. No matter how many times Armando corrected his bosses, *Arnie* stuck; he preferred it to the alternative nickname, "Mondo". Paula considered Arnie management material the day she met him. That was the day, he told her how nice she looked. From that day forward, Paula never left her trailer without raspberry lip-gloss in her pocket, whenever she thought Arnie might be around her.

Armando "Arnie" Ramirez spent most of his childhood in Southern California. His parents crossed from Tijuana into San Diego, five days a week, for ten years, on work visas. When they had enough money to buy a two-bedroom ranch style home, they moved to San Diego. Young Armando became the first Latino in the school's history to have a perfect S.A.T. score. Although there were minority based scholarship offers from colleges around the country, he had other plans. The day after graduation, his father gave him the keys to an old work truck, several hundred dollars and the telephone number of his famous uncle who lived in San Diego. He arrived at his uncle's sprawling mansion with nothing more than a backpack, never to live in Tijuana again.

Armando was proud to be the namesake of one of the most powerful drug lords in Mexico, and boss of the Sinaloa Cartel, but there was an inherent risk that could be fatal. Although he knew, "Uncle" had the nickname, "El Diablo", he would never refer to him as a devil. "Uncle" taught Armando, his only nephew, everything he needed to know to become a successful in business.

Under his uncle's tutelage, Armando spent his first year in his uncle's San Diego home building a lucrative marijuana distribution network catering to the wealthy La Jolla business executives, attorneys, and their spoiled teenage children with substantial bank accounts. However, everything changed when the Tijuana Cartel's bosses joined forces with the Cali Cartel from Columbia and ordered a hit on both of them. The Sinaloa Cartel, who was vastly superior in Mexico, reconsidered the dangerously competitive drug market in San Diego. During a secret meeting of cartel bosses, they yielded the West Coast and U.S. Pacific to the Cali Cartel along with their Tijuana partners to avoid an all out war. The Columbian's offer came from an imprisoned insider by the name of Guzman known only as "El Chapo". In exchange, The Sinaloa bosses set their sights on the Juarez territory and the entire Gulf of Mexico.

"Armando, I have to return to my Sinaloa home, it's time for you to get out of San Diego. It's too dangerous for you to be here without the family's protection. Besides, I want you to expand our territory. You will be an unknown when you get there, but your safety will only last for a very short time if you're not careful."

"Uncle, where do you want me to go, and what am I going to do when I get there? My parents and cousins count on me. I am finally able to provide for them, and now, you want me to leave?"

"We are all family. I'm honored my brother gave you my name; it gives us a special relationship. You are a man now, so I'm going to speak to you as one, it's time to leave. I give you my word; you will never have to worry about taking care of them. You are going to be wealthy one day, if you can stay alive. If you choose to stay here, the Tijuana Cartel will not stop until you are eliminated, you will be heading to Juarez."

"You want me to go to the most violent city in Mexico, Ciudad de Juarez?"

"That is the last place they will be looking for you. I don't want you to tell anyone who you are when you get there; you will assume a new identity. If the Juarez bosses find out the nephew of the Sinaloa's boss is in their territory to expand operations, it will become a blood bath. I don't want you messing with the low-level operations, it is way too risky. You are going to be my Lieutenant and in charge of our distribution out of Texas. I'm sending your cousin Carlos with you to get you started; let him handle the day to day operations and manage the sales. He will be *your* right hand and *you* will be mine. There's one more thing, your name is now, Armando *Gonzalez*, not Ramirez."

"Uncle, if I need to go, when will I leave?"

"My plane and pilots are ready to take off after you say your goodbyes. Armando, I am sorry, you cannot tell anyone that you are leaving. No one can know where you went, or that you changed your name to Gonzalez. It is for your family's safety as well as yours. Do you understand?"

"I understand, but I don't have a clue how to get started when I get there. I don't know anyone and I won't know who to trust."

"I have a man that lives on the other side of Interstate 10 in El Paso but he doesn't work for me, his orders are coming out of the Cereso jail in Juarez. He's a general with the Barrio Aztecas; I pay him for his assistance."

"I'm going to be dealing with the Barrio Aztecas? Why would we want to be involved with a gang from El Paso, especially one that works for the Juarez Cartel?"

"Don't be fooled into thinking they're just a gang. Whether they are on the street, or behind bars, they're still very dangerous. The Juarez Cartel recruited Azteca members to fight and kill every Sinaloa member they could find. I'm afraid my delay in sending you there will make your job harder than I anticipated."

"The Juarez Cartel uses the Aztecas as their soldiers?"

"The Azteca controls the drug market for them and joined forces with the Juarez's armed thugs, La Lineas. We need to make sure the Aztecas become as powerful as a cartel. You are going to be a Padrino for my man in El Paso. He is now getting orders directly from the cartel's boss in Juarez; he'll be able to give you information on the cartel operations and their La Linea enforcers, without drawing any suspicion."

"I'm going to be a *Padrino*? You want me to be a money source for a gang? Uncle, the Sinaloa's are going to finance the Barrio Azteca's operations?"

"Nephew, I promise, they are not merely a gang. You will supply my man in Juarez with as much money as he needs for the *all* of the Barrio Aztecas. If I'm right, they are going to make a move to break away from the cartel's La Linea and continue to make their own money. They're well on their way to becoming as powerful as a cartel, the more we help the Aztecas, the less they will rely on the Juarez bosses and work for the Sinaloa family. Once we have control of the Barrio's finances, we'll make our move on the Juarez Cartel; they won't know what hit them."

Armando's safety in Juarez didn't last very long; the general he befriended was found shot execution style, minus his hands. The amputation let anyone who dared, know what happens when you steal from the Aztecas. A shipment of illegal guns, financed with money coming from Armando, turned out to be too much of a temptation for the general. The departure from the normal drugs-for-guns transactions proved costly for him. The general paid the ultimate price for making a private deal with the funds that came from Armando, the Aztecas money. Even though the general never revealed Armando's true-identity, the Juarez cartel ordered a hit. So, Uncle Ramirez told Armando to take the financial loss and leave Juarez.

Out of concern for his own personal safety, Armando moved his operations to El Paso, where he built a successful landscaping business to funnel the ever-increasing amount of drug money he shipped out of Mexico. Juarez suffered with abject poverty, carnage, and misery, while El Paso prospered on the north side of Interstate 10. The lucky ones, issued work visas, rarely returned to Juarez when their permits expired. Everyone else entered the U.S. illegally with the help of expensive "coyotes" and arrived penniless. Consequentially, the constant supply of workers wanting a job allowed Armando to staff one of the largest and most respected Mexican owned businesses in El Paso.

Many of his struggling compatriots, who had been desperately looking for work, considered Senor Gonzalez a hero. He helped them get their green cards with the assistance of well-paid immigration officials employed by Armando's uncle. He provided living accommodations in the many homes, trailers, and motels he owned. When they were established and able to provide for themselves, they could buy the homes, interest-free. Employees, whether full-time or part-time, proclaimed their loyalty and dedication to him for giving them a job and a place to live. More importantly, they were proud to work for him and wore the landscaping company's uniform shirts even on their days off.

As the landscaping business expanded, so did the needs of his ever-growing workforce and their families. He built Gonzalez Urgent Care to provide medical services and dental care as well as drug treatment counselors to take care of their health needs. He also used the landscaping business to funnel profits from his drug business, until it started making too much money. He had to stop, out of his fear of the I.R.S., as much as the police did.

Armando's reputation as a legitimate business owner, and respected member of the Hispanic community, kept him under the radar. He maintained a squeaky-clean image by never being involved with the street level marketing and he kept the drug shipments to destinations outside of the state of Texas. From their first days on the job, workers understood, drug dealing was an offense, serious enough for immediate termination of employment.

When the wife of a shuttle driver went into labor, the morning work shuttle that provided transportation for the daily laborers needed a driver. Armando lived up to his reputation as a hands-on employer, by filling in and driving the work van to the Home Depot parking lot off I-10 in El Paso. His arrival sparked an enthusiastic applause and pats on the back from the workers.

Minutes after his arrival, a nondescript van, with Florida license plates, pulled into the parking lot and honked several times as it approached. The driver painted a picture of paradise in Florida, and offered to anyone willing to make the journey, a job at his landscaping business. Armando, the only man fluent in English, served as interpreter and explained the stranger's offer to all the workers. The "gringo's" instructions were simple, they needed to pack light and be ready to leave the following morning. The man in the van made it clear not to disclose where they were going, even though he never said exactly where in Florida they would be going.

"Pack light? Deez men are wearing everything they own. Where we go in your Flor*eeda*?" Armando spoke with a phony accent to maintain his cover as just another worker.

"Look here 'beaner'; you wouldn't know the name of the city if I told you," Carl said.

Geography happened to be one of Armando's favorite subjects in high school and said, "Amigo, why don't choo' try me."

"Okay, smart ass. It's near a big city called Pensacola. How about Fort Walton Beach or Destin, you heard of them?"

"Si, where you call Panhandle on dee' Gulf."

"How in the hell do you know all that?"

"I see on travel channel. I am, how you say en English…, *honored* to go with you."

"What's your name Amigo?" Carl said.

"Armando. My pleasure to meet you…" Armando Gonzalez extended his hand and waited for a handshake to bond with his new employer.

"My name is Carl, just Carl. I want you and your friends to come with me to Pensacola in the morning."

Armando gave the instructions, minus the baggage restrictions, to the men who wanted to join him. Not once did the topic of pay come up; they knew, by reputation and personal experience, their hero would take care of them. He spent the rest of the day traveling between Juarez and El Paso, meeting with a Sinaloa captain, speaking with his uncle, and arranging for one of his cousins to manage the El Paso businesses in his absence. By the time he traveled the twelve hundred miles to his new home in Florida, his Uncle Ramirez had arranged for him to expand the cartel's operations in the unclaimed market of the Florida Panhandle.

Paula stood in amazement when the van returned and the side door of their van opened. The male bodies pouring out reminded her of a clown car she had seen at the circus as a child. The new recruits expected to see the emerald green waters and white sand beaches Armando had described. Instead, all they saw were towering pine trees sprouting up from beds of palmettos. Although they had seen the Gulf waters several times on their trip, the palm trees changed to pine trees when they left the coast and headed north.

Paula began counting aloud, "Uno, dos, tres, uh…four, five, six, seven…, ocho? Damn it, why can't you just go to Home Depot like everyone else?"

"What the hell do you mean?" Carl, exhausted and irritable from the non-stop, eighteen hour, cocaine assisted drive, barked out so quickly and loud, everyone jumped.

"I just thought it would be easier to find men at Home Depot. I see a bunch of 'wetbacks' there every time I drive by there." Paula wasn't sure why they were called wetbacks; she assumed it had something to do with how much they sweat in the sun.

"You're such a stupid bitch. There has to be at least a dozen cameras on the building and half the light poles. I don't want them taking my picture, do you?"

"I ain't seen any cameras," Paula said.

"They're everywhere. Hell, everybody gets their pictures taken whether they like it or not, and they show em' to the cops."

"You're teasing me. They don't really have cameras on poles, do they? Paula said and truly didn't understand the concept of unmanned remote security cameras.

"How can you be that ignorant? There are cameras at Home Depot, Wal-Mart, the mall, convenience stores, and every damn place you go. 'Big Brother' is everywhere."

Embarrassed by her naiveté, and fearing Carl's temper, she changed the subject by asking in the sweetest voice she could muster. "Honey, can I get you sumptum?"

"You're damn right you can. Don't just stand there, get em' some bottles of water." Carl gave a quick nod to the new men as a display of machismo and to show them, he's the boss. He forgot, only one spoke English.

In their first year of their marriage, Carl attacked Paula with his words. She took his verbal abuse and pretended it wasn't a big deal. Over time, she could tell by his tone, when it would be best to do what he told her to do. Even though only Armando spoke English, the workers understood Carl's tone in the same way as Paula, and a few of them already feared their new boss. Armando stared down Carl then reassured his men they had nothing to fear, she went to get them "agua".

Paula returned, pulling a cooler on wheels and filled with bottles of cold water. Every man and teenage boy emptied his bottle in seconds. Paula looked to Carl, who just shrugged his shoulders and then said, "I didn't want to stop for piss breaks, whatever goes in, has to come out."

In honor of the new arrivals, Paula wore her "business-look" ensemble: a collared white shirt with a brown calf-length skirt matched with open-toed, imitation brown, leather sandals from Payless shoes. She tolerated the painful odd shaped bubbles pushing out of the sandal's webbing for as long as she could before her feet began to blister. So, while Carl was getting information on each man from Armando, Paula went back to the trailer to change into and outfit and more comfortable footwear. Her new ensemble was one of her many multi-colored Hawaiian Muumuu dresses and flip-flops that exposed her bizarre curling toenails. The look was simple and a little understated, but it gave her freedom of movement while concealing her shape.

"Start right off whiff a good 'ampression'. Let em' see I'm not just a bizness woman," Paula explained when Carl looked her up and down.

Carl laughed and said, "If you want to impress them, give em' a dollar. They want to make money, not look at your sorry ass."

He turned towards the workers and gave the international sign for money by rubbing the tips of his thumb and index finger together. Instantly, they replied with a chorus of "Si! Dinero! Si! Si!"

The mobile homes provided for the new residents of Powder Sands Trailer Park were just outside of the city limits of the bayside community of Niceville. Carl inherited the trailer park and a large building adjacent to its gated entrance when his father died. His mother decided she couldn't run the business alone and purchased a home in town with the proceeds from several life insurance policies of various amounts. The day Carl returned from Vietnam, she gave him the property. It included a spacious and functional building for the landscaping business, but the park needed immediate improvements, including its name. So, he removed *Trailer* from the name, and used his landscaping skills to beautify the entrance. Then, he had his workers build an expensive eight-foot tall wooden security fence to conceal the weed-infested rows of slab concrete hidden behind it. Although Carl didn't need his mother's or Paula's permission, he convinced them the property would be perceived as a classy gated mobile home community.

Next to the road, a flashing neon sign now read:

POWDER SANDS PARK
VACANCY! ONLY A FEW PIE_ _S OF PARADISE LEFT!

From the road, Powder Sands Park appeared to be the kind of place anyone would want to live. The front entrance of the property was a beautifully landscaped a beach façade created with brilliant white sand illegally taken from the beaches near Destin. The sea oats, native grasses, and protected plants Carl dug up and transplanted, came from the areas ancient dunes. Carl stole the plants from the Gulf Islands National Seashore's dunes before the protection laws were passed, and thanks to the "grandfathered" clause, he wasn't charged with theft.

Behind the fence, concrete slabs dotted the park. Lined up by size of cement pad, were twenty single-family trailers, twelve multi-family doublewide homes, and five abandoned trailers in various stages of deterioration. The numerous unoccupied slabs were utilized to build a couple of improvised basketball courts with pyramids of massive steel oil barrels for backstops, and broken landscaping equipment served as bleachers for onlookers. The rest of the property was a graveyard for earth moving machines, tractors, and other pieces of rusting farm equipment. Every time it rained, puddles of water stained the road and concrete pads with a rusted metal color.

The most interesting piece on the property was a fire-gutted motor home that "accidentally" exploded and burned. The motor home was adjacent to an old barn that Carl's father had built before turned the land into a mobile home park. Most of the residents believed "the fire" was arson committed by a Niceville Police Department's detective. The privacy fence blocked the entire trailer park from public view, and only the residents witnessed what actually happened. When the fire investigators sought potential witnesses, no one claimed to have seen anything. After all, they weren't only neighbors of the men arrested, they were clients.

CHAPTER 6

*H*e wore the uniform of student freedom fighters, a dark green military jacket with an American flag sewn upside down on the sleeve, and spoke in a whispered voice that reeked of wine, hashish, and cigarette smoke.

Reality returned when the pickup hit a small rut as they turned into the designated parking area. Even though his gaze never left Carl, he had been out the entire half-mile ride to his Explorer. The dreamy memories of his college days left a distorted look of confusion on Bonn's face as he tried to separate the past from the present.

"Are you going to make it old friend?" When Carl spoke, the stench of his breath and the green military jacket he was wearing, jolted Bonn's memory of the first time they met.

Bonn painstakingly shook his head to remain conscious, almost to the point of being involuntary, and it sent a shiver down his body. The moment he grimaced, Carl gently braked to a stop, and the pickup's keychain reflected several flashes of light that hit Bonn's face. The flashes coming from the ornament radiated a halo of three letters: C-A-P.

Bonn didn't look up to confirm if they were at his Explorer. Instead, he reached behind and groped until he could feel the door handle. Using his body, he pushed open the door enough to slither out. He planted his feet firmly on the ground, and pointed his unloaded gun through the open door.

"Turn it off. Get out on my side," Bonn emphasized his demand by pointing his gun directly at Cap's head while backing away from the truck. Although he anchored his shotgun's butt on his hip, the gun wavered as he trembled to keep his balance.

"If I feel like I'm going to blackout, I *will* shoot you," Bonn said, then clicked the gun's safety off. "The way I'm feeling, it could be at any minute. Toss me the damn keys."

Fortunately, the keys came at him in a gentle arc and to everyone's surprise, caught them left-handed and threw them into the knee-high grass; he looked like a child throwing a ball for the first time.

Bonn indicated with short strokes of his barrel, where he wanted him to sit. "Get on the ground!"

Almost instantly, after hitting the ground, Carl began yelling and swiping at his arms, then jumped up and danced with insane gestures. Florida's fire ants have a burning bite that leaves a painful blister. They were feasting on Carl.

Bonn got the chance he had been waiting for since discovering he had an empty gun. Without hesitation, he reached into his pocket, grabbed a shell, and loaded his gun in seconds. His training taught him to disassemble and assemble a weapon as simple as a shotgun in less than a minute, blindfolded. By the time, Carl heard a shell racked into the Remington 870, Bonn had locked and loaded.

Now, with his shotgun at ready, Bonn casually pushed a second shell into the magazine.

"What the hell?" Carl asked, as he slapped his neck. "I can't believe your gun was unloaded," he said while brushing off non-existent ants, the phobia had taken hold.

"That's right asshole, get back on the ground," Bonn said, then slid in a third shell then fired a warning shot at Carl's feet. A few of the BBs hit Carl's foot, sending him to the ground. Even though Bonn heard a death threat, he smiled as he calmly ejected the spent shell and shoved in a replacement.

The warning blast had been deafening. The roar in Bonn's head returned and affected his balance; he grabbed the truck's hood ornament to stay on his feet. Carl appeared to be shouting at him, but the roar drowned out the string of expletives and threats. He blinked repeatedly to stay conscious and leaned into the pickup; he didn't fall, he drifted back to his college days.

"When the first bomb detonated at noon, thousands of demonstrators, law enforcement, and** National **Guardsmen at the university crouched in disbelief before they scattered in mass hysteria."

The scent of the gunpowder wafting in the air had Bonn thinking there had been an explosion. When he snapped out of his past, he said, "I know you from… I don't understand. I can remember when you…set off a bomb."

Carl smirked but remained silent.

"I saw you, I remember when you…" Bonn said and as he was about to collapse, ready to accept defeat, he looked up; a faint metallic rattling in the distance grew louder by the seconds. The old green truck, owned by Carl's accomplice, fishtailed on the soft-packed sand road and judging by the growing dust cloud, he was coming with a purpose. When he cut across the field, Bonn raised his shotgun and shattered glass of his front windshield with a single shot.

Twenty feet away, the old truck came to an immediate stop when it smashed into an oak tree, sending the driver face first into the steering wheel. Unsure if the man was armed, he shifted his aim to the driver's window.

"What's your friends' name?" Bonn wasn't sure why he asked.

"Armando." "Just Armando," Carl said.

"*Just* Armando? What is it with you guys?"

"Arnie, he goes by fucking Arnie," Carl said with a degree of irritation.

"Well, 'Just Carl', you can get out of that ant hill," Bonn said. "Let's see if Arnie is still with us."

Bonn succeeded in making it to Arnie's window for an up-close look at him. Arnie's face had a slimy sheen of beading sweat gathering in collective puddles on the edge of a pencil-thin mustache. He remained conscious with his hand on his head and glared a hatred-filled expression towards Carl, not Bonn. The bump on his forehead had grown to golf ball size, matching the one he received earlier from the butt of Bonn's shotgun.

"'Arnie', turn off your truck and throw the keys out the window," Bonn said. "Get out and keep your hands where I can see them." When the door opened, he could see Carl's shotgun was jammed, muzzle down between the brake and clutch, and bent from the crash.

Arnie's first step out of the pickup sent him staggering towards Carl, who grabbed him in time to keep him from falling to the ground.

Arnie refused to take the blame for Bonn's attack, "I dint' choot you, *he* did."

"Shut the hell up," Carl growled through a clenched jaw.

"Did he say *choo-choo?*" Bonn asked Carl, who had moved a couple of steps closer. Bonn blasted a hole in the side of Arnie's truck when anger replaced his confusion. "You're next if you take another step."

"Shoot me or get the hell out of here," Carl said.

"Shut up," Bonn said. "Alright, both of you get on the ground." Reluctantly, 'Just' Arnie" and 'Just' Carl dropped to their knees. Arnie began to vomit from an obvious concussion. The wafting odor and retching sounds coming from Arnie made Bonn swallow repeatedly and cover his mouth.

Before he puked, Bonn lunged towards the stability of his Explorer's rear bumper to retrieve the keys hidden behind the tire. He pushed the *unlock* button without hearing the SUV's distinctive beep, and kept pushing it without success. Just as panic began, he saw the brake lights flashing and relaxed.

While Carl and Armando were swiping at the fire ants, Bonn slid ass first into his SUV and caught the first glimpse of his face in the mirror. His worst fear became apparent when he raised the lid to his blood-covered eye to a world cloaked in darkness. Undeterred, with a will to survive, Bonn dead lifted his legs inside, turned the key, and let the surge from the vehicle slam his door shut.

Adding insult to their blistering injuries, a sandy dust cloud enveloped them. "I will get your ass. If it's the last thing I do," Carl yelled and coughed.

The inevitable became a losing battle, Bonn's dry heaving turned to violent vomiting. Now, his clothes and car smelled as horrific as he looked. When he floored the gas pedal, his head flopped back and lolled. The last thing Bonn saw as he sped away was Carl screaming into his cell phone.

"Four miles to pavement, you can do it," Bonn said to himself as he leaned in, with his hands wrapped white-knuckled on the steering wheel, and concentrated on staying out of the ditches. The loss of peripheral vision caused him to over steer, but he managed to keep his vehicle on the road, and then began chanting, "Make it to the highway…make it to the highway…"

CHAPTER 7

Niceville's Police Chief Barnes planned to be out of the office for two weeks. He always scheduled vacation time for his two favorite things, hunting season in the fall and fishing in the spring. The annual Cobia World Championships are in the coastal town of Destin during the month of April, he hoped to be on his boat from sunrise to sunset, it would be his office. Even though he was on a fishing vacation, he couldn't stand not knowing what was going on in the field with his fellow officers. Therefore, Chief Barnes equipped his boat with a police scanner and a satellite phone for the times he ventured offshore.

In the spring months, the highly valued fish known as a Cobia, migrated in the Gulf of Mexico. They left their wintering grounds in the Keys, and then swam northward along Florida's west coast to their spawning grounds off Texas and Louisiana. Cobia fishing tournaments take place in most every port along the fish's migration route, but none compared to the annual World Championship in Destin. The prize money in other cities paled in comparison to its $250,000 prize for the largest Cobia caught and another quarter of a million in cash and prizes for the winners of various categories. Chief Barnes intended to win the fishing tournament and earn as much of the $500,000 total prize pool as possible.

The main migration push through the coastal city of Destin brought droves of anglers and millions of tourist dollars to the entire area. The "good ol' boys", who owned weekend project boats, had to compete with the million dollar fishing machines owned by wealthy professional fishermen. While most contestants dreamed of winning a life-changing amount of money, the affluent anglers in their expensive boats wanted the prestige that went to the winner.

Chief Barnes preached to his friends and family, "*When* I win the money, I'm going to retire." As a trained detective he knew whenever a large sum of money was up for grabs, there would also be trouble. In his wildest dreams, he never envisioned the problems that this year's tournament would bring.

The city of Niceville was on the southern border of Eglin Ari Force Base and only a few miles from the beaches of the Gulf of Mexico. The area, considered an ideal place to retire from the service, kept Chief Barnes' police force loaded with former or retired military; they trained to follow orders and they *usually* obey them.

During his first run to be elected as police chief, he had a self-proclaimed moment of brilliance and wrote his own campaign slogan, "Our Military – America's and Niceville's Force". During the Cobia tournament, he would tell the citizens of Niceville not to be concerned about their safety while he fished. "The public has nothing to worry about; the military will be in charge during my absence."

Detective "Mac" McCain was the only exception to the obedient ranks on his force. Mac's calm demeanor, analytical problem-solving skills, and battlefield experience were attributes Chief Barnes wanted in his officers. Shortly after his retirement and few special assignments as a civilian contractor, Mac experienced the boredom that many retired military face. Hoping to find a little excitement, he accepted a position with the Niceville Police Department.

Mac spent most of his military career at Hurlburt Field, the Special Op's base built on Eglin's southern most boundaries. Everyone, except Chief Barnes, felt a little intimidated by Mac's physical appearance. The chief was of average height, his barreled chest and massive biceps made him an imposing figure. If Mac's six and one-half foot, two hundred and twenty pound frame, topped with a short military haircut weren't intimidating enough, the battle-worn intensity in his eyes would get anyone's attention.

Most of the significant military contractors, the DOD, and numerous mercenary groups attempted to recruit Mac at his retirement. After his illustrious Special Op's career, he received offers of clandestine missions that paid well, but he considered them hazardous duty and chose his assignments wisely for a few years. After building a substantial financial portfolio as an independent contractor, he accepted the position with the Niceville PD, but maintained his military contacts as a consultant.

Shortly after his retirement, Mac testified in front of the Armed Services Committee about a solo clandestine operation where innocents were lost. Major McCain USAF-retired testified, "I mourn for them, but I have no regrets for my past service. If I'm asked to serve again, I will come to the aid of my country."

His patriotic answer, precipitated an onslaught of offers from private contractors, he rejected them. The word finally got around, Mac only accepted missions in the name of national security that came from Washington. He didn't care that the White House assignments were more dangerous, and in most cases, paid less than the private sector. He chose to work exclusively for the government because of the unlimited resources available to them throughout the world. For now, as mundane as being a detective in a small-town police department could be for him, he accepted his new life without regret.

Mac stayed true to his "national security only" commitment until he received a call from a freshman Cuban-American senator from Florida, who was also, the newest member of the Senate Intelligence Committee. The senator had been present for Mac's infamous speech and used that as the reason for his call. The request from Senator Julio Diaz turned out to be a personal plea for Mac's assistance in rescuing a kidnapped American missionary imprisoned deep in the Columbian jungle. Mac and his men were in a bloody battle that left all the rebels dead without any loss of American lives. During a tearful reunion in front of the press, Senator Diaz revealed the rescued woman was his cousin.

After returning from the mission and unexpected press conference, where he learned the woman he rescued was Senator Diaz' cousin, Mac received a second call.

"I want to thank you for a job well done," Senator Diaz said.

"You are welcome, but I wish you hadn't left out a detail like the woman we were going to rescue was your cousin," Mac said, but he didn't know why it made a difference. "Twenty men paid the price for their actions."

"Major McCain, I hope you can find it in your heart to forgive me, I didn't want you to feel any added pressure by knowing…," Senator Diaz sounded remorseful and unable to continue with his apology. "I should have respected your professionalism and realized…"

"Thank you for understanding."

"I will forever be grateful, and I will never forget the courage you and your men showed. Major, it has come to my attention that you have made the decision to retire from the service and live in the Destin area," Diaz said, "I own a Gulf view condo at the Palms Condominiums in the Crystal Beach area of Destin that I am going to be putting up for sale. If you have an interest…"

"Senator, what's the catch?" Mac asked.

"There is no catch. I acquired it from my ex-business partner. It can be yours for the money I gave him to pay delinquent taxes owed to the IRS. It's the least I can do to repay you for everything you've done for me."

Mac didn't realize there was an ulterior motive for the phone call. The Palms condominiums were on prime beachfront and next to one of the most luxurious hotel resorts in Destin. Ancient sand dunes, covered with picturesque sea oats and grasses, separated the two complexes.

Sitting in the middle of the sand dunes between Mac's condominium and the resort's hotel, was a beautiful, old native Florida home built in the late 1800's. Its owner turned out to be Mac's closest friend, General M.D. Bonner. When Mac realized they would be neighbors, he accepted Senator Diaz's offer. As thrilled as he was having Bonn for neighbor, he wasn't the only one. Before Mac took occupancy, the senator had several listening devices planted inside the condo, and a micro-camera hidden on the veranda, pointed directly at Bonn's house.

Mac found life as a small town policeman boring, compared to military life. He tried to build some excitement by working on the edge of regulations, and at times, failed to call for backup. Mac obeyed orders on an as-needed basis unless they came directly from Chief Barnes. Despite receiving many commendations in the military, he seldom followed *all* procedural policies as a police officer, and teetered on the brink of insubordination. Mac applied his military training on his cases, and went methodically by the book, *his* book.

A few years prior, McCain was on paid leave over the way he had taken down a drug lab and methamphetamine distribution ring operating out of a trailer park north of Niceville. Based on the results of an internal investigation, he received a demotion for not working through the Drug Task Force and for procedural violations too numerous to count. Mac, with the help of Bonn, busted the drug ring using questionable methods; he never revealed the role Bonn had in the arrests.

They took down all three "cookers" at the same time without backup, a grievous violation of department policy. Mac brought them to the station, zip-tied together in the back seat of his vehicle, by himself. Chief Barnes laughed and called the methods used by his detective, "unconventionally effective, definitely impressive, and in violation of Departmental procedures."

The photo of Mac marching his captives, single file, into the county jail appeared on the front page of the Destin Log and the NWF Daily News. City officials seeking camera time, called him "a hero". Privately, they demanded disciplinary action. In his defense, the mobile homes, R.V. and barn were already on fire when he arrived at Powder Sands Trailer Park.

As far as the military was concerned, Mac always made righteous arrests; his methods were never in question. Eglin's Public Affairs office raved about Mac's military training in their official statement, "The community of Niceville is fortunate to have Detective McCain on their police force". Off-the-record, Mac admitted to Chief Barnes that he waited until the structures were in flames before he called it in to dispatch.

The barn that burned to the ground housed a "kitty" farm, along with everything needed to manufacture enough methamphetamine to supply every speed freak in the Southeastern United States. One of the "meth cookers" claimed to be an innocent breeder of show cats, not a drug dealer.

Neither Bonn nor Mac was fond of cats, but they released all the feline critters from the barn before they torched the lab. Immediately upon their release, the cats became a game of chase for "Lexi", Mac's canine partner. She was pursuing one of the dealers trying to escape on foot when a band of smoldering feline fur balls scampered out of the burning building. Lexi's training trumped her instincts and she knocked down the suspect, held him until Mac could put on the handcuffs, and then she took off in pursuit of an award winning, long-haired, Himalayan show cat. Sadly, dozens of cats and kittens had scattered in the woods. Mac and Bonn left them to fend for themselves without reporting the incident to animal control.

Animal lovers called Mac a hero for saving dozens of their furry friends from the burning inferno, but his notoriety only lasted a day. The ensuing feline problems made national headlines. Kitty road kill littered the highways, county roads, and the city streets. The city of Niceville had a legion of roaming and starving cats foraging through its trashcans and dumpsters.

One group saw the opportunity to further their own cause. PETA arrived in Destin several days before the beginning of the National Shark Fishing Tournament and spent most of their time in front of the reporters. The People for the Ethical Treatment of Animals attending a shark-fishing tournament went over as well as representatives from the ACLU attending a skinhead convention. They were making unsubstantiated claims that local anglers were using their feline friends as bait. They didn't know that large, longhaired cats were going for a premium among the local shark anglers; their undulating hair was enticing to the sharks. The ultra liberal left-wing organization took advantage of the controversy to launch their new campaign to ban all fishing. They claimed, "hooks and gaffs cause pain, and the fish suffer a slow, cruel death by suffocation when they are taken out of the water".

Mac and his "kitty fiasco" took the blame for PETA's presence and the subsequent drop in chartered fishing trips taken by the tourists. The county commissioners wanted to avoid bad press and they pressured Chief Barnes to make an example of Detective McCain.

In response to the disciplinary action, Mac laughed and said to Chief Barnes, "Don't you see the irony of being demoted for making the largest drug bust in Okaloosa county history and setting free some stupid cats?"

"I wonder why the animal rights nuts didn't come to your rescue for helping out the poor caged animals they are supposed to protect." Chief Barnes said. "They're a bunch of nuts."

Although Internal Affairs couldn't prove Mac started the fires or set free "the furry critters", they busted his rank, assigned him to a desk for ninety days, and only used Mac as a consultant in robbery-homicide investigations. Chief Barnes was so disgusted with the system; he reassigned Mac to run the new Violent Crimes Unit where he worked *less* hours at a desk for *more* pay than he earned in the field.

It wasn't about the money. Mac's retirement benefits from the Air Force, and the small fortune he saved from working as a contractor, made the pay decrease irrelevant, except in principle. He considered leaving the department, but unknown to Mac, Senator Diaz had already taken proactive steps to ensure Mac's job was secure, and his rank reinstated.

The morning before turning in a well-composed resignation letter, he sought the advice of his friend. If he had followed Bonn's advice, although it seemed to be a good suggestion at the time, it might have cost him his life.

"Bonn, I can't take the politics anymore…I don't need this job. I have Senator Diaz covering my back; he can make all this crap stop. The problem is…, I'm not sure I'm cut out for the civilian life."

"Mac, having political friends is power. Never forget that. But… you have to keep the relationship with Senator Diaz to yourself until you absolutely need him. That being said, the only person who truly has your back…is *me*, take some time for yourself and think about it? Go fishing or better yet, why don't you go turkey hunting with me tomorrow morning; it's opening day."

"I'll make a deal with you, when you get back tomorrow, call me and tell me how many '*big ol' gobblers*' are out there and we'll go the next morning," Mac said. "I'm going to give it one more week and if Barnes doesn't take me off the desk, I'm out of there and we'll be turkey hunting and fishing every day."

CHAPTER 8

While flying down the road, Bonn glanced at the side view mirror long enough to see trailing dust billowing behind his SUV like a plume of spent rocket fuel. No one would be able to follow him closely and not choke blind by the spewed cloud that extended above the treetops. The knowledge that two killers were going to be coming after him, made his attempt to reach pavement even more desperate. Bonn suspected Carl would have at least one handgun in his truck, and if they found the keys, they would be armed and pursuing him. He chastised himself for not thinking clearly.

"Why didn't I take his damn keys, instead of just throwing them? I should have shot both of them. Damn it!" The adrenaline surge brought on by his anger, matched his increasing paranoia and he pushed his SUV to dangerous speeds. He let his subconscious steer the eight miles of sand and dirt on his journey to reach the highway.

The trail of dust behind his Explorer settled like a heavy fog bank on a becalmed morning. Unfortunately, the dusty haze left a marked trail, easily followed. Since the highway's asphalt would be his only hope for escape, he continued chanting, "Make it to the highway. Make it to the highway."

The true severity of his injuries became apparent when he leaned over to get another look at his face in the rear view mirror. His reflection confirmed, if he didn't receive immediate medical attention, death was a certainty. His swollen right eye had hemorrhaged and there were copious amounts of dried blood streaked across one side of his graying face. As disturbing as he found his appearance, there was something missing and his anger surged; he realized he wasn't wearing his favorite camouflage cap. In its place, a wad of leaves stuck to his bloodied hair. After his first shot, Carl laughed and said to Arnie, "Did you see his hat? It jumped off his head like a damn firecracker had been placed under it".

While Bonn fought to stay conscious and obsessing about his hat, he lost track of how far had he driven or if he had been driving in the right direction. The loss of visual acuity distorted the passing landscape to the point of becoming unrecognizable streaking ribbons of colored light, which added to his nausea. Just as the sensation of being lost entered his mind, the stop sign for the highway magically materialized directly ahead. Unable to judge distance, he slammed on the brakes and the Explorer began to fishtail wildly before coming to an abrupt stop, a hundred yards from the pavement.

After driving in a timeless Nirvana for miles, the sight of pavement brought back a degree of clarity. Bonn's autopilot guided him to the "T" where dirt met asphalt. Still disoriented, he didn't have a clue which way to turn for the hospital. The previous night's pre-hunt ritual of calculating the time and distance to determine to what time to set his alarm helped him in his decision. If he turned the right direction, he had a chance to survive. Bonn turned right and correctly. "Twelve miles, you can do it Bonn. Stay awake."

In what seemed to be a matter of minutes, with no recollection of the dozen miles driven, a bank of blue and red lights blocked the intersection leading into town. The unbelievable and rapidly approaching scene didn't make sense and when he spotted the armed barricade beneath the multi-colored display of lights, his world darkened. He braked hard into the parking lot of a KFC and came to an immediate stop when his Explorer crashed into the restaurant's sign. It had been a tough morning and the afternoon wasn't going to be much easier.

The 911 operators and dispatchers for the law enforcement agencies were jammed with calls from drivers on the two-lane highway leading into Niceville. One caller frantically reported, "A maniac in a late-model black SUV is weaving all over the road at a high rate of speed." Another call, filled with expletives, reported a drunk driver had just forced a lumberyard's truck off the road, and its entire load emptied into the inter-coastal waterway.

Niceville, the epitome of small town America, loved the amount of money tourists brought to their economy, not the traffic jams. If the SUV made it into the heart of the town, an ensuing calamity could occur.

In Chief Barnes absence, an old school captain called Mac to his office. "What are you still doing here? You've heard the reports. Get out to Highway 20 and stop that son-of-a-bitch before the boys from Destin get there, this is a Niceville case. Mac, use whatever force necessary to stop that SUV."

"Copy that! There is no way I'm going to let those 'Damn Destin Divas' get credit for this one. Finally, there's a little excitement!" Mac saluted and sprinted out the door as a kid released from school for the start of summer vacation. The tires of his Ford Expedition were smoking as he left the department's parking lot and he made the five minute drive, in three and a half.

Mac had jurisdiction over the county deputies in *his* town. That's when an idea came to mind; the sheriff's deputies had to cross the bay from coastal Destin to inland Niceville, via the mid-bay bridge. The dispatcher for Niceville P.D. didn't know the extent of Mac's authority when she radioed for any available unit, to stop all north bound traffic coming to Niceville from Destin. The double lanes at the tollbooth backed up across the bridge that spanned the entire width of the bay from Destin to Niceville. The County Sheriff's 'Divas' leaving Destin were livid and kept their sirens wailing when they were stopped by the endless string of cars blocking them from crossing.

With-in seconds of Mac's arrival at the intersection of Highway 20 and Mid-bay Bridge Road, the in-coming SUV had grown from a distant black spot, to a lethal 4000-pound projectile approaching at a high rate of speed.

"Ready your weapons… on my command." The orders coming from a bullhorn triggered the clicking and clacking of ammunition clips slammed into the arsenal of handguns and assault rifles. Suddenly, to the relief of few, and the disappointed of many, the SUV veered into a parking lot then crashed. Mac drew his weapon as he jumped out of his vehicle and ran towards the lunatic behind the wheel. Not knowing if they were dealing with a drug-crazed lunatic or a drunk, a dozen officers surrounded the Explorer and prepared to empty their guns.

Mac approached from the rear of the SUV with his hands wrapped around a Glock 40 and aimed at the driver.

"Driver, show your hands and exit the vehicle," Mac shouted. While his target's body slumped motionless against the steering wheel, Mac heard the staccato gurgling of blood and flashed back to his time in Southeast Asia. As he cautiously approached the driver, waves of sirens were drowning out his hearing, and he strained to make sense of the driver's words.

"Shot...following...Choo-Choo."

Mac wondered if the man was on drugs and hallucinating. He repeated his orders for a "show of hands…", and then wheeled and shoved his weapon at the limp body. To the dismay of his fellow officers, Mac lowered his weapon and let it hang by his side. There, pressed against the steering wheel and with a shotgun across the seat next to him, was the blood-streaked face of his best friend and would-be hero to cat lovers everywhere.

"Bonn!" Guilt overtook Mac for not recognizing the vehicle or noticing the front vanity plate that read, *FlyH2o*.

Mac holstered his weapon and his fellow officers followed in unison. The sight of Bonn brought on a personal déjà vu' as he returned to an unforgettable time etched in his memories. Major McCain, USAF, began shouting.

"Medic, Medic! Man hit, man down!" Several officers, who were also veterans, instinctively echoed his request through the ranks.

"General Bonner! Can you hear me?"

The air reeked of vomit when the one-eyed soldier forced an exhale as he tried to speak.

"Following me…kill…"

"Who's following you? Who wants to kill you? Stay with me buddy!"

Sounding as though it may be his last breath Bonn said, "Just… Carlin'…mando."

"What do you mean? Who's Carlin Mando?"

Bonn remained unresponsive, and the unmistakable coppery odor of blood permeated the air. The stench triggered another emotional reaction from Mac, who suddenly drew his weapon and searched the area for an unseen enemy. When Mac assumed a shooting position and searched the area with his Glock, some of his fellow officers drew their weapons while others hit the ground. Nearly everyone scanned the area for the threat Mac must have seen.

One of the paramedics who was anxious to get to Bonn, cautiously touched Mac's shoulder and spoke calmly, "Detective, we need to check him out, Detective?"

"What? Medic, we have a Cat Alpha. It's General Bonner!" Mac came out of his stupor, holstered his weapon, then grabbed the paramedic by the shirt and swung him towards Bonn without releasing his grip.

"Sir, you need to let go of me; we need to check his vitals."

Mac released the paramedic appeared to relax, then stiffened when he heard a voice yelling, "Damn it detective, your status!" The on-duty captain had taken over the radio communications by plugging his headset into the dispatchers control board. The authoritative voice jolted McCain back to the present and said, "Highway Twenty; four-thousand block, requesting immediate chopper, Cat Alpha. Pilot needs to 'mask up', bad air!"

Whoever requested Mac's status on the radio never served in the military and didn't understand what Mac said. 'Cat Alpha', most critical injured, and 'Bad Air' were meaningless terms but he assumed it was military jargon. To Mac, the air from the fast food restaurant smelled like the Napalm-burned flesh of the enemy he encountered in Vietnam. The scent of fried chicken had become a stench that permeated his soul and kept him from eating almost anything fried.

Dispatch informed Mac, the Med-I-Vac helicopter would transport the patient to Okaloosa County Regional or Sacred Heart in Pensacola if needed.

"Detective, his pulse is dropping; we need to get him on the chopper now! He's Tango One!" the paramedic shouted above the chaos to let Mac know Bonn required immediate surgery.

"Take point, give cover!" Mac commanded to everyone.

The other officers within earshot stared with their eyebrows raised, uncertain what to do. Some were shaking their heads in pity, while others searched for an explanation. Mac's contagious emotions had a few die-hard veterans entering into their own former roles, and for a second, started to "take point".

"Keep your eyes open and try to breathe General," the paramedic said when he put a portable incubator over Bonn's face and squeezed the soft rubber bulb.

Bonn rewarded the medic's efforts with a gasping breath as they lifted him out of his vehicle and placed him on a stretcher. He looked at Mac and tried to say something then stopped as his open eye glazed over. For the first time since leaving the military, Mac encountered the hypnotized stare of the rheumy-eyed wounded.

"Don't try to talk General," Mac said and wobbled slightly.

"Detective, are you okay?" the paramedic asked.

"Medic, I'm fine. Get him on that chopper!"

The paramedic pointed to the bumper of the ambulance and said, "Sir, have a seat and let me take a look at you. General Bonner is being loaded right now, there's nothing more that you can do."

"I told you, I'm fine. Where are they taking him? I have to go," Mac said, he refused the invitation to sit.

"Mac, sit down." Chief Barnes, who had heard the dispatcher's call on the way to his boat and sped to the scene, gave the order in a clam, assertive voice.

"Chief, what are you doing here? Is there a problem?" Mac snapped to attention and struggled to appear in control.

"The problem is…you're talking and acting like you not with us. Sit your ass down! That's an order; I'm the commander on this battlefield."

Mac returned from his delusion, and while perched on the bumper, explained his actions to Chief Barnes, "Bonn and I are old friends, we served together. I was trying get to him tell me what happened."

Although skeptical of Mac's mental health, the medic confirmed he could find nothing physically wrong with him and appeared to be in charge of his faculties. As soon as Med-I-Vac lifted off to Okaloosa County Regional in Fort Walton Beach, Chief Barnes allowed Mac to leave, and then said to the on-scene officer in charge, "I'll deal with Detective McCain later; he's not your concern. Now, get this traffic moving again and open up that bridge, toll-free, before those idiots from Destin have their own break down." Chief Barnes had already heard from the Okaloosa County Sheriff who whined and complained about his men stuck on the other side of the Bay. The chief had no doubt, who gave the order to shut down the tollbooth for traffic coming into Niceville from Destin.

Bonn's blood coated him like the juice from a bloody steak and his matted hair struck a punk rocker's pose that would have looked comical if it had not been so grotesque. The Med-I-Vac paramedics found their patient's status disconcerting and attempted to keep him conscious.

"General, what happened? Can you hear me?" The paramedic pleaded with no response then made rapid circles with his finger as an indication for the pilot to hurry. The pilot pushed the multi-million dollar helicopter to its limit and gave the initial status report to the ER staff that scrambled to the hospital helipad.

"We have a 50-55 year old Caucasian male, six foot, 185. GSW head wound with multiple cranial contusions, vomiting, and possible concussion. Doc, there is massive swelling to right orbit and rupture to eye. There are many secondary GSWs upper torso, possible internal bleeding. HR is fifty-two and irregular. BP is eighty over fifty and falling. Doc, this is going to be a tough one, possible Tango One, scrub up. Six minutes out."

CHAPTER 9

P aula hated hunting season. Carl would get up hours before sunrise to head off to the woods and return in time for lunch. When Carl's pickup slid into the parking lot and sprayed gravel against the aluminum skirting of their doublewide trailer, Paula thought bullets had riddled her trailer. Petrified, she belly-flopped on the trailer's burnt orange shag carpeting and managed to maintain control of her giant mug of Diet Coke without spilling a drop. When she heard a door slam, followed by Carl screaming a profanity, the hairs on her arms rose, and she subconsciously began to wring her hands.

Outside, dressed in hunting clothes, Carl stood next to his truck rubbing his head and Arnie staggered around like a spring breaker after too many Jell-O shots. In their haste, both men had jumped out of their trucks, hitting their heads on the cab's roof. Her attention shifted from their head banging, to the holes in the door and windshield of Arnie's pickup. Judging from the knot on his forehead, the starburst crack in the windshield came from Arnie's head.

"What kind of a mess have you two gotten' into?" Paula said with her hands on her hips and tapped her foot.

"What the hell are you looking at?" Carl said and continued rubbing his head.

"You tell me. What did ya'll do?" She regretted her question immediately.

"Nothin', mind you own *damn* business. Get your fat ass in the trailer and make us a couple of sandwiches," Carl said, then leaned in to Paula's face and shouted," Now!" His tone not only frightened her, it caught the attention of the workers who were inspecting the holes in Armando's pickup.

When Paula came back holding a tray of food, she heard Carl talking on his cell phone, "Don't worry about him, he won't make it out of the hospital alive."

"Who were you talking to? *Who* won't make it out of the hospital?" Paula knew when the word left her mouth, a line was crossed and she would pay a price for asking about his personal business.

He ignored her question, stared at her chest and started laughing. "Did you stop at the slop bucket while you were in there?" Carl asked then pointed at her white blouse where a glob of peanut butter and jelly had landed on one of her giant breasts.

"You are such a pig. I should just put you on a skewer and roast you."

Paula pretended to take the ridicule in stride, and to the amusement of Carl but not to Armando, hoisted her F-cup and licked it off her 'bizness' blouse. "I hope it doesn't leave a stain. I need to go soak it in bleach."

Carl laughed when her shoulders slumped forward and she blushed. His throbbing foot was more important than hurt feelings. He needed a couple of painkillers, plus a cocaine boost, both were in the office and that is where he was going before he did anything else.

"Keep an eye out for the pigs while I figure out what to do."

"We got no worries amigo, he dint' know us."

Carl pointed at his truck and said, "Do you see the *Beachside Landscaping* on the tailgate and doors?"

"Si," Arnie said.

"Well dumb ass, you can bet he saw it too! If he is alive, this is the first place they'll come! You 'dint' think of that did you?"

Paula could not help herself and jumped into the conversation. "Alive? What are you talking about, Carl? I heard you talking about someone not making it out of the hospital when you were on the phone. And, what the hell happened to your foot?"

The moment she saw the look on Carl's face she covered her mouth. It was too late; he turned and backhanded her so hard, flashbulbs went off. She wanted to avoid another blow, and waddled to the trailer as fast as her short stumps would take her. *Swisht, Swisht.* When she reached the grated metal steps to the trailer's front door, she pulled her cell phone out and punched in a number. While rubbing her cheek with one hand and holding her phone with the other, she gave Carl a hatred-filled stare and disappeared behind a slammed door.

Carl hobbled to the business office and walked straight to the desk where he retrieved his .38 caliber, Security-6 revolver and set it down with the barrel pointed at the door. The next minute involved refilling his little brown bottle with cocaine and inhaling a small pile of the crystalline rocks. When the initial rush subsided, he looked up to see Paula standing at the office door with her cell phone in hand and staring at the revolver on her desk.

"What'd ya' need that gun for?" Paula spoke with an uncharacteristic air of confidence.

Holding his six-shooter of manliness and rushing with a drug-induced courage, Carl jumped up and shoved his gun inches from her face. "If you say another word to me I'm going to blow your fat head off! Tell me who you were on the phone with when you went in the trailer."

Shocked by the gun in her face, Paula gasped and clutched her enormous chest. Bug-eyed and with her hand on her heart, Paula fell back and cracked her head on the corner of the small metal filing cabinet next to her desk. As she lay limp and lifeless, Carl's anger overcame him and he ground the muzzle to her forehead, ready to shoot, but decided not to pull the trigger when she didn't open her eyes.

He didn't care if her heart stroked, or the impact of hitting her head killed her; he wanted to see who she called ed couldn't find her phone. Her blood pooled on the concrete floor and added to his paranoia as it oozed towards the rug covering the trap door. His mind raced from the mix of cocaine and adrenaline as he debated what to do next.

Carl decided it would be a great misdirection if he called 911 and acted like a panicking distraught husband reporting a heart attack. Convinced that no one would argue with him that her obesity caused her stroke and subsequent fall, he adopted the explanation as his story. Confident in his ability to play a grief-stricken spouse, he lifted the handset of Paula's pink phone and dialed.

"911. What is the nature of your emergency?"

"Help me! My wife just had a heart attack and hit her head when she fell! There's friggin' blood everywhere and I don't know what to do!"

"Sir, calm down and tell me the address of your emergency."

"I'm at Beachside Landscaping, next to Powder Sands Park; a quarter mile off 85 on Dolphin! Hurry…Pleeeeze." Carl tried to sound choked up. Thanks to the surging effects of too much cocaine, his words came out strained and distorted.

"Did you say, Dowlfin? Sir, Dowlfin?" The 911 operator, a New York transplant, found Carl's southern drawl foreign.

"You know…the fish? Dolphin? Damn it, Mahi-Mahi!"

"Sir, please remain calm. You said 'Beachside Landscaping, a quarter of a mile off 85th and Dolphin? Do you have an address?"

"Off Highway 85, not 85th, on Dolphin. That *is* my address you stupid bitch! Now send a damn ambulance! She's bleeding all over the place!" Finesse wasn't Carl's strong suit when under the influence.

"Sir, is she breathing?"

"No, goddamn it." Then, just as gracefully as his answer, he slammed the receiver down with enough force to shatter Paula's pink princess phone. While transfixed on the pieces of pink plastic littering the desktop and floor, paranoia hit him; his loss of composure might complicate his story of Paula's demise. Carl devised a plan out of the fear of charges, under a liberal law, for swearing at the 911 operator and hanging up. Carl made an effort to add credibility to his story and ripped open one of his Camel cigarettes, rubbed the tobacco between his fingers, then wiped the nicotine-laced digits on his eyes.

The ensuing tears and bright red eyelids made the role of a distraught husband in shock, Oscar worthy.

Unbelievably, after picking up Paula's pink princess phone, the twisted metal bell began ringing a muffled chime. Impulsively, Carl ripped the cord out of the wall then stuffed the shattered phone and all the scattered parts in the desk drawer and sat back down to go over his cover story. The tears coming from his burning eyes helped him portray the role of a grieving husband, but he needed to gain some composure before the authorities arrived and spent the next few minutes taking slow, deep breaths.

When the first two sheriff's deputies arrived, they encountered a scene played out daily in America's southern border towns, not in northern Florida. At least a dozen Mexican men were milling around, drinking from paper bags and grinding cigarette butts into the ground. By the look on their faces, the deputies suspected not all the cigarettes were tobacco.

The curious group of workers standing by the office door parted to make room for the deputies. A deputy asked no one in particular, "Habla English?"

Arnie lied by omission and displayed a small gap between his thumb and index finger then said, "Si, a leetle'".

"Where's the injured woman? Do you comprende?"

The urgency in the deputy's voice wasn't met with much enthusiasm as Arnie, already nervous, hitched his thumb towards the office's front door. He couldn't help remembering doing the same thing in the woods when Bonn asked where he and Carl parked their trucks.

Before following his partner into the landscaping office, the deputy commented to Arnie, "That's a pretty bad bump on your forehead 'Taco'. Do you want to tell me what happened?"

"No comprende," Arnie said and touched his forehead with his middle finger.

"If you didn't understand, why did you touch it? What's your name potner?"

"Que?"

"We'll talk later, don't go anywhere. Comprende that?" The deputy said then followed his partner.

The stream of police, ambulance, and fire trucks arriving at the same time created a panic throughout the workers. Most of the men were undocumented and eased their way in different directions.

Since Arnie held a Green card, he had no reason to leave. Against his better judgment, he stayed to see what Carl had done.

CHAPTER 10

The deputies entered Beachside Landscaping and through the wire cage surrounding the office, could see Paula lying motionless in a pool of her own blood. Carl, teary-eyed from the nicotine rubbed into them, knelt next to her and held her hand for all to see. The deputies assumed they were witnessing a husband on the verge of a breakdown.

"I think my wife had a heart attack. She grabbed her chest then fell back and hit her head," Carl said while holding his hands over his heart then pointed to the corner of the two-drawer metal filing cabinet smeared with blood.

As EMSA personnel ran in carrying their orange medic bags, an officer said, "Sir? I'm Deputy Stevens, please step over here and let the medics do their job. What's your wife's name?"

"Paula, Paula Perkins. I'm her husband, Carl."

"I'm sorry for your loss Mr. Perkins. How long ago did this happen?"

"What the hell do you mean? It just happened and I immediately called 911."

The deputy hesitated after Carl's passive-aggressive response; he was more interested in the drops of dried blood trailing through the office left by Carl's bloody foot. "Was your wife already bleeding when she came in here?"

"Already bleeding? No, she was standing right there and fell," Carl said and glanced at the paramedic performing CPR. Carl rocked from one foot to the other, wobbled ever so slightly, and the deputy grabbed Carl's elbow to steady him. Some feelings never went away, and Carl fought to contain himself when he felt the deputy's hand. He vividly recalled an incident, decades earlier, when he plunged his knife into a university policeman who grabbed his arm and forced him to stand during an anti-war protest.

Deputy Stevens recalled the bump on Arnie's forehead and asked, "Were you in a fight?"

"No, I shredded it with a weed eater and it hurts like hell." Carl lifted his foot for the deputy to inspect. While the deputy stared at the tip of his peppered and slightly pink Nike, Carl realized he wasn't asked about his tennis shoe.

Deputy Stevens had a good idea what made the holes and played along until he could piece together the connection between Carl's shoe, the death of his wife, and the injury to the Mexican worker on the porch. He diffused the situation by pretending the explanation was plausible and said, "Well potner', let's have the medics take a look at your foot while they're here. Okay?"

"It's not that bad, I'll be..." he wanted to dismiss the severity of his injury when he heard a medic shout the one word he didn't want to hear, "Clear!"

"Stay here, I'll be right back," the deputy said as he rushed to join his partner.

"Clear? What the fuck?" Stunned, Carl had spoken aloud. Both deputies turned when the supposedly distressed spouse cursed. They knowingly glanced at each other to confirm each other's suspicions.

The workers who had not gone into hiding, stood next to Arnie and watched the scene playing out next to 'Miss Paula's' desk.

"What are you looking at? You've never seen a dead person?" Carl asked.

Startled, half of them answered in unison, "Que?"

"What happened to Miss Paula?" Arnie whispered.

"That fat bitch had a heart attack and cracked her head when she fell. I thought she was dead, now I don't know. It sounded like they were trying to shock her back." Carl noticed the deputy was trying to hear what was being said and followed with, "Please Lord, help her."

"Que? Miss Paula is dead?"

"Why do you care?"

Before Arnie could respond, another team of paramedics entered the building with a gurney. Carl leaned against the wall to give them room and felt the pistol tucked in the waistband of his lower back. After turning his back to the deputies and standing face-to-face with Arnie, Carl smiled and spoke with clenched teeth, "I'm going to give you my piece. Put it somewhere and make sure nobody is watching."

Arnie vehemently shook his head until he felt the barrel pushing into his gut.

"Take the damn gun," Carl demanded without moving his lips.

Arnie, blocked from view by Carl's body, slid it into his waistband. The gun, hidden under his shirt, hung heavy and started pulling down his already low-riding britches. When Carl dropped his vial of cocaine into Arnie's shirt pocket, he grabbed Carl's wrist and held tight.

"What 'choo' want me to do with that?"

"You'll do what I tell you," Carl retorted furiously and jerked his arm free.

Inches from Carl's face, Arnie, who usually spoke with a heavy accent, spoke in perfect English, "I'm not going down for you, and it ends today."

That's when Carl felt the pistol he gave Armando pressing into his stomach. He whispered angrily, "You have just messed with the wrong guy."

Deputy Stevens split the tension from across the room when he said, "Mr. Perkins, would you come here?"

Carl spun around and saw the deputy pointing to a spot next to him, the same way his father used to point, prior to beating him.

While Carl walked towards the deputy, Arnie eased out of the office and dumped Carl's gun into a 55-gallon drum used to burn trash.

As Carl approached the deputy, he regretted giving his gun to Arnie. When he was on the way, his jaw dropped and he stopped. The gurney with Paula on it was making its way out the office cage and the deputy straight-armed him to the chest. Carl could barely control his rage and instinctively checked the accessibility of the deputy's weapon. He trained for such predicaments in the military, and he visualized snatching the deputy's gun, shooting him first, and then his partner.

Standing next to the gurney, Carl stared at the bright-red blemish on Paula's forehead. The bruise he made with the barrel of his gun had grown, but only one of the many spots on her face and neck. It wasn't the first time he had seen her have an allergic reaction, but he couldn't figure out when she might have eaten nuts. Although she kept, Epinephrine pens in the desk drawer, in their trailer, and in her purse, Carl refused to disclose the fact that she even had an allergy.

Paula was unable to speak through the respirator and tell the paramedic about her pens, glared directly at Carl. He didn't care why other blemishes were covering her arms and legs; he needed the deputy's focus to shift away from the one he had caused.

"I thought she was dead, thank you for saving her." Carl said, and tried to divert attention away from her face by waving his hand over her arms, "What the hell, does she have chicken pox?

"It looks like hives. Sir, your wife had a fatal stroke. Fortunately, we were able to get her breathing again. I'm sorry; we need to move her… now."

Carl reclaimed his role as a despondent loved one, then spoke softly, just loud enough to be heard, "Thank God. Praise Jesus. Thank you Lord."

The paramedics, with the help of several officers, groaned as they lifted the stretcher in the back of the ambulance. Eerily, Paula never tried to speak; her eyes remained locked on Carl. As the ambulance's back doors closed, the rock song *Stairway to Heaven* started playing from inside one of the gigantic pockets of her Hawaiian dress. A paramedic emptied the contents of her pocket into Carl's hands; he began with her pink, rhinestone-covered cell phone. When the Led Zeppelin song she used for her ringtone, finished playing, Carl recognized the caller's number, it was a number he knew by heart. The paramedic continued to pull out treasures from the pocket, including a crinkled granola bar wrapper rolled out on the floor and landed at Carl's feet that no one seemed to notice.

"Potner', they're taking her to Fort Walton. Are you able to drive?"

Carl, still mesmerized by the number that appeared on Paula's phone, didn't respond. The number belonged to the same person he called as Bonn drove to freedom after being shot.

"Mr. Perkins, can you drive?" the deputy repeated.

"What? Drive? Yes, of course," Carl said.

"If I could see some ID and get a number where you can be reached, then you can go be with your wife."

"No problem." Carl snapped his driver's license out of his wallet with the skill of a magician making a card magically appear.

"I'll be brief," the deputy said as he studied Carl's license. "I need you to start at the beginning, and tell me one more time…what happened."

After repeating his story exactly and getting permission to leave, Carl hurried towards his vehicle. He spotted Arnie leaning against the bed of the pickup, and said with a wink, "Let's go, they've taken her to Fort Walton, we need to talk to her before she talks to anyone else."

"What do mean, *we* need to talk to her?" Arnie said in perfect English, and then reluctantly climbed into Carl's truck.

When the dually's four rear tires scratched at the gravel, the first words out of Carl's mouth angered Arnie, "We, me, us…whatever, just give me the coke."

"This crap is going to kill you," Arnie said, again without an accent, and he handed Carl the little brown bottle.

"Shut the hell up and give me my piece too."

Arnie gingerly touched the tender bump on his forehead in the visor's mirror, and said without any hint of his heritage in his voice, "I hid it. I didn't know if the police were going to question me or not, and I wasn't going to get caught with *your* gun. Screw you."

"Damn it Arnie, tell me where you put it…I need my damn gun," Carl said and again, still had not noticed the change in Arnie's demeanor or his sudden loss of a Mexican accent.

Arnie pointed to an area on the opposite side of the parking lot, and then pulled down the pickup's visor to get a better view of the lump on his forehead.

"Listen to me 'beaner'; I don't give a damn about your little bump. Tell me where you pointed so I can get my gun." Carl said. "Do you comprende?"

"It's in the…burn barrel." Arnie's cold stare went unnoticed by Carl.

"Well, you better hope no one saw you put it there. Go get it. You won't be seen; the truck will block anyone's view," Carl said then made a u-turn and pulled up to the barrel.

After reluctantly retrieving the pistol, Carl tucked it under the front seat and began mocking the local law enforcement for not piecing together his role in Paula's unfortunate accident.

Arnie had enough, and said in perfect English without a hint of an accent, "My name is *Armando*, not *'Arnie'*, and my last name isn't Gonzalez. Right now, I'm worried about Miss Paula; she has always been good to me and my men. What did you do to her?"

Carl, shocked by what he had just heard, pulled over on the shoulder so fast; he almost slid into a drainage ditch. "Listen to me asshole, I don't care who you are…, and let me make this clear…, you are a nothing but a foreman, they are…*my* men."

"No, they work for me; you just think they work for you. I'm not going to play the dumb Mexican with you anymore. Let me make something perfectly clear to you, get your shit together, lay off the drugs, and make plans to lay low for a while. The cops aren't stupid, and they're going to figure out whatever it is you did to Miss Paula. And, if you're not careful, they will find out about your screw up with that guy you are calling, Bonn," Armando said, and put his finger in front of Carl's face. "I have too much invested to lose everything because of a cokehead like you; I'm not going to go down with you."

Armando pulled out his own Glock to make his point and get Cap's undivided attention. While staring down the barrel of Armando's gun, Carl started laughing hysterically and began drumming the steering wheel to the beat of the 1960's drum solo, "Wipe Out".

"I'm not going to fall for that crap, if your hand leaves the steering wheel, I will shoot you the second you reach for your gun," Armando said.

Carl stopped drumming and glared at Armando, then said, "Everything has been an act since I met you in El Paso, hasn't it? Who the hell are you anyway?"

"I'm a pissed off Lieutenant of the Sinaloa Cartel who wishes it was you in that ambulance. I should have eliminated you the day I realized you were a drug addict. While you've been moving kilos of pot, I've established a distribution network from Tallahassee to Pensacola, and guess what, I'm going to let you keep your little growing operation. If I wanted to get in the pot market, I'd have a ship bring in a ton at a time. What you do is…nothing." Armando said, "I bring in kilos of that crap you keep putting up your nose, and I make a lot more money without the hassle. Now, I have to tell my boss why it's going to stop because of your stupidity. You will be lucky if he doesn't kill you."

"You're lying," Carl said.

"Are you really that stupid? Do you really think I've magically lost my accent, and I'm making up a story?" Armando said and looked down while shaking his head in disgust of Carl's stupidity.

That's when Armando's gun was snatched from his hand. "Who's stupid now?" Carl said, and tapped Armando's tender forehead with the pistol's barrel.

Armando appeared unfazed, and kept looking at the visor mirror, then said with an air of confidence, "Take a look in your mirror, here come some of my men right now," Armando smiled,. "In case you're wondering, they grew up with assault rifles and are expert shots. My men are ruthless former military and elite 'policia'. If anything happens to me, they will feed you to the gators."

"Do you really think a couple of 'spics' are going to scare me? I've worked for the military for decades, and I've used more weapons than you've seen in your life," Carl said, "Amigo, I don't give a crap about some cartel in another country, but if you can supply 'kilos' of coke, then there isn't any reason we both couldn't benefit from that money train; I want in…"

Armando waved off the men in the pickup that pulled next to Carl's truck, then extended his hand to get his gun back, and said, "If a cop pulls up to see why we're sitting on the side of the road, both of us will be going to jail. We'll talk about this later. Let's go check on Miss Paula. I have an idea that could benefit both of us."

Carl handed Armando his gun, and continued driving to Fort Walton to check on Paula. After a minute of silence, he said, "Alright, what's this idea of yours?"

"If the cops don't arrest you, I want you to sell us the landscaping business and trailer park. Sell it to us for half its market value and we'll give you the difference in cash or cocaine, at a discounted price. You can take the money and buy an island somewhere that you can play soldier, or sell the coke and triple your money." Armando said.

Carl drove for miles before saying, "Why wouldn't I just sell the business to someone else at full market value and then buy product from you?"

"You're not very bright; we can pay cash for the business, and do it off the books. If you have the time to put your rundown business on the market, and wait for a buyer, go ahead. But don't think for a second, we'll sell you any product at a discount, we won't." Armando knew he made an offer Carl wouldn't refuse.

Carl didn't respond, he stared straight ahead.

"I want an answer today. You're either in, or not. There isn't anything to negotiate, don't try. If my people don't accept my plan, we can both kiss our asses' goodbye. They don't give a damn about anything except their money, and they're not going to be very happy about their cash flow stopping because you tried to kill your wife and got caught.."

"I didn't try to kill that bitch, she had a heart attack. She's a traitor, and called someone who can take us both down. She knows way too much about my operations and therefore…" Paula's phone interrupted Carl with another rendition of *Highway to Heaven*. The call was coming from the same number he saw when the paramedic emptied her pockets and gave him the phone.

Carl put his finger to his lips, answered the call, and said, "The next time I see you, I'm going to kill you. No bitch double-crosses me."

Immediately after the call ended, the phone let out a series of beeps. When Carl opened the *NEW MESSAGE*, from *UNKNOWN*, two old police mug shots, decades old, appeared with the caption, Carl A. Perkins-Julio Diaz. With-in seconds, the images collapsed like falling dominos, one small square at a time, until the photo completely disappeared.

CHAPTER 11

U pon entering the posh and tasteful cherry wood office from her personal back entrance, one of the Air Force's only female commanders overheard her personal assistant on the verge of yelling.

"Yes...sir. Yes... sir. Yes...Sir," Jenn said then slammed the received down.

The commander walked into the reception area, and saw her assistant Jennifer staring in disbelief at her phone. Eglin AFB's Wing Commander Cari Bentow, walked up from behind and said, "Yes...sir?"

"Commander!" 'Jenn' almost wet herself. I liked it better in the old days at Wright-Patterson; at least I could hear you coming." *Your heels clicked on the tile as you walked, but not here with all this damn carpeting.*

"You could hear me coming? I don't know what the hell that means." Commander Bentow emphasized her words with hand gestures. "So, are you going to tell me who gave you orders?"

"General Hearns... he..." Jennifer choked on her emotions.

"Damn it, Jennifer. Speak up, he...what?" The commander asked with an attitude that demanded an immediate answer.

Jenn wasn't surprised by the sudden appearance of Cari's military persona; she had seen her friend switch personality roles many times. After retiring as a communications specialist with the Air Force, she went to work as Cari's personal secretary. They were close friends, and on a first-name basis, except when they were at work, where Cari insisted on military decorum. So, Jenn addressed her as, Colonel, Commander, or Ma'am.

"Commander, are you ready for a story that will make your week?" Although she separated from the Air Force a few years prior, Jennifer tried to maintain her military decorum.

Cari mumbled, "Damn, I need a cigarette."

"Go ahead and light one up, I can wait," Jenn said, even though she knew her friend would fight through the urge.

Jenn had witnessed Cari's constant struggle during her year of tobacco abstinence and tried to help her by making sure containers of cinnamon, carrot, and celery sticks were always on the commander's desk. The pacifiers served as a gauge to her friend's mood, Jenn stayed out of Cari's way whenever a stick was in hand.

Cari held a cinnamon stick between her fingers and pretended to take a drag, then said, "I'm sorry for the temporary insanity. *Jennifer*, go ahead and tell me your little story."

"*Commander*, I don't think it's a story," Jenn cleared her throat and said, "I was told, around 0800 this morning, in Sector six, a civilian was shot while hunting." Then, she grabbed her water bottle and took a long, slow drink to buy a little time before she had to tell the whole story.

"Alright, I'll bite. It must be good, you look a little nervous. What... exactly, did General Hearns say happened?"

"When the call came in, security was already in the area, eradicating dozens of marijuana plants that were found during a training exercise. The plants were in large black plastic containers and appeared to be strategically placed along the edge of a creek to help conceal them," Jennifer said with a hint of excitement.

"Why are you telling me about the pot? Did the victim get shot for trying to steal someone's crop?" Colonel Bentow also showed some enthusiasm, she wasn't a stranger to the evil weed.

"That isn't what Security thinks. The area where the shooting took place was approximately one klick from where the plants were found," Jenn said.

"I f they were a little more than a half of a mile away, why he was shot?"

"Ma'am, I don't think General Hearns knew, if he did, he didn't say."

"It had to be some kind of drug deal that went bad," Cari said.

"They don't think so; they thought it was just a random shooting until the shooting victim told a Niceville detective to look for pot in the area.

"The shooting victim's alive? None of this makes sense. The victim wasn't' anywhere near the pot, and yet, he knew enough to tell the authorities to look for marijuana? It still sounds like a drug dispute," Commander Bentow said.

"I don't think so, Ma'am."

Commander Bentow rubbed her temples and the impatience in her voice served as a warning for Jennifer to get to the point. "Give me something besides a theory; did the 'vic' have a history?"

Jennifer swallowed again. "They ran a background check and discovered he's a contractor on the base and works in military intelligence. They don't believe he had any prior knowledge of the pot, they think he might have been hunting. According to General Hearns, most of background information on the man who was shot, is classified."

Jennifer was dreading the inevitable line of questions that would be coming about the wounded contractor. She remembered hearing rumors a few years back, but she didn't give them much credence until General Hearns referred to the victim as, "Cari's old flame".

Cari picked up a carrot stick and began to chew furiously as her eyes narrowed. "Damn it Jennifer, your giving me a headache... there's something you're not telling me. What's... the victim's... name?"

"Well...uh..."

"I'm not going to ask again." Cari braced herself for the answer she didn't want to hear.

"Retired General M.D. Bonner from Destin, he's a military..." Jenn stopped when she saw her friend turn as white as a snowbird from Michigan.

"I knew it! He went and got shot, *again*. Is he all right? Where is he? What's the diagnosis?" Cari's frantic series of questions left Jenn at a loss for words.

"General Hearns didn't say what General Bonner's condition is right now. Why, do you know him?" Jenn asked suspiciously and tried not to appear coy.

"Yes," Cari said quietly and turned her back to indicate, the end of the conversation.

"Yes? What do you mean? Yes, you know him. That's all, just yes?" Jenn wasn't going to tolerate a simple answer without elaboration, then she saw Eglin's commander choking up, it took her by surprise.

The only time she had seen her friend cry, had been when Cari's mother died. Treading on unfamiliar ground, it felt like she was trespassing on Cari's private feelings and asked, "What's wrong?"

After a few moments of silence, Cari said, "A few years ago, I dated him for about six months.

"Six months! You dated General Bonner for six months without telling me?" Jenn spoke a little too loud.

"Turn it down a notch sweetie. I didn't tell you because it wouldn't have been kosher for me to be dating a government contractor, who just happened to have contracts with this Base, my Base."

"And...?

"And... now, I don't care who knows. The General and I are just friends," Cari said, and picked up her purse. "I need to go see him."

"Stop right there *Cari*..., it's been two years since my last serious relationship and I'm not going to let you leave without giving me the details," Jenn said.

"Excuse me?"

"I'm sorry; I didn't mean to say that. *Please*, don't leave without filling me in on this little romance of yours." Jenn spoke in her sweetest voice.

"*Jenn*, you have an unbelievable imagination. It wasn't a big deal, we had a few dates," Cari said with a smile and took her turn at being coy with her friend, not her assistant.

"If it's not a big deal, then tell me…and don't leave anything out," Jenn continued with her own orders while rubbing her hands together in anticipation.

"Well…" Cari hesitated as she recalled seeing his sleek fly-fishing skiff glide to a muffled swoosh against her dock while toting a fly rod in one hand and a bottle of Chardonnay in the other.

Cari popped out of her trance with a single tear trickling down her face, which she quickly wiped away. Embarrassed that she might have been reminiscing aloud, Cari headed for the door.

"Please don't stop now, I'm not finished! I mean, you're not finished. How romantic is that?" Flustered, and possibly a little jealous, Jenn took her turn at being uncomfortable. "Please continue…he picked you up at sunset in a boat?"

"Well…, I thought Prince Charming had come by water. I felt like whipped butter and I melted." Cari laughed from the relief of finally telling someone how enamored she had been with Bonn since that date.

"A blind beggar on the streets of Bombay could see the way you're glowing right now, you wear it well."

"If you ever tell anyone, I'll kill you. I have deep feelings for him and I think I would die if…"

Jenn dropped her pencil and legal pad and rushed around the desk to embrace her friend.

Cari drew a deep breath and exhaled, which seemed to bring her back to a composed mental state. "Where did they take him?"

"He was airlifted to Okaloosa Regional in Fort Walton." Jenn left out one important fact; the prognosis was dire.

"I have to…go." Cari's voice fell like a soufflé and trailed off to a sweet hush. She knew Bonn would laugh if he could hear her reminiscing about their brief, intense, and memorable relationship. "He loves strong women, and what he calls, their 'gentle gene'.

"Cancel anything I have scheduled, and don't you worry about that prick Hearns, I'll handle him. Call me if you hear anything else," Cari said, and pivoted on one heal, and turned in true military fashion.

Jenn smiled at the sound of clicking heals when Cari marched out of her office and onto the tiled floor.

Less than a minute later, on her way to relieve the bladder pressure that had been building, Jennifer's cell phone vibrated. Even though she saw COMMANDER on the screen, she had to make it to the stall.

"Ma'am?" Jenn asked.

"Jenn, when I walked in, you sounded like you had just been given an order, he can't do that. What did Hearns say to you?"

Now, as she relieved one pressure, another replaced it. Although, both Hearns and Bentow had the authority to make her life hell, her friendship meant more than her job.

"Ma'am, he told me not to tell you anything, except that a civilian contractor had been shot. He wanted to tell you in person, and ended the conversation by saying, I quote, "Listen to me you little bitch, I better not find out you told her it was Bonner who got shot, or you will...."

"Or...what? Damn it Jenn, spit it out." Although Cari's anger wasn't directed at her, Jenn felt the wrath and sat in silence, not knowing what to say next.

"Jennifer, he threatened you with your job, didn't he?"

"Yes Ma'am," she whispered.

"I'm going to have his ass for calling you a name and for ordering you to withhold the details, it's ludicrous. He just wants to rub it in; he knows I have a past with 'Bonn'. He will find out what a real bitch is like when I talk to him," Car, said even though she knew his rank made him almost untouchable.

Jenn, touched by her friend's loyalty, said, "I would never keep anything from you. You know that, don't you?"

"Yes, of course. We are best friends. I told you not to worry. When I get through with him, he'll be asking for your forgiveness!"

"That's not necessary."

"Yes, it is, and I'm sorry he involved you with the intention of getting at me." Cari pushed END on her phone and wept.

CHAPTER 12

Harold "Hank" Hearns first claim to fame, began in Vietnam when he claimed his jet took a hit from anti aircraft fire. Actually, there had been an engine malfunction and he set down his F-4 fighter jet on a North Vietnamese landing strip. The war had been over for 3 days, and the enemy soldiers were too busy celebrating their victory to imprison him. Instead, they requested a plane to pick him up and take him to an American base so they didn't have to deal with him.

The propaganda machine in Washington viewed the release of an American pilot as good fodder for the media and Hank's story took on a life of its own. Hank received the Purple Heart for falling off his jet's ladder and twisting his back. Then, while recuperating, he chipped a tooth trying to remove a beer bottle cap with his teeth, he claimed he was a victim of prisoner abuse and they beat him.

When he returned to the United States, and was introduced to a nationwide audience as "…an American hero, a Purple Heart recipient, a *former* P.O.W., and a God-fearing man, the legend of Hank Hearns was born."

During his first public interview, when the reporter asked about his hero status, he spun the praise perfectly, "I'm just a simple soldier who loves his country". His response made the cover of the Saturday Evening Post, Time magazine, and the Air Force News, it became his go-to answer for almost any question asked.

From that day forward, he requested the word "legend" added to every introduction, article, and interview his publicist could control.

He became obsessed with the acclaim he received upon his return and rewrote his story. Audiences were in awe as they listened to him weave his recollection of events. His story included a gun battle before his capture, then unspeakable torture by the enemy, and it ended with a fabricated story about his escape. If the facts became public, he would be humiliated and the "Legend" would die.

Decades later, as the commander of Security Forces on Eglin AFB, Brigadier General "Hank" Hearns, was listening to his lead investigator finish with the details of the shooting, when his cell phone chimed.

He dismissed the investigator with a wave of his hand, and focused on his phone without saying a word. He had never received, or sent a text message, and yet, 1NEW MESSAGE-UNKNOWN stared back at him. Once he figured out how to read it, a picture of an army operative, in a Vietnam era uniform, appeared with the caption, *Bonner's assassin* written in the subject box. Before Hank had the chance to read the message, his phone rang.

"This is General Hearns, who the hell is this? Yes, I remember you, it's been quite awhile. How are things at the agency?"

He wasn't' sure if the call would be of a sensitive nature and continued with small talk while he closed his office door.

"Yes, I know the senator *and* her. What does *she* have to do with anything? Damn it, I had a feeling this would...I'll take care her as soon as you tell me he's onboard...I don't care, *you* are his handler, handle him," Hank said and ended the call.

Even though Hank just solved the mystery of the message and photo, he summoned the Investigations officer that he dismissed only minutes earlier. When Hank attempted to show him the first text he's ever received, his enthusiasm dissipated rapidly, *Messages* and *Call History*, were empty.

"I'm telling you, I received a photo of a man in army BDU.s with a caption that identified him as General Bonner's assassin."

"When you called me, there hadn't been any information released about the shooting or it being an attempted assassination. Only a few people know General Bonner is still alive, your text messenger may have been the one who gave the order. The sender might have been gloating and giving you a warning. Do you know the soldier in the picture you claim to have received?"

"I'm not *claiming* anything; I've never seen the man in the photo," Hank said and hoped he sounded credible.

"I don't mean to imply anything…Our tech specialists will need access to your phone. They'll be able to determine what number sent the message, as long as it's not one of those throw-away phones."

"There's no record I received a call or text message. I need to think about it before I turn over my personal phone," he said without missing a beat in the conversation, and then Hearns dismissed the security officer, as though he was brushing away imaginary crumbs. Hank wanted to find a way to share the spotlight when the news story broke, but he feared his phone might end up linked to a murder, or attempted murder. That is, if Bonner was still alive.

Paranoia crept into Hanks thoughts as he deleted his cell phone's voicemail messages, cleared his search history, and even though he didn't know what to look for, removed the battery. His biggest concern was the possibility that someone recorded his conversations, especially the call he got after getting his first text message.

When his secretary buzzed on the intercom and said, "General Hearns, Commander Bentow is holding on line two…she doesn't sound very happy." Hank swallowed and took a deep breath.

Worried his warning to Jennifer went unheeded and Cari knew about the threat, he mumbled to himself before picking up his phone's handset, "If that bitch said anything..."

"Cari, Cari, Cari. How is the most beautiful lady in the Air Force?" Hank shoveled old-school sweetness in an attempt to calm the fast approaching storm heading his way.

"You will address me as Commander Bentow, and you won't think I'm a lady when I'm through with you," she said and resisted the urge to verbally castrate him.

"Now, Commander, is it that time of the month again?" Hank continued to try to charm her with sexist understanding; he just lacked any tact and remained oblivious to the possible repercussions his words would bring.

"Listen to me, and listen very carefully. If you want to keep that little dick of yours in uniform, you'll cut the bullshit and tell me what happened."

He lowered his voice for dramatic effect and tested his authority. "I'm going to give *you* a little advice, Commander; you need to be very careful in the way to talk to me."

"Hank, you may outrank me, but I don't answer to you! This is *my* base, I'm Wing Commander. In case you forgot, my orders come from Wright-Patterson, not from you. Tell me, why were you harassing Jenn? What the…" Cari stopped and bit her tongue to keep from cursing, a habit she was trying to break.

"I didn't harass anyone and its *General* Hearns to you. Don't you forget it *Colonel*."

"Didn't you just hear me? Don't try to pull rank. You're a one-star running *my* Security Forces, *for me*, on *my* base."

"I can, I will, and I just did…*Colonel*."

Cari, oblivious to Hank's notation of rank, continued to press the conversation. "What happened in sector six?"

"Well…your old *'friend'* Bonner…, seems to have been…, shot." The way Hank paused for dramatic effect, infuriated Cari.

"My relationship with him is none of your damn business. Just give me the report," Cari ordered.

"Security reported the shooting took place three klicks from that gigantic radar site in the middle of nowhere."

"That area is total wilderness. Why would he be in the woods, almost two miles from the Space Surveillance building?"

"It's not *where* he took the hit; it's *why*."

"I give up, why was he shot?"

"They're not exactly sure, but *we* have a few leads." Hearns decided to put a spin on what he knew. "A Niceville detective had a hunch the shooting was drug related and the M.P.'s searched the area for marijuana plants."

Cari already heard about the pot plants and the Niceville detective and played along. "What do you mean on a hunch? How did a detective know to search for pot in that locale?"

"Your buddy Bonner remembered seeing tools that could be used for pot cultivation in the back of one of the trucks driven by the guy who shot him."

"Wait, if General Bonner told them…that means he's okay?"

"They didn't say he died."

"You're telling me 'one of the trucks' had tools in the back?

So, more than one person was involved. How do they know how many trucks were there?" Cari asked.

"There were three sets of tire tracks leaving the parking area, which means there could be at least other two people involved. They didn't say exactly what was in the back of the trucks, but I would assume there had to be a shovel.

"How do I get you to give me a straight answer? That's it? All they have are some tire tracks?"

"No, they found a bloodied hunter's cap on the edge of the woods; they believe that's where they shot him. It looks like your *friend* could have been ambushed; he probably didn't know what hit him. They also found a shotgun with a bent barrel in the parking area, ballistics is checking to see if it's the gun used on General Bonner. "One of the trucks was a pickup with four rear wheels; I can't remember what kind of truck he called it…"

"It's a damn pickup called a 'Dually', it has one rear axle with two tires on each side," Cari interjected.

"That's it, a 'Dually'. Anyway, there is evidence that one of the pickups crashed into a tree at the parking area but was able to drive out of the area." General Hearn's pretended he didn't know what it could be, even though he owned one and used it to pull his travel trailer.

"Damn it Hank, you are giving me a headache. You've told me about three vehicles, two shooters, a bent shotgun? Get to the point."

"Patience…Commander, they were able to follow the tracks from all three vehicles. We haven't had any rain for a couple of weeks; the roads are dry and dusty, and easy for them to match-up the treads."

"Where exactly did the dirt road lead?"

"Well, civilians called and reported a black Explorer, driving at a high rate of speed and forcing motorists off the road. As you know, Bonner drives a black Explorer. When he came into Niceville's city limit, he crashed. By back tracking the origin of the cell calls, they were able to determine he entered Highway 20 near the entrance to Sector 6."

Cari still wasn't sure she understood exactly what happened, but she didn't want to speak with, or listen to Hank for another second and hung up.

CHAPTER 13

Detective "Mac" McCain's blacked-out Expedition squealed to a hard stop at the valet pulpit at the hospital, and had every head turning with the expectation of seeing a horrendous wreck. Before the fast approaching and irritated attendant had a chance to tell him he not to park where he had stopped, Mac stepped out and flashed his badge.

"Son, I'll be down to move it to parking when I can. I don't believe I've seen you before, are you a new hire?" Mac asked hoping to diffuse the situation.

"Sir, yes Sir. First week…, Sir," replied the recent Air Force veteran with closely cropped hair and a physique worthy of poster model. Although Mac obviously worked for the police, the hospital's attendant could spot a military man when he saw one, and subconsciously stood at full attention while keeping his gaze straight ahead.

"Thank you Smit, there's one more thing I need you to do," McCain said after glancing at the *R. Smit* name badge on the attendant's pocket.

"Sir, yes sir, whatever you need…, sir." Smit's military decorum wasn't helping Mac stay in the present.

"Tighten the perimeter soldier. Don't worry about the vehicle, my dog is in there. She won't let anyone in without paying a price." Mac tapped on the darkened back window, gave a command in a foreign language, and then rushed through the double doors of the hospital.

R. Smit couldn't hear a dog in the SUV, and he didn't know if *"tighten the perimeter"* had been a joke. Regardless, R. Smit had always followed orders and scanned the area's perimeter. The Expedition's darkened windows kept him from seeing inside the vehicle. When his curiosity got the best of him, he casually walked towards the back window, then stopped, mid-step, after hearing a menacing growl.

Mary, the 70-year-old hospital greeter, spotted McCain the moment he burst into the lobby. She knew he worked in Niceville P.D.'s Violent Crimes Division and saw him many times at the hospital.

After acknowledging Mary with a wink and a nod, McCain followed the red line to the Emergency Room as it wound through the hallways. This wasn't the first time he walked the line, and it wouldn't be the last. Before he reached the ER, on his way to inquire about Bonn's condition, his cell phone vibrated.

"McCain here, this better be important."

"Detective, this is Deputy Stevens with the Okaloosa County Sheriff's office. Sir, I know you're at the hospital on a high priority, but I have information on case you may want to look into while you're there."

"What is it Stevens, make it quick," Mac said.

"I responded to domestic at Beachside Landscaping which is next to Powder Sands Park…where those meth dealers were busted? The same guy owns both places, sir."

"That's right. Tell me something I don't know. I'm a little busy right now deputy, what's the problem?"

"Well sir, the wife of the owner had a heart attack, collapsed, and hit her head. When we arrived, EMSA was about to declare her DOA, until they put the paddles on her. The husband's story seems to go with what appears to have happened, but I don't trust his explanation. She should be arriving in the next few minutes; her husband should be there fifteen or twenty minutes later."

"What is it you want me to check out, Stevens?"

"My instincts are telling me the husband had something to do with her heart attack. Detective, when she started coming around, she looked directly at her husband and looked like she wanted to kill him. If she had been able to speak, I believe she would have told us what he did to her. When you talk to him, you will understand why.

He couldn't take his eyes off her and was in shock to see her alive. I'll let you draw your own conclusions. The word around the station is that you and a *friend* know them…Mr. and Mrs. Perkins.

"Perkins? Yeah, I remember them. She's a very large woman who's married to a dirt bag with long hair. As soon as I have a minute, I'll talk to both of them. Officer Stevens, I'll get back with you. Good work." Mac intentionally avoided acknowledging the officer's insinuation about Bonn and continued to the ER wing.

Smit greeted Mac at the E.R's double doors entrance and together, they approached the triage area where two Ft. Walton officers stood outside of the closed curtains surrounding the room holding Bonn. One of the uniforms, who knew Mac and Bonn were friends, spoke as they approached.

"Detective, the trauma team is getting ready to take General Bonner to four-south."

"Four-South means surgery," Mac said and pulled out his cell phone. "Smit, I have a call I need to make, can you stay with these officers then let me know when Bonn's on his way to the OR?"

"Yes sir. If there is anything I can do to help, please don't hesitate to ask."

Mac stepped close to hospital's security guard and said, "Well, there is one more thing; we have a female heart attack victim on the way that may turn out to be a domestic assault. Make sure the husband doesn't see her until I've talked with her?"

R. Smit, placed a hand on Mac's shoulder and said, "Sir, yes sir. From what I have heard, General Bonner is tough. If at any time, I can be of assistance in the search for his assailant, do not hesitate to ask."

"I promise you this much Smit, whoever did this is going to pay, I may take you up on your offer."

"Yes sir," Smit said and his arm started to rise in salute.

"I'll be in the hallway on my phone. Keep me informed and shoot first, if it comes to that," Mac said with a smirk.

Confused by Mac's choice of the words, "shoot first", Smit instinctively felt for his weapon.

CHAPTER 14

D uring her divorce from the Post Commander at Fort Benning, Georgia, Colonel Rebecca Fagan learned her new assignment would take her to Northwest Florida's Eglin Air Force Base; she stayed adamant in the property negotiations over a condominium located in nearby Destin.

Until recently, Ft. Benning, an army post in Georgia, had been Rebecca's "long distance" home during her deployments around the world. She figured she spent a total of six months in base housing with her husband at Ft. Benning. The other four and a half years of their marriage, she lived alone in base housing provided by the Air Force, a different temporary home came with every new assignment.

Her marriage to the post's commander had been tumultuous; the only time they really spent together happened when she had an extended leave. Rebecca didn't know if she disliked the army or just loved the Air Force more, whenever she returned to their house at Fort Benning, she couldn't wait to leave. As it turned out, she had an aversion to both, and they spent most vacations at the condo he owned at the Fort Benning Army recreation center in Destin. The allure of warm, emerald green water and sugar-white sand beaches persuaded her to go after the property when she filed for divorce.

Rebecca's efforts paid off when the court awarded her the property in the divorce settlement. She spent long hours admiring the view from the veranda, and reminiscing about what could have been decades ago with Bonn. Being the owner of a condominium in a prime location with a million dollar view was a dream-come-true, no one to share it with left her feeling incomplete.

Although the official announcement of her return to the area wasn't made, she already received congratulatory calls and emails from those "in the know". Officially, she would be the new Interagency Liaison to the Air Force, which was a title unfamiliar to everyone. Unofficially, Colonel Fagan worked for joint covert operations with the C.I.A, in the overseas arena; this assignment would be in her old stomping grounds. Her previous deployments with the Special Activities Division landed her in the Middle East; she hoped this domestic deployment to Eglin would be less stressful and safer.

Rebecca's return to the area brought back memories of happier days. As a young airman, and prospective Special Op's candidate, she received orders to meet with a superior officer who would put her through the initial screening process for membership into the elite group. A woman gaining admission in the 1-S.O.W. or Special Op's Wing was almost unheard of at the time. Disclosing the possibility of a woman being in one of the country's elite covert operations organizations would be unthinkable, and definitely unacceptable to the American public.

In contrast to the stereotypical image of a female soldier, Rebecca was a dark-haired, brown-eyed beauty, with a towering five-foot nine-inch frame. While wearing her uniform, she appeared to be on the thin side, but her body mass index tipped the charts toward the muscular side. If being gorgeous and walking with an air of sensuality had been a requirement, she would have received immediate membership. In addition to an Ops consideration, her name was on the short list of candidates for Delta Force.

Officially, The White House, Department of Defense, and the Secretary of the Air Force, denied the existence of Delta Force along with the possibility of a female becoming a member Special Ops.

Early in her career, Rebecca excelled during her Ops training and hoped Special Ops would be in her future. When she began to doubt her chances, Rebecca received orders to meet with the officer who would make the final decision. He didn't want to meet her at Command and Control. Instead, he chose a place where he could judge her hands-on skills, and to meet him at the Hurlburt Field pistol range.

She arrived an hour early for the appointment with the officer she only knew by reputation as the "best of the best", but she didn't have a clue what he looked like. It wasn't the first time she followed orders without knowing what to expect and never questioned the location. Rebecca wondered why he chose the range for their meeting; she assumed it had something to do with her efficiency and skills. Unable to resist the opportunity to practice her skills while she waited, she stepped up to a shooting station and emptied her weapon. As she stood and admired the grouping on her target, a round of perfectly placed shots from the station next to her shredded the blackened center of *her* target. The shots hit so rapidly, small bits of paper were floating as though suspended before they fell in a confetti shower.

Rebecca stepped back from station's partition, ready to say something to the shooter who cleaned up on her target. Standing stone-faced with his gun holstered, and his arms crossed, was an officer in his BDU's; the name on his jacket identified him as Col. Bonner.

"I'm sorry, is that your target?" he asked innocently, he wanted to say, "Oh my God, you're beautiful."

"Sir, yes Sir!" she answered while coming to attention and saluting.

"Encounters with the enemy rarely last more than a couple of seconds. If you're going to survive, you need to improve your speed and work on your aim." With that said, he turned and walked away with a simple promise, "I'll be in touch."

Humbled by his display of marksmanship and the seriousness of his statement, she spent countless hours at the range practicing.

A month had passed without any word from him. Then, at an Intel' briefing, she found herself face-to-face with the man who held her fate in his hands.

"Colonel Bonner, it's good to see you again."

"Airman, it's good to see you again as well. I want you to know, even though you haven't heard from me, I didn't forget about you. Word has it; you've been spending time at the range, is that true?"

"Yes, that's one rumor you can believe. I've been working on my target shredding skills." Rebecca smiled ever so slightly.

"That's good because you're going to need them. I wanted to tell you in person, you're accepted into the program, actually, for several programs, besides our Ops."

When he shook her hand to congratulate her, he held it a little longer than expected and they both felt a degree of discomfort. With-in weeks, and on the first date, he revealed he had just ended a relationship with a woman he met at Quantico.

"She's one of the first female agents to work with the Special Forces and worked for the Agency's Special Activities Division, it's sad. I don't mean emotionally, I mean S...A...D., get it?"

Rebecca didn't respond to Bonn's corny attempt at humor. "Anyway..., my time at Command is very demanding but that's not the real reason the relationship failed. Uh...long distance relationships are very difficult and..."

Again, Rebecca remained motionless and relished in watching him squirm. And...we were miles apart in philosophy when it came to covert strategies. She worked under the constraints of men in suits that stayed with a plan, and rarely deviated from it. As you know, many times, our Ops' teams have to learn to adapt their strategies in the middle of the operation."

Rebecca understood the differences between military operations and the "suits" from Washington. She didn't care about Bonn's recent breakup or his ex-girlfriend's expertise, and made sure he dropped both subjects.

"Do you know the difference between going on a date with a man who talks about his ex, and one who doesn't" Rebecca asked.

"No," Bonn said.

"Obviously," Rebecca said with a hint of irritation in her voice.

Early in their relationship, Rebecca and Bonn were solid in their commitment to each other. Unlike with his ex, they agreed on military strategies, and wore the same wardrobe. Unfortunately, the Air Force's first female Special Ops member had to keep her association with SOW Commander, confidential. Her secret became easier with each of his TDY orders that turned out to be longer than temporary, and his duties always required him to be in other countries. As Bonn's extended absences lengthened, Rebecca's heart didn't grow fonder.

History repeated itself when she learned, Bonn left for an assignment, in the middle of the night without contacting her. By the time he returned to Florida, Rebecca was gone, and they both inherited the title of "ex".

Now, decades later, she was back in Destin and spending a Sunday afternoon at *Beachfront Bar and Grille*. The moment she sat down at the bar, she daydreamed of her past life with Bonn. Rebecca always considered the elevated deck with the postcard view, "their" spot. After all, it was the site of their first date and first kiss.

Most tourists leave Destin by noon on Sundays. The tourists came to Destin to fish, party, and relax and by Sunday morning, they were usually exhausted, sunburned, and heading back home on the Interstates and over-priced flights. Absent of the crush of tourists, Sunday afternoons became a traditional time for the locals to gather at Beachfront's open-air upper deck for a shrimp boil, listen to their favorite bands, and dance. On her first "local's" Sunday, back as a single woman, Colonel Fagan wore her 'civvies for an afternoon of music and people watching. She wanted to blend in while relishing in her new found freedom and to celebrate her new assignment. She drew in a deep breath of clean Gulf air as a symbolic gesture of *out with the old and in the new*; her new life.

Even though it had been twenty years since the last time she and Bonn were together, Rebecca defied the aging process and didn't hide it. Subconsciously, the civilian clothes she chose were tight designer jeans and a white, button-down shirt, which happened to be the only thing he left at her place; she couldn't throw it away. Her mind kept drifting to daydreams about a time she served him breakfast in bed wearing it, and nothing else.

Unexpectedly, she saw Bonn standing at the rail of the upper-deck club. He was gazing out at the constant stream of bikini-clad boats showing off their bronzed bodies. Although there were fishing charters, manned with sunburned land lovers showing off their catch after a hard day at sea, his attention stayed on the coming and going of the bikinis.

The sight of him and his thick wavy hair blowing in the Gulf breeze, revived the memory of their first kiss, and made her heart ache. She wanted to hear him call her name at that special moment, and how it pushed her over the edge. The very thought of being joined with him, made her squirm. Somehow, she needed to muster enough courage to walk up to her former lover and act surprised to see him. She had to talk to him, no matter how nervous she felt; losing him again was not an option.

When her iPhone vibrated and chimed, she snapped out of the erotic daydream and almost threw the phone over the bar. Rebecca frantically scanned for him in all directions, and then realized her imagination had been at play.

NEW TEXT MESSAGE-BBB appeared on the screen of her cell phone. According to the message, her Big Brother Bob, a Med-I-Vac pilot and paramedic, wanted to know about the man in her thoughts. At first, she didn't understand the message and sent a text back. *Wats name of Colonel u dated, Bonner?*

Unconvinced the text from her brother wasn't a dream as well, she responded, *Bonn. Why r u asking?*

BBB texted back, *Flew 2 ORMC. Shot. Can't talk. W C ASAP*

With trembling hands, Rebecca immediately sent another text message to her brother, *WTF? SHOT?*

After a very long minute without a response, she hoped the delay did not mean...Confused and concerned, she sat in stunned silence reading and re-reading the text. Without dawdling, she gulped down her Margarita and got up to run to her car, only to stop in her tracks. When brain-freeze stuck her to the bar, her daydream turned into a nightmare. She held her head in both hands, moaned, and shouted over the music, "Damn."

The cute bartender with coal black hair and ice-blue eyes, who caught her staring at him earlier, told her to push her tongue on the roof of her mouth to get rid of the headache, amazingly it worked. She reached into her purse, grabbed a ten and slapped it down on the bar, mouthed a sweet *thank you*, then sprinted to her car.

Rebecca could cut the drive time from Destin to Fort Walton Beach and Okaloosa Regional Hospital in half by following the Air Force 'flyboys' racing their Mustang GT convertibles and crotch-rocket motorcycles. Her classic red Porsche Carrera GT drafted in the air current of a candy-apple red convertible running interference from the radar-wielding officers patrolling coastal Highway 98 until her cell phone alerted with another message. Assuming her brother Bob sent an update; she braked hard, and parked on the road's shoulder.

The cell phone's screen read, New Message UNKNOWN. When she opened it, a picture of Bonn appeared with the caption, HE IS MINE. Stunned by the anonymous message, she gasped for air and cupped her hand over her mouth to stem the uncontrollable sobbing as it surged. After regaining control of her emotions, Rebecca looked at her cell again, but the photo and bizarre message were gone. "I can't believe I deleted it!" she screamed and pounded the steering wheel.

The hospital loomed like a monolith as her Porsche roared towards the designated Visitor Parking area. Her sleek, red car screamed, *Give me a ticket* whenever a cop saw its sleek lines. She didn't care, the thrill of being behind the wheel, made the trade-off worth it.

The only ticket, she received in the two years since its purchase, came when a 'butch' Deputy Sheriff made a pass at her. Any hope of just a warning, vanished, when Rebecca laughed at the deputy's advances then disputed the definition of speeding, the hand wrote in the violation line, *Speeding (flying too low)*.

Rebecca sent her Porsche into a perfectly controlled slide and came to a stop in a designated spot for compact cars. Judging by the sight of the hospital's security guard coming towards her at a pace worthy of a competitive speed walker, she realized that she must have set a new record for parking in the least amount of time. The guard's nametag read, R. Smit and included a picture of him with the standard military buzz-cut, which explained the way he addressed her. "Don't worry about your car Ma'am', I'll make sure that no one messes with it, Ma'am'."

"Thank you," rolled off her voluptuous lips before she caught him staring at her chest. "What are you looking at R.?"

He immediately recognized her attributes, as well as her authoritative demeanor. Even in blue jeans, he knew military when he saw it, and snapped to attention. "Nothing, Ma'am. The name is Rich…Richard."

Rebecca turned as red as her Porsche and thought her readiness to bust his balls may have been a little premature. The way 'R' addressed her sounded military, but she was in a hurry, and he blocked her from opening the Porsche's door.

"It's nice to meet you; I'm Colonel Rebecca Fagan…I need to get out, Rich Richard."

"Yes Ma'am," he said as he stepped away, still red-faced from embarrassment. Stunned by her beauty, he mouthed "Wow!" as she spun in perfect military form, and departed in a double-time step.

The moment she entered the hospital, the sound of her heels served as a warning, not to get in her way. The lobby's tile floors cracked and popped with every step as she made her way to the reception desk.

"Bonner, M.D., what's his room number?" Rebecca spoke in her most authoritative voice, hoping the aging greeter would respond to it positively.

"What did you say the doctor's name is, sweetie?" the southern, blue-haired volunteer asked.

"Not M.D. as in doctor; his name is M.D. Bonner."

Mary P.-Volunteer Hospital Greeter, still clueless, asked again, "What is the doctor's last name; I don't see a *Bonnet* on the list. Do you know what department he works in?"

"Not Bonnet. Bonnerrr…," Rebecca said. Instantly, she saw Mary P. had become even more confused.

Rebecca excused Mary's incompetence; the aging blue-hair reminded Rebecca of her "Nana". Besides, she found Mary's name tag refreshing; at least she knew her first name, unlike Rich Richard's badge. She changed tactics and spoke with a little more volume.

"Mary, could you *please* point me in the direction of the administrative offices?"

"Why…yes, sweetie," Mary said without making it sound like a question. "Are you here to see someone in administration?"

Rebecca fought the temptation to state the obvious. Instead, she replied with a mocking southern drawl, *"Why yes*, David Crain, your hospital administrator?" Rebecca still wondered if she and Mary were communicating.

"Oh, *why*…didn't you say so? His office is on the seventh floor. Don't you worry about it being Saturday, I saw him come in a little bit ago. Sweetie, get on those elevators over there." Mary pointed to a bank of elevators that had a freestanding sign in front of it. *Administrative Offices-7th floor*

Rebecca anxiously pushed the button repeatedly during the entire ride until the elevator doors magically opened. Directly in front of her, a bleached-blonde in her early twenties sat behind an expensive contemporary metal and glass desk. A large plate-glass window, with a view of Choctawhatchee Bay, framed her like a modern day Mona Lisa.

Ever so pleasantly, and in a valley girl accent, the girl said, "Good afternoon. Like, how may I help you?"

Somehow, Rebecca resisted the temptation to say, *"First, lose that voice..."*

"Please tell Dave, Rebecca is here to see him."

"Dave? Like, I don't know a Dave."

"Oh…my…god. Where did he find this one?" Rebecca spoke quietly into a cupped hand.

"Excuse me?"

"Where can I *find* him? Dave Crain?"

"Oh. I didn't know his name is, like, Dave. I always call him Mr. Crain. Who may I say is here? Or is it, like, whom? I never know."

"*Colonel* Rebecca Fagan." This time Rebecca stressed the word Colonel hoping the receptionist would respond to a title.

"You don't look like a Colonel. Like, are you really a Colonel?"

Rebecca decided not to take "like" anymore, and stormed straight into Dave's office, where he was sitting half asleep in his high-backed, red leather chair, facing the view of the bay. Startled by Rebecca's entrance, he tried to swivel towards her and smacked his knee on an open drawer.

"Damn! Colonel, you can't just walk in here like you own the place," Dave said while holding his leg with both hands.

"Or what, are you going to call security? Dave, I need to find a patient. Do you know anyone around here that has a clue and could help me?" Rebecca fought the temptation to ask Dave about working on Sunday with his receptionist.

"A clue to what? *Like*, what are you talking about?" Dave said and bent over, pulled up his pant leg, and inspected his knee.

Rebecca wasn't sure if it had been her imagination or if she really heard him say "like". "What is going on around here? Are all of you related?"

"Related? What?"

"Dave, I need to find about the status of a friend of mine. Someone tried to kill…"

Dave, who had the habit of stepping on other people's conversations mid-sentence, said "General Bonner? He is in surgery as we speak. Try not to worry; Benson and Levinthal are the best we've got on staff."

Dave respected Bonn, who happened to be the Chairman of Military Affairs; there were few positions as powerful in the area. Staying in the good graces of the Military Affairs Council was a mandatory job requirement.

"He's in surgery? What kind of surgery?" Rebecca held her breath in anticipation.

"I don't know. I was in the middle of a very important meeting when they rudely interrupted." Dave said while he continued rubbing his knee. "The last I heard, they were waiting on an ophthalmologist from Tallahassee to join Benson and Levinthal." Actually, Dave had just finished putting a golf ball into the cup of his, Tiger Woods and P.G.A. endorsed, practice green with ball return.

"Benson, Levinthal, *and* an eye specialist are going to work on him? Why does he need three surgeons? What's wrong with his eyes?" she asked and began to hyperventilate.

"I don't know exactly. All I know is the 'eye guy' is a consult. They just got started and it's going to be awhile. Why don't you relax and have a cup of coffee...or something a little stronger?" Administrator Cain said as he poured two fingers of vodka.

Now, Rebecca started to get scared at the thought of Bonn being blind, the color of his eyes were burned on her mind. When Rebecca began tear up, she turned and walked to the window. Gazing out with her eyes shut, and ignoring his offer of a drink, she asked pensively, "What kind of surgeries? What have you heard?"

"That's all I know. If you want, we can go down to the fourth floor and see how it's going." Dave said.

Rebecca turned and hugged him in gratitude.

Dave couldn't have misconstrued the hug anymore if he tried. Even with his reputation of being a womanizer, many women wanted to be on Dave's pedestal. Now, holding a tearful and attractive woman in his arms, a twinge of his manliness stirred.

Beautiful women had been Dave's downfall in his previous marriages. The panties found in the back seat of his second wife's Mercedes, belonged to the blonde-haired assistant he hired after his first divorce. For a second time, women's undergarments busted him; the first incident happened on the honeymoon of his first marriage. The black lace thong found in the back seat of his car belonged to his bride's maid of honor, who just happened to be her sister.

"I am so sorry for crying..." Rebecca started to explain then jerked away from his grip when she thought she felt something in Dave's pocket. Rebecca backed away, and deflated the situation by saying, "Dave, I know you and General Bonner are friends, I've forgotten how upset you must be."

"I'm fine. Let's go check on the patient," Dave said, then turned away to conceal his excitement.

CHAPTER 15

I t had been a chaotic morning, and the nurses' station had become as busy as a McDonald's counter at noon. So far, there had been a face plant into a windshield, two tourists with third-degree sunburns, one rip current patient survivor, and two Moped accident victims.

The star of the morning's show featured a hunter airlifted to the hospital with multiple gunshot wounds. Judging by the quality of surgeons arriving to work on the patient, he had to be someone important. The doctors called in were, Benson; the hospital's Chief of Surgery, Levinthal; a private Neurosurgeon extraordinaire, and Gupta; a renowned Ophthalmologic surgeon from Tallahassee. They would scrub and enter the surgical theater as one of the hospital's most impressive surgical teams assembled in quite some time.

The quality of visitors checking on the patient's well being was just as impressive as the level of surgeons who came to work on Bonn. The nurse's station buzzed with speculation about the people showing up to check on their VIP patient, they were a cross-section of *Who's Who* in local politics and they were taking turns at marking their territory as they entered the room. The visitors included, the hospital's administrator, who was escorting a gorgeous brunette with tears in her eyes. Following them was a beautiful, and busty, blonde Air Force commander, who got off the elevator and acted like she 'owned the place. Finally, an intense detective from Niceville, who paced like a caged animal, stormed in and repeatedly touched his weapon. When the representatives from the sheriff's department, highway patrol, city police, and the two Security Forces flanking Eglin's commander arrived at the hospital, there was enough firepower to make a stand against a small army.

The staff took the opportunity to analyze each visitor as they got off the elevator. The nurses, doctors, and orderlies concurred in their staff's evaluations: Rebecca had "an air of desperation", Cari came across as a "no-nonsense control freak", and Mac seemed to be a "little paranoid".

The surgical personnel knew the crazy morning would continue forward to a memorable afternoon when Chief Barnes walked off the elevator dressed in cargo shorts and wearing a t-shirt with *Fishermen Have Bigger Rods* silkscreened across the front. The Chief could have passed as a tourist if it wasn't for the gold badge clipped to his shorts.

Detective McCain approached Chief Barnes, who appeared to be slightly nervous. "Chief, what are you doing here? I thought you were going out on your boat."

"When I got to the marina, I received a call from a reporter who asked me why there were so many federal and state officers converging on the hospital. I thought I better make an appearance."

"Chief, I know I acted a little strange earlier at the blockade… I'm okay now." Mac feared the Chief might send him to a Psych Evaluation after witnessing his flashbacks in the KFC parking lot.

"I'm not worried about you Detective, what's *his* status?"

"No one has told me anything new since I got here, but it looks like we're about to get an update." Mac pointed in the direction of the nurses' station.

Together, they headed straight towards a huddled group having a hushed conversation with a charge nurse wearing her scrubs and mask.

"Why are they operating on him? When can see him? How is he …" Rebecca, uncharacteristically, sounded near panic as she kept asking questions without giving the nurse an opportunity to answer. Dave previously witnessed the temperament of the nurse that Rebecca grilled, and he smiled in anticipation of the battle he hoped would take place.

The arrival of Mac, who Rebecca had not seen in years, failed to deter her from wanting answers, and wanting them immediately.

Dave understood the nurse's hesitation to disclose any facts regarding Bonn's status then cautiously made the introductions: "Ashleigh, this is Colonel Rebecca Fagan, I believe you saw Detective McCain in the Emergency Room, and this gentleman wearing the fishing shorts, is Chief Barnes of the Niceville Police Department. The moment Dave commented on the chief's wardrobe, he turned bright red and forgot to introduce Mac and Rebecca.

Chief Barnes ignored Dave's fashion observation by asking Ashleigh, "What can you tell us?"

She took a deep breath, looked directly at the chief, and said, "Doctors Benson and Levinthal have been with the patient for about an hour and the Ophthalmologist from Tallahassee will be joining them as soon as he arrives. However, Dr. Gupta will not be operating today unless it is necessary; they want to stabilize him first."

"Ashleigh, did they indicate how long they're going to have him in there?" Dave asked as his way of letting Ashleigh know *he* was the one she needed to speak to, not Chief Barnes.

"Mr. Crain, I think it's going to be awhile before we know his actual status. He has many shotgun pellets in his head, neck and shoulder they are surgically removing. Dr. Benson indicated the procedure would be time-consuming."

"You said Gupta won't be operating today. Who is Gupta, the surgeon from Tallahassee? Is Bonn...," Rebecca held her breath and waited for the answer.

After looking to Dave for approval before responding, Ashleigh said, "They're concerned about damage to the patient's right eye. Dr. Gupta is a specialist in retinal detachment and optic nerve damage. Mr. Crain, I will keep you informed. That's all I can tell you. I have to get back in there or Dr. Benson will not be very happy," she said and turned to leave.

Rebecca, with tears in her eyes and her voice laced with dread, grabbed Ashleigh before she left and asked, "Is..., is he blind?"

Ashleigh jerked her arm out of Rebecca's clutches and gave her a hatred-filled expression. "You will have to ask the doctors. Don't ever touch me again".

Feeling disrespected, Rebecca asked Chief Barnes, "What's the current penalty for murder?"

"Well, I can see everything is under control here. I'm going to leave; I have an appointment with a fish on my boat. Mr. Crain, will you keep Detective McCain informed on the General's condition?" Chief Barnes said then winked at Rebecca and excused himself with Mac in tow.

Commander Cari Bentow couldn't recall the last time she cried. Just as tears started blurring her vision, she separated from the M.P. escorts. Cari feared if she showed any sign of weakness in front of them, it would tarnish her image as an officer and a leader. Tears were definitely not an option for her; they were a sign of weakness. Her military father would never have tolerated that kind of behavior, his words still haunted her as an adult, "Good soldiers don't cry."

Before she lost control, Cari walked towards the nurse's station in the Critical Care Unit, and took deep breaths with each step. Before she made it halfway there, she tried to change direction, but Chief Barnes and Mac intercepted her retreat on their way to the elevators.

"Commander, it's good to see you," Chief Barnes said softly.

"Chief, I...I can't talk right now!" an exasperated Cari, stutter stepped around them, and continued back towards the heated discussion unraveling at the nurse's station.

Although Chief Barnes feigned indifference, Mac noticed, both of them blushed at the sight of each other. He dismissed the thought with a simple, "Hmm."

When Cari reached the icy conversation, she witnessed *Ashleigh S.-RN*, squared off with a woman, restrained from behind with a bear hug by a smiling Dave.

Cari took advantage of a tense moment of silence between the two women and asked, "How is General Bonner doing?"

Ashleigh, irritated by yet another woman asking about her patient, put her hands on her hips, and asked, "Are you related."

Cari answered without hesitation. "I'm a very close friend. Will he be all right?"

Ashleigh rolled her eyes in response to Cari's claim and said, "Mr. Crain?"

"It's okay, she's Eglin's commander, that's where the shooting took place." Dave tried to place his hand on Cari's shoulder when he introduced her, but she managed to lean away.

"Whoever you are, keep your hands to yourself. Go ahead Ashleigh," Cari said.

"Alright, *Commander*, I'll tell you what I just told *Mr. Crain*, General Bonner is in surgery and he'll be in there for quite some time. Dr. Benson will be here when they're finished."

Cari shot back, "*Nurse*, just answer the question, will he make it?"

Ashleigh's answer had a touch of disdain and bitterness. "How the hell am I supposed to know? Ask the friggin' doctors. Tell them you're a friend, you'll see how far that gets you."

"What is your problem? I'm not just his friend, I'm also his fiancé'," Cari said, and then watch everyone look at her bare ring finger.

Rebecca's head snapped when she heard about Bonn's engagement. "What did you say?"

Now it was Cari's turn to look at Dave for help. He remembered her cold shoulder towards him, and just shrugged.

"Okay, I lied. As Commander, I need to know his status and if the situation is dire, I need to talk with him. Whoever did this has to be found."

"Of course Commander, I totally understand. If you want to have a seat in the waiting room, I'll ask Dr. Benson to come see you when she's finished."

Almost to the point of being obnoxious and condescending, Ashleigh said to Rebecca, "Why don't *you* have a seat in the waiting area, when there is any word on Bonn, I'll let you know. I have to return to the O.R."

No one heard Ashleigh mumble, "Bitch, threaten me again and you'll wish you hadn't."

Cari nodded at Rebecca, and ignored Ashleigh and Dave before she spun on one heel and left. They watched the most powerful woman in the area march in perfect double time with the clicking of her heals echoing off the walls, just as Rebecca had during her arrival to the hospital.

When Ashleigh started to leave, Rebecca sidestepped and blocked her escape, without grabbing her arm.

"You called him 'Bonn', do you know him?" Rebecca came to the realization that he had not missed a beat since their breakup.

"I've known him for awhile. Are you one of his girlfriends, or are you going to tell me you're his fiancé too?" Ashleigh asked.

The implication that Bonn had many girlfriends left Rebecca speechless, jealous, and a little angry. Not knowing what else to do, she headed to the elevators and while waiting for it, she overheard a nurse say, "They're taking Bonn to recovery. Thank God, he stabilized."

CHAPTER 16

T he moment Bonn was on his way to recovery, Rebecca rushed to his side. Hearts dropped when she reached the gurney and gently wrapped her fingers around his hand and kissed it. Rebecca wept silently but her tears didn't go unnoticed by Bonn's other "friends", who also fought to keep their emotions in-check.

Rebecca paced while waiting for him to wake up. A vast array of beeping machines tracked his progress while tubes strung out of hanging bags filled with clear liquids, and latched to him like tentacles. As she prayed, with her tearful eyes closed, Bonn called out in a weak, drug-induced slur, "Beshcca?"

"Bonn? Oh my God, yes, it's me…I love you," she said softly without thinking or caring who might hear.

He squeezed her hand, closed his good eye, and drifted back into unconsciousness. Worried he may have died; Rebecca desperately looked at the attending nurse.

"He'll be coming in and out of it for awhile. Why don't you get a cup of coffee and try not to worry. As soon as he comes around, and his vitals improve, we're going to move him to a private room in I.C.U."

"He hasn't seen me in years and…I can't believe he knows I'm here," Rebecca said then wrote down her cell number. "I'll be in the chapel, please let me know when to come back and see him."

As she turned to leave, Mac walked into the room. Even though she hadn't seen him in years, and earlier acted like she didn't know him, this time she embraced him and whispered, "Mac, get the fucker that did this to him."

Mac waited impatiently for the nurse to finish checking Bonn's vitals. The moment she left, he leaned close to Bonn's ear, gritted his teeth, and said, "Bonn, if you can hear me, I want you to know I will get the son of a bitch that did this to you."

Mac instinctively flinched for his weapon when he heard Bonn's door open. One of the uniforms that had arrived to protect Bonn escorted Rebecca back into the room. The guard raised his eyebrows and gestured towards Rebecca as his way of asking for Mac's permission.

Mac said, "She's fine."

Rebecca went to Mac for another embrace, and for the first time since her return to the area, felt like she had come home.

"I have missed both of you so much." Rebbeca confessed.

Mac took the liberty to speak on Bonn's behalf and said, "We've missed you. The last I heard, you were married to an army grunt and living in Georgia."

"I *was* married," she said as a matter of fact, and added nothing else.

Over the next few short minutes, Mac began with the last day they had seen each other, and told her why they had to leave without contacting her. "We received orders for immediate deployment during the initial surge into Kuwait. I know he wanted to call you and let you know what happened. Unfortunately, we were in lockdown at Command and Control for pre-deployment briefings along with the other members of our team. That night, we left for a six-month deployment in the desert that turned into almost two years. When he tried to contact you, he was told you were gone as well and your location was classified."

"Mac, that's the past. I understand. What you don't know… I boarded a C-17, two days after you and Bonn left. The day of my selection into Delta', my new team received orders as well. The next thing I knew, I was on a flight to…, hell." Rebecca swallowed and slowly closed her eyes.

"I understand. You're right; it's the past. Why don't we talk about your life, now?"

"Tomorrow, I move into a corner office on base. You are looking at the new Liaison officer; it's a title our friends in Washington created just for me. I would have been satisfied with being called just the Interagency Liaison; they want me to refer to myself as the 'I-A'. Regardless, can you imagine the shock when I received my orders and saw your name as someone to contact if I *needed* anything," she said with a barely detectable grin.

Before Mac asked Rebecca if she *"needed"* anything, Ashleigh walked in, and scowled at the sight of seeing two people with her patient, especially when she saw her nemesis, Rebecca.

Mac kept up the appearance of an ongoing conversation and said, "Where was I? Oh yeah, General Bonner is better than when I first saw him. You have nothing to worry about; he's not going to be moved to another room anytime soon."

Ashleigh acted as if she wasn't listening and proceeded to check fluid levels in the drip bags. While recording the levels on her clipboard, she constantly glanced at her watch, which both Mac and Rebecca spotted.

Despite the chill in the air, Rebecca asked, "Nurse, can you tell me what time a *doctor* will be in here to check on him?"

"*The* doctor will be in a minute," Ashleigh said and stormed out of the room.

"There's something not right with that woman. I think there's more to her than we are seeing."

"I totally agree. She is another one I've already added to my list of people who I don't trust. Mac, why would anyone want to do *this* to him?" Rebecca reached over and gently touched the side of Bonn's face.

One side of Bonn's head and face looked normal, if it wasn't swollen. The other side showed the horrific trauma he experienced. The surgeons needed to see where to cut out the embedded shot and carefully trimmed his hair close to his scalp.

From a different angle, it became grossly apparent where the shot hit him. Along the right rear side of his head, there were single, double, and triple stitched, knotted sutures running from his shoulder, up his neck, and into his scalp.

A circular splotch of blood, the size of a silver dollar, bled through the bandage where the main load of shot had hit the back of his head. An interesting sign of his recent surgery was a series of small black circles that isolated every red spot where a BB penetrated the skin.

There was an area that stood out in the middle of all the repair work The radiologist had drawn multiple circles around an innocent looking red dot on Bonn's the right temple, the exact spot where a single BB entered and clipped the back of his eye before it came to a stop.

"Mac, look at him, how can anyone take a hit like that and have a normal life? Do you think he will...I don't know what I'll do if he doesn't make it." Rebecca, known as a positive person, teetered on the edge of a fatalistic diagnosis.

"He's going to be around for a long time," Mac assured her, and added, "He has to..."

The constant negative thoughts regarding Bonn's welfare bombarded Rebecca to the point of exhaustion. Each possible outcome she could imagine had its own set of fears. Gupta's ophthalmology consult produced a fear that ripped through her emotionally as she studied Bonn's swollen face.

"His right eye...its pinched shut. Do you think he's...?"

A heavy silence engulfed the room; the possibility of Bonn being blind remained a taboo subject. Rebecca leaned over and positioned herself face to face with Bonn, swallowed for courage, and asked, "Can you see me baby?" The answer came from the partially opened door to his room.

"He's one lucky SOB. He'll be able to see you, but it's still too early to tell if *both* eyes are completely functional."

Rebecca wheeled to confront whoever had the audacity to use the word 'lucky' to describe Bonn's situation. To her dismay, she saw a gorgeous, strawberry blonde-haired woman in green surgical scrubs that had matching emerald green eyes.

While extending her hand, she introduced herself with a slight tone that Rebecca couldn't disseminate. "We haven't met, I'm Dr. Benson."

Rebecca didn't offer any personal information regarding her relationship with Bonn and just said, "Colonel Fagan."

Dr. Benson paused, surveyed Rebecca's clothing choice, and then asked, "You're a Colonel? Are you active duty?"

"Yes and...Yes, I'm active duty. It's good to finally meet you. Doctor Benson, this is Detective 'Mac' McCain."

"Doctor, we meet again," Mac said, and met her hand halfway.

"Unfortunately, it's always at the hospital and under depressing situations," Dr. Benson lamented and placed a hand on his shoulder. Rebecca noticed the physical contact and made a mental note to bring it up with Mac.

"General Bonner is one tough individual; even so, the next couple of days are going to be critical and crucial for him. We found a tremendous amount of foreign matter from his clothing had penetrated into his body by the sheer force of the shot. We had to flush each site repeatedly before we closed. We want to be proactive against infection. So, he will be on an antibiotic regiment for quite awhile." Dr. Benson spoke to both Mac and Rebecca in a way that only an experienced surgeon should: unemotional, factual, and proactive.

"There are so many wounds from all the different shot hitting him..." Mac wasn't sure what else to say besides stating the obvious.

"Detective, there is one pellet, or as you call it, a 'shot', that is of concern. It hit him and went through his temple, clipped the optic nerve of his right eye and shattered his medial orbit."

Dr. Benson described one of Bonn's most serious injuries and used her finger to show the path of the shot that concerned her the most. She pointed to her temple, ran her fingertip across her upper eyelid then circled her eye socket and stopped at a point where his "orbit" shattered.

"Dr. Gupta will make a decision on how to proceed with his eye, based on the scan results. As far as the rest of his wounds...well, you can see the cranial edema is severe, swelling of that degree is going to cause some problems with his skin, but he'll heal without any scaring. The prognosis for his recovery is good *if...*" Dr. Benson didn't intentionally ignore Rebecca, she was preoccupied with Mac.

"If what?" Mac and Rebecca asked in unison.

"I was about to say.., *if* we can control the clots. There are several areas where his clotting can be dangerous. We're giving him large doses of diuretics to thin them out and hopefully that will keep them from growing and breaking loose. That's..."

"That's what? That's it? What aren't you telling me?" Rebecca made her question sound like an order.

"The person, who shot Bonn, did so, with a hand load. Its ammunition that's been..."

"I know what a hand load means! I'm a weapons specialist and S.R.T. designated," Colonel Fagan interrupted, not because Dr. Benson referred to him as Bonn, she stopped her to disclose her Sniper Rifle Training.

"What difference does it make if its hand loaded?" Mac stepped between them with his question before the situation escalated. He didn't mention the fact that both he and Rebecca had been hand loading ammunition for years.

"There were steel, copper, and lead shot in his wounds. That shot load will kill with an impact that would be devastating to anything it hit. The heavy steel shot hold the lighter BBs together so it takes longer for the string of shot won't spread out as quick. At close range, it's almost like being hit with a solid lead bullet. We can't do an M.R.I. because the steel shot could be drawn out by the magnets, and that wouldn't be good for many reasons. The only way we can see the true damage to his eye is to go back in. Gupta believes Bonn may have lost vision in one eye when he took the hit to the temple."

Dr. Benson eyes shifted to Mac and Rebecca to see if they heard her refer to her patient on a personal level when she used his nickname.

Rebecca ignored the semantics of Bonn's name and focused on his condition. "Wait, that's it? What are you saying? Is he blind?"

"That's it for now, doctor and patient privilege. Colonel Fagan, it's been interesting. Detective…, until next time," Dr. Benson said and left without closing the door.

Rebecca had a fleeting thought that Bonn and Dr. Benson might have dated. She made *another* mental note to ask Bonn about his surgeon when he got better, her list continued to grow.

Rebecca locked arms with Mac as they stood at the foot of Bonn's bed and stared at him. Ashleigh, in her white nurse's shoes, walked silently through the door left open by Dr. Benson and sidled up behind them. When she cleared her throat, she made it sound as though they were not supposed to be in the room.

Rebecca considered decking her until she spotted how Ashleigh pulled off her sneak attack, nurse's shoes. Although the footwear looked comfortable *and* ugly, they were very quiet. From that moment on, Rebecca called them "Ninja" shoes.

"What is your real relationship with the patient?" Ashleigh made her point by not using his first name.

"We are *very* good friends," Rebecca said and pointed back and forth from Mac to herself.

"Really? You're *very* good friends? Well, before he went into surgery, he never mentioned either one of you when I asked him whom I should contact. He just told *me* to take good care of him, I'm sure he wasn't thinking clearly. Since he didn't mention you, I just assumed you were a *new* friend. How long have you known him?"

Rebecca didn't answer, she was thinking about using her hand-to-hand combat skills. Before she could act on her urges, Dr. Benson appeared at the open door.

"Detective, may I have a word with you… privately?" To Ashleigh's dismay, her boss added, "They can stay as long as they want."

"Stand down," Mac said to Rebecca, with a wink, before he walked out.

In the hallway, Dr. Benson got to the point. "Richard, our security man, told me you wanted to be notified when the heart attack patient arrived. Well, she's down in triage; I thought we might go see her."

"Alright then partner, why don't you and I do a little detective work?" Mac said to Dr. Benson who marched with a touch of pride when he called her, "partner". Mac had completely forgotten about the call from Deputy Stevens, his attention stayed on Dr. Benson as she walked a step and a half in front of him, possibly on purpose.

The standoff with Ashleigh still smoldered, and Rebecca continued to fan the flames. "Let's go back to your question. You asked me how long I've known him. How long have *you* known him?"

"Colonel, I don't know what your relationship is with him and I don't care. Many of us here know and love him. He is one of a kind, and we're all concerned about his welfare. I'm sure you wouldn't be here if you didn't feel the same way."

Rather than to respond to Ashleigh's hostility, Rebecca said,

"You're very perceptive for a nurse. I'm sure there's someone in your life that you love. Imagine if *she* had been shot; then you'll know how I feel."

The insinuation about her sexuality didn't draw a negative reaction. Surprisingly, Ashleigh kept her reactions under control and said, "As a matter of fact, I do feel that way about someone."

CHAPTER 17

D r. Benson wasn't aware of the call Mac received from the on-scene deputy at Powder Sands Park when she said, "Detective, before we go in and see her, I want you to know she has a wound that doesn't make sense to me. If you don't see it, I'll point it out."

Mac entered the triage area with his honorary partner and saw an overweight middle-aged woman attached to an array of monitors and drips. She had red spots of different sizes covering her body. One was slightly different, a purple contusion protruded in the center of a single red blemish. Mac pointed directly at it and said, "I have my suspicions, what do you think?"

"Someone pressed a gun into her face, literally." Dr. Benson pushed her finger to her forehead.

"I thought the same thing. The husband claimed she grabbed her chest, and hit her head on a file cabinet when she fell," Mac said.

"There's no way to tell if she stroked before or after hitting her head. If he shoved the barrel of a gun in her face, it could have scared her enough to have a heart attack."

Mac rubbed his beard while contemplating the possibilities. "I think you're right," Mac said and smiled at Dr. Benson.

"Detective, why are you smiling?" she asked and blushed.

"You are one special lady. She is covered with spots, and you keyed in on one, I'm impressed. It looks like one of those red dots people from India have on their foreheads. Do you know what I'm talking about?" Mac asked.

When Mac described her as a '*special lady*', it took a few seconds before she could regain her composure.

"It's called a Kumkum, and that's not one."

"Damn Doc, you would have made a great investigator."

"Thank you detective. Sometimes our patients can't tell us what happened to them and we have to figure it out. I've had way too many years of practice."

"Well it couldn't be too many years." Mac immediately realized how corny it must have sounded and changed the subject.

"How did you know I needed to see her?"

"Richard from Security told me you wanted to be notified when she arrived. I want to join you, I hope you don't mind." Dr. Benson blushed.

"Doc, you can join me anytime you want." Mac could feel the heat on his face and said, "I'm sorry; I didn't mean to be so forward."

"I wanted to be with you." Dr. Benson smiled and took her turn at being beet red.

"Would you mind if I took a picture with my cell?" Mac asked.

Dr. Benson instinctively ran her fingers through her hair then figured out Mac was talking about the blemish on Paula.

"No, take as many as you need," she said and ran out of the room leaving Mac puzzled and wondering if he said something wrong.

Dr. Benson returned in less than a minute with an old-school Polaroid camera. "I thought you may also want a paper photo to show, you'll get to see their reaction."

"You're good. There is nothing like catching someone off guard and watching them squirm." Mac snapped a picture and they stood together, with their shoulders barely touching, for the minute it took for the photo to appear. Although, the first attempt gave him a photo that clearly showed the spot with its purple center, he insisted on taking a couple more. When the last picture metamorphosed, he said, "Doc, there is one other thing, please call me Mac."

"Okay Mac, I'm going to go check on Bonn and I'll let you know if there are any changes. Call me if I can be of any further assistance."

She gave him a seductive smile and wrote her phone number on a sheet from her prescription pad. Next to the number and underlined, it read, *Call me, Susan.*

CHAPTER 18

After what seemed like an eternity alone at Bonn's side, Rebecca walked to the window and contemplated the circus of events surrounding the shooting. She turned when she heard the hushed opening of the door to Bonn's room, and to her surprise, saw the comforting smile of Mary, the hospital's greeter.

"Sweetie, I'm so glad you were able to find Mr. Crain's office and your friend. I will pray for him and for you. I thought you might want a cup of coffee, or maybe some nice tea?" Mary said in her nicest grandmotherly voice.

"Thank you. I don't think I would care for anything right now." The personal attention Mary offered, gave Rebecca some comfort in the middle of a stressful situation.

"Well Sweetie, you know where I'll be," Mary said as she held one of Rebecca's hands for a few seconds then hugged her.

Even though Rebecca didn't want to admit it, Mary's dedication to helping complete strangers was commendable, it was her communication skills that were a little irritating. Mary's critique ended when she heard a moan. She snapped her head around to the sight of Bonn bearing a Cheshire cat grin, and rushed to gently embrace him.

"Hello darlin', how are you?" Bonn said in a dry, gravelly voice.

His question lit a fuse. Rebecca pulled back and started to rant, instead of weeping in relief.

"Oh, I'm just great! You know how it is, the same old grind. What the hell do you mean, how am I doing? Bonn, if you ever go hunting again, I am going to kill you myself. Some hunter thinks you're a turkey and tries to blow your head off? Bonn, you were almost *accidentally* killed, and you want to know how I am? How can you even think about…?" Rebecca asked and showed her frustration.

"Rebecca, please stop. The guy who shot me and 'choo-choo' weren't hunting, it wasn't an *accident*."

She feared Bonn had lost it when he started talking about trains and her mothering instinct took over.

"Well there aren't any trains in here. Just try to sleep."

As she bent down to kiss his swollen and plum colored face, the doors opened and a parade of male investigators, led by Mac, filed into the room.

The kiss lasted long enough for the lead investigator to witness the not so public display of affection. He flashed his leather bound badge and ID that identified him as ATF investigator Kroch.

"Excuse me, who are you and what are you doing here?"

The first thing she noted was his *high and tight* haircut, a cutting technique used in the military that left a white stripe above the ears and braced for a conversation with a former military man who hated being a civilian.

"*Ish sokay, she's wish me. Dish is Becca,*" Bonn said, slurring his words and grimacing while his head lolled from Kroch to Mac, then back to her. His right eye remained completely shut and the narcotic painkillers had him to the point where he could no longer fight off sleep. So, Mac stepped in and made the introduction.

"General Bonner was trying to introduce you to Colonel Rebecca Fagan."

"Rebecca, are you involved in the investigation or just *involved* with the General?"

"You will address me as Colonel Fagan or not at all!" Rebecca spoke loud enough and heard in the hall.

"Is that clear agent Kroch?" She pronounced his name as *crotch*.

"Ma'am, my name is pronounced *croak*," he said over the snickers coming from the officers standing guard at the door.

"I will tell you this much Sergeant Kroch, whether or not I'm personally involved is none of your business. If you're asking me if I'm actively involved in an investigation, I am. Let me ask you, why does the ATF think someone would shoot General Bonner?"

"I'm sorry ma'am; I don't have clearance for you. I need to speak with the General alone. You'll have to wait in the hall until I call for you," Sergeant Kroch said.

"You want *me* to wait in the hall? You don't have a clue what my security level is, do you? This isn't the military, check the damn facts before you start giving orders." Rebecca's anger surged.

Her lecture ended when the door burst open and Dr. Benson, who had heard Rebecca's chastising remarks, entered and took control of the situation.

"I don't know what's going on, but know this; I'm the one in charge here. I want everyone out until I clear him for visitors, doctor's orders! You need to leave until I give you permission to return."

Rebecca planted a gentle kiss on Bonn's lips for Kroch to see as he stomped out of the room. Now that their relationship was out in the open, she didn't hesitate to give him a parting kiss before she followed Dr. Benson's orders to leave.

"Detective, I would like you to stay," *Susan* said and grabbed Bonn's chart to write down her implicit instructions that laid out who was allowed to visit.

After the room emptied, Mac's curiosity led him to admire her green eyes, and for a split second, peek at the perky breasts straining against her silk blouse.

Susan looked up from the chart in time to catch him surveying her attributes, and was actually glad she had taken off her white lab coat. She didn't want to discourage Mac's interest and said,

"I would like it if you called me Susan when it's just us. I hoped you understood my note...the one with my number and *Call me, Susan*. I meant for you to call me, and to let you know, it's okay to use my name when we're alone. Bonn's out cold right now, so he doesn't count. That being said, do you want to know the results of the blood work for the woman in ER?"

Mac didn't fully understand her note and began to stutter, "Su..., Susan? Doc, you want me to...I, I'm sorry...Yes, absolutely...*Susan*, you have the results?"

"Her blood panels were positive for marijuana, Benzodiazepines, specifically the drug Xanax, and a variety of opiates." She read directly from the report and kept glancing up to see if Mac would continue with her physical inspection. For some reason, she found his attention flattering and she pulled her shoulders back ever so slightly.

Mac didn't understand why Susan thought she needed to read the results of the blood panel and said, "So, she does drugs. Susan, why is that significant?"

"Detect...Mac, it isn't the drugs she took I find interesting, it's the presence of IgE and elevated histamine levels that showed up. I could tell she had hives, so I ordered tests for a food allergy. Individuals who are allergic to things like nuts are vigilant when it comes to what they eat. I wondered if she accidentally ate a food that caused an allergic reaction. Then I remembered when she came in, she had an area on her shirt that looked like a bloodstain. I had it tested; it turned out to be jelly with a trace of peanut butter. That could be the culprit, but I can't imagine her eating a PB and J, especially if she had a peanut allergy."

Mac's tried to tie all the clues together and stared at her in silence until it became so uncomfortable, she considered running out of the room.

"Anaphylaxis. Was she having trouble breathing?" Bonn asked.

His unexpected diagnosis came out of nowhere and caused Dr. Benson to juggle her clipboard and Mac to flinch.

"You're awake! Damn it Bonn. Don't do that, I almost threw this clipboard through the roof," Susan said then laughed, partially from knowing Bonn was better, and to some extent, from the sexual tension that had been building between her and Mac.

"What did I do? You two were talking in front of me like I was in a coma and couldn't hear a word you were saying. Who are we talking about...*Susan*?" Bonn relished the opportunity to tease Mac and glared at him with his one good eye.

Susan went into her role of doctor, oblivious to the emotional relief she felt hearing Bonn speaking well and more importantly, thinking clearly.

"Don't worry about my other cases. Be quiet and squeeze my fingers."

"Hey buddy, it's good to have you back. I need to ask if there is anything you can tell me about what happened to you?" Mac wanted to get as much information as he could from Bonn before he received any more Morphine from the auto-dispensing machine that was due to release another dose.

"I'm not sure what I can tell you. I'm having trouble when I try to remember exactly what happened."

"Who is Carl Armando? You gave that name to me when I asked you at the KFC who did this to you. That name doesn't come up on any database."

"Mac, there were two of them. One said his name was 'just Carl' and claimed he knew me. I didn't remember ever meeting him, but... he called me 'Bonn'. At the time, I wondered if he was doing someone's dirty work and...I don't know, I'm pretty sure I saw him on his cell when I got away in my Explorer, maybe he had to report in to somebody. Mac, he definitely wasn't calling 911."

"Alright, we'll look into it. Who in the hell is Armando?" Mac asked.

They found Bonn's story of Carl and his sidekick Armando as exhilarating as a good mystery novel. All of a sudden, the morphine dispenser's motor made a faint whirring sound, and within a minute, Bonn's eyes fluttered as he started drifting into an opiate induced dream.

"Bonn, stay with me. What were they doing out there? Were they hunting?" Mac asked.

"Grown weee..," Bonn slurred then closed his eyes.

"Bonn? Did you say growing? What were they growing, pot? Stay with me, buddy...Susan, what happened?"

"Don't worry Mac. He is going to be all right, he needs to sleep. Normally with a concussion, we would want him awake but the strain from his pain levels increases his B.P., and we can't risk a clot breaking loose."

"It appears we have *two* guys. How many hits did he take?"

"There were two; one to the head and another one scattered mainly over his torso. Do you think…?"

"Bonn said, 'Carl *and* Armando'?" Mac made the statement as though he asked a question, then pondered the possibility of more than one killer on the loose and repeated the names.

"Mac, we removed two different sizes of BB's from his wounds. I just assumed it was a hand load not from two separate guns. Ballistics will confirm if it's the same gun, either way, it appears there were two people."

"Bonn is a tough son of a bitch, who else do you know that can get shot twice, without it killing them? Doc…, Susan, I need to talk with him again. I have a gut feeling I know a Carl from somewhere, and so does he. How long do you think he'll be out?"

The anxious tone in Mac's voice alarmed Susan who took both of his hands. "Mac we can't press him too much. It may take a few hours for the morphine to ease up. When he does wake up, you can't drill him for answers, he needs to be kept calm and quiet. There is some bleeding on his brain, and he is still in danger. Even though we removed a couple dozen shot from his head, we couldn't get them all. Some of the BBs penetrated the skull; they are too deep to remove without causing more damage. The initial shots didn't kill him, but the secondary problems can be even more dangerous."

"Are you saying he might not make it?"

Susan squeezed both of Mac's hands and compassionately locked eyes with him. "He *is* going to make it, but it's way too early to say when he's going to be out of the woods. Right now, we can't risk any hemorrhaging. If one of those clots breaks loose, he could stroke out and we could lose him."

"Jesus Christ, Doc," Mac said with trepidation, forgetting to call her Susan.

"I'm glad you brought God in on this because Bonn's going to need Him over the next few days, and he's also going to need all the help we can give him. It's going to be a very, very, long recovery. Mac, I came here looking for you. I wanted to let you know, the husband of our ER patient arrived. He's higher than a kite, and a little paranoid."

"I've got it, I need to call and have them search for some weed, and put to out a B.O.L.O. for *two* guys. If I'm right, you may have one of them right here in your hospital."

Mac pulled out his weapon, checked his clip, and then spoke to the guards at Bonn's door.

"Remember, no one besides Colonel Fagan and his nurse is allowed in this room without Doc's permission."

Susan checked to make sure Bonn wasn't awake, and then whispered in his ear, "Bonn, I really like your friend."

CHAPTER 19

Mac arrived at the double doors, peered through the panes to see a scene that he had witnessed many times in his military career. The sight of the nurses, doctors, and staff scrambling didn't bother him, it was the antiseptic smell that turned his stomach and made the scar he got from a sniper's gut shot, ache. He subconsciously placed his hand on it, took a deep breath, and entered the chaos of triage.

Mac watched two orderlies, accompanied by several nurses, strain to slide Paula onto a different and substantially larger, gurney to take her for further tests. The husband, teary eyed from his own staccato laughter, sounded like a barking dog. Unbelievably, when his fit stopped, he leaned down and put his face next to his wife's, and took a "Selfie" photo with a bling covered cell phone.

Mac didn't want to encourage the outrageous behavior and ignored him. Instead, he shifted his attention to the task confronting the staff.

"Do you need any help moving her?

"We've got her," an orderly replied.

The husband, barely able to contain himself, continued with his attempt at humor. "You can have her."

Mac knew the man as Mr. Perkins from the trailer park fires, but asked anyway, "Are you the husband?"

Carl wiped the tears with the back of his hand and said, "Whew! That's *hilarious*. Yep, I'm her husband, and this is my wife Paula. Don't you remember us detective? You busted those meth dealers at the trailer park we own outside of Niceville. That's where Paula had some kind of heart attack, then fell and hit her head. It's horrible... what happened...I mean, you know?"

"Of course, now, I remember you and your wife. I can only imagine how frightening this whole thing must be for you."

Mac's training made him leery of anyone offering too much information, when he didn't ask a question, he believed Carl's interpretations were rehearsed. That, along with Carl's glassy eyes, heightened his suspicions about Paula's injury.

"Mr. Perkins, we'll be taking your wife to get an M.R.I. in a few minutes then to her own room. If you want to have a seat in the Critical Care waiting room, I'll come and get you once she's settled in," the nurse only offered because of her bedside manner training

"I don't want to leave her side; can I walk with her to Radiology, and then wait in her room?" Carl pressed his hands together in prayer hoping the nurse would allow his exaggerated and insincere request.

"Sir, it really would be best if you stayed in the waiting room until we're sure she's stabilized."

"Would it be okay if I have just a couple of minutes alone with her before you wheel her away?"

"I'll be right back when they're ready for her." The nurse's irritation showed when her ears turned red as she walked away.

Carl raised his eyebrows as a signal for Mac to step out into the hall. Mac took the not so subtle hint, and swiped the curtain closed with a snap of his wrist.

Standing next to Paula's gurney, Carl leaned in and whispered into Paula's ear. Mac peeked through a crack in the curtain in time to hear "trigger" and "fat ass" then witnessed Carl tapping her forehead with his index finger. Paula's eyes widened to the size of silver dollars and shook her head while letting out a high-pitched whine.

"That's right Miss Piggy. Next time you won't be so lucky," Carl warned and let out a chuckle.

At the sound of the curtain pulled back, Carl recoiled at the expression on Mac's face.

"Mr. Perkins, can you tell me what is so funny in here?"

After Mac asked, he moved his windbreaker enough to display the badge clipped on his belt.

"'Choo' had to be here," Carl said as his attempt at humor.

Mac's sensors activated even though he couldn't quite piece it all together. Then, he made the connection, Bonn had rambled something about a "choo-choo".

"Mr. Perkins, I would like to have a few words with you while your wife is getting her tests."

"Forget Mr. Perkins, you can call me Carl, just Carl. I didn't do anything to her. She had a heart attack and fell," he said and took quick glance at the police badge clipped on Mac's belt.

Mac caught Cap's propensity for the word 'just', and slid his hand inside his sport coat as he asked, "What did you just say?"

"I told you I didn't do anything. You're a pig from Niceville, so you don't have any authority here," Carl said and straightened to a fighting posture.

Detective McCain remembered Bonn identifying "Just" Carl as the person who shot him, so he pulled his gun.

"Okay, 'just Carl', I need you to turn around and put your hands on your head. You are under arrest for attempted murder."

"I told you once already, she had a heart attack and fell. What the fuck are you talking about? Attempted murder?" Carl misunderstood and didn't realize his arrest was for shooting Bonn.

"I'm not going to tell you again..." Mac said right before a chair hit him from behind. The force of the chair sent Mac's service weapon sliding across the floor, his vision filled with flashes, and he landed face first at Carl's feet.

"Take that asshole. Good job Arnie. Let's go!" Carl and Armando bolted for the exit, undetected by the staff. They were busy with a group of drunken spring breakers who swam into a school of jellyfish.

Susan eased into the triage room and gasped at the sight of Mac crumbled next to Paula's gurney.

"Nurse, get in here, STAT," Susan yelled.

Susan dropped to her knees and used two fingers on Mac's jugular to check his pulse. The only visible evidence of blood came from his matted hair. When he moaned and opened his eyes, Susan placed both her hands on his chest to keep him still.

Mac grimaced, blinked rapidly a few times, and struggled to get up, just as Susan predicted. He wanted to get back on his feet, more out of embarrassment, than for any other reason.

"Don't move. Let me check you out."

"I'm okay. Where did that that son of a bitch go?"

"I told you not to move. That's an order!" Dr. Benson pinched him when he braced himself for another effort to sit up.

"Ouch! Why did you do that?"

"Oh, you poor baby, if you move again I'll pinch you somewhere that will really hurt," she told him with a smile Mac found sexy.

Back to his senses, Mac whispered, "Right now, I have to go after him, that's the guy who shot Bonn. You can pinch me anywhere you want when I get back."

For the first time in years, Susan's heart raced. The chemistry between them was so palpable; his remark left her at a loss for words for the second time that day. Then she heard the nurse clear her throat and say, "Doctor, is everything all right?"

Doctor Benson flinched and looked up to see two orderlies and the nurse grinning with approval.

"Don't just stand there with those stupid grins on your faces. Help me get him up. Nurse, get me an icepack and hand me the scope."

While shining the pin light of the ophthalmoscope in his eyes, with her face inches from his, Susan's girlish nerves vibrated throughout her body. The thought of kissing him became a fleeting one with the staff gawking at her. Mac acted as if nothing happened. He jumped up, brushed off his clothing, and picked up his weapon.

"Gotta go," Mac said then sprinted out the doors and hoped to apprehend Carl. When she righted the chair, she spotted a rhinestone-covered phone under Paula's gurney. When she started to pick it up, she heard the nurse shout, "Doctor Benson!"

While everyone focused on Mac, Paula turned a light shade of gray and was nonresponsive. The "Grande Momma'" of Beachside Landscaping, and employer of the largest population of illegal immigrants in the area, became another one of Carl's many victims. When Dr. Benson's resuscitation efforts failed, and the sheet pulled over Paula's face, every member of the triage team hurried to the windows to watch the scene unfolding in the parking lot.

R. Smit, head of hospital security and a USAF Special Op's veteran, spotted two men running out of the hospital and heading straight for him. The smaller of the two appeared to be the one chased and he had a sizable lead on the man following him. Rich noticed the *chaser* ran with a limp, possibly from an injured foot, he heard him grunt every time it met the pavement. "Rich Richard" decided take them down, one at a time, and then ask questions. Instinctively, he waited behind a soccer mom's minivan until the last moment, and stiff-armed a direct blow to the throat of Armando.

Carl saw what happened and weaved his way to his truck, where he retrieved his handgun and crouched down in the front seat. Rich left the victim of his clothesline tackle, who appeared knocked out, and walked to the area where he last saw the limping man, but he was gone. To his surprise, when he returned to the minivan, Armando was gone as well.

Rich anxiously scanned every parking lot without success. Then, he noticed three vehicles leaving the lot. A Champagne-colored Mercedes followed a dark blue conversion van. In addition, a Japanese crotch rocket motorcycle with two riders, screamed away on the street. While Rich focused on the motorcycle, he missed seeing the taillights of a white pickup truck turning the corner behind him.

"Have they breached the perimeter?"

Rich wheeled to the sight of Mac with his weapon drawn and holding his hand on the back of his head.

"Yes sir, containment was...*is* breached."

"What direction did they go? Did they leave on foot or in a vehicle?" Mac asked without a hint of urgency in his voice.

Rich gave him descriptions of the two vehicles and motorcycle. The dozen or so Crown Vic's, police cars, and various other law enforcement vehicles that swarmed the scene, were too late. While the police stopped every champagne-colored Mercedes and motorcycle with two riders, Carl's white dually pickup slipped away on the back roads to Pensacola

"Detective, there's something unusual about one of the men when I first saw them running out of the doors."

"What is it Smit?"

"Well, I thought the big guy looked like he had been injured. Every time his foot hit the pavement, he cried out in pain. As far as I knew, he had been attacked; I didn't know *you* were the one who was assaulted."

Mac touched the back of his head and said, "I received a blow from one of those imitation leather and chrome chairs in the waiting room."

Rich's precise, almost photographic, description of the culprits, from their physical characteristics, to the color of their shoes, impressed Mac enough to offer Rich a job if he ever decided to leave the hospital.

When Mac returned, he could sense the panic in the air, and saw the intense concern on Susan's face.

"What's wrong Doc? If it's me you're worried about, don't be, I'm okay."

"It's our patient. I went to the windows to see what was going on with you in the parking lot. When I came back…she was gone."

"It wouldn't have made any difference. You can't blame yourself for her death, Carl and his friend killed her, not you," Mac said and embraced her.

"No, I mean, she's *missing*. When I found you on the floor and examined you, she stopped breathing. After you ran out of here, and we found not breathing and she was unresponsive to standard resuscitation…so, I left her and went back to the window. I couldn't have been gone for more than a minute…, when I returned her gurney was empty. She must have walked out of here; I guess she wasn't dead after all. Mac, there is something else missing besides my patient. In all the chaos, I spotted the woman's cell phone on the floor. When things settled down and I went back to get it…she must have taken it with her, none of my people have it."

"We have another problem." Mac said, and pointed to Rich sprinting into the Emergency Room with a couple of detectives from the Sheriff's office.

"Detective, we have a situation," Rich said.

"You're damn right we do. Get on that radio of yours and tell those uniforms outside of Bonn's room to come down here. Mrs. Perkins is missing. We thought she was dead, now I don't know. We need to lock this hospital down and find her." Mac's energy level increased.

One of the detectives from the Sheriff's office jumped in and said, "Detective, that's the problem. The two men I sent to guard the General, never made it to the room. I just received a radio call, they were found gagged and handcuffed in a supply closet."

"Then, who were the two officers guarding Bonn?"

"I don't know."

ORMC went on lockdown and after an extensive search, Paula couldn't be found and wasn't seen leaving or her body being taken out of the hospital. There weren't any security cameras on the triage area and the outside cameras hadn't worked since the last hurricane.

The only clue to Paula's disappearance came from a geriatric patient who had been wandering the parking lot looking for the hospital's main entrance. She ambled through the front doors using her aluminum walker adorned with two chartreuse tennis balls on its front legs, and asked Mary to take her to the boss's office. Mary followed the same instructions she had given Rebecca, and rode the elevator with the geriatric witness to the seventh floor where Dave and his receptionist kept asking, "Like, what's the problem?" She wanted to file a complaint about a vehicle nearly hitting her; it was the first lead in the quest to find Paula. She described the vehicle that almost hit her as, "a red and white truck, just like the other ones parked around the hospital." The all points bulletin for every red and white ambulance in the county proved futile.

CHAPTER 20

Bonn opened his eyes to the sight of Mac holding hands with Dr. Benson, and heard her telling Mac how lucky he was only to have a minor bump, and not a concussion.

"I can't wait to hear what happened to you," Bonn said.

"Damn it Bonn, I told you to stop doing that! I've had enough surprises for one day," Dr. Benson said and picked up his chart for a second time that day.

"Hey buddy. Glad to see you're still with us. It has been a rough morning. I took one for the team trying to apprehend a perp." Mac showed off the small gauze patch on the back of his head like a trophy.

"Be quiet, both of you, the updates can wait," Dr. Benson said as she plugged in her stethoscope.

After a cursory examination and a few positive affirmations from Dr. Benson, she asked, "Bonn, can you tell me when you were born?"

"What kind of question is that?"

"It's the kind of question I want you to answer. What year were you born?"

The far away expression on Bonn's face was a clear indication of what she suspected.

"Do you know what day it is?"

"No."

"Who's the president?"

"I don't know. What's wrong with me?"

"Do you know where you are?"

Bonn swallowed and looked to Mac for help. ""I'm in a hospital, but I don't know how I got here or why I'm here. This is crazy. What happened to me?"

Susan showed her trust in Mac and let him continue.

"You don't remember…,"

"Remember what?"

Mac looked to Susan for approval before he told Bonn the truth. "You were shot, at least twice. Does the name Carl mean anything to you?"

"Carl? Carl who? Doc, what is wrong with my eye? Why do I have a headache from hell?" Bonn wanted answers to the fleeting questions that were going through his mind.

Dr. Benson pressed the call button and asked Ashleigh to come to the room. "I'm going to give you something for your headache but we have to be careful. Bonn, you have a severe concussion and TBI. Traumatic Brain Injury is extremely serious, it's a miracle you're alive."

"TBI? Do you mean a brain injury?" Bonn wasn't sure he wanted to hear any more, and panic was about to become an issue.

"One of the shots hit the posterior section of your brain's Linea Temporalis." Dr. Benson put her finger on the right rear side of her head.

"Doc, what does that mean in layman terms?"

"Your brain slammed from one side of your skull to the other. The shot didn't have enough time to spread out at such a close range; it hit you like one huge bullet. Bonn, we spent hours removing buckshot from your head, neck, and shoulders. Hell, we also cut and picked dozens out of your entire body, we think most of those came from a second shot.

Bonn sat in stunned silence after hearing all the news.

"My eye… I can barely open it and when I do, I can't see anything. Did I lose it?"

Before she could respond, Nurse Ashleigh entered the room and said, "Doctor Benson, what can I do?"

"Ashleigh, I want you to meet General Bonner, I just told him about his injuries and how he got them. He needs four units of Diladid and eight milligrams, Zofran, I.V.; Keep a close watch on him."

"Hi Ashleigh, I'm sorry we had to meet like this. I hope I'm not going to be too much trouble for you." Bonn, always charming when meeting attractive women, actually smiled.

"It's a pleasure meeting you General, and you aren't going to be any trouble, I'll make sure you're as comfortable as possible. Let me know if there is anything, you need. I'll be right back with something that will help your pain."

Ashleigh had worked with enough patients to realize by Bonn's expression, he had no recollection of his stay so far. As Nursing Supervisor and Dr. Benson's lead nurse, she knew Bonn intimately from his surgery.

"Doc, where's Mac?" Bonn asked.

"I'm right here," Mac said and locked eyes with Dr. Benson who ever so slightly shook her head. Mac suddenly realized Bonn's right eye was his blindside, and eased around the bed next to Susan.

"You never answered me; did I lose my eye?" Bonn lifted his right hand to his eye. The I.V. tubes connected to his hands and arm trailed like pasta lifted off a plate of spaghetti.

"No, you didn't lose your eye. We've taken the bandage off because we want to know if...*when*, you start seeing more light. One of the best ophthalmic surgeons in the South has examined you; it's too early to tell exactly how much damage there is. His name is Dr. Gupta and he will be in to visit with you tomorrow. He'll be able to answer your questions."

All three watched Ashleigh immediately push the contents of two syringes into Bonn's I.V. tube. Awash with relief, his face relaxed and his body went limp. Sleep came rapidly as Bonn was staring directly into Mac's eyes and telepathically trying to tell him, he would be all right.

"Thank you Ashleigh, that's all for now. Detective McCain, he's going to be sleeping for awhile. I want you to go home and rest, Doctor's orders."

Mac, grateful for everything Susan had done, reached out and gently squeezed her hand with both of his, and said,

"Yes, ma'am, I'll get some rest," Mac said, then asked, "Doc, could you walk with me to the elevator?"

Mac blocked the elevator doors from closing and asked, "How well do you know your nurse?"

"Well enough to know she's the best I've ever had in surgery. Detective, why are you asking about my nurse?"

"I overheard her telling several people she knew Bonn, and she never referred to him as General Bonner. Then, she spoke with Colonel Fagan, and led her to believe Bonn was more than just an acquaintance. I don't believe anything she says and I find it interesting, as well as a little strange. I'll talk with you after I recharge my batteries, and if I remember correctly, you owe me a...'pinch'."

CHAPTER 21

R
ebecca sat with her feet propped on her desk and contemplated her decision to work as an undercover liaison officer or whatever she wanted to call herself, as long as she maintained her cover. Her cell phone vibrated on the wooden desk, but after what happened to her after the last few text messages, she hesitated to pick it up. After seeing 1 NEW MESSAGE – Unknown on the phone's screen, her fear gave way to an overwhelming curiosity. The message didn't help alleviate her pessimistic attitude; it justified her disdain for cyber communication. As soon as she saw BYE BYE BITCH in the message box, it disappeared one letter at a time and there wasn't a trace of the sender's number or that she even received the message.

"Whoever you are, you can threaten me, but if you try to hurt him again...," she said to her phone.

Her frustration level peaked and she threw the cell phone across the room.

A day never passed without thinking of Bonn or the messages she received since coming back to her old stomping grounds. The last text bugged her, it sounded familiar, like a name on the tip of the tongue that comes when you quit trying to remember something you know. So, that is exactly what Rebecca chose to do, quit thinking about it. Only then, did she realize how counterproductive her coping techniques were to her mental health, she quietly said, "I need a break from the daily trips to the hospital. And...I need to quit worrying about Bonn; he is going to be just fine." Rebecca stopped talking aloud but kept the conversation going in her thoughts, "If I keep having conversations with myself, I'm going lose my mind."

She wanted to do something she hadn't done for awhile, have fun. So, her decision was to buy a new bikini for the upcoming four day weekend. She hoped shopping and a therapeutic day on the water would be just what she needed to relax and relieve her stress.

The Memorial Day crowds gathered en mass on the beaches and emerald green water for three days of partying. The endless streams of multimillion-dollar yachts, boats, jet skis, and every other imaginable mode of water transportation, converged on Crab Island at the foot of the Destin Bridge, for the party of the year.

The submerged island was always under a few feet of gin clear water that allowed the watercraft to anchor and the partiers to wade waist high with their favorite beverages.

Rainbow-colored float tubes, holding drunken beer drinkers, drifted dangerously between churning outboards, inboards, and the obnoxiously loud roaring fans of several airboats. Viewed from the air, the shallow water island looked like a mass of living polka dots.

On one side of the island, *WDMM-99.5 Metal Mania's* barge floated in a sea of hardcore rockers, and played its music at deafening levels. On the other end, *Country-105's* barge had a makeshift dance floor crowded with barefoot line dancers and a few top-heavy cowgirls who opted to wear only one piece of their bikinis. The fumes of sunscreen, marijuana, and diesel fuel wafted the air at both locations. Rebecca relaxed for the first time since returning to Destin and blended-in with the hodgepodge of bikini-clad beauties, chiseled young servicemen, and beer-bellied rednecks fantasizing about the bikinis.

Relentless and overwhelming encouragement by her friends to "let her hair down", convinced Rebecca to go parasailing behind one of the boats offering a *thrill of a lifetime*. A voice of reason told her it wasn't safe; the homemade margaritas convinced her it would be "fun".

From the corner unit, on the top floor of the Emerald Pass Condominiums, Colonel Rebecca Fagan filled the lens of a 10x42mm Ultra M3A scope mounted on top of a M24 Sniper Weapons System rifle. The scope of the sniper's weapon rested on a telescoping tripod and tracked Rebecca's every movement. The military sharpshooter adjusted the scope for wind and distance as Rebecca lay motionless on an air mattress, working on her tan. Finally, to make ready for the shot, the shooter attached an AAC sound suppressor with a muzzle brake to the barrel.

As the assassin left the improvised shooting station to open the sliding glass door, Mick Jagger sang *Sympathy for the Devil* at a volume loud enough to drown out a muffled shot. The shooter was confident a shot coming from eight stories high would help dissipate any percussion the suppressor didn't conceal. Preparations complete, the sniper walked back to the locked and loaded rifle, then he could'nt find Rebecca's image in the scope. After frantically scanning an endless sea of bodies, the shooter spotted her friends waving and shouting at a bright yellow boat idling away from them. Refocusing the scope on the boat's stern revealed Colonel Fagan slipping into a nylon harness attached to a bright blue parachute.

Training kept any panic away and the sniper calmly moved the shooting station from the bay-view to the Gulf-view corner of the condo. Now, sitting on the veranda, new adjustments were dialed-in on the scope. The shooter knew to be patient and wait for her to make a pass eighty feet up and directly in front of the veranda.

The expansive view above the Gulf's green water was breathtaking, and although acrophobia might have been a problem, the vertigo Rebecca felt, she blamed on the tequila; Colonel Fagan would have stopped at two Margaritas. However, she was enjoying the view, until suddenly; she went limp and hung precariously in the harness.

The image of her white bikini top turning a pink hue had her friends screaming at the blond surfer boys running the boat and jabbing their fingers up towards their lifeless friend. Reeling her back to the boat was taking an excruciating amount of time, and the sobbing screams of her friends didn't help bring her in any faster.

Chief Barnes sat atop the spotting tower of his thirty-five foot Cabo fishing boat scanning the shallows and surf for the elusive Cobia that could win the Cobia World Championship fishing tournament. One good fish would earn him more money than he could in a couple of years of working as chief. He focused on the water and not in the sky or he would have seen the parachute that had been floating above his boat. By the time, he heard the *"Boater in distress"* call on his police scanner, boats from the Coast Guard, Marine Patrol, and Okaloosa County Sheriff's department were already speeding towards the bright yellow parasailing boat.

The chief began to climb down from his boat's tower, when directly off his port side; he spotted the largest Cobia he'd ever seen.

"It's a tournament winner!"

A thousand yards away, a yellow boat with *PARASAIL* and a phone number stenciled on its side, drifted with its engines turned off and its parachute floating on the water behind it. The chief was oblivious to the boat the people on the bow frantically waving their arms.

Chief Barnes ignored their pleas and he cast his live eel, five feet in front of the monster fish, the Cobia swallowed it instantly. When the drag of the Penn spinning reel started whining, he climbed down the tower's ladder while holding on with one hand and keeping the line taut by holding the rod high in the other.

"Catfish, she's a pig worth a quarter million dollars! We have to do this right! If we get her in, you will be driving a new pickup, she's a record!"

"Catfish", his first mate, took the boat out of gear while Chief Barnes fought the fish. However, there was a problem. For every hundred feet of line gained on the reel, the Cobia made runs of two-hundred feet, peeling line off the reel. They were going to have to chase the fish and get back most of the lost line, if they were going to have any chance of putting it in the boat.

"Chase that bitch down; she's spooling me," Chief Barnes said.

The chief started to panic as he ran, with rod in hand, to the bow of the boat while Catfish throttled the sleek fishing boat slowly towards it.

"Chief, try and turn her, she's heading straight to all those boats," Catfish said while frantically pointing in the direction of the boats that had surrounded and boarded the crippled Parasailing boat.

"I can't turn her! Keep following her and don't worry about those damn idiots."

Catfish mumbled to himself about where Chief Barnes could go. If it hadn't been for the new truck, and the notoriety that came with being the First Mate winner of the tournament, he would have sabotaged the chief's efforts. Nevertheless, the fish looked to be in excess of one-hundred and thirty pounds and close to a new world record.

Instead of diving to the bottom to escape, the Cobia decided to take refuge in the flotilla of boats that had gathered to help and jeopardized the chief's payday, plus, Catfish's new pickup.

Chief Barnes screeched in a high-pitched voice that made Catfish laugh, "Hard-to-starboard, hard-to-starboard!"

"I have to shut it down Chief. Look!" Catfish said as he pulled back the throttle and put the engines in neutral.

Two Coast Guard, and one Marine Patrol officer, were waving away the chief's boat and pointing their weapons in an attempt to get the fishermen to veer off. When the Coast Guard officer got on the bullhorn and told them they were going to shoot if the boat didn't comply, all they heard was the chief yelling back at them.

"No, I'm Chief Barnes, I'm Chief Barnes! I'm with the Niceville police department. I'm Chief Barnes"

"I don't care who you are. Stay clear!"

On cue, his fish of a lifetime made a run into the half-submerged parachute and the line went slack. The chief started reeling as fast as he could, hoping the fish had turned back towards them and not broken the line. Fortunately, the line tightened and the fish shook its head, causing the rod tip to vibrate. Wrapped into a snarl of silk and nylon cord, the giant Cobia cocooned itself.

Rebecca never lost consciousness or made a sound when they lifted her onto a stretcher and placed her on a Coast Guard boat. The orange Coast Guard Zodiac flew at full speed through the *No Wake Zone*. At the Coast Guard station, the helicopter pilot who transported General Bonner a week earlier, waited for a passenger who would get an emergency flight to the same hospital. This time, Rebecca's *Big Brother Bob* pushed the million dollar engines to their max.

CHAPTER 22

Fortunately, the high-powered 300 Win Mag bullet that hit Rebecca wasn't a hollow point, which would have expanded on entry and ripped a large exit hole. The bullet passed through her left chest just below the Clavicle or collarbone, cracking a rib, and fracturing the Scapula before exiting. A team of orthopedic, neurological, and vascular surgeons pieced together her broken and cracked shoulder during a grueling five-hour surgery. As a reminder of her stay, Rebecca inherited a variety of screws and pins that held her shoulder together. The near constant pain reminded her every day of how quickly life could change.

Representatives from every department and agency came to visit Rebecca during a surprisingly short stay, including the CIA agent who initially briefed her when she arrived to investigate the problems with the F-22 Raptor.

Special Agent Sienna Harris claimed to have received her orders, from the office for the Under Secretary of Defense for Acquisitions. Sienna deployed to Tyndall AFB in Panama City, where the Raptor pilots trained before they flew to Eglin AFB, their future home.

When Sienna walked into the room unannounced, Rebecca disguised her surprise as a twinge of pain.

"Colonel Fagan, I want you to know, we at the agency will use every resource available to catch the animal that did this to you. I take it personally when one of our agents comes under attack." Agent Harris spoke without making eye contract for more than a second.

"Thank you Sienna, please call me Rebecca, I have a feeling we are going to be seeing a lot of each other."

Caught off-guard by the reception she received, Agent Harris patted Rebecca's leg and said, "Thank you, Colonel."

Although puzzled by the refusal to reciprocate on a first name basis, Rebecca respected Sienna's wishes to keep the relationship strictly professional. However, she couldn't shake off the feeling that Agent Harris had been condescending towards her.

"As you wish…, *Agent* Harris."

"Colonel Fagan, is there anyone you can think of that might want you dead?"

"I've made many enemies in my career. I don't think what happened is a message from someone in my past. We need to figure out who knows about my assignment here and if that person has connection to the Raptor program."

"I agree, here's what I want you to do…,"

Agent Harris, let me stop you right there. You are strictly support if I need any. If you want to discuss possible options, I'm more than happy to have that conversation in a few days, we'll talk during a morning briefing. I'll call *you*."

Sienna didn't need further explanations to know she had just been dismissed. "As you wish, *Colonel*."

Out of safety concerns, Dr. Benson released Rebecca to the Air Force medical personnel awaiting her arrival at a fully equipped and secure house on Eglin. Right before the hospital's main doors parted to wheel her out; Mary spoke from behind the Welcome Desk, "Take care, Sweetie. Be safe." Uncertain if Mary was speaking to her, Rebecca ignored the statement.

An agent, disguised as an orderly, pushed her quickly outside, followed by an entourage of news photographers attempting the "money shot". To restrict her movement, she wore a mini version of an upper-body cast with a side bar running from her arm to her waist. A floating balloon tied to the wheelchair read, *Combat Tested*. Rebecca's body cast and floating balloon, along with the massive bouquet of flowers cradled on her lap, made a perfect front-page photo.

Security guard R. Smit had been anticipating Rebecca's departure and tried to pretend he didn't know she had been attacked.

"Ma'am, what happened to you?"

"Well, look who's here, 'Rich Richard.' I had a little accident. They tell me I'm going to be fine. I don't want you to worry about me, but I *do* want you to open the door for me," she said, and pointed to an approaching vehicle.

"You and I have a little problem with doors. Last time we met, you blocked me from opening my car door, and now, you're doing it again. Is there a reason you don't want me to leave?" she deadpanned before letting out a laugh that made her grimace.

"Ma'am. Yes Ma'am; I mean, no Ma'am." Rich blushed and agreed as he opened the door, then took her hand and assisted her to the front seat. As her ride started to pull away, Rebecca winked and silently mouthed a thank you through the glass window. The entire ride to Eglin, Rebecca kept her fingers tightly wrapped around the note he slipped her when he took her hand to help her into the vehicle.

Rebecca's departure was under the watchful eyes of two Secret Service agents sitting in a delivery truck while Agent Harris, posed as a newspaper photographer and took pictures of the agents. While everyone focused on Colonel Fagan, a lone observer stood in the glass walkway connecting the main building to the South wing and texted an update of the situation.

The subsequent investigation determined the shot that hit Rebecca came from one of the many buildings on the beach. The investigators were convinced; the trajectory of the bullet's entry and exit wound's wasn't consistent with a shot that would have come from the beach or a boat. The angle was consistent with a shot parallel to her, and not angled up, which had been the first assumption.

The number of multi-level condominiums and hotels in the general vicinity of where the shooting occurred was staggering.

Elementary calculations of rope length, and the boat's estimated speed, placed Rebecca at a distance of at least sixty feet above the water, which eliminated half of the hundreds of Gulf-view rooms. Unfortunately, there were a dozen condominium projects, two hotel resorts, and the roofs of multi-level parking garages that were six stories or more.

PART TWO

TEAM DESTIN

CHAPTER 23

U nder the pretense of solving a possible crime, Susan agreed to meet with Mac after she finished her rounds at the hospital. Mac couldn't believe how great she looked for someone who came straight from work to meet him. Susan failed to tell him, she had a resident cover for her so she could rush home to shower, primp, and go through half of her clothes to find the perfect outfit. They met at a quiet bistro for a glass of wine, to discuss the day's events at the hospital. Their chemistry became so intense; both forgot what they were talking about and why they were there.

Halfway through a $200 Cabernet, Susan feigned exhaustion and asked, "Mac, would you mind following me back to my house, in case I have trouble with my car."

"I had the same thought. I'm a man who knows automobiles, and it's always better to be safe than sorry when driving those unreliable foreign cars."

Even though she owned a mint condition, six-figure Mercedes, she found him endearing when he pretended to be naive to her real intentions.

During the entire trip to her million dollar mansion on the bay, his manliness strained at his zipper in anticipation of what he hoped would happen after they arrived at her house. Lost in erotic thoughts, Mac failed to spot the black Cadillac Escalade that had been following both of them since they left the restaurant.

The following day, Dr. Benson ignored a unanimous vote by all the nurses who didn't want 'Bonn' to leave. She released him to Mac and two intense men from Security Forces who were taking him to his beachside home in Destin. The hours he spent in surgery, to remove the dozens of buckshot, left him looking like a character out of a horror film. Dr. Benson informed Bonn, his edema and the discoloration on his face, would gradually go away, but his damaged eye remained a concern.

During the first few days of convalescence, Bonn learned that bright light triggered many of his headaches. During the early phase of recovery, only sunlight caused the headaches and the varying degrees of seizures. Later, he painfully discovered there were times the glow of a television, an overhead light, or even a table lamp could also cause a reaction. In an attempt to head off the onset of a headache, he wore a pair of Orvis fishing glasses with leather side blinders and a mirrored finish on the lenses. The sunglasses, made to reduce sunlight and glare, became part of Bonn's persona, even indoors.

Weight loss became an issue as nausea and the subsequent loss of appetite, persisted. The very thought of food made Bonn sick most every day. Dr. Benson demanded his diet include a regiment of protein drinks, Gatorade, lots of water, and vitamins to help him maintain an acceptable weight.

Bonn tried to conceal the problem with his memory, or the lack of it, even though he couldn't hide from his closest friends. There were many, he recognized without remembering their names. Several names came to mind. However, he feared the names he heard from his inner voices, and worried he might be losing control of his mind. It was a symptom of his injury, he never discussed with anyone. One name he never forgot, was Mac's. The other, he tried repeatedly to put a face with the name, Rebecca. Somehow, he knew her name, and thought he remembered her calling him, "Baby". He didn't have any memory of her being in his hospital room and concluded, she had been a dream.

The peril of being male, combined with his fear that people might perceive his memory loss as weakness, began to consume his thoughts and propel him into a deep depression. Any comfort Bonn relished in the comfort of his own home, dissipated as the prospect of a lifelong disability became his greatest fear.

Slouched in his favorite easy chair, Bonn realized, for the first time in his life, the sunset depressed him. He used to marvel at the Gulf's horizon. Now, a melancholy darkness enveloped his spirit and he refused to watch. Instead, he would stare at the cord grass and sea oats covering the ancient dunes that surrounded his house. The rhythm of their sway in the stiff southern Gulf breezes had Bonn contemplating their ability to bend and not break, even in the midst of a hurricane. The philosophical moment became an epiphany that brought him out of the darkness.

CHAPTER 24

T
he combination of anti-seizure, anti-anxiety, antibiotic, and anti-pain medications were affecting Bonn's read on Mac's protective demeanor. Mac refused to let anyone get to his best friend, and stood with his arms crossed in a way that made his biceps appear larger than they normally were at rest. They would have to go through him.

"Mac, you're being a "bitch" for hovering over me like a mother lion ready to tear apart anything that tried to mess with its cub."

"Ha! You're getting back to the ornery prick we all know and love."

Bonn's willingness to participate in juvenile male banter, gave Mac hope that his friend survived the worse, and would now make it. Mac felt it was time to share what he had been thinking about since his friend's release from the hospital. He wanted Lexi, his K-9 partner, to become a key player in Bonn's healing process.

"I've been thinking, maybe it would be a good idea for Lexi to stay with you while you're going through the initial healing process. She could double as your companion *and* security guard."

"I don't need a security guard! I may only have one good eye, and that's all I need. I can see just fine," Bonn said as he tapped the classic .45 Caliber Colt 1911 in his shoulder holster.

"I'm sure you can, but with her, three eyes are better than two. Whether you like it or not, Lexi is going to stay with you for a while. After what happened to you...Well, you shouldn't be alone."

Bonn smiled quizzically at his friend's statement and said, "I shouldn't be alone? There is something different about you today. If I didn't know better, I would say you are…what's the word, happy?"

Mac immediately bent over as though he had been gut punched and said, "I think you've taken too many pills. I don't have a clue what you're talking about."

Judging by Mac's response, Bonn knew he had struck a nerve and dropped the subject.

"Bonn, I know you think you could shoot a fly off the wall, but you're always in the dark wearing those damn sunglasses and you would be lucky to see what you're shooting at if anyone comes in here." Mac had to fight the temptation to open the blinds and turn on the lights.

"I appreciate your concern. Guess what, I can outshoot you with one eye shut, even in the dark." Mac's marksmanship was legendary; Bonn witnessed Mac's shooting skills when he took out an Iraqi sniper at a distance over a thousand yards.

"Why don't we get out of this dungeon you call home and go to the gun range? You can bring that cannon you call a handgun and practice shooting with your one eye closed. We'll *see* if you can still hit the target," Mac said then added, "No pun intended."

When they arrived at the pistol range and went to their shooting stations, Bonn stood with a faraway look on his face, and then closed his eyes and smiled as he visualized a time when he watched a young female airman shooting her weapon from the same station where he was standing. When he heard the whirring of the range's electronic target retrieval system, it reinforced the realism of his daydream. Although his hearing protection muffled the constant percussions of the weapons fired around him, the sensation pounded his chest with each shot, and shook him to his core. In that instant, he recognized the woman in his daydream *Rebecca*. As Bonn drifted in the memory, a surge of nausea hit him and right before his vision turned completely black, he aimlessly reached out to Mac for support of his buckling knees.

Mac wrapped his arms around Bonn, who was limp and sweating profusely, said, "Rebecca? Mac?"

"Hey buddy, you had me worried," Mac said then put Bonn flat on his back and used his jacket as a pillow to cushion Bonn's head, in case he seized and began thrashing.

"What happened?"

"You had some kind of episode. You were telling Rebecca she needed to improve her aim and speed. Don't you remember?"

"Rebecca? No, I don't remember. Where are we?"

Mac reached into his pocket and brought out his cell phone and after tapping a speed dial number said, "We're at the gun range."

"Wait. Who are you calling?"

"Susan. We need to go to the hospital and have you checked out."

"Hang up, I'm fine."

When Mac ignored him, Bonn pushed to a sitting position, rapidly shook his head to clear the cobwebs, and grabbed Mac's arm, "Hang up the damn phone!"

A small group of airmen huddled around them and offered their assistance. The staff sergeant, whose job it was to manage the range, kept insisting that regulation required he call the medics and report the incident.

Bonn stood, introduced himself as General Bonner, and told the young sergeant to "stand down" or he would make his life hell for the rest of his Air Force career.

Mac shrugged his shoulders when the sergeant looked to him for help.

"General, are you ready to leave?"

CHAPTER 25

B onn awoke from a fitful sleep filled with a cast of characters that he wasn't sure were real or imagined. He sat up in an attempt to orientate himself and flinched at the sight of Mac standing next to his bed.

Mac didn't try to hide his facetious tone when he asked, "Did you have a nice nap?"

"Mac…what are you doing here?"

"You don't remember what happened? We were at the range and you went stone cold. You wouldn't let me take you to the hospital. So, here we are."

"That's right; I was going to show you how to shoot. It's coming back to me. How long have I been out?" Bonn asked as he yawned and stretched.

"You've been snoring for a couple of hours, why don't you tell me how you're feeling?"

Bonn flung back the covers rolled out of his bed in his sports briefs. "I need something to drink, I could spit cotton balls."

"Well, you might want to put on some pants; you have company," Mac said and pulled back the curtains for Bonn to see his visitor's cars. The driveway and front yard were jammed with law enforcement vehicles from several agencies. Each agency had already claimed some jurisdiction in Bonn's assault case and they were waiting, impatiently, in the living room.

Two representatives from Eglin AFB sat next to a Florida Fish and Game investigator. One investigator in a suit, refused to take off her jacket, despite the Florida heat and humidity. Bonn walked into the living room and plopped down on his favorite chair, but it was too bright for his liking. After putting on his sunglasses, he turned the chair away from the sliding glass doors leading to his deck. That's when he noticed one of the vertical slats hung at an angle, letting in a ray of sunlight, straightened it from top to bottom, and checked it repeatedly. Then, he looked to Mac, who knew what to do. Before anyone said a word, Mac lit a series of candles throughout the room and then handed Bonn a chartreuse-colored tennis ball. His visitors watched the ritual with shrugged shoulders.

Bonn reclined, and was satisfied that everything was "just right"; he proceeded to toss the tennis ball straight up, and repeatedly made failed attempts to catch it. Lexi would snatch the dropped balls and immediately lay it back in Bonn's hand. When it was obvious everyone wanted an explanation, he just shook his head, mimicked them by shrugging his shoulders, and said, "I don't have a clue."

"Let's do this," Bonn said after successfully catching the ball. He made eye contact with each person even though they couldn't see his eyes through the mirrored lenses of his sunglasses. After a series of formal introductions that included Lexi, the female C.I.A agent took the lead role for the meeting.

"General, thank you for allowing us time today, if at any time you need to stop, please let me know, "Agent Michelle Milton said with an air of sincerity that she would dictate the flow of questioning.

Bonn turned his head to get a good look at her and asked, "Agent Milton, do I know you?"

She hesitated, and with all eyes on her, said, "I believe we met many years ago in Oklahoma ...my first year out of Quantico."

"Nope, I don't remember you. Why don't you tell me all about it?"

Mac detected the beginning of a twisted smile on Bonn's face and knew what Bonn was about to do and decided to become a "bitch" again. Bonn smiled for the first time in weeks.

"Drop it General, you don't remember a lot of things."

Agent Milton avoided an explanation of how she knew him and said,

"General, a lot of time has passed since we met, it's not important. I need to ask you if you know a man that goes by the name of Cap."

"No... I've never heard of him," Bonn said even though he had an uneasy feeling the name could be someone he might have known, and it showed.

"Sir, I'm sorry I have to ask, do you know a Colonel Fagan?"

"No. Why are you sorry for having to ask me if I know him?"

"It's not a 'him' I'm asking about. You might remember *her* as Rebecca?" Agent Milton phrased the statement as a question.

When Bonn snapped the recliner back to a sitting position and took off his sunglasses, he didn't appear to be self conscious of his swollen and bruised face; Mac knew his friend had returned.

"Did you say, Rebecca? I'm not sure. I have the feeling I know a Rebecca. Mac, do I know her? I remembered her at the range, right?"

Mac nodded one time as the entire room went still, and waited with abated breath for Mac to say something.

"You and Rebecca were a couple, it was years ago. More recently, the day you were shot, she came to your hospital room and you talked with her."

Mac remained motionless while he waited for the response he hoped Bonn would give him. If Bonn truly remembered Rebecca and their past as a couple, he would have to tell him about the recent attack on her.

Bonn got up and walked slowly to the bookcase. He ran his finger over the binders of several books until he found a photo album and flipped through a few pages until he saw a picture that made his body stiffen. Flipping the plastic pages of old photographs evoked a memory of a time many years earlier where he saw himself in a room with two FBI agents who were turning the pages of a photo album filled with mug shots. One agent was a beautiful young FBI agent with high cheekbones and dark eyes, who went by the name Milton. Bonn's head snapped towards her and he squinted.

Agent Milton asked, "What is it? Are you all right?"

"It's nothing I can put my finger on, you remind me of someone I knew with the Bureau many years ago." Bonn dismissed the possibility with a wave of his hand.

"General, we met at the beginning of my career with the Bureau, a rookie." As much as she didn't want to continue, the opportunity to build rapport and cooperation with him was crucial in her investigation.

Bonn saved her from having to continue with her explanation when he pulled out a picture of an elegantly dressed woman taken at a Commander's Christmas Ball many years ago. Rebecca's scarlet evening gown fit her body like a glove, and the three-quarter slit exposing one of her long slender legs had Bonn's heart racing, just as it had decades earlier. He held it out for Mac to see and asked, "Rebecca?

"Yes," Mac and Agent Milton answered in unison.

A wave of nausea overcame him as his teeth clenched and his eye rolled back before collapsing into Mac's arms. Bonn opened his eye to the sight of Agent Milton straddling him and doing chest compressions.

"What's going on, Mac?" Bonn asked as he started to come around.

"You had a seizure and went out like you did at the range. Just lay there and be quiet," Mac ordered. "We have paramedics on the way and Dr. Benson will be here as fast as she can."

"I'm fine Mac."

"Damn it Bonn, that's what Rebecca always says too. What is it with the two of you? You are not 'fine'. Stay put and don't argue with me. That, is an order

The paramedics' arrival caused Bonn to recoil when the front door opened and filled the room with sunlight. Their bright orange medical bags hung heavy and glowed with an aura when Bonn looked at them.

The young paramedic hesitated when he saw Bonn's grotesque appearance and asked Mac, "What the hell happened to him?"

The answer came from the front door when Dr. Benson walked in carrying an old-school medical bag and said,

"He's a gunshot victim and my patient. Let me in there."

Watching Susan take charge, reminded Mac of their first night together in her bed where also she showed her assertive side and when he caught himself shifting his focus to carnal visions, he intended to say under his breath, "I'm such a pig." Everyone turned and looked at him. To his relief, the only one who knew what he meant smiled knowingly.

Once Susan determined Bonn had not suffered a heart attack or any major setback, she gently patted his cheek. Almost instantly, his eye opened, and he tried to push himself up to a sitting position.

"Just be still for a minute General. How are you feeling?" Susan asked.

"My head is killing me. Will someone close that door and find my sunglasses, Bonn said while shielding his with a full salute."

Susan took charge of the situation. "Let's get him to bed."

The paramedics helped Bonn to his feet and escorted him to his bedroom. After giving him a shot to ease his pain, Dr. Benson returned to the living room and made eye contact with each person while shaking her head in disgust.

"This man is not well enough to be grilled. I've seen enough, it's time for everyone to leave. I'm sure there are questions that need to be answered," Dr. Benson said.

One of the two investigators from Eglin decided to end his silence and said with conviction, "I have orders from Commander Bentow to get to the bottom of what happened. The incident occurred on her base and unless I'm told something different, we have jurisdiction over this case."

"I can appreciate the fact you want to do your job Sergeant. Please feel free to call Commander Bentow if you think you are in violation of orders. I've spoken with her several times, and she knows my role here is as lead investigator. Tell her, Agent Milton said to call."

Mac wanted to diffuse the situation and said, "We all want to do what we can to help without running the risk of killing him by pushing for answers too soon. I will be with him, and you have my word, when he is well enough to answer questions, you will all be notified."

"Detective, I can appreciate your offer to be his caretaker and I'm sure your intentions are good. The problem is, I'm afraid it's not up to you to decide when I get to speak with him. As a detective, you're aware that every day that goes by is going to make it more difficult to catch the person who did this to him. I *will* talk with him. Is that clear?"

"Only one thing is clear to me. Dr. Benson is the only one here that has the training to determine what is best for him right now," Mac stood his ground. "No matter what *I* think, I'll leave it up to Dr. Benson. I'm sure your bosses at the agency wouldn't be happy if you didn't follow his surgeon's advice and Bonn had a setback."

After hearing the conviction in Mac's voice, Susan fought a temptation to kiss him.

"I'll tell you what detective; I'll give him 24 hours. My job is to protect him and everyone who is close to him. There are things going on that even *you* don't know about. I have my orders, and I'm going to do my job. Is *that* clear?"

Susan respected the agent's commitment to protect Bonn and said, "Mac, she's right. He is going to have these bouts, and we can't predict when. All we can do is protect him from himself and let her do her job."

Mac didn't question Susan's change of heart, he let it go and followed her lead. "Why don't we all meet back here at noon tomorrow? I'll call you if we need to reschedule."

CHAPTER 26

Mac sat in bed with Susan, his honorary partner. Both were exhausted after a third round of lovemaking and role-played their version of Sherlock and Watson as they tried to figure out the relentless chaos in their lives. While Mac shared his views, Susan took notes on separate Post-it note sheets and laid them out on the mattress in the order they happened. They had two columns: one had notes with events written on them, for things that happened before she came to the hospital and one for events that transpired after her disappearance.

"Beachside Landscaping has been on lockdown since Carl and his friend knocked me out," Mac said and subconsciously rubbed the back of his head. "Write that down and place it with the other more recent events under the Paula's disappearance column."

"Why don't we break down the events leading to her demise, then see if we can connect the dots?" Susan wrote, *Lockdown* on one of the yellow square notes and arranged it with the other notes of known facts underneath a picture of Paula. A triangle formed from the yellow Post-it notes that had information on them, not clues. They hoped by arranging the notes in the right order, a clearer picture would appear. They began with the first two notes below Paula's photo and worked down, line by line, from left to right.

"Let's start with *Heart attack* and *Head wound*, then *Hives*. Now, place the *Peanut Butter* note next to the *Knife with Paula's Prints*," Mac said, and then scratched his head.

"What are you thinking about?"

"Susan, I don't get it. If her medical records indicated an allergy to peanuts, which is something she had to be hyper vigilant about, how did she ingest the peanut butter?" Mac asked. "She wouldn't have licked the knife. The only worker, who spoke English, confirmed that she made a tray of sandwiches, and brought them outside for them to eat, but he didn't see her eat any of them."

"That's only one of the things what we need to figure out." Susan wrote *PEANUT BUTTER* on a note and set it down on the triangle that had doubled in size.

"Mac, even though I initially suspected anaphylaxis, I'm not sure. Without a body, we don't have any stomach contents to verify she ingested a peanut product, it's a guess based on her medical history."

When Mac didn't respond, Susan looked up to find him holding the note that had *PEANUT BUTTER* written on it.

"I'm starving, let's eat," Mac said.

The D.A. "temporarily" cleared the Carl of any wrongdoing in Paula's death since they didn't have a body. The name Armando Jesus Gonzalez wasn't found in any database, and they had to rely on an artist's sketch.

Armando was on the phone in Carl's truck and talking to his uncle in San Diego before he walked into the ER. When he entered, he saw a man in a sport coat, holding a gun on Carl. Instinctively, he looked around and did what he felt he had to do. They escaped and drove the back roads to Pensacola and hid in the back room of a Mexican restaurant owned by the cartel until Armando's men assured him, the police were gone. When one of his men arrived at the restaurant to pick up Armando, Carl became even angrier than usual, and left in his dually pickup. That was the last time Armando would see Carl.

A drug-induced paranoia transformed Carl A. Perkins to his "Cap" persona and convinced him the police would be on the lookout for a longhaired, tobacco-chewing redneck, not for a clean cut member of the military. The next day, Cap set off on his plan by trading his easily identifiable "dually" to a less than reputable car dealer for an untitled used gray Ford F-150 pickup, and enough cash to buy a few basic supplies.

Cap went into military mode and chose the pre-operational tactic of surveillance as the first step after he established a base. So, he checked-in into the *Flyboy Inn* on the edge of Niceville. After paying cash for a room at the "by-the-day, week, or month" motel, he buzz-cut his hair, shaved clean, and put on one of the two sets of BDU.'s he purchased at a surplus store. Cap posed in front of the bathroom mirror, wearing a woodland green camouflage pattern and said, "Perfect, just perfect." The reflection staring back in the mirror would be invisible when he mixed it with the military personnel coming and going from one of the military bases in the area.

To compensate for the swelling of his foot, he bought a pair of black jump boots after he switched one boot for another, two sizes larger. Although the roomier boot felt better, his foot pain became unbearable. Cap *needed* his painkillers, and he *wanted* more cocaine. After snorting a couple of lines of coke on the Gideon bible in his room, he made a paste with what he had left and applied it to his throbbing big toe, it numbed his entire foot and up his leg to the knee.

The Ruger Security-6 revolver he kept in his truck held six rounds, but it wasn't his weapon of choice for what he had planned. It became clear; a return to the scene of the crime was inevitable if he wanted to retrieve his favorite handgun, a .40 caliber Glock 22 with a 15 round clip. Although his rifle would give him a substantially better kill range, it would deprive him of seeing Bonn up close and personal when he killed him. Cap took one more look in the full length mirror screwed on the back of the bathroom door and saluted.

Cap made his way towards Beachside Landscaping in his nondescript gray pickup and looked like any of the other active duty personnel in their vehicle. Driving at a snail's pace, he eased past his business and saw a group of workers milling around their trucks, drinking beer, and smoking. Cap worried about what they might do if they spotted him without Arnie and drove aimlessly until the sun had set.

Darkness came, and with lights off, he eased into a field across from Beachside Landscaping and the trailer park, and parked behind the dam of a pond until everyone went to their trailers for the night. When the last man left, he slipped into his trailer, grabbed his drugs, and stayed in the shadows as he made the short walk to his office. Once inside, he removed a drawer with a false bottom from Paula's desk and added the stashed semi-automatic Glock to his arsenal. After ingesting enough painkillers and cocaine, to numb his throbbing foot and mind, he plopped down on Paula's overstuffed Lay-Z-Boy, and then scanned the dark office with his penlight.

The beam lit up a framed photo on Paula's desk that Cap remembered taking of her while on a trip to Mexico. At the time, Paula thought they were on vacation, and didn't know Carl planned the trip as his cover to meet with one of the most notorious Cartel bosses in Mexico. While she floated on a doublewide air mattress and worked on her tan, he met with Armando's uncle. The photo became another reminder of the unbearable time he spent living off the grid with her, and smashed the framed picture against the wall.

As the pain levels subsided and his focus returned, he moved the rug that concealed the entrance to his growing operation. The second he lifted the hatched door, a stench drifted out that Cap recognized immediately. He racked a shell into the chamber of his Glock and eased his way down the hole leading to his growing room. In the middle of an empty room, he found Armando, gagged and bound to a chair with a single bullet hole in the center of his forehead. Cap resented the attempt to implicate him by using his signature shot, but he didn't dwell on it; the mature female pot plants, worth over a couple hundred thousand dollars, were gone, and Cap believed Armando's demise was a robbery-murder.

He wasn't sure who tried to make it look like he shot Arnie until he noticed the white tip of a business card sticking out of Armando's front pocket. The card had a line drawing of a Mayan Chief that initially had no meaning to him; he dismissed it by flipping it to the floor. Only a few people knew of his signature, and most of them worked for the government who they would blame if he didn't dispose of the body.

Working as quickly as possible, Cap combined several fifty-pound bags of ammonium nitrate fertilizer with diesel fuel and built a crude fertilizer bomb that would destroy the growing operation, as well as Armando's body. As a symbolic gesture, he set the timer from the growing lights to one hour and three minutes. Finally, the one year and three months he spent married to Paula, and living in self-exile as a civilian, had ended.

Satisfied with his work, he removed a section of flooring and lifted a dark green ammunition box crammed with tightly bound bundles of one-hundred dollar bills and a sealed plastic bag holding several different passports. Lastly, he pulled out a small military issued rucksack that contained several pounds of C-4 explosive, a small bundle of detonation cords with blasting caps, and a spool of detcord.

In the side-pocket of the rucksack were two plastic tubes with eight, one-ounce gold Krugerrands, one of the best currencies to exchange for cold, hard cash.

Sleep deprived, and on edge from too much cocaine, Cap strapped on his rucksack, grabbed his ammo box, and turned on the timer. Again, he stayed in the shadows while zigzagging his way back to his truck.

After returning to the *Flyboy Inn*, he stretched out on the lumpy mattress in his darkened motel room, looked at his watch, and according to plan, a distant explosion rattled the windows. Minutes later, the sound of emergency vehicles wailing outside his window confirmed his success; uncharacteristically, Cap lamented, "Rest in peace Arnie."

CHAPTER 27

T he physical effects of Bonn's seizure, combined with the handful medications he had taken, finally wore off enough for him to come out of a deep sleep. He had no memory of undressing to his sports briefs or going to bed. Although his headache had eased to a dull pain, the dehydration from vomiting left him craving water. He sat on the edge of his bed rubbing his temples, and then moaned as he tried to stand. The medication still had a grip on him, and combined with his loss of peripheral vision, he veered a little as he tried to walk a straight line down the hallway. When he turned towards the kitchen to get a bottle of Gatorade, he froze at the sight of Mac and Dr. Benson locked in a passionate kiss.

Oblivious to Bonn's presence, they both let out a shriek when they heard Bonn say, "Well, well, well. Now, I know what is different about you Mac."

"Jesus Christ Bonn! Are you ever going to stop doing that?" Dr. Benson's familiar rebuke came instantly.

"Stop what...stop watching? I wouldn't miss this for anything." Bonn smiled with the same Cheshire cat grin he had recently shown more than once.

"Susan and I were just..." Mac looked to her for help.

Susan stepped in to help and said, "Just...thanking him for his help."

"That's it...thanking me," Mac said and winked at her.

"Susan? *Susan* thanked you by doing a tonsillectomy with her tongue?" Bonn laughed so hard it hurt; literally.

The esteem Dr. Benson felt like a teenager who just got caught making out with her boyfriend, while Mac, just stuck his chest out with pride and began strutting, she told him to, "grow-up".

Bonn wiped a tear from his good eye and held on to the doorjamb to keep his balance then said, "Stop making me laugh. It hurts."

"Okay, you caught us. I can see you're feeling better. How's the headache?"

"What headache? I don't feel a thing. Doc, what are you doing here? The last thing I remember is sitting there tossing my ball," Bonn said and pointed at the tennis ball on his recliner.

"You don't remember?" Susan stole a quick glance at Mac who also tried to hide his concern.

"I think, I recall a couple of security guys from Eglin, a female 'Fed', tossing my ball, and... Hell, I don't know."

"That's right. We were in a meeting and right in the middle of a question, you had a seizure. I caught you before you hit the floor." Mac omitted the part about doing C.P.R. and shuddered at the thought of having to do mouth-to-mouth if Bonn's breathing hadn't returned to normal.

"The EMSA boys were trying to agree on what to do with you when Doc arrived and gave you a shot of the good stuff. You were out cold, so, I carried you into your room, tucked you in bed, and rescheduled the meeting for tomorrow. Maybe you can put on some clothes before they come back."

Bonn slipped on his jeans, asked for something to drink, and slowly made his way to his recliner where he plopped down and grabbed his chartreuse tennis ball.

When Mac tried handing him an orange-flavored Gatorade, Bonn got another reminded of his vision problem when he jarred it out of Mac's hand.

"Doc., what the hell is wrong with me? Everything is little off. If it's the drugs, I want off them."

"Do you remember me telling you in the hospital your peripheral vision has been compromised? It's going to take a lot of work in rehab to get accustomed to a new perception." She used the word 'new,' instead of 'loss,' in an attempt to reassure him without bringing up the worst scenario.

"A *new* perception? Why don't you just call it what it is, *blind* in one eye. My career is over. Mac, what in the hell am I going to do, wear a damn eye patch and be a pirate?" Bonn showed his agitation and squeezed the tennis ball with such force his fingers turned white.

Susan knelt in front of Bonn, cupped his face with the delicate touch of a surgeon and said, "Bonn, this isn't like you. Are you going to give up? What would you tell your men in battle…man-up? I'm not going to lie; you are in for a battle." Susan said. "Listen to me, Dr. Gupta is one of the best eye surgeons in the country and specializes in retinal detachment; I believe he can fix your eye."

"Doc, all I see with this eye, is a dot of light. Other than that, it's black, and my balance is off. Everything seems to be…off," Bonn voice trailed off with every word.

After pacing for a few seconds, Mac turned to his friend and scolded him, "I have never seen this side of you, didn't you hear a word she said? If you're going to surrender, you'll do it by yourself. We won't help you." Mac's anger was evident. "Either fight back, or find someone else to join you in that pity party. The man I know is better with one eye, than the rest of the world with two, you are a warrior!"

A tear slid down Bonn's face, where minutes earlier, he wiped one away from laughter. Susan had seen depression end more than one life, and wrapped her arms around him. She whispered in his ear, "If you're getting ready to tell us good-bye, keep your tongue to yourself. The world would *not* be better off without you."

Bonn whispered back in Susan's ear, "Don't you worry about me; my thoughts were about killing Mac for being a bitch. I'll keep my tongue to myself, unless you have an interest."

Susan burst out in laughter. She didn't find his remark humorous; it was a release of sheer happiness to hear his twisted and off-color sense of humor again.

"You wish, you 'perv'," Susan said, and then pinched him.

"What's so damn funny? I know he said something about me," Mac said.

"It was nothing, 'bitch'," Susan said, winked at Bonn, who loved her play on words, and doubled up in pain from the laughter.

"I have to get back to the hospital; I want you to keep the faith… don't stop playing catch with your ball."

"What is this ball thing about?" Mac asked.

Dr. Benson took his hand and walked across the room to the kitchen. "You're the detective. Look at the countertop and tell me what you see."

"Hmm, I see a toaster, a coffee pot, an empty Gatorade bottle, creamer and sugar bowls. They're on a black granite countertop. How did I do?"

She ignored his question, and then escorted him into the bathroom, where she pointed at the black sink in the center of a grey counter. Susan couldn't help thinking how black on grey was *so Bonn*. It wasn't Bonn's taste in bathroom colors she wanted Mac to notice, the grooming products and five prescription bottles were lined up in the order he used them. Every military man she had known embraced the habits they developed during basic training, and maintained their proclivity neatness and organization.

"Tell me detective, what do you see?"

"I don't get it sweetie." Mac didn't think he would ever use that word after hearing Mary, the hospital greeter, repeat it so many times, it stuck in his head like a song.

Susan melted when Mac called her "sweetie" and stood on her tiptoes to give him a kiss.

"My big bad detective doesn't notice everything is skewed to the left side of the sink? What about the kitchen…did you see the creamer, sugar…, the spoon?"

"Well I'll be…," Mac said.

"Bonn's brain is adapting to his vision loss." Susan said. "I have him tossing the ball because of his *temporary* loss of peripheral vision. When a person's depth perception changes, the mind starts compensating. As he practices tossing the ball up and catching it, he's training his brain to adapt at a faster rate."

"Have I told you how sexy your mind is?" Mac asked.

"Hello…, I'm still here, get a room," Bonn said.

The laughter comforted Bonn as much as any shot for pain. Convinced her services weren't needed any longer; Susan gave Bonn a peck on the cheek, Mac received a more substantial show of affection before she left.

"Lord that is one special woman," Mac said and continued to stare at the spot where her car had been.

"Mac, close the damn door and tell me when the two of you became an item. Give me details and don't leave anything out."

"Huh? Oh, you mean Dr. Benson?"

"No, I mean *Susan*. Never mind, I don't want to hear your denials. I think the two of you are perfect for each other. I say, go for it." Bonn gave his blessing yet he felt a twinge of jealousy.

"You know what?" Mac asked.

"What?"

"Years ago I used to watch you and Rebecca. It made me sick every time the two of you were together. You were like animals with that PDA crap, that's for young people with raging hormones."

"And now…?

"I 'm not sure, I'm a little…confused."

Bonn tried and failed to give him a fist bump, and as quickly as the elation, he felt when he saw Mac happy, a wave of depression replaced it.

"Let it go Bonn. There are things more important than a perfect fist bump; you'll get your vision back. Don't let the guy who shot you win. *We* are going to beat this. Anyway, I'll bet Rebecca will think an eye patch is sexy. Pirates are dangerous, and women like men who are a little dangerous."

Bonn's mood switched at the speed of light. He laughed, then sat back down and stared pensively as he rotated the tennis ball in his hand.

"What's wrong? I've seen that look before. I'm just kidding about being a pirate," Mac said.

"That's not it. I remember her. I'm just not remembering *us*. I don't know, maybe it's the medications that are making me dreaming about her. The dreams are so real, it's like she came back and we were together again. Watching you and Doc brought back the memories. Maybe, I'm losing my mind."

"We need to talk. You didn't hear me; I told you 'Rebecca *will* think an eye patch is sexy.' But…" Mac dreaded the prospect of having to tell him again about Rebecca's return; this time, he would include the news that Rebecca had been shot.

Over the following hour, Mac stayed in the role of a detective. He went over the events, in chronological order, from the day of the shooting and included the gruesome details of Rebecca's ordeal. Bonn, mouth open, listened in amazement and kept repeating "No way."

"I remember a "Cap" from my college days. When I met him, he wore a green military jacket with an American flag on his sleeve, sewn upside down. Even back then, it bothered me. I asked him about his outfit, and he described it as the uniform of 'student freedom fighters'. I will never forget. He smelled like wine and an ashtray. I had a dream about him the other day."

"That's Carl Perkins. You may know him as Cap. He's the one, and the same." Mac watched Bonn's demeanor change.

"The guy who owned the trailer park where we busted those meth dealers is…Cap? Plus, you're telling me Rebecca is back, and someone tried to kill her? I'll kill that bastard. What are we going to do now?"

Although Mac understood Bonn wanted retribution, he needed to temper the enthusiasm and said,

"Whoa cowboy, only one question at a time. *We*… aren't going to do anything. You're going to heal and play with your ball; *I'm* going to get that SOB and everyone who helped him. Tomorrow at noon, Agent Milton and the guys from Eglin are going to be back. All of us have questions and we hope there's something you can tell us that will help figure this out." Mac wanted to add, "If you don't zone out on us".

"I'm overwhelmed and exhausted from trying to process all the information," Bonn said.

So, Mac pulled out a printed sheet of paper Dr. Benson had given him and read her instructions. "I'll get you another Gatorade and all your meds, according to this schedule; it's time for at least a couple pills. Plus, you have to try and eat something. She said you have already lost too much weight and need to eat."

"The thought of food makes me sick; I'll eat later." Bonn cringed and shivered.

"The last thing we should do is piss her off. She's not the kind of person we want to mess with."

"It says right here..," Mac said while jabbing her instructions with his finger, "Eat small amounts of food 4-5 times per day. Avoid citrus, salt, dairy products and anything not easily digestible. I don't know what the hell that means, but she had me buy some protein drinks for you in case I couldn't get you to eat."

Bonn hadn't heard a word Mac said and put up his hand to get him to stop reading the list. "Where's Rebecca?"

"She is in a GQ house at Eglin, under guard. It's the same Gentleman's Quarters used by every dignitary who comes to Eglin, and it's being guarded around the clock. She's couldn't be in a safer place, and she isn't going anywhere. The doctors come to her, and she has a nurse at her beckon call."

"Mac, I need to go see her and let her know I'm okay."

"Negative on that, Commander Bentow has approved a small security detail to bring her to you when you're ready for company. Now, be a good little soldier, take your medicine and eat something. Then, and only then, will we talk about having company. Do we have a deal?"

"Deal, you're a pain in the ass. Do you know that?"

CHAPTER 28

Early the next morning, refreshed after a rare and peaceful night's sleep, Cap admired his transformation from a longhaired southern redneck. Although he gained a few pounds and had a few more wrinkles, he thought he still looked as handsome as he did in his twenties.

Thanks to the surplus store, he now had two complete sets of Air Force BDU's. One, a camouflaged green, with black and brown splotches for the woods, the other was a light tan and brown set for a sandy environment.

Cap paced until he caught a glimpse of his new appearance. Confident he would be mistaken for one of the thousands of men and women who worked on one of the bases, he put his plan in motion. First, he needed to stash his newly acquired supplies; only one spot came to mind, a remote area outside of town, not far from where he failed to take out Bonn. After slinging the explosives-filled rucksack over his shoulder and picking up the green ammo box, he looked at himself in the mirror on his way out the door, one last time, and said, "Perfect, just perfect".

While driving along one of the sand roads that wove though Eglin's 400,000 acres, he spotted the "Perfect, just perfect" place to stash his explosives. The wilderness area had wrecks of old Vietnam era F-4 jets littering the reservation. Stripped down, and radio equipped for remote control flights, the old jets became target practice. When he looked across a controlled underbrush burn, Cap spotted the tail section of a jet that could become his safety deposit box.

Cap crossed the field, and parked just inside the tree line where his pickup wouldn't be seen, but he would still be able to spot anyone coming towards him from the road. He opened the ammo box on the tailgate and removed the bundles of cash and passports. Cap wrapped the tubes of gold coins in a bandana and secured them with a rubber band, and stuffed them in the cargo pockets of his uniform. Lastly, he pealed the cellophane wrapper from a few putty-like blocks of the C-4, and placed them, along with a bundle of pre-cut 120-second fuse and blasting caps, on the pickup's tailgate.

He assembled the bombs with an expertise that came from years of practice. Individually, they were capable of blowing down a steel door or part of a house. Cap planned to place several charges at strategic locations, and take down an entire structure.

Satisfied with his work, Cap shoved the ammo box, stuffed with the extra blocks of C-4 and fuses, behind a massive bird's nest of wires hanging from the stripped dashboard of the wrecked F-4 fighter.

Cap tossed his explosives-filled rucksack in the bed of his pickup. Having worked with the ordinance many times, he didn't worry about the assembled charges exploding. C-4's composition allowed it be transported safely and wouldn't detonate if dropped, shot by a gun, or exposed to fire. The only way it could occur, would be from a charge that emitted heat *and* shock. Carl had an abundance of blasting caps and a roll of detcord.

Before heading to Destin to conduct initial surveillance, Cap stopped to take a little target practice and release some of his pent up aggression. He drew his Glock from its holster, and unloaded the entire clip at a small sign attached to a fence. Every shot rang true as it punched holes in a *WARNING! UNEXPLODED ORDINANCE AREA* sign. Throughout most of the Eglin Reservation, there were unexploded missiles, rockets, artillery shells, mines, and grenades that either malfunctioned or were duds. The Air Force and Army used the base's reservation as a training ground for troops and aircraft since the 1940's. Live ammo, either lost or left behind, littered the ground.

Impressed with the expert grouping he shot in the sign, and with his confidence back after over a year out of action, Cap paced fifteen steps to the sign and said, "Fifteen paces, that's more than enough."

Cap wanted to get Bonn with-in his thirty-foot kill zone and finish the job he originally set out to do. The shredded sign was a cause for celebration, and he thought of something else that would make him feel even better; he jumped in his truck, snorted a pile of cocaine, and took off. Suddenly, he braked hard to a stop when he noticed he had a visitor, his euphoria turned to anguish. A U.S. Fish and Wildlife game warden blocked the open gate leading out to the road.

"Keep your cool Cap; this is a 'nobody," Cap said and dropped his bottle of coke in his pocket then reached under his coat and ripped open the holster's Velcro flap securing his gun.

The game ranger walked up to Carl's window and said, "Sir, could I see your hunting license and a form of identification?"

"Not huntin', just doing a little plinkin'."

Cap spoke with a deep southern drawl and hoped the warden was a good ol' boy. Cap ignored the request and sat motionless with his hands on the steering wheel without making any effort to get out any identification.

The wildlife officer asked again, "Sir, could I see some ID?"

Cap stepped out of the pickup, taking care not to expose the pistol concealed under his jacket, and pulled his wallet out of his BDU's back pocket.

"Sho nuf, but why do you want to see my ID? I'm active duty; I don't need a license while I'm stationed here. Look, I gotta git back to Eglin, or my Sergeant is going to kick my butt."

The warden inspected both sides of Carl A. Perkins driver's license and asked, "What do you do for a living Mr. Perkins? Where do you work?"

The cocaine had kicked in, and the faster Cap's heartbeat, the angrier he became. Whether he portrayed himself as Carl or Cap, he hated any authority, especially someone like the asshole in front of him, prying into his personal business. Pissed and not intimidated, he said, "I can't stand assholes like you, who act like they're so tough. You're a damn animal cop and nothing more."

"Carl, I'm sorry to hear you feel that way. I'll ask you one more time, where do you work?"

"I'm Air Force. Are you blind? Can't you see my damn uniform?"

"Your jacket doesn't have any patches or anything that identifies you as Air Force. As a matter of fact, you're wearing army BDUs."

"I'm cross-training with the Army Rangers. I just got this uniform and haven't had time to have my patches sewn on."

"Carl, a new uniform would have crisp lines, and you gave me a driver's license, not a military ID"

The game warden's tone became more severe with each fact he pointed out. Cap sensed what was coming, and put his hands on his hips, for easy access to the pistol under his jacket. With Cap's license in hand, the warden took a few steps towards his truck to check for warrants.

"Officer, wait," Cap said with his arms fully extended, gun in hands.

When the warden turned, Cap placed his deadly signature shot, front and centered. He dispatched the officer with the speed and accuracy of a trained assassin. The "animal cop" never stood a chance.

"The name is *Cap*, you ignorant hick. That's what you get for calling me 'Carl' and for trying to impress me by pointing out everything wrong with my uniform. How observant are you now?"

Cap immediately picked up his driver's license and pulled the warden's body into the palmettos, covered it with a layer of leaves and pine needles, and raked through the drag marks. Assuming the game ranger had radioed his location into dispatch when he stopped at the gate, Cap wanted to have as much of a head start as he could get before they started looking for him. Cap drove the wildlife officer's truck a few hundred yards past the downed jet and sent it cascading to the bottom of a ravine. Cursing himself for missing the details in his disguise, Cap stripped off his jacket to his nondescript black t-shirt, and drove to Destin for some reconnaissance work on Bonn's house.

Driving at a snail's pace behind two aging snowbirds, gave Cap the opportunity to case the area for any sign of a stakeout at Bonn's house. He eased his way along Old Highway 98 with its million dollar homes on the north side of the road and a mix of condos, resorts, and beach houses on the Gulf side. He eased to a crawl in front of an older Florida "cracker" house that stood alone among the sand dunes. The nineteenth century house had a native wood frame with a metal roof, raised floors, and a large porch that wrapped that halfway around the house.

As Cap drove behind cars with passengers who were also looking at the classic home, he sensed 'eyes' on Bonn's place that weren't sightseers. To make sure he didn't stand out, Cap stayed in line with the tourists, but he never turned his head when he checked out every driveway and condo parking lot with-in 200 yards of Bonn's house.

That distance would fall in the minimum shooting parameter for a sniper to take a shot. Although Cap didn't see any suspect vehicles or shooters, it didn't mean Bonn's house didn't have the watchful eyes of any number of agencies. There were two exceptions parked in Bonn's driveway, a Niceville Police Department's SUV and a sleek black Mercedes.

When Cap saw the ten-story resort hotel adjacent to Bonn's property, he selected it as the location for his base of operations. This time, Cap left his jacket in the pickup and wore only a black military t-shirt when he requested a corner room atop the Crystal Inn Hotel and Beach Resort. He enthusiastically accepted the ten-percent discount for paying cash, and the additional ten-percent for being active-duty military, his disguise passed the test. The discounts were irrelevant considering the bundles of bills and gold coins in his pockets. Just for kicks, he signed-in under the name of *Capt*. C. Weatherman USAF, a name that reflected his 'college days' relationship with Bonn.

CHAPTER 29

C ap awoke, still dressed in his BDU's and boots. He had slept soundly which helped alleviate his stress. Reinvigorated, he stepped out on the veranda of his room, excited and extremely anxious to settle the score. The warm rush of adrenaline pumping through his veins satisfied him in way cocaine couldn't duplicate. Scanning Bonn's house with his field glasses, he tried to pinpoint areas of the house where the charges would cause maximum damage to the structure, and kill his mark at the same time.

The old cracker house, with its elevated floors, would provide enough crawl space behind the latticework that encircled the foundation, to plant enough of the explosive to send the house into the Gulf. Without electronic detonators, he would have to light the fuse while staying concealed under the house's flooring.

He decided to wear his desert BDUs to blend in with the sand dunes while he did dry run at dark to set the charges, and return the following day at sunset to finish the job.

The time fuses on the blasting caps he assembled before his altercation with the game warden were 120's, which would have been sufficient time for a 'light and leave'.

However, Cap determined it would take four minutes to light them and make his way to his vehicle, before the fuse hit the blasting caps and set off the C-4. Cap replaced the 120's on three charges, in favor of 240-second lengths of fuse. He planned to use a technique he called "the golden triangle" to bring down the house. He needed to place two blocks approximately ten feet apart, and a third one, directly under the front door to form the deadly triangle. The resulting explosions would bring down the house and bury Bonn under the rubble.

While Cap changed out the components of his bombs, he failed to notice the Air Force-blue Chevy Impala that pulled into Bonn's driveway, dropped someone off, and left. Although Cap missed seeing the car and the passenger it delivered, the "eyes" Cap sensed during his drive-by surveillance of Bonn's house, didn't miss anything, including Cap's coming and going.

CHAPTER 30

Bonn sat in the low light of his living room at sunset petting
Lexi, Mac's blond Labrador retriever. Although he had half-
heartedly protested Mac's suggestion to have her stay with
him while he healed, he welcomed the companionship. Mac trusted
Lexi, who was a recipient of the Silver Star for Valor and a purple
heart, to serve as a sentry for Bonn.

Bonn read a list of Dutch-to-English commands aloud and
laughed as he tried to say them properly. The seriousness on Mac's
face wasn't humorous, so Bonn listened intently to the correct
pronunciations. Bonn had seen military dogs used by the Special
Forces and Navy Seals in Vietnam, Afghanistan and Iraq. Their
performance and fighting ability convinced him, Mac wasn't just
leaving a guard; he was leaving a weapon, if needed.

"Mac, she's a beautiful Lab. Where did you find her?"

"Lexi's been working in the Middle East for a couple of years.
They retired her after an injury in Iraq; her handler, a friend of mine,
died at the same time. When his wife called me to break the news, she
told me, she had a gorgeous blond girlfriend with a beautiful body
that she wanted me to meet. I drove to Pensacola one evening and
met this sweet girl; it was love at first sight."

"Well at least you didn't meet her online," Bonn joked.

"I had just picked her up and brought her to the station when I
got the call about a crazed driver; it turned out to be you. Since then,
Lexi and I have gotten very close. I know she looks like a sweetheart,
but don't be fooled. She is as gentle as can be, except when she's

working. Lexi is known for her ferociousness, intelligence and for having the best nose in the military," Mac said with the pride of a new father.

"Are you sure she'll obey me?"

Mac went deadpan and said, "As long as you can speak Dutch and pronounce the commands correctly."

"I don't speak Dutch. I can't even pronounce the words on this list. Mac, tell me you're not serious."

"You'll be fine. She was trained with a breed called the Belgian Malinois, it's a breed that has been used extensively by the bomb units and if you give a command, Lexi will do whatever you tell her. I'm going to teach you the basic ones, when to use them, and more importantly, how to give them. Lexi is very smart. Even if something happens and you're not able to talk, her instincts are unbelievable; she'll know what to do. Trust me, the two of you are meant for each other."

"I don't know her, and she doesn't know me. Are you sure she'll listen to me?"

Mac decided to have a little fun with Bonn and said, "She knows you're a good guy because she's here with me right now and I haven't given her the command to attack. She's been with several units and got to know everyone, and the difference between friend and foe."

Just in case, Bonn went to a knee and stroked her coat.

"Lexi became a hero to a Navy seals unit out of Pensacola for her ability to find caches of ammunition and unexploded Russian bombs left over from their turn in Afghanistan. That's not all she can do."

"I have a feeling you're going to tell me how she earned her Silver Star," Bonn said.

"You're going to love this; during a routine search for the Taliban, Lexi discovered a booby trap seconds before she and her handler were shot. Even though she also had taken a bullet, she fought off two insurgents who were trying to drag off the Navy Seal's body for propaganda. Didn't you girl?" Lexi stood next to Mac while intently looking up at him and started wagging her tail upon hearing her name.

"Mac, she never takes her eyes off of you. It's like she's waiting for you to do something or give her a command."

"She will make eye contact with me, and hold it until I put her at ease, or give a command. I'm her new handler and she'll do what I ask of her or die trying. Again, even if I can't speak, she has the uncanny ability to know what to do on her own. I'm convinced you can handle her, she'll obey your commands as well." Mac reached down, scratched behind her ears and she licked his hand clean.

"Are you ready for training?" Mac asked Bonn then said, "Zit". Lexi sat down and shivered in anticipation another command.

"Her body language changed immediately, she's ready to go to work. I have 'Zit' down pat, keep going."

Mac was encouraged by Bonn's enthusiasm and hoped the healing powers of dogs, especially one like Lexi, was just what Bonn needed. Mac took Bonn by the arm to the other side the living room while Lexi remained in the sitting position.

"We'll start with the basics. Lexi, Heir." Lexi came to Mac's side at lightning speed.

"There's nothing to it." Bonn kept his attitude cocky.

"If you remember nothing, remember this, she is a *dog* not a human. Give her one-word commands. If you speak to her in complete sentences, what she'll hear is your tone. It's just like when new parents talk to their baby. The child doesn't know what they're saying, they're comforted by the tone of mommy or daddy's voice. She'll sense if you are in danger or just talking to her, she know the difference. The average person can give her all the commands they want, but she won't respond if she doesn't know you."

"I get it. Okay, we've covered the 'come', command," Bonn whispered, "Heir?"

"I think you need to be able to have her stay alert and guard when you sleep. She'll stay awake and God help anyone who tries to get to you if you're getting some beauty sleep or if you have one of your seizures and you're unable to move."

The seriousness of Mac's demeanor changed, and instantly, Lexi stiffened and appeared to hold her breath when she noticed the change of nuance.

"I want you to practice giving her commands in a stern and semi-hushed voice. She'll know it's time to go to work when you say her name followed by an order. Lexi, *Bewaken.*"

Lexi froze and her muscular back rippled while she surveyed the entire room to guard against any threat, perceived or present.

"*Kalm,*" Mac said and gave her a hand signal that put her at ease.

"It's pronounced *bay…walkin'?*" Bonn made sure to whisper when he pronounced the words separately, in case if she thought he was repeating the command.

"Close enough. Let's try several commands at once. You have to be able to put her at ease if you've been asleep and she has been on guard the entire time. If you want her to come to you and sit, just say, "Lexi, Kalm. Zit," Mac said with an accent that sounded German.

"Lexi, be patient with him," Mac said.

"I'm comfortable with giving you the basics and leaving. Bonn, whatever you do, don't give her the command to attack if no one is around," Mac said and took a step toward the door.

"What? Wait!" Bonn yelled to Mac who was still laughing when he slammed the door to his Expedition and drove away.

A short time later, Lexi jumped to attention at Bonn's feet when she heard the sound of gravel displaced in the driveway. Bonn pulled his Smith and Wesson Model 19, Combat Magnum .357 and said to Lexi, "*Bewaken*", and he watched the hair on her back stand straight up and bared her canines.

Bonn made his way to the window, stood to the side and lifted a slat to see three visitors. He holstered his weapon when he saw Rebecca escorted from an Air Force blue Chevy Impala to his front door by two large MPs from the base.

"Lexi, kalm. Zit," Unintentionally, Bonn spoke with a German, not Dutch, accent.

Lexi sat 'at ease' while Bonn opened the front door. Even half-blinded by the light, he froze. There, in the skintight jeans he daydreamed about, stood the woman of his dreams, past and present. She wore a loose Florida Gator's sweatshirt with the sleeves cut out. Down one side, the seam split down to her waist to make room for a sling.

"Quit staring at my fashion statement. It's better than what I wore a couple of days ago. I never thought I would be happy about wearing a sling, but compared to the body cast that I was wearing, it's great."

Bonn, twenty-plus pounds lighter from his hospital stay, didn't look any better. Before his reunion with Cap, Bonn looked cut and fit, the recent weight loss left him looking gaunt and sickly. Rebecca noticed his face wasn't as swollen, and the black and blue undertones, from the trauma and surgeries, weren't as pronounced as they were when she saw Bonn in the hospital. Through the narrow slit of his partially opened eye, she could see a bright red maze of broken blood vessels.

The moment of silence broke into laughter from Lexi's whining and tail wagging.

"Well, it seems at least one of you is glad to see me," Rebecca teased.

Bonn became self-conscious when he heard the word "see" and put on the sunglasses hanging on his lanyard.

"I'm sorry, please come in," he said and gave Lexi, who kept spinning circles, the command to heal.

Bonn was in shock from seeing her injuries and asked, "Can I hug you without hurting you?"

"You better, or I'm going to think it was a bad idea to come here."

Bonn, ever so gently, embraced her and placed his lips against hers. Rebecca made a whining sound, mimicking Lexi, and in the voice he had longed to hear again, said, "I have missed you so much baby."

"Darlin', you never left my heart. Ever since Mac informed me you were in my hospital room, and it wasn't my imagination, I've been consumed with the thought of seeing you again."

"I promise you, this isn't a dream," Rebecca said, then kissed Bonn passionately until he began to whine. Lexi followed his lead with a little howl that lightened the mood of the darkened room with laughter.

"I didn't know you had a dog. Who is this pretty girl?"

"This is Lexi, my body guard. The way she's acting, it appears you aren't a threat. She is Mac's dog and one of the Air Forces finest."

Rebecca saluted and Lexi went to full attention. The small talk ended abruptly when Rebecca grabbed her shoulder, in obvious pain.

"I heard what happened, I'm so sorry. They'll get the bastard that did this to you," Bonn said.

"I want to be there when they do. We have figure out why a hit was ordered on me, then we'll know who gave the order. Everything points to a military operation, but as far as I know, there's hasn't been any reasonably explanation as to why I'm a threat to them."

"There's also a rumor, you have a new job. Do you think there might be a connection?"

"I'm convinced someone definitely doesn't want me here and knows why I'm down here in Florida. My new job is on hold while they are... *we* are, trying to find the connection. When I hear anything I'll let you know, I promise," Rebecca said. "For now, let's get back to you. Mac has been updating me daily on your condition. Baby, we're going to get through this *together*. Do you hear me?" A tear ran down Rebecca's face, and she squeezed Bonn's hand.

"Yes ma'am," Bonn said and gave her an appreciative peck on the cheek.

"Rebecca, I know you have been grilled and don't really want to talk about it, but I need to ask you some questions." Bonn's rare moment of clarity helped him realize that the limited information Mac had given him wasn't a complete briefing about Rebecca's assignment or her attack. He assumed Cap's contract targeted both of them and came from Washington.

"I was told me you're a liaison for the Air Force...who are you really working for? My sources say you're interagency."

"I've heard that too. Bonn, I can't confirm or deny your information, all I can tell you is we're on the same team."

Like Bonn, she worked with the NCS or National Clandestine Service. While Rebecca remained active duty, he worked as a contractor. The NCS helped end the DOD and CIA rivalry.

"Officially, you work for the Air Force?" Bonn asked.

"Yes, but we're parting hairs. There are so many agencies involved; I quit trying to understand who wants what. Ultimately, we both answer to the same person. I know this sounds convoluted, but the Deputy Director made the request to look into the DOD's Office for Acquisitions…the trail begins right here at Eglin."

Rebecca paused and her silence spoke volumes. "You understand how it works; a request is made, and the next thing I know, I'm getting my orders from an Agency A.I.C. stationed at Tyndall AFB in Panama City. I'm Air Force and I'm not accustomed to taking orders from an agent."

"I'm going to surmise you've been assigned the domestic operative role. If we have an embedded mole here at Eglin then I'm going to assume it has to do with the Raptor program. I'm going to also assume our old friend Sienna is the A.I.C. working out of Tyndall. Who recommended her, and why were you picked?"

"I don't know if the Senate's Committee on Intel recommended her or someone else. I only know my nomination for the job was because of my work at a couple of 'Black site'," Rebecca said in reference to the secretive international prison system used by the U.S. Intelligence and its allies.

"What do our holding sights have to do with anything?"

"I conducted an interrogation at the black site in London where an Iraqi official was being held by the Brits. They were tracking him before his capture. Then they discovered, he was in communication with a foreign pilot, who was training at Tyndall. I don't believe the pilot had any role beyond supplying low-level classified information on the F-22's computer capabilities. He's most likely a diversion from what the Iraqis really wanted; I'll know more when I get to work in a couple of days. Until then, let's focus on us."

Bonn thought he understood her role, although, he wasn't sure. The trepidation on his face showed his concern. "Promise me you will be…careful."

He tried to tell her to be *very* careful, when out of nowhere, his field of vision inundated with flashes of light and a wave of nausea overcame him.

"Baby, what's wrong?" Panic rapidly filled Rebecca's voice. "Should I call the doctor? Talk to me baby." She pleaded to no avail as he half-collapsed on the couch in a heavy sweat, and his eyes were rolling back as he asked her in a weakened voice, to get his meds out of the bathroom.

Lexi ran to Bonn's side to see if he needed help. He was unresponsive, so she rested her head on his leg, and waited for a command. Rebecca returned with prescriptions in hand and a wet towel that she used to wipe his brow and hold on the back of his neck.

"I need the one that says it's for nausea, and my Gatorade. Please…," Bonn said and then patted Lexi.

Bonn didn't have to wait long for what he had been anticipating; the roar that always came with the nausea, arrived full force.

"Baby, what is happening to you? I'm calling the doctor," Rebecca said and saw her soul mate grimace in pain.

"No darlin', don't call anyone, this happens several times a day. I'm starting to get one my headaches from hell and possibly, a seizure. I need a couple of pills from the bottles for pain before it gets worse; it's too late for the seizure meds."

After handing him what he requested, Rebecca tucked an afghan around him in a tight cocoon and said, "I'm going to give you an hour, and if you're not better, I'm calling the doctor. Don't argue with me."

Lexi curled in a ball next to the couch when Bonn awoke. He sat up and assumed they were alone.

"Well, girl, I guess I was just having another one of those dreams."

Lexi cocked her head, and then jumped when a voice in another room let him know he was not alone.

"I'm in here resting," Rebecca said with an inviting tone.

"Lexi, go get her and bring her to me. Good girl."

She burst at top speed towards Bonn's bedroom to obey the retrieval command even though it wasn't in Dutch and promptly began tugging at Rebecca's jeans until she got up.

Rebecca appeared in the doorway with a quirky smile and asked, "Do all females do what you ask them to do?"

"I wish. Darlin', get over here."

"You're right, keeping wishing." Rebecca sashayed and pretended to be obeying Bonn's order as she approached the couch.

Bonn smiled and got up to meet her halfway. They were embracing in a full body hug, with lips locked, when they heard Lexi whining and scratching frantically at the pine floor.

"Lexi, Foei! What are you doing?" Bonn said, and just-in-case, he reached into his back pocket for the list of commands Mac had given him to make sure he had told her *no*.

"Phooy? Is that what you said?" Rebecca asked.

"That's the Dutch command for no or stop, I think an enemy can give her all the commands they want and she's not going to obey them if they're not in Dutch," Bonn said, then realized he needed to ask Mac what would happen if the enemy spoke Dutch.

"Bonn, I'm impressed. I didn't know you were such an expert on dog training. She's trying to tell us something, you better give me a crash course."

Bonn didn't tell her he only became an expert a few hours earlier and handed the list to her. "Here are the basic commands you to learn."

"Heir. What's wrong girl?" Bonn patted the top of her head when she obediently came to his side and waited for a command that never came, and she ran back to the corner, sat down and growled.

Rebecca and Bonn looked at each other quizzically and were unsure what to do next. "I don't like this, especially her attitude," Rebecca said as she pulled a 9mm semi-automatic out of her custom fitted sling with a built-in holster, and Bonn grabbed his pistol that he kept under the sofa cushion, and turned out the light Rebecca had turned on.

"Just like old times darlin'," Bonn whispered.

"We're getting too old for this crap," Rebecca said as she flattened against the wall and peeked out the blinds.

"I'm the one getting old. You are still the young, and beautiful, and sexy woman I fell in love with years ago."

Lexi shivered, spun in a circle, sat down next to the spot she had already identified, and started whining again.

"She is *definitely* trying to tell us there's something wrong, I trust her instincts. There's only person who can tell us what the hell she's doing." Bonn waited on his cell for a few seconds and said, "Mac, my house. *Flywater.*", then slid it back into his pocket.

"Mac knows your safe word? If I remember correctly, 'Flywater' is the word you used with your children and me. Well, he knows you are in a desperate situation and need help. So, what are we going to do till he gets here?" Rebbeca asked.

"*We* do nothing. Lexi, *Bewalkin*," Bonn said the command with the tone of a professional trainer.

Rebecca remained silent and went on guard with Lexi while she tried to read the list of Dutch commands.

"I can barely read anything in the dark, did you say *bay walking?*"

"That's close enough. You don't need to whisper, I told her to *guard* and she's knows by the tone of my voice how serious I am about what I said. Let's keep quiet, stay alert and watch her. Mac will tell us what's bothering her when he gets here. All of this is just like the old days isn't it?"

"Damn it, quit saying *old*," Rebecca said and nudged him.

Bonn put his finger to his lips and cocked his head exactly like Lexi when they heard the sound of feet pounding on the driveway's gravel. Rebecca peeked through the blinds, in time to see someone dressed in battle dress uniform. When the sensor activated a security light, the person took off running towards the beach.

"It's one of ours."

Bonn who had both hands wrapped around his weapon and pointed at the front door, asked, "How do you know?"

"Wait, maybe not…there's something strange going on…whoever it is was wearing our desert pattern BDU's. We haven't used that pattern for years. I don't even know where someone would get them unless they were kept as a memento. It's an outdated pattern used almost exclusively in arid regions," she said then relaxed and tucked her gun back into her sling.

Bonn let his weapon fall to his side, and repeatedly put a hand in front of the damaged, checking, and double checking, to make sure what he discovered wasn't his imagination. "Oh my God!"

Rebecca, startled by Bonn's statement, instantly reached in her sling for her weapon. "What is it? What are you doing?"

"Rebecca I can see again."

"What? What do you mean you can see again?"

"I don't know why…, I have most of my vision back, not all of it, but enough. The edges aren't as black and I've got some depth perception back. When I aimed my gun, I used both eyes without realizing it."

Rebecca's face relaxed and her eyes filled with tears.

CHAPTER 31

C ap just finished placing the final charge of his "golden triangle" under Bonn's living room floor, when he heard scratching directly overhead. Motionless on his hands and knees in the crawl space he entered from the broken lattice ringing the old cracker house, he heard a dog whining and scratching directly overhead. During the time he had Bonn's house under surveillance, he never saw a dog, a cat, or any other pet. When he heard another voice, a woman's, he made the decision to go back to his room and regroup.

The charges were set for detonation at sunset the following day, and his pilot had the plane ready to take him to Belize. Cap refused to let a woman with a dog, sidetrack his plans and crab-walked his way to the opening in the lattice.

After wiggling out from beneath Bonn's house, a flood light lit up the parking area. Exposed, Cap scrambled across the drive and disappeared into the adjacent sand dunes that bordered Bonn's house. He knelt in a patch of sea oats, pleased with his choice to wear the desert camo, and safely observed an impressive display of police force converging from all directions.

Caught off-guard by the cavalry's reaction time, Cap began to question some aspects of his plan, and unnecessarily belly-crawled his way to his hotel parking lot. Once there, he casually walked to the side entrance and took the stairs to his sixth floor corner room. While sitting on his veranda, he replayed the details of his plan, and wished he had taken the time to find electronic detonators instead of fuses. If he had electronic detonators, they could have been set off from his room.

Regardless, Cap remained confident; the four-minute burn on the detcord would give him ample time to escape before Bonn's house blew, it would take less than a minute.

Yawning and exhausted, Cap dug into his pocket for the small glass vial that held his cocaine. Unable to find it, he cursed his luck and feared it came out in the dunes. At first, he didn't obsess about it and just swallowed a handful of painkillers. But, his drug addiction fed the obsession and he searched his pockets repeatedly for the vial.

The army of responders who arrived at breakneck speed, returned to his thoughts when he caught a blue reflection from a police cruiser on his windowpane. Cap began talking to himself. "Someone was watching Bonn's house. Damn, how could I have not seen them, he heard me and flipped on that damn light. It's time for plan B."

Although there were still plan B details to work out, Cap began to fixate on the lost bottle of cocaine.

"I'll bet it came out in the dunes, if it didn't fall out under Bonn's house or on the ground between the house and the dunes, or maybe I…"

Engulfed in a mild mania, and convinced he couldn't complete his mission without the assistance of his drug, he opened the in-room safe grabbed the rest of his money, the gold laden plastic tubes, and then stuffed them in his bag.

After wiping down everything in the room, he made his way down the stairs to the side exit where he had disabled the parking lot's security camera and floodlight. As he started his pickup with one hand, he pulled out the disposable, untraceable cell phone and placed a call to a number that he called many times over the past year. Cautiously, he drove along the coast watching his mirrors for any sign someone might be following him; he never saw the eyes that had been on him since he checked-in to the hotel. Unknown to him, a GPS device was on his bumper, giving his stalker the ability to track him from a considerable distance.

CHAPTER 32

Bonn and Rebecca leaned back to back in the dimly lit rooms as one deadly fighting machine while Lexi took point. In case there was more than one intruder, all three of them waited and listened for any sound construed as danger. Heavily armed and with some of his vision back, Bonn started to feel whole again. He moved his hand until it touched hers; she laced her fingers with his and squeezed gently.

"I don't know when…the last time I've told you…"

"I love you too, turn around," Rebecca said, and pressed her lips against his.

Their declaration of love, brought Rebecca to tears of joy, unlike the last time she wept for him. This time, when Bonn pulled her close to comfort her, she pressed hard against him and had to catch her breath when he lowered his hand. The moment ended when Lexi let out a bark that made both of them jump. Whatever she heard made her tail wag rapidly and she could barely contain her excitement.

The sound of gravel crushed by a controlled slide into Bonn's driveway shattered the stillness, and alternating blue and white flashes sliced through the blinds into the darkened room. Mac had come in, silent and fast. Now, as Mac ran, with his weapon drawn, towards the front door, Lexi barked and spun like a puppy. Bonn and Rebecca, locked in a passionate embrace, looked at each other, and in unison said, "Wow".

Bonn found it difficult to break away from the heat of Rebecca's body. "Darlin', hold that thought and we'll finish this later."

The instant Bonn opened the door; Lexi charged through the screen and almost knocked him down on her way out.

Mac holstered his weapon and brushed a double ear rub greeting on Lexi. He spotted Bonn calm and smiling in the doorway.

"Bonn, what's going on? You used the safe word," Mac said with a hint of confusion and intensity.

"I was hoping you could tell us," Bonn said.

"Tell us? What do you mean?" Mac asked.

"Hello Mac. It's only Bonn, Lexi, and little ol' me," Rebecca said.

Mac flinched for his weapon when a voice came from the shadows of the already darkened room. Luckily, he recognized the voice.

"Rebecca? I didn't think you weren't coming over till tomorrow morning. I spoke with Commander Bentow this afternoon and told her to make sure you had a couple of escorts when you came over here."

"That's sweet Mac, you want to protect me." Rebecca leaned in and kissed his cheek. "You forgot I'm a big girl now, I dismissed my bodyguards. I've waited so many years, I couldn't…I *wouldn't* wait until morning," she said and locked arms with Bonn to convey her reasoning.

"Rebecca, you are lucky I didn't pull my gun… Look, when I tell I want you to have protection…"

Bonn listened to the banter until he got irritated watching his best friends go at each other.

"Excuse me for interrupting the debate. Mac, I appreciate you looking out for me, but keeping her away is not going to help. And Rebecca, Mac's intentions are good and are out of concern for your well-being, you need to meet him halfway." Bonn said to Rebecca, "I'm glad you didn't wait."

"Thank you baby," she said and sensually squinted at Bonn.

"You're welcome darlin'."

"Excuse *me*. Bonn, this baby darlin' stuff is so romantic; it had better not be the reason you called me and said, 'Flywater'. Why *did* you call me? Don't tell me it's Rebecca."

Bonn nodded towards Lexi, who went back to the spot where she had scratched the floor. This time, she pawed the air, which changed Mac's demeanor drastically. The moment he noticed the deep gouges in the native pine, he pulled out his pocketknife.

"What the hell? Did you spill something here at one time?"

"No, she just went crazy and began scratching up my floor. Even after I '*Foei'd*' her, she didn't want to quit. I hoped you would know what she's trying to tell us."

Mac snapped his fingers once, "*Reveiren*." Lexi, the bomb specialist, pawed at the corner again, and sat back down. Mac carefully ran the tip of his knife between the spaces of the tongue and grooved boards. After tapping them with his knuckle, Mac spoke directly to Lexi. "I don't get it girl, what do you smell?"

Bonn and Rebecca put their heads together and studied the command list to see what 'Reveiren' meant.

Mac led Lexi away from her find and repeated, "Lexi, *Reveiren*," She performed with the precision of a fine-tuned machine as she went nose-to-floor and room-to-room, smelling every inch of every room without any further commands. When she got to Bonn's bedroom, the hair on her back rose and she hunched low and eased to an area next to Bonn's bed.

"That's exactly what she did in the living room."

"I think we need to get the hell out of here," Mac said and reminiscent of a scene from a Hollywood movie, they bolted through the front door.

In Bonn's front yard and driveway, three Okaloosa County Sheriff's cars parked next to Mac's Expedition with their lights flashing. Two paramedics halted from exiting their Fire Rescue truck when they saw Mac waving everyone away and shouting.

"I'm Detective McCain with the Niceville P.D. and I need everyone to get back behind your vehicles," Mac yelled and held his credentials out for all to see.

With Bonn, Rebecca, and Lexi safely behind a police cruiser Mac said the word they feared would be coming, "Bomb".

"Are you sure?" Bonn asked.

"We have the best explosives detector right here. I've got to take a look at something." Fearlessly and without safety gear, Mac pulled his belt off to use as a lead by looping it through Lexi's collar before taking her back to the house.

A middle-aged, pot-bellied deputy stepped in front of Mac. "Hold it right there, no one is going anywhere near that house if there's a bomb."

"There are at least two bombs," Mac said, in fact.

"That's it, I'm calling the bomb squad," The deputy said and unclipped his radio from his belt.

"Deputy, there isn't time. Sergeant Lexi will let us know what we're dealing with," Mac said.

"Who is the hell is Sergeant Lexi?" He turned to Rebecca then to Bonn. In turn, they shook their heads and said, "I'm a Colonel."

Bonn followed when he said, "I'm a retired General."

The deputy pointed at Lexi and said, "It's a dog?" "Show a little respect, she's an officer and our bomb squad," Mac's demeanor drastically changed.

"No, detective, we do it by the book. I'm going to radio my Captain and get the ATF, SWAT, and *our* bomb squad here. You have no authority, I'm in charge here and we'll do it my way."

"Deputy, go ahead and call it in. While they're trying to get the teams together, we're going to find out what we're dealing with." Mac sidestepped around him and mumbled, "Damn Destin divas, they are all spoiled bitches."

When the deputy heard the comment and grabbed Mac's arm, Sergeant Lexi introduced herself by latching on deputy's arm and shaking furiously.

"*Loslaten!*" Mac commanded and Lexi released, then crouched for round two.

"That bitch bit the hell out of me," The unsuspecting deputy said and drew his weapon to shoot Lexi who strained on Mac's belt, ready to finish the job.

Rebecca drew her weapon out of her sling with her back to the growing number of responders and kept it hidden from their sight, and then said, "I would put that gun away before you really get hurt."

Bonn found it funny and actually laughed at the sight of Rebecca holding her weapon in one hand and wagging a finger of the other hand that was peeking out of the sling.

"Have I ever told you how sexy you are when you're pissed off?"

"No baby," Rebecca said.

"Well you are," Bonn said.

"What the…? That goddamn dog just bit me," the deputy said. "If you think you can draw down on me, and laugh about it, then talk like love-struck teenagers… I'll have charges brought up against all of you."

They laughed at him as he coddled his arm, and for some reason, limped around in a circle as though his foot or leg was injured.

"Screw all of you, that bitch bit me. She needs to be put down." The deputy wanted to do it himself.

"I saw a sweet little puppy protecting her owner from a big bad deputy who had no right to pull his gun on a military officer," Rebecca claimed.

"I didn't draw my gun."

"Yes you did, we are great witnesses." Mac and Bonn both nodded in agreement with Rebecca.

"She's an American hero. I don't think your Sheriff would want any bad press about one of his hot-headed men blaming a military hero for doing the job she had trained to do." Mac wanted to get in on the lunacy.

"She is such a sweet girl," Bonn said to Lexi.

"Yes, she is, come here girl. Did that nasty man scare you?" Rebecca concurred with Bonn's assessment and stooped to pet Lexi who licked her hand and whined while her tail smacked the deputy repeatedly.

"What do you think deputy?" Mac asked.

"All of you are fucking crazy. I don't care what you do…, if I get rabies, well…I better not!" the deputy said and sidestepped around Sergeant Lexi. The paramedics ran a cursory examination on the 'Diva', thanks to the padding of his windbreaker, found only a bruised ego.

"Lexi, 'Reveiren.'" As soon as Mac repeated the command to search, she started on one side of the wooden steps and worked her way around the house. As they rounded the first corner, she sat down at a break in the latticework. Mac zipped the belt off her collar and it cracked like a bullwhip. When Mac released her, she shot between two support posts and disappeared in the crawl space.

Mac yelled, "Deputy, how about a flashlight?"

His request came as seconds later, when a beam of light spun in the air and headed straight for his head. Mac caught it mid-air and heard something about his mother coming from the deputy.

"Now, that's a picture that I'm going to have trouble getting out of my mind," Rebecca laughed as she commented on Mac's butt crack that disappeared through the crawl space.

Several minutes later Lexi emerged from the darkness with Detective McCain in tow. In his hands were two balls of putty in one and two blasting caps with fuses in the other.

"All clear," he said and proudly displayed what Lexi had found.

Rebecca identified their find immediately and asked, "C-4?"

"Roger that, one charge under the living room and another under the master bedroom, right where Lexi showed me," he said and then reached into another pocket.

"Plus, we have a bonus." Mac proudly held up Lexi's other discovery, a small brown bottle wrapped in his handkerchief.

Rebecca asked, "What the hell is that?"

"It's a little nose candy, cocaine. I'm going to see if we can get a print off the bottle and run it through AFIS. Hopefully, we'll find out who paid you a little visit before he tries again."

"It's amazing Lexi could smell the explosives under the house."

"Military grade has a marker added to it, that's what Lexi smelled below your floor."

"Well, I'll be...what happened here?" SAIC Milton, who arrived along with several other vehicles, asked.

"Agent Milton, what are you doing here?" Bonn asked.

"We need to talk. Can we go inside?"

Lexi, sniffing every inch on the way, led the way into the house.

As soon as the front door shut, everyone reached for their weapons when the Sheriff's deputy, who had an encounter with Lexi, pounded his fist on the front door.

"Everyone needs to leave the premises. You are all contaminating a crime scene. If you don't leave right now, I'll arrest each and every one of you.

"Deputy, stand down *now*, unless you don't want to spend the rest of your career as a crosswalk guard at the elementary school," Agent Milton said as she flashed her credentials and slammed the door so hard, even Lexi jumped.

"Diva," Agent Milton said and instantly bonded with the close friends who shared her opinion.

Agent Milton addressed the entire group and began by passing on information that only Mac had heard.

"Earlier today, someone shot a Federal wildlife officer on the Eglin AFB reservation. He had been on the lookout for poachers and called in his 'twenty' after hearing shots and spotting an older grey pickup in the area. Dispatch repeatedly attempted contact him after he gave his location and failed to check back with them. Another wildlife officer found where the last radio communication had come from. When they arrived at the location, there wasn't any sign of the officer or his truck."

"Why would you, a government agent, get involved with the murder of a game warden?"

"He wasn't a state game warden, he worked for the U.S. Fish and Wildlife Department, and any act of violence against a government law enforcement officer is a federal offense. When I heard about a murder in the woods on Eglin, just like the attempt on General Bonner's life, I had to check it out."

"Agent Milton, why are you telling us?" Rebecca cut to the point she wanted answered.

"Bear with me Colonel. A helicopter from Hurlburt Field spotted the warden's vehicle down in a ravine. Security personnel swept the entire area with their dogs and found the officer's body in a shallow grave; he had a single GSW to the forehead. From what we've been able to determine, the shot that killed him, came from a distance of twenty to twenty-five feet."

"Either the shooter was very lucky or extremely skilled," Bonn said.

"I don't believe luck had anything to do with it. The shot came from a very dangerous individual, the same individual we suspect is responsible for several murders and… *attempted murders*". Agent Milton directed her statement towards Bonn.

"We also found cellophane wrappers for three blocks of the explosive, and one of the dogs led us to a stash of several more pounds hidden in the wreckage of an old target practice jet. He assembled at least one IED, if not more, at the location. He plans to use them soon.

"Like these?" Mac reached into his pocket and brought out the C-4 he retrieved.

"Where did you get those?"

"Right under where you are standing, Lexi sniffed them out. Didn't you girl?" Lexi perked up when she heard her name.

Agent Milton scratched behind Lexi's ear as a reward and said, "Damn good work girl."

Bonn could tell Agent Milton had more to say and encouraged her to speak her mind. "Obviously, you think the same guy who shot the game ranger came after us. Anything you can share with us will stay right here. Have you been able to identify him?"

"We were able to retrieve one partial print. That print was common on eleven points with a paramilitary operative who has been living in the area for a little over a year." Agent Milton waited to see if the Bonn could predict her next statement.

"Cap? Don't tell me the son-of-a-bitch who shot me, also shot the wildlife officer…*and* he's military?"

"That's what we suspect. We have every airport within five-hundred miles under a twenty-four hour alert for him.

"I'll be damned; 'Just Carl' and Cap are one in the same. We have a history, I owe him," Mac said and felt the back of his head.

"He also owned the landscaping business next to the trailer park where you arrested the Methamphetamine dealers. That is, until yesterday, when an explosion left a hole the size of a semi where the building once stood."

"I heard the explosion and thought it was another one of Eglin's bomb tests. We hear them all the time," Bonn said.

Agent Milton went on to explain, "Mr. Perkins most likely blew up his building as a cover-up for the pot growing operation he had under the building."

"Then it was Cap and his Mexican buddy who shot me, and possibly Rebecca too."

"I'm sure Mr. Perkins tried to kill you, but his friend…, I don't think he'll be bothering you anymore. They found the scattered remains of a young Hispanic male who had a single bullet hole in his the decapitated skull; the explosion was also a possible cover-up for murder. Although it's going to be very difficult to positively identify the victim, the investigators believe it could be one of his workers…" Even Agent Milton could hear the lack of conviction in her voice; she knew the man's identity.

"Armando," Bonn said as a fact.

"Yes, and he wasn't just a worker, he partnered with Mr. Perkins in a drug trafficking ring that has ties to Mexican cartels."

"Let me guess, other than the drugs on his property, there's no evidence linking Mr. Perkins to the explosion or the murder of Armando."

"It's a little too early to know. The initial ballistics report shows the slug used on the Hispanic male was a smaller caliber than the one that killed the wildlife officer. In addition, the bomb wasn't from C-4; a crude fertilizer and diesel fuel bomb did the job. We are not sure if it is Mr. Perkins work or not. If it's his work, why wouldn't he use his military explosives? It appears he had a good supply," Agent Milton said.

"Plus, it doesn't make sense for him to destroy his business to conceal a murder, when he could have dumped the body anywhere and let the gators take care of him," Mac said.

"The strange thing is, there was very little evidence of there being any plants. There should have been remnants scattered over the area. This was a huge operation where hundreds of mature plants worth several hundred thousand dollars could have been growing, I believe someone removed or stole the crop before the explosion. All they found were pieces of equipment scattered over the property."

"Cap probably moved them then went back to take care of his partner," Mac concluded.

"There would have been no way for one man to harvest and move a crop the size of one that was growing in that building. Mr. Perkins wouldn't have had the time, and he knew it. He's much smarter than he looks."

"I still think he's a sociopath," Mac said.

"Detective, I'm not so sure. The psychopaths are highly organized planners, and they live what society calls a 'normal' life as upstanding citizens and they may even have a family. They also have an uncanny ability to stay under the radar; Mr. Perkins has successfully done that for over a year while he's been living in this area," Agent Milton said, and then hesitated to collect her thoughts.

Bonn joined in on Cap's diagnosis and said, "Sociopaths are often 'loners' that act out impulsively, and often violently. Cap is impulsively violent, *and* he plans his heinous acts. I believe that trait comes from his military training."

"Everyone knows him as the owner of a landscaping company and trailer park. Although he's been living off the grid as just another member of the community, he is *still* an assassin. And now, *that* man is back," Agent Milton said.

"You're absolutely right, but there's another problem; he's strung out on drugs, and that makes him even more dangerous," Bonn nodded as he spoke. "He'll start acting impulsively out of anger and make mistakes. When he does, it will be our chance to stop him."

Rebecca repeatedly tried to speak to speak during the team's assessment. Frustrated, she blurted out, "Wait!"

Everyone, except Bonn, flinched in response to her unexpected demand. Once she had their attention, Rebecca spoke directly to Agent Milton. "I concur with your profile, but let's get back to *why* he shot Bonn. Security personnel reported they discovered pot plants in the area of the shooting, isn't it possible Cap thought Bonn was a hunter who stumbled upon his crop?"

Agent Milton shook her head and said, "At first we thought the same thing. No, the pot had nothing to do with it. We have evidence; Mr. Perkins had been following General Bonner's every move for months."

"*We?* I assume you mean the Agency. Why is the CIA so interested in what happened to me?" Bonn asked.

"Actually, we..., *I* was sent here to provide security for Colonel Fagan, my priority shifted when you were shot."

"You were sent to protect...*me?* Why the hell would I need your protection?" Rebecca interjected before Agent Milton could elaborate.

"Colonel, we uncovered a document regarding your selection and assignment to Eglin. The memo stressed the need to "protect" you, as well as the Raptor program. Even to this day, there are a still couple of things we haven't figured out."

"Such as...?"

"Such as...we discovered the memo six months before you were given your orders, whoever nominated you was most likely the author of the memo. The Agency wants to know why that person felt you needed protection, and why the jet was in jeopardy too. Did anyone contact you *before* you received your paperwork?"

"Yes..., your office. Well, actually, the Associate Director of your agency followed protocol with the NCS when he called me to outline what my job would be when I got here. He said nothing beyond investigating certain individuals with the DOD and a couple of contractors; he never mentioned protecting the F-22's." I only learned of the Raptor's problems after I received my orders to come to Eglin."

"Darlin', I think Agent Milton is asking if your boss told you something different than your written orders. And, who did you report to when you got here."

"That's classified," Rebecca said, with a slight grin. She was aware of Bonn's clearance level, which actually exceeded hers; she didn't know about Mac's or the agent's.

The frustration of protocol could be seen on Agent Milton's face when she said, "If we're going to figure out who shot you, we need to know who besides my office knows what you are up to and what your next move might be. I'm convinced the answer is in the paperwork. I've read your qualifications and accomplishments; they are impressive to the point of being over qualified for a domestic deployment like this."

"Know this, if the Raptor's problems are a result of foreign sabotage, I'll find out. If I discover the jet's problems aren't the work of another government that leaves a DOD employee or a defense contractor." Rebecca looked to Bonn to see if he thought she might have revealed too much by using the word "sabotage".

"Agent Milton, does Cap have anything to do with the jet that crashed at Tyndall?" Bonn asked the question for Rebecca.

"That's very perceptive General. Within twenty-four hours of the crash, the Pentagon's Office of the Inspector sent a memo to the US Senate committee on Armed Services. That committee is chaired by your local representative, Senator Diaz."

"Agent Milton, my job is to gather any information I can find relating to the reason one of our jets ended up in the Gulf. Did the memo regarding my assignment specifically mention Senator Diaz? If it did, I need to know," Rebecca spoke emphatically.

"The Pentagon warned the intelligence community a possible sabotage of the Raptor by foreign nationals who worked for a contractor that wants the F-22 scraped. That contractor lost the initial bid on the Raptor contract, and has the inside track on improved versions, would only benefit if the Raptor failed."

Mac remained silent until his curiosity finally got the best of him and he spoke up. "If Rebecca uncovered anything that implicated a defense contractor, it could jeopardize billions of dollars in future contracts with the DOD. Senator Diaz is connected with a contractor that's developing a replacement, correct?"

"This is the end of the discussion. No matter what our clearances are, this meeting needs to end. We need to see if we can find out who is giving Mr. Perkins his orders," Rebecca said.

"Regarding Mr. Perkins, there's something else you need to know," Agent Milton said.

"He knows Senator Diaz,"

"Kudos General. A press release announcing Diaz as the keynote speaker at the upcoming Military Appreciation Days banquet appeared in your local paper. Normally, Public Affairs would make the announcement and give the paper an approved news release. Instead, your paper received a carefully scripted release from the Senator's office. There's an embedded message for Mr. Perkins in the release, whatever Senator Diaz has planned, it will be the day of his speech."

"I find it hard to believe Cap and Senator Diaz know each other," Bonn said.

"We discovered some interesting things about Senator Diaz and his connection with Mr. Perkins. A computer whiz, who works for us, does routine random web searches on people we have an interest in, and came across a news story that ran at the end of Vietnam War. The story is about a young Private J. Diaz, saved by a Corporal C. Perkins.

"Cap is old enough to have served in Nam' but Senator Diaz is way too young. Are you going to tell me…?" Bonn stopped mid sentence when he figured out the connection.

"Yes, not only did you know Cap back in the day, you also knew the Senator's father."

"I knew his father? I don't recall meeting anyone named Diaz."

"You met him in college. Actually, we both did."

"This is unreal. You're telling me that we both knew Cap and the senator's father? Come on Agent Milton, this has to be more than a coincidence," Bonn said.

"I don't believe it's a coincidence. Do you remember, when you were in the 'Underground', meeting someone by the name of Julio? He was a logistics specialist and helped Mr. Perkins coordinate the bombings of a Bank of Americas branch in California. He was also instrumental in the...*incident* that happened while you were a student at the University of Oklahoma.

Rebecca mouthed the word 'Underground?' to Mac. He raised his eyebrows in response.

"I don't remember anyone named, Julio," Bonn said.

"Julio and Mr. Perkins were close friends and political activists in California, back in the late 60's. Their involvement with a group known as the *Weather Underground* put him on the FBI's radical political activist watch list. They left California to avoid arrest, and ended up in Oklahoma, that's when Mr. Perkins started going by the name 'Cap', and his love affair with explosives began,"

Agent Milton said and never took her eyes off Bonn. "I arrested both of them at the University of Oklahoma. That is also, where you met Julio..."

"When I..., *we* were at the University in Oklahoma...in the middle of an anti-war protest..." Bonn went into a trance for a few seconds then said, "There were at least a thousand demonstrators, cops, and National Guardsmen... that's when Cap chose to detonated a bomb. It turned into a nightmare, everyone crouched down when it went off...mass hysteria...we ran..." Bonn turned pensive and hung his head with his shoulders drooping.

Agent Milton swallowed after seeing the toll her discussion was having on Bonn. The expression on everyone's face confirmed her suspicion that he wasn't the only one who found the topic arduous.

Rebecca asked, "What were you doing with a bunch of left-winged radicals like ones in the Weather Underground?"

Bonn had everyone's attention as they waited to hear his explanation. "It happened a long time ago darlin', I haven't always leaned to the right."

"The past is the past, you can tell me about it some other time, if you want. If not, that's okay too."

"Darlin'? He called you Darlin'," Agent Milton said and smiled at Rebecca.

"What? I can't have a social life?" Rebecca slowly turned her head towards Mac to get some help.

"Leave me out of this." Mac gave the international signs to stop by holding both of his hands up and showing his palms.

In the uncomfortable silence that followed, Lexi went to the front door and whined. Bonn was grateful for the diversion and said, "Every time that dog whines, she's trying to tell us something. I think she needs to go out and do her business."

"She did her business when we were outside earlier. I think she wants to find Cap or whoever put those bombs under your house." Mac clipped a leash on her and said, "Lexi, *Zoek.*"

Lexi tracked the bomber's scent into the dunes then headed straight to the Crystal Inn's side door. Agent Milton immediately ordered the deputies to "secure the premises and call ATF".

CHAPTER 33

Just like most addicts, Cap couldn't resist the urge to replenish his cocaine supply. He didn't care about the police activity at Bonn's house; he needed to feed his addiction before returning to finish the job he started.

Wearing a military hat on his new buzz-cut hair, and dressed in an Air Force uniform, made him nearly unrecognizable when he stopped at the dealer's house. Adding to his disguise, the old pickup he bought in Pensacola made him almost unrecognizable.

He knocked on the front door, and the occupant pointed the barrel of a small pistol poking through a small crack and said, "Take one more step and I'll pop a cap in your ass."

The dealer's use of the word "cap" didn't go unnoticed by Carl, who then removed his hat and said, "DJ put that piece away. Look again 'Bro', it's me. Cap."

DJ laughed and said, "You white boys all look alike. Why you all pimp'd out as a soldier? Get yo' white ass in here."

Cap walked into the house and pulled out a wad of hundred dollar bills that would more than cover the cost of the 1/8 ounce of cocaine, and said, "I need an '8-ball."

"Whew, look at all that green, yo' sure that's all you want?"

Cap's anxiety surged as he watched DJ open a drawer, pull out a bag of white powder, with a quantity far greater than the eighth of an ounce Cap wanted, and drop it on his glass coffee table.

"I'll take it all," Cap said and peeled off a stack of bills that would more than cover the street value of his dealer's entire stash.

"No honky, I'll take it all," D.J. said and then pointed the small .25 caliber pistol at Cap.

"Please…, don't shoot. You can have it, don't shoot me," Cap made his plea in jest.

All of a sudden, Cap threw the entire wad of hundred dollar bills in the air and said, "Here, you can have it."

When the dealer's eyes locked in disbelief at the fluttering bills, Cap pulled his Glock and placed his signature shot squarely on the supplier's forehead. The deafening percussion of the gunshot silenced the breaking glass, as his dealer's body crashed on the coffee table.

"What an idiot," Cap said, then grabbed the bag of cocaine and ran out to his truck and left the scattered money. Money wasn't his problem; he needed a little energy and dipped his key into the bag, twice. He didn't care if the neighbors heard the gunshot, or if they saw him leaving, he would be long-gone by the time anyone identified him.

Cap was curious if there was still activity at Bonn's house and drove back along the coast until he saw the flashing lights of a roadblock in the distance. Instead of making an attention-grabbing U-turn, he turned into the parking lot of the *Fish Tale Seafood Restaurant* and watched the activity from a few blocks away.

On the other side of the roadblock, a swarm of law enforcement vehicles, including a SWAT truck, sat in the Crystal Inn's parking lot. Cap was concerned about the status of his bombs, and the reason a SWAT team converged on the hotel next to Bonn's house. So, he continued with his Plan B.

Right after starting his truck to leave and relocate for the night, a classic Mercedes convertible, driven by a classic beauty, pulled in and backed her car in a slot several spaces away. While exiting her two-seater convertible, she spread her long legs and exposed the sheer white panties under her miniskirt. When she stood, her purse spilled on the pavement and a lipstick tube rolled next to Cap's door.

Being a true southern man, Cap said, "Why the hell not?" and decided to assist the damsel in distress. Although she kept her knees together while scooping up her contents, Cap couldn't get the image of the sheer white panties out of his mind.

"Let me help you," he said and picked up her wallet along with a cosmetic case, then hesitated when he saw a condom packet.

"Thank you so much... Oh my god, I'm so embarrassed," she said when he handed her belongings back.

"No, please, it is always best to be safe; you have nothing to be embarrassed about," Cap said.

"I am such a klutz sometimes. Thank you for helping me, and thank you for your service," she said after seeing his military uniform.

"I'm Carl; it's nice to meet you." The fire in his loins that had been doused for the past year, quit smoldering, and flamed up.

"I'm Ashleigh; it's nice to meet you too. Carl, I know this might sound weird, I was supposed to meet a girlfriend who called and cancelled. Do you want to have a drink…with me?"

Cap couldn't believe his luck and said, "I would love to have a drink with you, Ashleigh. Why don't you grab us a table, and I'll join you in a minute, I need to make a call."

Senator Julio Diaz II was one hour out of Tallahassee, on his way to Fort Walton Beach for a "Military Appreciation Day" speech he would be making the following evening. While reciting his speech aloud, the glow from an *Incoming Call* glowed bright on his phone and lit up the back seat of his limo. Anticipating a positive report, he answered. "Tell me about our late and great friend."

"He's not late, he's a little behind schedule." Cap reassured Senator Diaz that he would succeed their desire to eliminate Bonn.

"Is there anything I can do to help him get there on time?" Senator Diaz nodded to the reflection of his driver's inquiring eyes.

"He would *appreciate* a ride tomorrow and then I would be able to meet with him. Maybe you could find a friend to give him a ride and I will handle everything when he arrives," Cap said.

"I'm sure that can be arranged. I will personally invite him, and his friend, to meet me at 17:00 in VIP parking. If for some reason I'm running a little late, be sure to thank *both* of them for me."

Senator Diaz was convinced Detective McCain would eventually figure everything out and he didn't want any loose ends.

"I understand your concern; I'll *greet* them right after they arrive. Regretfully, I won't be able to stay for your speech; I believe I have a flight to catch," Cap said.

"The weather is great for flying and your flight has been confirmed. Have a safe trip and thank you for your help. Be sure to stay in touch once you get settled." With that said, the Senator found on his speed dial, the one person who could convince General Bonner to attend the event.

"Driver, head straight to Gentleman's Quarter's on Eglin and call my friend, tell him to have his plane ready at…*5:30* pm tomorrow evening," Senator Diaz said when he wasn't able to convert 5:30 to military time.

"You've reached the voice mail of Detective McCain; please leave me a message…"

"Detective, this is Senator Diaz, please give me a call tonight. I have a favor to ask."

Cap was relieved everything was still a go and wanted to party. He got back in his pickup and inhaled enough cocaine to drop the average person to their knees. Almost immediately, his field of vision exploded with a veil of flashing lights while his brain numbed, and his blood pressure shot up from the dopamine surge. As his heart pounded at a life-threatening rate, he drifted to unconsciousness.

When he came to, Cap didn't know how long he had been sitting in his truck, he hoped "white panties" was still inside. While checking out his appearance in the rearview mirror, he saw a pony-tailed young man in a black van pass behind his pickup.

For an instant, under the light cast from the parking lot's floodlight, the man behind the wheel looked like a younger Senator Diaz. His hair and age weren't close to the senator's but his face was close enough that Cap wanted a second look. All he saw was the van's taillights as it turned onto Coastal 98 and sped away.

"I've got to cut back on the coke," Cap said and slapped himself repeatedly then hustled into the restaurant. After scanning the tables without success, Cap started to panic until he glanced out the window and saw her Mercedes still parked and empty.

"Where are you...whatever the hell your name is," Cap said on his way out to the deck. A local was belting out a Jimmy Buffet song that Cap heard at every beach bar in Florida so many times, he wanted to pull out his gun and shoot the singer, just to shut him up.

"Buy me a drink soldier?" a voice from behind asked.

"I thought you left. I couldn't get my mother to shut up. She kept going on. You know how they can be when you call them."

"So you're a momma's boy?"

"Yes, guilty as charged."

"Yeah, I'm a daddy's girl. How about that drink...daddy."

The air hung heavy and pungent with the scent of passion, tobacco smoke, and alcohol in the room at the Holiday Inn Express. Unexpectedly, Ashleigh enjoyed the thrill of having her way with a man as dangerous as he has. She rested her head on his shoulder, breathless and drenched in sweat, and traced imaginary circles on his chest.

"You know something Carl? You and I have a lot in common."

"You're damn right we do; we're both animals in bed. By the way, you can call me Cap."

"I like Carl, Cap sounds childish. I can't argue with your assessment about our compatibility in bed, there's more to us than we've let the other one know. For example, I don't know if you're married, not that it matters," Ashleigh said and gave him seductive smile.

Carl was afraid Ashleigh might think Paula was his type, and began to stammer. "Why do you want to know, are you married too? Not that I'm still married, I was married until recently...I mean I wasn't really married, it...she was a joke."

"I know all about your wife, or should I say, *deceased* wife?"

Before she could say another word, Cap pulled a gun out from under his pillow then asked, "Who the hell are you?"

"I'm a very dangerous woman, a registered nurse, and someone who has an unfinished job that needs to be completed; I think you understand what that feels like, don't you?"

"You work at the damn hospital? I knew there was something familiar about you, I saw you there when I was visiting…a friend."

"General Bonner is a friend of yours? Carl, that's a good one."

"I've never heard of him," Cap said, then tightened his grip on the Glock.

"Easy cowboy, we're both on the same mission. That's what I wanted to tell you, listen to me," Ashleigh said and hoped to diffuse her situation by letting the sheet fall when she sat up.

"You have ten seconds... Nine, eight, seven..," he said and kept his eyes glued to her nakedness.

"Put the damn gun down, I want Bonner dead too."

Five, four, three..." Carl's voice lost its intensity as his countdown approach zero.

"Carl, we can both have what we want, let's work together."

"Tell me, how do you know Bonner?" Carl asked.

"I don't really *know* him, not the way you know him. Did he recognize you after you shot him? That's right big boy, I also know about you and that Mexican shooting him."

"Arnie won't be talking."

"So his name was Arnie? Did you kill him too?"

"No. He was already dead when I found him and what do you mean kill him *too?*"

"You're a very popular man on the news. Let's see, they want you for the murder of a game warden, as an accomplice to the assault of a police detective, *and*…you're wanted for questioning in the suspicious death of your wife. Do I need to go on?" Ashleigh caught the slightest twinge of pride on Cap's face.

"That's it? Wait till they add murder of a local nurse."

"You think I'm just a nurse and I'm here by accident? I have to admit our little encounter has been quite remarkable, but know this, I wouldn't hesitate to take you out for a second," she said as she pulled a pistol from under *her* pillow and held it inches from Carl's chest. He laughed so hard, the bed shook. "We both had guns under our pillows? Now, that is funny." Carl continued to laugh until he started coughing uncontrollably. When she leaned back, to avoid any spray from his fit, he knocked her gun to the floor. After pinning her down with a vice lock grip, he began kissing her passionately.

CHAPTER 34

Bonn's driveway was a crime scene, again. Inside his house, four determined individuals huddled in the dimly lit room, while Lexi, Mac's military and combat tested canine soldier, guarded the front door.

This time, Bonn sat in his favorite chair and caught his ball effortlessly. Rebecca, the only one who knew Bonn's vision returned, smiled. Mac and Agent Milton found his behavior amusing.

"By morning, the alpha boys from the FBI are going to be pissing on everything, trying to mark their territory," Agent Milton warned.

"I guess that means Cap is a serial, which qualifies him as their property." Mac didn't bring up the fact Agent Milton used to be in the FBI and continued to mark her territory as an agent with the Central Intelligence.

"I'm trying to hold them off as long as possible; my boss is telling me they're raising hell. The only reason they've stayed in the shadows is because I help them whenever I can, they owe me. I've asked for a day."

Although his sunglasses helped conceal Bonn's intentions, Rebecca she could tell by his body language, he wanted to take charge of the entire investigation.

"Baby, let Agent Milton do her job, she'll handle the federal boys and Mac will make sure the locals won't bother you."

Lexi nuzzled Rebecca. "Lexi will also make sure you're not bothered; won't you girl?"

"Rebecca's right. Why don't we call it a night and get back together in the morning? Agent Milton, would you mind giving her ride back to GQ? As much as I would like to find Cap right now, I'm feeling a little rough," Bonn said.

"No problem. Colonel Fagan, shall we go?"

Mac's cell, which had been on Silent Mode, beeped to let him know he had a voice message and he held up a finger. Moments later he said, "Well, well, well. Guess who wants to talk with me."

"My guess, is Susan. In case you ladies haven't heard, Susan is Mac's new girlfriend; you may know her as Dr. Benson. I caught them giving each other mouth-to-mouth earlier today." Bonn laughed and jabbed his finger in Mac's direction.

Mac turned bright red as he went on the offense. "You're one to talk, '*baby-darlin'*.'"

"Susan is absolutely the right one for you. She is smart as hell, and she doesn't take any of your crap. It helps that she's a real looker. Case closed," Rebecca said with an approving smile.

"Doctor Benson is your girlfriend? My job is the only relationship in my life," Agent Milton unintentionally vented about her current relationship status.

Mac could feel the heat rising in his face. ""Let's get back to the phone call. The message was definitely *not* from my 'friend', Dr. Benson. It was Senator Diaz; he has a favor to ask of me. It must be a big one; he wants me to call him tonight. How's that for timing?"

"I don't think his call is a coincidence," Bonn said.

"Mac, why does the Senator have your private cell number?" Rebecca asked, Agent Milton wondered the same thing.

"He helped me get my condo; I always knew there would be a price to pay for that favor. I have a feeling, whatever he has in mind for me, may be the repayment." Mac stared at his phone and before he placed the return call, asked, "Any thoughts?"

"First, find out what he wants, and then we can give you our input," Bonn said, Agent Milton and Rebecca concurred.

"Lexi, what do you think?" As part of the team, she let out a single bark of approval.

"Then it's unanimous, he's going to be my bitch," Mac said and hit *Return Call.*

"All of you are crazy; crazy good," Agent Milton said and for the first time, felt camaraderie with them.

Mac held his finger to his lips and while he waited for Senator Diaz to answer, put his phone on speaker.

"Detective McCain, I was hoping you would call tonight. I trust all is well with your condo and it survived the last hurricane?" Senator Diaz said in the voice of a politician or award-winning actor.

Just as Mac predicted, the senator opened with a reminder of the favor he had done for him.

"I love my place and I'm eternally grateful for your help in getting it," Mac said and winked at Agent Milton who gave him the thumbs up.

"It's nothing compared to the years of service you've given this country. I'm the one who's eternally grateful."

"Senator, you mentioned on your message, you needed a favor?" Mac wanted to get to the point.

"Not really a favor, an invitation. I wanted to see if you and General Bonner would be my guests at tomorrow's Military Appreciation Day banquet. I believe the 'meet and greet' starts at six; I thought we could get together and discuss a few things before it gets going. Let's meet around five, if that works for you."

"Senator, the general is still trying to recover from his injuries, but I think it would do him some good to get out." Mac raised his eyebrows and everyone turned their thumbs up.

"That's great. I'm looking forward to seeing both of you. Just follow the signs to VIP Parking and you'll see my limo. I'll be waiting for you, we can go in together. Alright, five-o'clock it is, or should I say 1700 hours?"

"Roger that Senator. Thank you for thinking of us. I'm looking forward to it as well." Mac disconnected and said, "I hate it when civilians try to speak in military jargon, it's like white people trying to talk like they're from the hood."

"You heard him. He invited us to the Military Appreciation Day dinner that's sponsored by Military Affairs. That is so thoughtful of him, I'm the Chairman and you're a member." Bonn shook his head in disgust and said, "What an idiot."

While his partners discussed the senator's intent, Bonn sat in his easy chair, and continued tossing his tennis ball without missing it once. Rebecca watched in awe, and wanted to share the good news, but he had a concerned look on his face.

"Baby, what are you thinking?"

"I smell a setup. All of us, except Agent Milton, have received invitations to the banquet; we don't need to be anyone's guest to attend. Senator Diaz is the keynote speaker at the request of Military Affairs; I guess it's possible his assistant didn't tell him who extended the invitation.

"I find it strange he wanted to meet in the parking lot when we could meet inside. I'm with you, he has a surprise planned," Mac said.

"Let him think his plan is perfect. I have a few surprises in mind, just for him. Why don't we get some rest and meet for breakfast, we need to be alert and ready for anything tomorrow. Right now, I'm feeling weak and I'm not sure how much more I can do tonight." Bonn didn't know how much longer he could hide the nausea and headache.

Mac learned all the little nuances associated with Bonn's as his caretaker and had seen the headache coming on at light speed before Bonn. "Do you want me to call Susan? She told...*asked*...me to keep her informed if you weren't feeling well."

"I think you're just looking for an excuse to talk to her. Don't call her for my benefit, if you want to tell her goodnight, go for it." Bonn relished every opportunity to give his friend a hard time.

Rebecca could tease with the best and said, "Mac, calling her would be sweet. A woman likes a man who calls and let's her hear his voice before she goes to sleep. Isn't that right Agent Milton?"

"I wouldn't know. I go to sleep with Conan, Leno, or Letterman every night. Colonel, let's head to the base and get a good night's sleep. I have sneaking suspicion General Bonner is right and we're going to need to be alert and ready."

"Please call me Bonn, Agent Milton."

"Okay Bonn, call me Michelle. Please, all of you, its Michelle." Agent Milton smiled when Colonel Fagan echoed the moment by saying, "It's nice to meet you Michelle, call me Rebecca."

"I have to tell you, it gets confusing when I'm talking with all of you. Bonn, you're a General, Rebecca, you're a Colonel, and Detective McCain will always be Mac to me. I hope there aren't any other names to remember."

The ensuing laughter eased her confusion and everyone decided to call each other by their preferred names when they were together and by rank in public.

Michelle put her hand out for everyone to join in a circle and then she said, "Let's get this bastard, Team Destin!" A chorus of laughter preceded a rousing "Team Destin!"

"Wait a second, Lexi, heir." Mac then led a four-person, one dog cheer and let out one more "Team Destin!"

Commander Cari Bentow greeted Senator Diaz when he arrived at GQ and entered the VIP house. Always courteous, he asked how she was doing and got a tedious rant about spending the evening bailing out a friend charged with assault while he was out fishing.

The Senator didn't understand the connection between fishing and fighting. He disregarded her previous ramblings and hesitantly asked, "What? A friend of yours got arrested for assault when he went fishing?"

Cari saw another opportunity to grate on the senator's nerves with another tedious, rant. "The dispute began when he brought in a tournament winning fish at the World Cobia Championships. It was officially weighed in, but the tournament officials argued he didn't actually catch it. I know what you're thinking, and the answer is no, it didn't jump in the boat. Apparently, when he reeled it to the boat, the fish entangled in a parachute that was hanging behind another boat. The officials considered the fish to be "netted" by someone else and disqualified it until a decision could be made whether or not to let it count."

Senator Diaz got to a point where he just kept nodding, as though he understood what she was saying. Even though he didn't understand the part about a parachute, he didn't want to hear the explanation, but the fish story caught his attention.

"What is the big deal about a fish?"

"What's the big deal? The fish is worth over a quarter of a million dollars! Even in Destin, that's a lot of money. When there's that much cash involved, there are potential problems."

Cari took the opportunity to change the subject and steer the conversation to the attempt on Rebecca's life. "Destin may be just a tourist town, but it has big city problems. The woman parasailing behind the boat that wrapped up my friend's fish in its parachute is a Colonel in the Air Force. She is also the girlfriend of a well-known person in the area. You may have heard of him, General Bonner?"

Senator Diaz maintained his poker face and said, "I seem to recall the name…but I don't *know* him."

Cari acted as if she believed him. She clearly remembered seeing them at the same table at a fund raising event during the senator's first election campaign. As plausible as it was for him to forget someone, considering the number of people he met as a public figure, Bonn wasn't someone easily forgotten.

During the election campaign, Bonn's support, as Chairman of Military Affairs, helped swing the county for him. In gratitude, Bonn received a personal, hand written letter of thanks, from Senator Diaz. Bonn displayed it on his office wall along with many other acknowledgements; she had seen it on several occasions. Cari wanted to refresh his memory, but his cell phone chimed, and by the expression on his face, it was her time to leave.

"Senator, please enjoy your stay, I'll see you tomorrow at the banquet." Cari sat in her car trying to decide who to tell about her observations until it hit her; there was only one person to call.

The fifteen-minute ride to Eglin was a comfortable, silent, and welcome experience for Michelle. When a James Taylor's song about having a friend came on the radio, she and Rebecca sang soulfully.

"Rebecca, you are very lucky to have friends like Bonn and Mac."

"*We* are lucky Michelle." Rebecca assured her by patting Michelle's leg.

"Where am I taking you?"

"I'm staying at the Gentleman's Quarters housing complex. They have me in a beautiful house, right on the water. I need to give Commander Bentow a call and let her know I'm headed back," Rebecca said as they approached the main gate.

"Whoa, you may want to hold off for a second." Michelle was stunned to see the gate heavily manned with personnel carrying automatic weapons. Waving them through were several very large MP's indicating they should pull over to the side, just past the gate. As Michelle braked to a stop, the MPs saluted Colonel Fagan and then pointed to a blue Chevy Impala in the center of a roundabout.

An intense looking, young staff sergeant appeared at the passenger's window, starling Colonel Fagan, and he saw the business end of Rebecca's Glock come out of her sling. Although he was a little shaken, from the sight of Rebecca's gun, he couldn't wait to get off duty and tell his story. The legend of Colonel Fagan and her skills were born.

Michelle's mouth hung open for a second then said, "Remind me not to piss you off girl. I don't think I've ever seen anyone draw down that fast. That is one fancy sling you have there."

"Ma am', I'm sorry if I surprised you. There is no need for that, please forgive me. The commander would like to have a word with you."

Commander Cari Bentow exited the Chevy, and slipped into the back seat of Agent Milton's vehicle. "Good evening Colonel, Agent Milton. I spoke with Detective McCain, and learned you were headed back to Eglin."

"Commander, is there a problem?" Rebecca asked.

"I'm not sure. I would like to visit with you at headquarters before you go back to your housing. There's a guest staying in the place next to yours that you might want to hear about."

Escorted by the armed guards, Michelle and Rebecca followed Commander Bentow to her offices and as Rebecca fiddled with her sling, Michelle subconsciously kept checking and double-checking for her gun by squeezing her arm against it during the short drive.

Commander Bentow led Rebecca and Michelle into her cherry wood paneled office, decorated with mementos from around the world and included a painting of President Obama above her desk.

"Please have a seat. Would either of you care for coffee or maybe something stronger?"

"I'll go with the stronger, Jack neat. I'm done with my antibiotics," Rebecca said.

"Make that two. Commander, who is this "guest" you want to tell us about?"

"Senator Diaz."

"We knew he was coming to Fort Walton, I had no idea he would be staying at Eglin," Michelle said.

"For obvious reasons, whenever dignitaries are visiting, the base is the safest place for them to stay. He checked-in tonight and I welcomed him at the house next to the one you are staying in, Colonel."

"Why did you think it necessary to let me know he was next door?"

"When we were having a casual conversation at the house, I mentioned what happened to Bonn… he acted like he barely knew him or knew he had been shot. The story has been all over the news for weeks. Regardless, I know they've met, and that 's why I found his cavalier attitude, a little disconcerting. Something is up. I can feel it. I don't know if it has to do with the attempt on your life or the General's, maybe both."

Michelle and Rebecca looked to each other for direction. Michelle said, "Team Destin is aware of the Senator's strange behavior. Mac spoke with him right before we left to come here."

"I don't know what Team Destin means, what's up?"

Agent Milton and Colonel Fagan extended their hands and introduced themselves as Michelle and Rebecca. "Cari" reciprocated.

While throwing back several shots of Tennessee's finest whiskey, the three power women planned a course of action and promised Cari they would share it with the other members of Team Destin over breakfast. They were sure Senator Diaz wasn't aware, Rebecca occupied the house next door, but to ensure her maximum security, Michelle agreed to stay with Rebecca. Cari, the Honorary Member of Team Destin, ordered two of her M.P.s to contain and secure the house.

Mac called Susan and completely forgot to mention anything about Bonn's condition or the events that had happened that night. Instead, he spoke in a low seductive voice, telling her the things he would do with her the next time they got together.

When Bonn knocked on the guest room door, which happened to be open a few inches, Mac said in his best official voice, "Dr. Benson, I have to go. Yes…me too. Good night."

"You are so full of crap. Who do you think you're fooling?" Bonn asked.

"I don't have a clue what you're talking about," Mac said.

"I think we need to work in shifts tonight. As you know, I only sleep for a couple of hours at a time, mostly during the day. I'm usually up all night, why don't you get some sleep and I'll wake you up when I start to get tired."

"You look like walking death right now. Are you sure you're up for all of this?"

"Thanks for the compliment, I'll be fine," Bonn said.

Mac strolled around the house checking locks, windows, and popped the clip out of his gun to be sure it was full before saying, "Lexi, Bewalkin'".

"Bonn, it's like a dungeon in here. Why don't you turn on a light and see if you can handle it. That pervert doesn't know you're sensitive to light and if it's dark in here, he's more likely to think you're asleep and try something."

"You're right. I'll wear my sunglasses and watch a little TV. Go ahead and crash, Lexi and I will be fine."

In the bright light cast by his floor lamp and the television, Bonn tossed his ball in the air while trying to figure out Cap's motive. Watching a ball that never came her way, wore Lexi out and as soon as she heard Bonn snoring, she walked a tight circle at the front door a dozen times, then curled-up and slept with one eye open.

Bonn spotted them first. The police and National Guardsmen surrounded the students like a pack of wolves. The screams of the innocent young girls pierced the air as the batons spewed blood and ferocious dogs ripped the flesh of those who dared to resist. Cap screamed, "let's get out of here", all Bonn could hear was his own heart beating.

Bonn awoke from his college nightmare when Lexi tugged at his sleeve. He cringed, and thought Lexi was one of the police dogs used at the student strike in his dream and was attacking.

Drenched in sweat and in the middle of an intense headache, he told Lexi to go get Mac. She wheeled at lightning speed and nosed her way into Mac's room barking incessantly.

Mac arrived in time to see Bonn's eyes roll back and his body seize as he spasmodically dry heaved. "Bonn, talk to me."

When Bonn finally relaxed his clenched jaws and opened his eyes, Mac said, "Hang in there, buddy.", and gave him a sip of cold water and used damp towel to wipe the beads of sweat trickling down Bonn's face. "You scared me this time. How are you feeling now?"

"I need a couple of minutes. I'll be fine."

"There you go again with that "fine" shit. You're not fine, I'm calling an ambulance."

Bonn grabbed Mac's arm with enough force to confuse Lexi who had been watching helplessly. Her growl stopped with a simple 'Kalm' and Mac removed Bonn's hand, one finger at a time.

"I'm sorry Mac. This happens several times a day. It takes me a few minutes to come around…once my meds kick in…I'll be…all right."

Mac and Bonn couldn't believe their eyes when they heard the sound of pills rattling in the bottle Lexi had in her mouth and was bringing to Bonn.

"This dog is not normal," Bonn said as he wiped off the slobber coating his prescription bottle.

"You're not going to believe this; she brought me the ones I needed," Bonn said and took threw a couple in his mouth, still shaking his head in disbelief.

"This is my special girl; there isn't anything she can't do. Isn't that right girl?" Mac rubbed both her ears and kissed her.

"Is that what you told Dr. Benson you were going to do to her?"

"What did you hear?" Mac made his question sound like a warning.

"I didn't hear anything, I swear. You were blushing, so I just assumed I interrupted phone sex."

"Well, you didn't. Quit changing the subject, if you don't want me to call an ambulance, what do you want me to do?"

"I didn't change the subject, you and that super dog of yours did. I'm getting better by the minute. Go back to bed, if I need anything I'll have Lexi get it for me."

"This is nothing to joke about Bonn. If you're still zoned out in the morning, you're not going anywhere. I'll figure something else out."

"I remembered Cap," Bonn said so quietly Mac wasn't sure if he heard correctly.

"Did I hear you right? You remembered Cap? What do you mean?"

"I had a dream about my college days and some extremely unpleasant memories. I remembered how his mind works; I doubt he's changed over all these years."

"Is that why you to got so messed up tonight?"

"I don't know if it was the dream or these damn lights that brought on the headache. I remembered, *exactly* how he thinks, and we are going to use that to our advantage." Bonn turned off the light and rubbed Lexi's belly until she quit chasing bunnies in her dreams. He wanted her to be rested, just like the rest of Team Destin. Confident in Lexi's ability to guard, he fell asleep without giving her the command to guard.

CHAPTER 35

T he round table in the giant booth at the IHOP overflowed with: stacks of pancakes drowned in syrup and melted butter, eggs cooked in various stages of consistency, piles of pork products, fresh-squeezed Florida orange juice, and enough coffee pots to bring the stares of anyone who passed by.

No one spoke about the day that lay ahead, or what role each team member would play in the coordinated effort to apprehend Cap. Team Destin wanted to help him get the retribution and closure he needed, and kept the conversation light while they waited for him to take the lead. They didn't have to wait long.

"I have a plan, and if everything goes according to that plan, there will be one less maniac in the world. When were finished here at the feeding trough, I'll lay out the details."

Mac loosened his belt, picked at his teeth with a toothpick, and made sucking sounds to remove any remnants of the half pound of bacon and sausage links he might have missed.

"Mac, if Susan hears you making those god-awful sounds, it will be the last time you will see her," Rebecca joked.

"Sorry, I don't remember eating yesterday at his guy's house, it's no wonder he's as skinny as a bird; all he has is bottled water, Gatorade, and some crackers in his kitchen. I almost ate some of Lexi's food just to keep my stomach from rumbling."

"The only '*crackers*' I saw at my house last night were you and that deputy Lexi wanted for dinner," Bonn said and had them near tears from laughter.

Once the laughter wound down, an eerie quiet became the signal for Bonn to proceed with his plans.

"I want each of you to know, I am honored to be a charter member of Team Destin and today, God willing, we will take down a deranged killer. Does anyone have any updates before we get started?" Bonn set the mood for everyone.

Michelle began with her update. "Last night, a local drug dealer took a point-blank shot with the same caliber gun used on the game ranger."

"*His* shot?" Mac asked even though knew the answer.

"It was definitely Cap's signature but what happened, doesn't make sense, the room where they found the victim was littered with several thousand dollars in large bills. Cap's prints were on the bills, nowhere else. The strange thing is how reckless he's getting. He's trained to move undetected, and now, he seems to be killing indiscriminately without caring who knows."

"With that much money lying around, it doesn't sound like a robbery to me," Rebecca said.

"I'm not sure. The victim had less than a gram of coke on his person, which means Cap probably has the main stash. If I'm right, it's going to add fuel to his fire…if he wasn't rapid cycling before, he will be now. We have to assume his psychosis is getting dangerously out of control.

Bonn asked, "Agent Milton, where's the dealers house, in Destin?"

"The house is approximately a mile from your place. Mr. Perkins is close and up to something, he's going to lash out again. I believe it will be today, and if his pattern stays true, you are the target," Michelle said. "I stayed with Rebecca last night and my phone rang nonstop. Erroneous reports came in from three counties, all fitting the description of a man with long blond hair, we're checking on some of the more legitimate tips. However, I have no doubt, he's changed his appearance and we can't rely on them."

Mac gave the local report. "Cap's picture is plastered on the front page of every newspaper and the lead story on all the television news reports. So far, there hasn't been a single positive ID, we now know why. The night clerk at the Crystal Inn gave a description of a man dressed in military BDU's and sporting a short military haircut. Guess what, he signed the hotel's register, Captain C. Weatherman USAF."

"Cap had to be who I saw leaving Bonn's house the night Lexi found the bombs. He was wearing a military cap and I didn't see a ponytail, it had to be him. Mac, what did the hotel's security tapes show?"

"Unfortunately Rebecca, the security camera at the front desk wasn't operational. Somehow, he went into the controls and disabled every camera by frying the main circuit board. Trying to recognize him from the thousands of military men around here, is going to be next to impossible."

"We're focusing on the wrong things. It's irrelevant he didn't leave any prints or hard proof at the hotel, he wants us to waste our time trying to figure out the clues he's leaving while he charges ahead with *his* plan. I don't think there are clues, they are nothing but distractions. We need to figure out what his plan is and who's helping him carry it out." Bonn looked at each member of Team Destin, all agreed.

"The answer is Senator Diaz is working with him," Michelle said.

"Cari met with Diaz when he arrived at GQ housing, he was in the house next to mine. That's why Michelle stayed with me."

"Now it's Cari, not Commander Bentow?"

"Bonn, she is definitely a friendly; we made her an honorary member of the 'Team'. The resources available to her are invaluable to us," Michelle said.

"Why didn't you call us? Diaz is a very dangerous man. We would have come to protect you women." Mac's comment brought a kick from under the table; he wasn't sure who did it.

"I think we can take care of ourselves." Rebecca tapped the weapon concealed in her customized sling to make a point.

"Yeah, why didn't you call us? Mac's right," Bonn said facetiously, given that Rebecca's extensive training made her more dangerous, handicapped with one arm in a sling, than most men with two good arms.

Rebecca played along and said, "I'm sorry baby, I call next time."

"Here we go again with that 'baby' stuff, it may work on him, it's not going to work on me." Mac beat his chest and said, "There isn't a woman that could play me."

"All joking aside, did you and Michelle watch the Senator's house to see if he had visitors?" Bonn asked.

"Of course we did, he didn't have single visitor and his limo never left. He wouldn't risk exposing his relationship with Mr. Perkins, especially on the base, where security is tight as hell. Cari seemed a little spooked after her visit with him. She had patrols cruising throughout the night; we spotted one of her men across the street wearing night vision gear."

"Cari told us, she mentioned you to Senator Diaz and he acted like he didn't know you beyond a fleeting introduction a few years ago. She distinctly remembers the two of you having dinner together, and she never let Diaz know that she caught him in a lie."

Bonn found the senator's behavior interesting but not surprising, considering the incriminating evidence piling up against him.

"Darlin', even though we were together when Cap was crawling under my house, I'm not convinced the attempt on your life is connected with mine. I think it's a coincidence. Someone could be working with him; it is even possible they have teamed up. Regardless, we need to be cautious."

"Here's my plan for this evening..." Bonn, ever vigilant in his details, proposed the entire team attend the Military Appreciation Day's celebration. After hearing each of their roles, they joined hands in the center of the table and gave a subdued *"Team Destin"*.

CHAPTER 36

The annual *Military Appreciation Day* commenced on proclamation by the mayor of Fort Walton Beach to the delight of thousands.

The vendors of "handcrafted" goods made in China, pitched their goods on the main runway, and weekend pastry chefs deep fried funnel cakes for the current and future diabetics. Across the way, beer-guzzling rednecks washed down fried mullet then cleansed their palates with a generous portion of fried ice cream. While the patrons devoured the carnival cuisine, steel guitars wailed in a sympathetic harmony with heartbroken country singers on the entertainment stage

The crowd came together as one big party when Lee Greenwood sang a tearful rendition of *God Bless the USA* followed by *Proud to be an American*. The entire mass of people united in a mass salute to the giant American flag that hung as the stage's backdrop. The milling throng of off-duty military personnel wore civilian clothes and blended with the general population. The shift-ending personnel, dressed in their BDU's, created a security nightmare for law enforcement. They were on the lookout for Cap dressed in uniform and they hoped he was still in the outdated desert pattern uniform he had on when Rebecca saw him leaving Bonn's house.

While Bonn and Mac were in route to their five o'clock meeting with Senator Diaz, Rebecca and Michelle mingled in the crowd wearing floppy straw hats, sunglasses, and nursing Bud Light bottles filled with water. If their suspicions were correct, Cap was already there, and waiting for his opportunity to take out Bonn, and anyone else who got in his way.

Sitting atop the exhibition building and overlooking the swarms of people showing their appreciation of the military men and women, Cap and Ashleigh prepared for another kind of climax.

Ashleigh scanned the crowd with the same high-powered scope with her scope while Cap used his field glasses until they were able to find the Air Force Blue sling holding Colonel Fagan's arm.

Satisfied her bullet would hit center mass this time, Ashleigh said, "The instant I hear your signal, I'll finish that bitch off and clear the way for you. Be careful soldier."

Cap felt re-energized from the previous night's carnal release and slept for the first time in days. Now, coked-up and hyper, he paced in circles while clapping his hands and saying, "Here we go; perfect, just perfect".

Bonn sat in the passenger's seat of Mac's Expedition and said, "Mac, it's just like old times, I'm honored to have you with me."

"The privilege is mine. Are you sure you're up for this? Do you have any signs of a headache coming on?" Mac asked and showed his concern by resting his hand on Bonn's shoulder.

"I've taken pills to prevent seizures, nausea, and a mild dose of painkillers. If I have any more drugs, I wouldn't be able to function. *I'm fine.*" Bonn couldn't resist using his infamous self-diagnosis to alleviate some of the tension.

Two young MPs assigned to observe all incoming vehicles, waved Mac's easily identified police SUV through the gate. When they saw Mac's passenger was wearing Orvis sunglasses with leather blinders, they came to attention and saluted. Bonn didn't realize his look had become the rage. While following the arrows to VIP Parking, they canvassed every vehicle and the space between them. When Lexi barked from her built-in K-9 cage, Bonn turned and said, "What is it girl?"

Lexi was bearing her teeth and refused to take her eyes off the roof of the main building.

"What did I tell you? Old habits are hard to break." Bonn pointed to the figure of a man wearing the current Air Force BDU's, silhouetted against the piercing blue sky.

"I'll be damned. Do you think that could be one of ours?" Mac asked.

"No, he's not a friendly. It's not the outdated camo pattern he wore when he paid me a visit, but he's our man."

"Do we keep going or call in back-up and take him down now?"

"Keep going. I'm going to have another reunion with him, and maybe a little payback."

"What if he's up there with a rifle?"

"Cap's an explosives expert and proficient with a hand gun, not a snipers rifle. He's going to come to us, trust me."

Senator Diaz's limo, adorned with both Florida State Seminole and Florida Gator flags, stood out from the other limos chauffeuring the wealthy and powerful to a side door that let them avoid the unpleasant task of waiting in line with the commoners.

A giant of a man, dressed in a black-on-black chauffeur's uniform, stood next to the Senator's black stretch limo and signaled for Mac to park his SUV a few slots away.

"Gentlemen, the Senator apologizes for not meeting you out here and wants you to meet him inside," the driver said, then left without saying another word.

"Did you get the impression he didn't want to stick around?"

"That's one less person to worry about Mac. I wonder how the girls are doing."

The lack of sophisticated communication didn't deter their confidence or ability in mounting a coordinated effort. The familiar beep of an incoming call came from Bonn's cell and he said, "Great minds think alike…, Talk to me, Darlin'."

"Baby, a uniform's coming down from the roof on the south side of the Expo building, that's right next to the woods. If you're right, it's our man. Be careful, Michelle swears she saw two bodies up there.

"Roger that, we've just parked. I'll send Mac and Lexi to check it out. Make your way to the main gate and have Michelle cover the entrance to the stage. Out," Bonn said.

"Mac, Rebecca spotted our guy man leaving the top of the building and is convinced Cap has a friend who stayed up there. Why don't you and Lexi go check it out? I'll slip into the woods and see if I can mark him, he will either try an ambush or a surprise attack out here. I guarantee he's smart enough not to get trapped in a building that's jammed with cops."

"I'll neutralize anyone up there, and then Lexi and I will join you. If you don't hear from me in ten minutes, send the Calvary," Mac said.

As Bonn disappeared into the bordering woods running the length of the parking lot and next to the building, Mac leashed Lexi and started towards the rusty metal stairs leading to the roof. They found it difficult to pass through the crowds without stopping for people who wanted to pet Lexi. Mac was already three minutes in, and he hadn't quite made it to the stairs when a Staff Sergeant, walking with the masses of people, reached to pet Lexi. She uncharacteristically snapped at his hand and raised her mane.

"I am so sorry Sergeant; I don't know what got into her," Mac said.

"Don't give it a second thought. I'm a stranger and I should have known not to pet a dog who doesn't know me."

Mac and Lexi rounded the corner of the Expo building, when he saw her bristled again and asked, "What's wrong girl?"

Straight ahead, a naked and bloodied body, still wearing metal dog tags, lay under the stairs. Balled up next to the body, was a pair of desert camo pants with a matching jacket. Mac knew instantly who owned the camo when he saw a hole in the man's forehead. Mac's phone shook as he tried to send Bonn a text. *FLYWATER! CAP ON WAY!*

Lexi led the way as they sprinted up the stairs, two steps at a time, towards the rooftop. Mac let Lexi scramble up the final few and jump on roof's ledge. As they reached the roof, an explosion, followed by the unmistakable crack of a high-powered rifle, caused all hell to break loose. The mass of people converging on the exits slowed the swarm of police and military charging in from the parking lot, displaying an astounding number of weapons.

The explosion triggered a chaos where brave enlisted personnel who tried to subdue the wrong individuals jumped undercover cops. Identifying the difference between the uniformed security forces and personnel became futile. Finding the individual who shot the woman wearing the sling was next to impossible since the shot came a split second after the explosion.

Ashleigh pulled the trigger of her M24 SWS hitting Colonel Fagan almost instantly after Cap's signal, and through her Leopold scope, she confirmed her kill. Horrified men and women, unaware of what happened, knelt next to a motionless Colonel Fagan lying on the ground.

When the explosion's shock wave hit them, Mac duck walked to safety behind the building's air conditioning unit and shockingly, found Rebecca with her finger to her lips then giving hand signals, one combatant and its location. After Rebecca's barely perceptible nod, they burst to the open, Mac went high and Rebecca went low; they both hit Ashleigh multiple times as she ran towards the stairs.

"Bitch, payback is hell." Rebecca lowered her gun when Lexi ran to the body and clamped down on a lifeless body.

"Lexi, Foei! What is going on Rebecca? Where's your sling? Where's Michelle?" Mac asked.

"Michelle? Oh-my-God! Michelle!" Rebecca sprinted to the roof's ledge and frantically searched below until she saw the crowd surrounding her friend. Michelle remained sprawled out on the ground with a quarter-size hole in her Air Force-blue sling.

"The explosion! Mac, where's Bonn?" Rebecca asked.

The desperation in her voice was contagious and brought on an air of panic in Mac, "I left him down at parking. Shit. Let's go,"

"Drop your weapons and get on the ground, now!" The orders came from two FBI agents who had scrambled to the roof. As soon as they recognized Colonel Fagan, they holstered their guns but kept their eyes on the yellow Lab displaying her teeth and ready to attack.

Cap slithered from vehicle to vehicle until he reached where he last saw Bonn and Mac split up. Free of the security rushing towards the explosion and into the crowds, Cap figured he had a precious few minutes to finish the job he started in the woods with Arnie. The area surrounding the limo was void of any sign of Bonn and he wondered if his explosive diversion had driven him away.

"Bonn, it's me! Your old buddy Cap! Come and get me."

When no one answered, he tried again. "That bitch girlfriend of yours is dead! You heard what I said, show yourself!"

Cap stood mystified as he watched a chartreuse tennis ball rolling towards him and hitting his jump boot. When he reached down to pick it up, his hand burst into a pink mist when the bullet shattered several bones as it passed through. A dull thud came from Cap's thigh, followed by a hail of bullets that shattered the windows around him. He raised his hands in surrender, and then, slowly locked them behind his head.

As he hobbled into the opening, Cap said, "You win Bonn. Stop shooting, I'm unarmed."

Bonn came out from inside Senator Diaz's limo and said, "If Rebecca is hurt, you will suffer in ways you can't imagine. Kick your gun away and get on the ground; keep your hands where I can see them. Do it, now!"

Cap kicked his gun and watched it slide across the asphalt, but he didn't unlocked his hands from behind his head.

"Get on the ground, now!" Bonn yelled.

Cap went to his knees, then rolled to the pavement and held out a small black object, no larger than a matchbox, and pointed it directly at Bonn.

"I'll see you in hell," Cap said as the limo exploded, sending Bonn into the air.

CHAPTER 37

Pieces of the limo were scattered in all directions, and the limo's burning tires filled the air with a thick black smoke. The smoke screen provided the perfect cover for the stranger who had been watching everything from the safety of her car.

The only significant evidence found, besides a string of blood drops from Cap's hand, was the electronic detonation device he used to set off his one remaining block of C-4. Investigators traced the device's serial numbers back to a local Radio Shack. The store's security tape showed an unidentified woman, wearing a baseball cap and sunglasses, paying for the detonator.

Every major airport in the Southeast went on high alert while the local hubs in Pensacola, Fort Walton Beach, and Panama City went on locked down. The numerous private airports and landing strips were either closed or under drone surveillance by orders from Commander Bentow. An updated picture of Carl A. Perkin's, taken from security cameras at the Holiday Inn Express, was circulated to every law enforcement agency, news organization, and military base within several hundred miles. The Coast Guard, Florida Fish and Game, and two rapid deployment watercraft from Pensacola Naval Air Station, patrolled the Gulf of Mexico, searching every boat along a one-hundred mile shoreline and up to one-hundred miles out at sea, without success.

One-half hour after the carnage at the annual Military Appreciation Days, Ashleigh's classic two-seater Mercedes pulled up to Senator Diaz's vacation home in a remote region of Choctawhatchee

Bay outside of Destin. The driver was weak and tried to stem the blood loss coming from his hand, by using his belt as a tourniquet. He stumbled as fast as he could behind the Senator's mansion, and staggered to the home's private pier and dock.

The massive gunmetal gray Grumman C-111 Albatross HU-16, used in Vietnam for combat rescue and extradition of Special Forces, fired its engines, then slowly built speed as it left the dock. The heavy-bellied seaplane lifted off the water on its way to Belize. By the time authorities confirmed Cap's connection to Senator Diaz, he had become a recluse resident of Belize.

Reports came in from around the world claiming Cap was working as everything from a bartender in Cancun, Mexico, to a hunting guide in South Africa. Intelligence agencies immediately placed him on their most wanted list and offered one million dollars for any information leading to his arrest on murder, attempted murder, treason, and drug charges.

Senator Diaz disappeared in the middle of the investigation that was looking into his dealings with Carl "Cap" Perkins. The authorities found a skiff adrift along the south shore of Choctawhatchee Bay that had copious amounts of the senator's blood covering the bow. A suicide note in the senator's handwriting, stuck to the boat's windshield. The dragging operation that cost the taxpayers a quarter of a million dollars, turned out to be an unsuccessful staged event.

Due to the lack of evidence or a body, Senator Diaz received an impressive and highly publicized memorial with a twenty-one gun salute. Although the F.B.I and the CIA objected, the White House sent the Vice-President to avoid any possible negative press. After all, a United States Senator had taken his own life.

CHAPTER 38

Ashleigh's bullet hit Special Agent Milton when she decoyed herself as Colonel Fagan by wearing Rebecca's customized sling and a large floppy sunhat at the annual celebration honoring the military. Fortunately, for Michelle, the sling's built-in holster holding her Sig Arms P229 pistol served as body armor when the bullet hit it.

Officially, Michelle received a reprimand for conducting an operation without clearance from her superiors. Unofficially, they praised her plan and gave her a suspension with full pay while she recovered from her injuries. The political machine in Washington put their own spin on the events by praising each other.

The Director of the FBI received a verbal reprimand from the White House for giving a CIA agent time to implement an unauthorized plan before they took the lead in the case. Behind closed doors; the CIA's Director thanked the Bureau's boss for helping Michelle and promised to bring them in on a soon-to-be high profile case involving a Mexican cartel boss, known as "El Diablo".

For the first time in her life, Michelle had true friends, and as a charter member of *Team Destin*, she didn't feel alone. The strength she felt from having friends, helped her find her smile again and gave her the courage to leave the Agency. The day her suspension ended, Michelle hand-delivered a letter of resignation and moved to Destin where she opened a private security firm with Mac and Rich. Team Destin used their high-profile contacts to make T.D. Security the most sought-after investigative firm in Florida.

Michelle spent her first month away from the government, sunbathing on the white sand beaches, sipping fine wine, and decompressing while taking her personal inventory. After the initial burn, she proudly displayed her newly bronzed body in the first annual <u>Women of Destin</u> swimsuit calendar and donated all of her Agency's black sport coats to Goodwill. Rebecca, Michelle, and Cari became Sunday regulars at the Beachfront Bar and Grill where they drank Margaritas, listened to music, and laughed at the sunburned tourists.

Ashleigh's skill as a sniper impressed the military and government investigators, but it was her choice of weapons that helped them identify her. The rifle and scope combination found next to her lifeless body, after Rebecca and Mac shot her, were army issue and reported stolen from Fort Benning. Although the serial numbers had been ground off the rifle, Ashleigh forgot about the numbers on the folding bipod she attached to the bottom rail of the sniper rifle. The gun's rail allows shooters to add optional accessories from specialized flashlights for their night vision goggles, to telescoping shooting sticks used to stabilize the rifle when taking a shot.

Ashleigh's personal items included a military coin. Also called a "challenge coin", it bore an insignia of an elite group of military specialists. The coin presented to her in recognition of her membership into that organization, all of whom had at one time, performed heroically in combat.

Serving as a military-trained assassin, Ashleigh eliminated several of Saddam's generals and two Iranian warlords. The existence of the classified operation and her accomplishments went unsung to the public and press.

The coin in her possession bore the emblem of the army's 1st Cavalry Division on one side; the coin was given to her by the commander of her unit during Operation Desert Storm. She received the coin at an undisclosed forward position in Iraq, in recognition of her performance as a member of an elite four-man sniper team during the initial surge into Bagdad. Ashleigh, the first female presented such a coin, regretfully accepted it as the lone survivor of the team.

The Commander of the 1st Cavalry Division in Iraq was none other than General Charles Fagan. His relationship with Ashleigh resumed when they returned from deployment and General Fagan accepted the position of Garrison Commander at Fort Benning. While Ashleigh had to fly back from Iraq in an Air Force transport, Charles relaxed on a private jet filled with politicians that included Senator Diaz and news reporters, returning from a PR trip to the frontlines.

Just as their relationship began to bloom, Ashleigh received orders to live "Dark" with rewritten records that showed she had been 'discharged with honors'. She relocated to Mexico, and enrolled in nursing school, which meant her romance with Charles was going to be on hold until she received new orders to return to service.

At first, investigators believed it to be a coincidence that both Rebecca and Ashleigh had lived at Fort Benning while General Fagan served as Post Commander. A review of Ashleigh's travel records showed she and Charles were together, one year before Rebecca filed for divorce.

Ashleigh made bi-monthly flights back to Georgia, where she stayed at the posh St. Regis-Atlanta hotel, in a room already occupied by General Fagan. Although there were government records of her flights between Mexico and the States, nothing existed in her records about her life in Mexico.

While Ashleigh attended nursing school at the University of Guadalajara, a reputed drug kingpin of the Sinaloa Cartel fell seriously ill. He ended up at the University Center of Health Sciences, in a wing built with drug money donated by the cartel.

Ashleigh happened to be on rounds with other graduate students when he came in for evaluation, while surrounded by men who were obviously armed and there to protect him. Ashleigh asked about the new patient and learned about the notorious El Diablo; Ashleigh knew she had to meet him.

She "borrowed" a white lab coat and stethoscope, grabbed a clipboard, and entered Armando's room without knocking. Once his men put away their guns, she examined him for something she saw when they brought him into the hospital. It didn't take long for her to come up with the diagnosis, arsenic poisoning.

"Do you see the slight discoloration and white lines running across his fingernails?" Ashleigh asked the bodyguards. "That is a symptom known as 'Mees lines', it's a classic sign of arsenic poisoning. He's going to need blood transfusions immediately."

Hemodialysis performed on the drug boss saved his life and Ashleigh became a hero to the cartel. One person didn't think of her as a hero, the CIA agent who worked as his private chef and had to be extracted to avoid a certain death by execution. The agency's new plan included, Ashleigh applying for the position of his personal nurse, befriending the cartel boss, and act as a bodyguard during his recovery. Her altered military records showed her as retired Army, with a sharpshooter designation, and currently pursuing a new career in nursing.

Just as the agency suspected, the cartel did a background check and actually learned the truth without knowing she was undercover until called for service. After finishing her academic requirements, Mr. Ramirez had a short conversation with the hospital's CEO and Ashleigh's employment started immediately. She assumed the duties as his personal nurse, bodyguard, and more importantly as "mole" during his stay.

When Armando Ramirez left the hospital and returned to his hacienda, the head of his security team tried to rape Ashleigh while his boss was heavily sedated and asleep. She crushed his trachea with one blow, snapped his neck, and then shot him twice. One shot to the throat covered up the broken neck and she finished with a single shot through the heart, for good measure.

Ashleigh's handler in the States gave her the personal number of the Tijuana Cartel's boss and used the would-be rapists' cell phone to call the rival cartel's boss. When the drug lord answered her call,

Ashleigh disconnected. Just as she predicted, a call came back to the bodyguard's phone, leaving it in the phone's call history. When confronted by Mr. Ramirez for killing his bodyguard, Ashleigh insisted she overheard his head of security having a conversation about killing him, and when she tried to slip out of the house undetected, he spotted her and threatened to kill her, so she shot him.

Her story wasn't believed until Mr. Ramirez personally went through the bodyguard's phone and found the calls Ashleigh had made and received from his arch nemesis. From that day forward, one of Mexico most notorious drug lord considered Ashleigh his "guardian angel" and the only person, besides his nephew in Florida that he truly trusted. Following Ashleigh's diagnosis, and for killing his former bodyguard, he made a deposit of one million dollars into an account for her. She never disclosed the reward to her handlers and continued working in the joint Military-CIA operation, undetected as an operative. The information she compiled on the inner workings of the cartel's operation proved to be invaluable. Whenever the Mexican authorities shut down an operation, he blamed his former bodyguard and never suspected Ashleigh.

Her time with the leader of the Sinaloa Cartel allowed her to live the life of the rich and famous. She bonded with the cartel's boss, stopped giving information on his organization, and completely broke contact with her handler. She realized the money she could earn working for the cartel, dwarfed her military pay. Her new plan was to make enough money to retire and go into business with Charles at her side.

During her employment with the cartel, she used her military training as a sharpshooter, to eliminate several of his enemies. The single 600-yard shots she took were a first in the war between the cartels. The distances she was shooting from kept her location a mystery and earned her the nickname, "El Fantasma". Everyone thought "the ghost" had to be a man since no one considered the possibility a woman could make shots of that distance.

To maintain her cover, Ashleigh decided to complete her nurse's surgical training during the day and do her work for the cartel on her days off. At graduation, Ashleigh kissed her boss on the cheek, proclaimed her loyalty to him, and revealed she would be leaving. Ashleigh assured him, she would always be at his calling. When she made the commitment to "help" him whenever he needed her services, he agreed to let her go. She called Charles with the good news and asked him to help her get a job at the Fort Benning hospital. He used his influence to grant her request with the intention of using her skills to eliminate his wife. Months before she moved to Florida, Ashleigh already had Rebecca in her sights, literally.

One afternoon, during a surprise visit to her husband's office, Rebecca caught Charles in an embrace with a strange woman.

"Excuse me, am I interrupting something important?"

"Rebecca! No, you're not…well sort of…I mean, this is Captain Smit. She served with me in Iraq…I was thanking her for service and welcoming her back. Ashleigh, I would like you to meet my wife, Colonel Rebecca Fagan," Charles said.

Ashleigh snapped to attention when she heard Rebecca's rank, then relaxed when she saw Rebecca's Air Force BDUs.

"Colonel…, Mrs. Fagan, it's nice to meet you. I wanted to thank General Fagan for the combat award he presented to me."

Ashleigh pulled out her coin and showed it to Rebecca. The explanation led Rebecca to believe their embrace was nothing more than a hug by two people who had served together. The close call prompted Ashleigh to share her plan to use her skills as a sniper and shoot Rebecca from a safe distance.

"I'll wait until you think the time is right."

"You're right, undetected is the only way this is going to work. Thank you 'Ash', I'll be in touch." Charles said and embraced her one more time.

Over the following months, Ashleigh's impatience grew and if she hadn't made the promise not to wait until *he* gave the order, Rebecca wouldn't have made it to Florida.

At the time of the embrace, Ashleigh had her short dark hair under her army cap, and never made direct eye contact with Rebecca. When they met again at the hospital in Fort Walton Beach, she had light-colored hair with long flowing strawberry-blond extensions and was convinced Rebecca didn't recognize her.

General Fagan used his trips to Mexico to see Ashleigh, and hide as many assets as he could before he filed for divorce. He counted on Ashleigh's skills to avoid years of alimony and keep his financial losses at a minimum. His decision to keep it amiable would make it appear as though someone killed Rebecca for her role in the investigation of the F-22, and thereby eliminate him as a suspect.

When Rebecca received her assignment as the lead investigator in the case, she didn't know Charles had been offered a position with the defense contracting company that lost the initial bid for the jet's production. Charles feared Rebecca would jeopardize his post-retirement job offer and gave permission to proceed, but she would have to follow Rebecca to Florida.

Ashleigh had her pick of openings for nurses in the Florida Panhandle, and accepted a Surgical Nurse position at Okaloosa Regional.

PART THREE

DARLIN'

CHAPTER 39

T he last thing Rebecca wanted to do alone, was attend the Commander's Christmas Ball at Eglin, and it showed. She couldn't stop thinking about Bonn who had been laying in a coma for six weeks from the injuries he sustained when Senator Diaz' limo exploded. Instead of putting on an evening gown and wearing her collection of jewelry, she came in her full dress military uniform, adorned with her medals. In true military form, she entered the receiving line of dignitaries, politicians, and officers with her shoulders back and stepped in perfect time. The stern look on her face let everyone know she was not just a woman in uniform, they were seeing a veteran warrior. Her eyes had the intense and sometimes faraway look seen in the eyes of every soldier, sailor and pilot who experienced the horrors of war. Rebecca held her gaze straight-ahead, as she sat at the head table, and struggled to hide the sadness growing with each day Bonn remained in a coma. Already filled with regret, she pushed her food around without taking a bite, while she tried to think of an excuse to leave. Her answer came when she received a text message from Dr. Benson.

Rebecca arrived at the hospital and headed straight for Bonn's room to meet with Dr. Benson. The sound of her heals on the polished tile floor cracked like a gunshot as it echoed off the walls. Ahead, standing at attention, were two armed men in battledress uniform. Although the city and county police departments objected to a support role, a call from the Governor's office ended any speculation about the Air Force's influence.

"At ease," Colonel Fagan said after giving them a smart salute. The guards spread their stance with clasped hands behind their backs and appeared to be more 'at attention' than 'at ease'.

"Is there anyone with him?" she asked.

"Yes ma'am, Detective McCain and Dr. Benson are with the general, Ma'am".

Rebecca eased the door to Bonn's room open and heard, "Mac, it is nothing short of miraculous he survived, it's the secondary complications that have me worried. That's why we put him a medically-induced coma; it will give him time to recover from the trauma."

"Susan, I got your text. How is he doing?"

"Besides looking like hell, he's going to make it. I can't remember anyone who fought to survive the way he has, and I wouldn't be surprised if in a few days, he tells us he's 'fine' and wants to go home."

"I'll tell the security detail outside to shoot him if he tries to leave," Rebecca joked.

"I'm not sure they could stop him if he really wanted to get out of here," Mac said.

"Rebecca, I'm glad you got my message and came to see him. We put him in the medical coma for his own good, and now…, his vitals are normal and the only way we'll know how much damage has been done, is to wake him." Susan said.

"What if he doesn't wake up?" Rebecca asked.

"He'll wake up, I'm sure of it. I stopped the drugs that were keeping him under. It's going to take awhile for the barbiturates to wear off, but his blood pressure is already starting to get back to normal. We never know how long it's going to take; you need to be prepared for when he comes around."

"Prepared for what?" Mac and Rebecca asked in unison.

"It's not unusual for the patient to wake up confused and a little frightened. They don't know what's happening or why they're in a hospital. In addition, it takes awhile for the drugs to get out of their system before their short-term memory returns. We'll have to wait and see."

"Susan, what do we do if he's confused and begins asking questions?" Mac asked.

"Tell him the truth without overloading him with too much information all at once. Initially, we'll give him some of the basic information when he asks the normal questions. I'll give him some time to become more coherent, and then I'll answer his questions as he asks them." Susan paused and held up a finger to them wait before asking her anything else.

"But…, there is one other thing you need to be aware of when he comes around," Susan said without a hint of trepidation in her voice.

"Will he forget who I am?" Rebecca feared losing Bonn again and ignored Susan's request to wait.

"No, no, no. I didn't mean to alarm you. Although it's rare for a patient to have a degree of amnesia from the drugs used to put them in the coma, it does happen, it's almost always temporary." Susan began to wonder if she was sharing too much about Bonn's condition.

"Amnesia?" Rebecca asked.

"Rebecca, that's not what I wanted to say. Occasionally, they have dreams that they feel were so real, they insist the dreams had to be premonitions of something that's going to happen. *We* know they were only dreams, but the patient has a hard time shaking off the memories of it, almost to the point of it becoming an obsession."

Mac started to worry and said, "I guess I've been a little naïve thinking he would wake up and be right back to ornery old Bonn."

"Hold it big boy; I said he *might* have some of these symptoms. He could also just be groggy for awhile before he starts bossing us around." Susan's observation brought out a stress-relieving chuckle from both Mac and Rebecca.

"What did you mean when you said he'll ask the 'normal' questions when he wakes up?"

"He'll want to know: Where he is, why he's here, when he will get out, *and* when he'll get out. If he keeps asking when he can leave, I'll know he's doing well and turn him loose."

Almost on cue, a moan came from Bonn followed by a few a few twitches of his fingers. Susan immediately went into her physician's role and instinctively plugged in her stethoscope. While checking his pulse with one hand and placing the scope's chest piece at various locations, she tried to coax him awake.

"Bonn, wake up. General, this is Dr. Benson. Rebecca and Mac are here. Can you open your eyes just a little?"

"Hi baby. It's time to get up. Can you open your eyes for me?" Rebecca's voice trembled as she fought back tears.

Susan turned up the oxygen and watched Bonn's eyes open.

"Hello General…it's Dr. Benson. Everything is okay. Rebecca and Mac are here. Just take a few deep breaths and relax."

Bonn looked at her with a confused expression, exactly as Susan had described. A shiver of fear went through Mac and Rebecca when he didn't respond. A few minutes of slow, deep breathing, with his eyes closed, seemed to awaken his entire body as he pointed his toes, extended his fingers, and arched his back. Rebecca had seen him stretch the same way every morning when he woke up. A smile appeared on her face for the first time in weeks.

In a weak and slightly raspy voice Bonn whispered, "Waaerr." Susan scooped a few ice chips from a cup with a plastic spoon and eased them towards Bonn's parched lips. It only took a few seconds for him to raise his chin and open his mouth, like a baby bird.

"Welcome back. I want you to suck on those ice chips nice and slow until they melt. We don't want you choking, doctor's orders."

A few clearings of his throat later, Bonn spoke in a much clearer voice. "Darlin'…, Mac." Hearing their names opened a floodgate of tears.

"Hey buddy, it's good to see you." Mac, barely able to speak, needed his own ice chips.

Rebecca's tears were flowing in relief; she gently touched her lips against his and whispered, "Hi baby."

It didn't matter how many times Mac wiped away his tears; they were replaced with fresh ones. Seeing the vulnerable side of Mac tugged at Susan's heart. Seeing Mac express true feelings for his friend, confirmed her decision to be with him, a good one. Following

Rebecca's lead, Susan leaned into Mac, and with a loving smile, whispered in his ear, "Hi baby".

Rebecca was surprised to hear *her* line used by the normally reserved Dr. Benson. Mac had been her strength during Bonn's first hospital stay and after her encounter with a sniper. Mac's presence helped alleviate the anxiety she had to endure while waiting to see if Bonn would survive. Susan, in her own way, had given her emotional support as well; Rebecca gave *Susan*, a smiling nod of approval for calling Mac, "baby".

"What happened? I'm back in here," Bonn asked his first "normal" question, just as Susan predicted.

Susan prodded Mac to answer the question. "You had it out with Cap…, again. Do you remember?"

Bonn never broke his eye contact with Mac during a minute of silence. Everyone waited, for what seemed like an eternity, to see if the coma affected Bonn's memory.

Bonn didn't give a hint if he remembered anything. It was obvious his mind reeled as he tried to process the simple question. The staccato sound of him trying to clear his throat preceded a simple and raspy request, "Ice".

Rebecca started shaking when she tried to get the crushed ice out of the Styrofoam cup.

"Are you okay?"

Bonn nodded and gave her the same Cheshire cat grin he wore when he awoke during his first hospital visit. He didn't want to send mixed signals by delaying a direct answer to her question, and gave his classic response, "I'm fine."

"Whenever I ask you how you're doing, you always say 'I'm fine'. You've said it so many times I'm going to quit asking. Since you're fine, I'm going to go back to the house, get out of this uniform, and take a long hot bubble bath. I'll be back later."

Rebecca couldn't conceal her excitement and relief, and Bonn couldn't hide the fact he remembered that whenever Rebecca took a hot bubble bath, she planned to be close to him.

As she headed towards the door, she added, "Oh yeah, I forgot; I also need to feed the puppy."

"Hold it right there. You're going to feed the puppy? What puppy?" Bonn wondered if 'puppy' was a code word he couldn't remember or if he forgot what it meant.

Mac pulled his phone out, and after looking at it said, "Got to go, it's the Chief. I'll see all of you later," He smiled at Rebecca, then Susan, and disappeared out the door.

"Bonn, I need to feed *our* puppy."

"What do you mean *our* puppy? We don't have a puppy."

"We do now. Do you remember when Lexi discovered bombs under your house? Well, she was carrying a 'singleton' in her belly. When Mac got her from the Navy Seal at Pensacola NAS, no one knew his top stud dog, a Belgium Malinois, bred her. Mac offered to give 'Doe' to *us* when she weaned him. It felt the right thing to do, and now, *we* have a puppy."

"We have a half-Labrador, half-Malinois puppy named 'Dough'? Like money or bread?" Bonn asked with the pride of a new daddy.

"It's neither; it's like John D...O...E, Doe. I figured we would name him when you got out of the hospital. Right now, he's a little confused by his name. I didn't understand the confusion I was causing every time I said 'No' until I started housebreaking him. When I yelled, 'NO Doe', he thought I called his name and came running to me. We need to name him quickly; he's going through an identity crisis." Rebecca found the best of a few dozen pictures of Doe on her phone, and showed them to Bonn.

"He's a white fur ball with long hair. Lexi is blonde, Belgium Malinois look like a German Sheppard. Are you sure about the father?"

Rebecca laughed and said, "I wasn't there for the main event. If you want, we can have a paternity test done when you get back home."

Giddy from relief, Rebecca sashayed out of the room, causing Bonn's heart monitor to beep rapidly as he enjoyed the rear-view exit she gave him.

"She felt like it was the thing to do? Get a puppy? I think she would have killed me if I hadn't come out of the coma. Whew…, I wonder what else she did for *us*. I have some catching-up to do."

Susan didn't feel the time was right for her to tell him, "what else" Rebecca had done during his two months in a coma; he would eventually find out, she marked her territory. Every female who had contact with him, including Mary the hospital greeter, understood Bonn was in a committed relationship with Colonel Fagan. Rebecca used a black permanent marker and drew her own custom-made tattoo on his arm, the word, **Darlin'**, was large; it could be seen across the room.

CHAPTER 40

The good news, the coma didn't seem to have any major residual effect on Bonn's body. The bad news, his mind constantly churned as he tried to comprehend the events leading up to the present. Not only did it frustrate him, it brought on a depression that concerned Susan greatly.

The relentless questions he asked, were grating on everyone's nerves, until the frantic episodes turned to sadness and Bonn would go silent. Surprisingly, his memory of the fateful day and the events leading up to Senator Diaz's limo exploding was spot-on. Beyond that terrible day, so many things had happened while he recovered in a coma; the answers to all his questions only brought more questions.

Bonn became restless and bored when Mac and Rebecca were at work, and he sat alone in his bed. Dr. Benson took the opportunity during their absence, to give him every test she could think of, mainly to keep him occupied and quiet. Although the results were better than expected, he followed the pattern Susan predicted.

"*When* can I go home?" Bonn asked.

"You are still in serious condition; let's give your body a little more time to heal."

"I promise you, I would be better off at my house…, surrounded by…my things."

"Bonn, I'm not sure Rebecca would appreciate you calling her a *thing*." Dr. Benson smiled knowingly and gave him a wink.

The nurses taking care of him were emphatic when they heard his constant complaining; in private, they said he was worse than the kids on the pediatric floor were. The payback for his orneriness came from the running joke played on him, the tattoo Rebecca drew on his arm with permanent ink. The nurses responsible for Bonn's care knew it would eventually wear off, and made sure to avoid it during in-bed, bath time.

"Doc, I'm remembering more everyday but for the life of me I can't remember getting this tattoo," Bonn said while tracing the letters with his finger. Although he liked it, **Darlin'** wasn't the kind of tattoo he envisioned, if he ever decided to get one.

Dr. Benson continued with the ruse and said, "It's so sweet of you to have that done, but I'll never understand why anyone would want to disfigure their body with tattoos."

As Bonn stared in disbelief, it took every bit of restraint for her to keep from bursting out in laughter.

"Well, some of those meds you were taking a few months back were pretty strong; I guess they could cause a type of amnesia. You didn't drink anything while you were taking them did you?"

"I don't drink. I thought you knew that."

She couldn't resist the opportunity to twist the knife one more time and said, "I never took you as the kind of guy who would get a tattoo. Why would you permanently scar your skin?"

Bonn turned bright red and just lowered his head, shaking it slowly, ashamed of what he did. Susan hoped when he started taking showers on his own, the tattoo didn't fade too fast.

"General, there is something I would like to talk to you about."

"Doc, please call me Bonn."

"Bonn, please call me Susan. This is so weird. I had the same conversation with Mac. He also wanted me to call him by his first name; the two of you are so much alike, it's scary."

"Susan…, I've never seen Mac as happy as he's been since he started dating you. If I didn't know better, I would think he took some of my meds. He is my closest friend and there isn't anyone, I trust or respect more than Mac. I think you are good for him but…,"

She was caught off-guard by Bonn's hesitation, and the use of the word "but". Susan stiffened, and waited in anticipation for whatever bombshell she was getting ready to hear.

"But…, I don't know if he should be with anyone who would take advantage of a defenseless, injured, and wonderful person like me."

Confused and taken aback, Susan wondered if she had heard him correctly.

"What? Who are you talking about?"

"I'm talking about *you*, Susan."

"Me? You think I'm taking advantage of you? What are talking about?"

"I'm talking about my tattoo. The very first day I woke up from the coma, I could smell the ink from a *Sharpie*. I wanted to see how far everyone would take Rebecca's little joke." Bonn started laughing until it hurt so bad he had to cover his face with a pillow so he wouldn't see Susan's expression.

"Oh…my…God," Susan said. "I guess I deserved that, I should have known you would figure it out. Just so you know, I promised Rebecca I wouldn't say anything."

"I won't let her know, if you don't tell her that I've known all this time. To use her expression "Payback is hell", and I'm not done paying her back. All kidding aside, I really like you and so does Mac. You're the best thing that has happened to him in a long time."

"I am so glad to hear you say that, I like you too. But…"

"But? That's my line," Bonn said.

"But… I don't *like* Mac, I love him. There, I've said it, I love him. I love who he is, not the military hero or detective. Beneath that hardened exterior is the sweetest man I've ever met."

Susan put her clipboard in front of her face and said, "There's one more thing. Mac will kill me if he finds out I told you. His flashbacks of Vietnam disappeared after we…consummated our relationship." Then she peeked over the top of clipboard and added, "multiple times".

"Now I know why he has been acting like a prepubescent little boy and sucks in his stomach every time you're around."

"While you've been here taking it easy in a coma, something else happened that I hope you approve of as well, Mac moved in with me. It feels so right. I've never had anyone who made me feel as safe as he does."

"You're telling me, I've lost my neighbor?"

"You can come visit him anytime you want."

"I can't believe he didn't tell me."

"That's my fault. I asked him not to overload you with too many personal changes that happened while you were hibernating. There's one more thing, this is as good as time as any…he left the police department and went into business with Agent Milton."

"He did what? There is no way he…wait a minute, that would mean Michelle is no longer with the Agency! Where is he anyway? Now that I think about it, I haven't seen either one of them for a couple of days."

"Mac came by the other night to discuss it, you were asleep. He's on a business trip for a few days. He left you a letter updating you on everything that has happened while you were incapacitated. He's been keeping a journal on your case and Colonel Fagan's; it helped him with his stress. He shared some of what he's writing with me, I have to tell you, it scares the hell out of me. What I've read is more like a case study of Cap and Ashleigh. There are all kinds of documents with his journal, stamped *Classified*. He calls the journal, his 'therapist'. I think writing helps him organize his thoughts and make sense of everything that happened. Right before he left on his trip, he made a copy for you. When he handed it to me, he said, 'just-in-case'".

"Susan, did you ask Mac what that meant?"

"You know better than anyone what it means; he uses homonyms all the time, expects everyone to get what he's trying to say. He emphasized the word '*just*'. Susan paused.

"I will quote *his* words when he gave the envelope to me, 'you know how Bonn is when he's taking all those meds'; he could get spaced out and forget where he put it'.

When Bonn didn't speak, Susan continued, "You were still in a coma, and he *told* me to give it to Rebecca for safe-keeping until you felt better. Mac is usually so polite and always asks me to do things; he never tells me to do anything. The change in his demeanor scared me."

"After you get off work, will you go get it from Rebecca and bring it to me?"

"I can do better than that, I brought it with me to give to her tonight, and I don't think there's any reason not to give it to you now. I'll be right back, don't leave," Susan said, but she wasn't totally kidding about Bonn going anywhere.

A few minutes later, she returned holding a bulging manila envelope with *FLYWATER* boldly written and underlined across the front.

"You call this a letter?" Bonn put it flat on his palm and pretended to be checking its weight.

"I think he had a lot on his mind." Susan said.

"He told me if anything happened to you before you had a chance to read it, Agent Milton and Colonel Fagan would know what to do. Something tells me, whatever is in that envelope is…dangerous. I know this might sound selfish, but I hope Michelle can take care of any problems before Mac comes back."

"Speaking of Michelle, what is she doing?" Bonn asked.

"She and Rich are holding down the business while Mac's away. She has been here a couple of times, and you have either been asleep or gone for tests. She wanted talk with you about the day you were injured."

"Are you talking about Rich, the hospital's security guard? Hey, what happened to Cap when the limo exploded? What about Michelle and Rebecca's plan to get Ashleigh, did it work? Did they get her?" Bonn asked while clenching and unclenching his fist.

Susan decided, after watching Bonn's body language, and the speed at which he asked questions, he needed something besides a sedative. Instead of medicating him, she unclipped her cell phone from her clipboard and dialed.

"Who are you calling?"

"I think your better half needs to come and see you. She should be the one to fill you in on what she knows. The answers you're looking for may be in that envelope, I don't know. You have a lot of questions and I don't have the answers, she will."

Susan spoke with Rebecca while Bonn stared at the envelope and tapped the word *FLYWATER*, letter by letter, with his finger.

"No, he's doing very well. I won't be giving him anything to help him sleep for a few hours if you would like to come see him. I'll let him know. I'll see you later."

"Bonn, I'll be back in a few hours to check on you before I call it a day. Enjoy your dinner tonight, I've ordered some solid foods for you. It's not hamburgers and fries, it's better than the mush you've been getting for dinner. Rebbeca will be here later and wanted me to tell you, she would be 'all clean from her bath and wearing your favorite perfume'. I want the two of you to behave yourselves," Susan warned with a coy smile on her face.

Rebecca gathered, the call from Susan wasn't a cordial request to come to Bonn's room and assumed she would find out what Susan wanted to say, but didn't. The entire drive there, Rebecca checked her hair and makeup in the mirror, just as she did on their first date. Before walking into the hospital, she dabbed a drop of Bonn's favorite perfume on her wrists and rubbed them together. Then, "Darlin'" undid one extra button on her blouse and dabbed a drop on her chest.

Mary wasn't at her station when she entered the hospital, as irritating as Mary could be; Rebecca felt a twinge of disappointment. In her opinion, a smiling face, greeting people at a place as depressing as a hospital, had to be better than no one at all. Rebecca headed straight for the bank of elevators that Mary had directed her to on her first visit and when the doors to the elevator opened, David Crain let go of his secretary's hand when he saw Rebecca.

"Colonel, it's good to see you again. I heard General Bonner is awake…uh, out of his coma. You remember Tiffany, my receptionist?" Dave asked.

"Yes, it's good to see you again Tiffany." Rebecca couldn't remember if she ever knew her name, she would always be Dave's "Valley Girl".

"It's *like*, good to see you too," Tiffany said as a painful reminder of their first encounter.

"Have a good evening Colonel. Let me know if there is anything I can do for you," Dave said.

"If I need anything, I'll have Mary get it for me when she gets back. I'm sure you have more important things to do," Rebecca said in jest and looked directly at Tiffany.

Dave was oblivious to the implication about Tiffany when he asked, "Mary?"

Bonn blinked awake from an unintentional short nap he took while waiting on Rebecca and stretched the way he always did when waking up. The night-lights Susan left on, gave the room an ambiance conducive to sleep, but kept it bright enough for nurses and doctors to make their rounds without waking the patient. It had been an hour after his first meal of solid food and his stomach rumbled for more.

Although he never enjoyed the taste of boiled chicken breast, it was real food and not like the gruel, he had been eating. He closed his eyes and fantasized about cheeseburgers, grouper sandwiches, a T-bone steak and French fries. He caught himself drifting off and opened his eyes to the sight of a friendly, silver-haired candy striper; he assumed she had come to get his dinner tray.

"Please give my compliments to the chef. The chicken's great," Bonn said as he pushed the rolling table holding his emptied tray towards the aging volunteer.

"Oh my, I am so sorry if I woke you Sweetie. I'm glad you enjoyed your dinner. Is there anything else I can get you?"

"As a matter of fact, would you be so kind as to get me a pen and some paper to write on? I have a few ideas on how to catch the man who did this to me, and I want to put them on paper before I forget them. I'm still a little groggy from all of the medication."

"I don't think so, there's no need for you to write them down. In fact, no one cares what you think. As much as I would love to continue this little chat with you, I think it would be a waste of time.

So, why don't you be a good boy and give me whatever it is that detective friend of yours left for you," she said.

"How do you know about…?" Bonn didn't have time to react to the strange request made by the geriatric volunteer; he saw the business end of a silencer, inches from his face.

"Sweetie, if you think I will let you harm my baby boy, you are terribly mistaken." Mary sounded like a cold-blooded killer.

Under the glow of the dim lights, Bonn couldn't see her face clearly but she saw the glinting name badge with the name **Mary** clearly embossed on it and said, "I'm going to assume, you're Carl's mother. Is that right, Mrs. Perkins?"

"That's right General Bonner, and now it's time to pay for what you did to my son. You ruined his life. You made him a killer the day you decided to be a traitor. I've heard the story so many times, I have it memorized. He told me how you gave him up to the FBI back in college to save your own ass, and you were the reason for his arrest. You were able to finish your education at the Air Force Academy; Carl got the choice of going to prison or the Army. He died inside over there, and now, you're going to die."

The soft night light became slightly brighter when a vertical line of light appeared behind Mary, and Bonn asked, "Mrs. Perkins, would you mind turning on the light behind my bed? I want to see the face of my killer before I die."

Mary laughed at Bonn's request and pulled the cord swaying from the florescent light behind his bed. The split-second distraction gave Rebecca enough time to put a perfectly placed round into Mary's head, plus three more to her chest while she was falling.

Rebecca kicked Mary's gun across the floor, more as a response to her training, than for any concern about Mary's ability to retrieve it and shoot.

"Are you okay?" Rebecca asked, but she had to watch Bonn's lips for an answer. Bonn, unable to hear anything either, just nodded. The percussion of four shots coming from Rebecca's 40-caliber Glock fired in his room left them temporarily unable to hear above the ringing in their ears.

The two military guards who let the kind, gray-haired lady into Bonn's room, rushed in with guns drawn. The bloody collage of skin and hair plastered on the wall, was proof positive, Mary was no longer a threat.

After moving Bonn to a temporary room, the forensics team photographed Mary's body, including the carnage. Agent Milton wanted to see if she could use the photos of his mother to root out Cap. Even though every agency wanted to question Bonn about what happened, Dr. Benson, who had gone home and returned, cleared the room.

"Do you think the two of you can make it through the rest of the night without any more drama? I have to get a few hours sleep before my first surgery in the morning."

Bonn's sarcasm returned as Susan walked out. "Yes Ma'am, we promise to do our best, not to be attacked by any more insane killers."

Rebecca displayed her own ability to match Bonn's cynicism by saying, "I'm going to get a private security detail to camp out *in* your room. First, it's you, then it's me; now, you...*again!* I don't want another turn; I'm starting to think people don't like us."

"Don't worry about me. I'm going to be released in a couple of days, until then, I want you to bring me my 9 millimeter. I don't trust anyone, especially after a little ol' lady tried to take me out. Rebecca, you and I both know Cap isn't going to be very happy when he finds out his mother is dead, he may decide to pay me a visit."

"Mary is Cap's mother, I can't believe it! I just remembered something that happened when you were here after Cap shot you; she walked into your room while I was waiting for you to wake up. She pretended to be there to see if I wanted some coffee or tea. I realize now, a 'greeter' had no business being in your room, she intended to kill you then. How could I have missed it? That's a damn rookie mistake!"

"Don't be so hard on yourself. You were stressed, and she doesn't look like a killer. By the way, I can see you took the advice I gave you years ago. Your aim and speed is much improved from the first time I saw you shoot at the gun range." Bonn waited to see if she remembered.

"I will never forget that day, you were right. Don't change the subject, let's get back to *her*. How did you figure out she is...was, Cap's mother."

"She told me her baby boy has been trying to kill me because the thought I turned him in to the FBI when we were in college. She let me know, I was the reason he had to go to Vietnam. She also insinuated he became a psychopath because of me. There is one thing I haven't figured out, she also knew about this..." Bonn reached under his covers and brought out the manila envelope Mac had left for him.

"What's that?"

"It's something Mac left for me before he went out of town. He *told* Susan to give it to you if I wasn't better. She said I was doing great and decided to give it to me tonight. We were alone when she handed it to me, yet, somehow, Mary knew I had it, and she wanted it. How is that possible? I didn't tell her, and there wouldn't be any reason for Doc to tell her...I think there were 'ears' in my room."

"Let's go and see what we can find."

After a heated discussion with the representatives controlling the crime scene, Bonn and Rebecca promised they wouldn't jeopardize the integrity of the scene and agreed to have one of the agents accompany them in the room. Against their better judgment, and mostly likely their orders, the M.P.'s blocking the entrance into Bonn's room allowed the three of them to go under the yellow crime scene tape.

Rebecca asked, "Okay, where would be the best place to hide a small listening device?"

Bonn pointed to the garden of delivered flowers that had taken over one end of his room and said, "What are the chances there are two bouquets exactly the same?"

He answered his own question when he wheeled himself straight to them and picked up a potted plant holding a single dark red flower surrounded with the tiny "Babies Breath" flowers used as fillers in most arrangements. A cursory examination, revealed a "bug", which the agent wrapped in his handkerchief.

"There's another arrangement exactly like it, how did you know it was in that particular one?" Rebecca asked.

"I learned about that flower early in my career when I was stationed in Japan…that is a Red Spider Lily, they're known as the flower of death. It's the only one that doesn't have a message card. Anyone who has ever served in Japan, or has been there for any length of time, could have known the symbolism and sent it. I have a feeling they were from Cap or his mother. The other one has a card with it, let's see who sent it," Bonn said.

"They're from me, baby. I saw them at a high-end flower shop in the mall and brought them in a few days ago. You were in radiology having your picture taken, so, I just left them. I thought you read the card and just forgot to mention you got them. I didn't want to say anything, in case…" Rebecca wasn't sure if she should continue with her explanation.

"In case…I have some memory loss? You're right darlin', my memory isn't all there, but I did see them and I read your card. I'm sorry I forgot to thank you. When I woke up the next morning and saw another one just like yours, I just figured I forgot there were two delivered."

The agent's head turned from Bonn to the Rebecca as they talked, and then said to Bonn, "Your tattoo. I get it now."

"You 'get' what, my tattoo? Oh, right…I call Colonel Fagan 'Darlin', we're a couple. It's not a secret. The tattoo is another thing that I don't remember getting. I'm so fortunate to have someone in my life looking out for me so I don't do anything foolish that might *permanently* affect me. Isn't that right, 'Darlin'?" Bonn looked up and glared at Rebecca.

"How long have you been playing me?" Rebecca smacked him on arm when she realized the joke was on her.

"The second I detected the scent of Sharpie ink. I love that smell. Be careful, you might wake up one morning and have your own tattoo somewhere you might not want it. Payback is hell."

"What do you mean have my own tattoo? You better not; do you hear me? You have that stupid grin on your face," Rebecca said and pinched him.

"Then, you owe me, and I want to collect the first night I get out of here. I know something else; you're wearing my favorite perfume," Bonn said and put his finger on her lips then traced a line down her neck and stopped at the button she left undone, just for him.

The agent cleared his throat. "Why don't we go back to your room…I mean *you* go back…*we* will go back, and *I'll* leave…hell, I don't know what I mean! Let's go and I'll get a forensic team in here." The guards were puzzled why only Colonel Fagan and Bonn were laughing when they came out of the room; the agent shielded his eyes with his hands.

Bonn received a suite on the hospice floor, and both adjoining rooms emptied, to isolate him. Armed guards manned the door, as well as every possible entrance to the floor and hospital. Members of Eglin's elite Security team, on orders from Commander Bentow, guarded the hospital's perimeter. The press wasn't allowed in the hospital and anyone not on staff had to be cleared to see him.

ORMC hoped to salvage its reputation from the political and public relations nightmare caused by the Perkin's family, and they had to find a way to get the press on back on their side.

Although the initial press interviews were done by the Hospital Administrator, David Crain, he was replaced as the official spokesman when he made an off-camera comment that played on every news program and was a front-page headline throughout the print media, "The Air Force has the toughest bitches in the military; Colonel Fagan gave Mary Perkins what she deserved."

Rebecca didn't have a problem with his politically incorrect comment, she actually agreed with his assessment. The comment set off a dispute when a male Army P.A. Chief *and* a female Marine spokesperson claimed to have the 'tougher bitches'. The Army P.A. Chief regretted his statement, he was condemned by every woman's group; the Marine's claim was ignored. The Navy's personnel said they would let the other branches have the title. The only comment from the Air Force came out in a press release that read, *Colonel Fagan is indeed a woman, and a United States Air Force trained professional.*

Dr. Benson replaced Dave as the official spokesperson for the hospital, in spite of her protests to the Board of Directors. Her retaliation came when she limited the number of press conferences and interviews by scheduling as many surgeries as possible, and thereby limiting their access to her.

CHAPTER 41

Commander Bentow received orders directly from her superiors at Wright-Paterson to protect Colonel Fagan with a military presence, more competent than the one that failed to guard General Bonner. The embarrassment became part of Cari's record and she needed it to be reconciled. Now, with Bonn out of the hospital and back at his beach-front home, Cari used everything at her disposal to keep not only General Bonner safe, she had to make sure nothing happened to the other USAF officer living with him.

At first glance, the only obvious security was the deputy sheriff's cruiser parked in Bonn's driveway, and the constant surveillance by Air Force's drones that Eglin's commander ordered went unnoticed. Cari authorized the use of the newest aircraft in the Air Force's arsenal, a drone so small, it couldn't be seen or heard at a distance greater than half the length of a football field. Bonn and Rebecca spent many balmy Florida nights on the deck counting stars and listening to the faint sound of a micro-drone's engine as it circled the house. There were very few places as heavily armed; there were none with high-tech military drones, equipped with infrared cameras, providing protection from above.

"I need to call, uh…Commander Bentow, and let her know the drones are overkill. Excuse the expression," Bonn said.

"Baby, it's okay to call her Cari; she's your friend and I don't want that to change because we're back together. Even though the tattoo I gave you wore off, she knows you're taken. Besides, she's engaged."

"I've thought about her engagement to Chief Barnes, guess what, I don't know his first name, and I've only heard him called, 'Chief'. Now that he's left the department, what do we call him?" Rebecca laughed as she came to the same realization.

"Let's keep calling him 'Chief' until he tells us different. I was shocked when Cari told me they were engaged, I'm happy for them. I wonder if he's advising her on the best way to keep Cap or any other killers from trying to get to us." Although Bonn spoke in jest, he couldn't hide the concern in his voice.

Rebecca stretched and gave her opinion, "I don't know if Cap's in Destin or if he's even in the country. When he finds out I shot his mother, it will only be a matter of time before he comes to avenge her death."

"If the story made the news outside of the United States, I don't think it would be front page headlines. The internet is another story; I've seen the picture of you leaving the hospital in a wheelchair on every major search engine. The 'Combat Tested' balloons were a nice touch," Bonn said.

"It doesn't matter, we have a mole. I'm convinced someone we know, helped Cap and his mother. We have to be careful to only share our plans with Team Destin, and I have a feeling, we can't discuss anything on the phone. Somehow, Cap's been able to stay one step ahead of us."

"There has to be a way to get to him before he gets to us. I'm beginning to think he's an asset for the Agency and was reporting Diaz. It's possible his handler works as an agent, and when Diaz disappeared, Cap went rogue. I'll bet he quit listening to anyone's orders, including his handler's. Don't forget, he's rapid cycling in his mania and doing a lot of drugs, which makes him even more dangerous."

"We have one big advantage he doesn't know about, Alex." Bonn received a thorough face licking when Alex heard his name.

"It's hard to believe he came from Lexi. He's only six months old, and weighs as much as her. Judging by the size of those paws, he's going to be larger than either one of his parents. Plus, he's as smart as any pup I've ever seen. We need to talk to him about joining the military," Rebecca said.

"You sound like a proud mother and I agree with you, he's smart and already one tough stud. He's definitely a Special Op's candidate, without question. In the journal Mac left for me, he wrote about the day a PETA rep. came to see him to ask for permission to take a picture of Lexi with Alex. They wanted both of them on the cover of their magazine with the caption, *Sergeant Lexi-USAF, America's K-9 Hero with son.* The leader of PETA's group accidentally stepped on Alex' paw and Mac had to say, "Foei!" more than once to keep Alex from taking a chunk out of her. Alex hadn't been through training yet and didn't know what Foei meant, so he bit the PETA woman's ankle," Bonn said. "She didn't file a complaint, because she repeatedly tried to kick a little puppy, which wouldn't be considered 'Ethical' by the very group she represented. It also helped that Susan caught it on her phone's camera, while documenting Lexi's first photo shoot, she had a record of exactly what happened."

Rebecca, still laughing, wiped the tears from her eyes when her cell phone chimed-in with a *New Text Message* from Michelle. *Lunch tmrw? Bonn 2. Pick me up? 11 Am.?*

"It's Michelle, how would you like to have lunch with two beautiful women tomorrow?" Rebecca asked, even though she had already texted back, K *C U @ 11.*

Bonn regretted his attempt at humor as soon as the words left his mouth. "Where are you and Michelle going to be?"

"Alex, *Bewalkin*," Rebecca commanded.

"You told him to guard?"

"That's so you won't touch me tonight." Rebecca held Alex up next to her face and growled. Alex didn't seem to know why, but he followed Rebecca's lead and growled with her.

"I'm sorry, I couldn't resist teasing you. It will be good to see Michelle and have lunch with both of you. I read about her leaving the Agency in Mac's report or journal, whatever. In the parts I've read, he talks about her decision to leave the agency, her partnership offer helped him with his decision to leave the police department.

I found it intriguing, Mac hired a security guy who worked at the hospital and turned out to be Ashleigh's long-lost brother. The hospital became a family affair, didn't it? I think it's strange, Cap's mother and Ashleigh's brother, both worked there at the same time and they didn't know each other. There has to be a connection we don't know about," Bonn said.

"Rich, that's the hospital guard, slipped me a note as I left the hospital from my parasailing incident; it warned me about his sister," Rebecca said.

"You knew he and Ashleigh were related? What else haven't you told me?"

"You were fighting to stay alive, give it a rest. I have a feeling when you read on, you're going to find out that Rich wasn't really a civilian security guard; he was still active duty and working covertly in an on-going investigation of his sister as an operative gone bad. Michelle and I met with him several times; it was his idea for me to switch identities with Michelle at the Military Appreciation Days fiasco. Mac and I discussed it and kept it from you…we were afraid it might have been too stressful for you, I'm sorry." Rebecca gave Alex the command "Kalm" and hoped that taking Alex off 'guard' would suffice as an apology.

"Apology accepted. I have to ask if that little traitor you're holding really understands your commands." Bonn tentatively reached out and scratched Alex behind the ear.

"He seems to understand the Dutch commands better than the English ones. I can tell you this much, he's very aggressive on the command 'Bewalkin'. The same Navy Seal who trained Lexi went into private business, and he's training Alex. The day I dropped him off at canine boot camp, Alex tried to bite him when he got close to me. He is going to teach him about 'controlled aggression', he'll be going back for a refresher course tomorrow; I'll take him after you have lunch with those *"beautiful women"*. Rebecca's raised eyebrow warned Bonn to keep his mouth shut.

CHAPTER 42

W hen the call came on Mac's cell phone, the word *Private* blocked its identification. Aware that it might be from one of the agencies he worked, he answered.

"McCain."

"Mr. McCain, you don't' know me, but please hear me out before you hang up." Mac never liked a conversation prefaced by a voice he didn't recognize, especially one that hinted he wasn't going to like the topic.

"Who is this, and how did you get my number?"

"Mr. McCain, I am someone who wants the man who tried to take both of your friends from you. I have information you will find helpful in your pursuit of him *and* the person he's working for."

Mac found the phasing a bit strange, and he detected an accent, but the caller was getting Mac's attention. He had been working on the theory that Cap acted alone; however, Mac never discounted the possibility that someone gave Cap the orders to kill Bonn.

"I don't know what you're talking about. I'll ask you one more time, who is this and how did you get my number?"

"Obtaining a phone number or any information is, as you know, not difficult. By the way, how is your new life with Dr. Benson? Susan is her name, correct? I also want to wish you the best in your endeavor in the private sector with Agent Milton. Please understand, I wish you no harm; we have the same goals when it comes to Mr. Perkins. You may know him as 'Just Carl'."

Mac and the rest of "Team Destin" were the only ones who knew that Cap's downfall began when he referred to himself as "Just Carl" and said, "All right, you have my attention."

"I need for you to trust me and meet with me. I give you my word; no harm will come to you or anyone you know, even if you choose not to meet. If you agree, all the information you need to find Mr. Perkins, I'll give to you. What you do with that information, and him, is up to you."

"I don't know you, and you want me to meet with you? Fine, I'll put my assistant on, and you can make an appointment." Mac said, even though he didn't have an assistant.

"I'm afraid that is not possible; you need to come to me, I am not in your country. However, there are a couple of terms you must agree to before we can meet. First, you cannot speak with anyone about this call. Secondly, you must come alone."

"Let me make this perfectly clear, I don't know you, I don't take orders from anyone, and you can go fuck yourself." Mac had enough of the mystery man's games, and just before he pushed *End* on his cell phone, he heard the last word he expected to hear, "*Flywater.*"

Mac almost dropped his phone when he heard Bonn's safe word. As far as he knew, the word had only been used a couple of times, including the night Lexi found the bombs planted under Bonn's house. Initially, he considered the possibility that Cap worked with the caller; his suspicion eased when he heard a hint of sadness in the man's voice.

"Mr. McCain, I will guarantee your safety and I would personally consider it a favor if you would just hear what I have to say, it must be in person. Mr. Perkins must suffer for what he has done…; I will pay whatever your services cost."

After hearing the details of the proposed meeting, Mac packed his bag. He considered a variety of lies he could tell Susan as a reason he had to leave first thing in the morning. Instead, he chose to tell her the truth and prepare for a lecture.

To his surprise, Susan listened without any negative body language, she kept her body open and repeated what she heard, the way she heard it.

"I don't know his name or why he wants to hire T.D. Security; he knows things about all of us and sounds like he wants Cap as bad as we do. Against my better judgment, I trust him. I should be gone for at least a week, I'll call you every chance I get." Mac said and hoped Susan could hear the seriousness in his voice.

"Let me get this straight, you don't know who you are going to see, where you are going, and you will be gone at least a week, but it may be longer." Susan said then stared directly into Mac's eyes and waited to say what she had on her mind.

"Mac, I don't like this. I'm sure you've considered the possibility it could be an orchestrated trap, I have to trust you and your instincts. You trust him for reasons you can't share, or you would have told me why, that's okay, if you think you need to go…and you promise to keep your promise to call me every chance you get…, then go. I love you, more than any man I've ever known. I don't want to lose you. I will be the strong basket case waiting by the phone."

"I feel like the luckiest man on earth with you in my life," Mac said right before the other lady in his life, whined and nudged his hand with her cold, wet nose. "No girl, I can't take you with me."

The pilots were the only people Mac had seen since boarding a private jet on the way to a private landing strip outside of Cabo San Jose. As a gesture of good will and trust, they only confiscated Mac's service revolver for the flight then returned it immediately when they landed.

When Mac stepped out on the paved asphalt strip in the middle of nowhere, there weren't customs agents, police, or other planes waiting to greet him. The black Mercedes waiting at the end of the runway drove him to an exclusive resort with a presidential suite overlooking the Sea of Cortez.

The suite came lavishly stocked with fresh fruit, trays of caviar, cheeses, bottled water, and piles of carved meats that Mac devoured. The selection of Mexico's finest tequila would have to wait. The entire time he stuffed himself, he stared at the large envelope that was waiting for him on the bed. When he saw *Team Destin* written across the front, it struck him as eerily similar to the envelope he left for Bonn.

Mac threw back a shot of tequila for desert, and then dumped the envelope on the dining table. Inside, he found an old style flip-phone, twenty thousand dollars in cash, and a parking stub taped to a car key. Seconds later, when the old cell phone rang, Mac immediately scanned the room for a camera.

The sound of the crashing waves was having a hypnotizing effect. Mac yawned and stretched while he waited in the parking area at a public beach side park. Lights swept the asphalt as it turned in, then stopped on the opposite end of the parking area with its high beams blinding Mac's vision. When the lights flashed twice, then turned off, he patted the bulge in his windbreaker for the umpteenth time since arriving for the clandestine meeting.

Under the glow of the parking lot's single flood light next to Mac's car, the figure of an extremely large man in a black suit appeared.

"Senor' Ramirez would like to talk with you Mr. McCain." The request came with a sweep of a hand towards the black limo that almost disappeared on the moonless night.

Mac didn't sense any danger when the limo's rear door opened; he slid into the backseat of a limo owned by one of the most wanted cartel bosses in Mexico.

"Mr. McCain, please accept my apologies for being so secretive. I want to express my gratitude for your discretion. It's obvious you recognize my face. I'm sure you now understand why I've requested our meeting so far from your home, when you could be with that beautiful doctor friend of yours. Susan, isn't that correct?"

"Well, well, well, look who we have here. Should I call you 'El Diablo' or Mr. Ramirez? Any information about Cap is between us. Leave her out of it. This is a warning, not a threat. If any harm comes to her, you will be known as the *late* Mr. Ramirez."

"Please hear me out; working with me will not be a deal with the devil. I'm a businessman in a very dangerous country, and no matter what your opinion is of me, you will get the information you are seeking. I have a proposition, if you have no interest; you are free to go on your way. I will understand."

"If you have something regarding Cap, give it to me and quit wasting my time."

Mac witnessed the legend of Mexico tear-up, took a deep breath, and quietly said, "Armando."

"Did you say Armando? Are you talking about Cap's right-hand man, *that* Armando?" Mac subconsciously rubbed the back of his head where Armando hit him with a metal chair while he tried to arrest Cap.

Mr. Ramirez wagged his index finger back and forth and gave the appearance of being truly offended at the accusation. "My Armando was not that cockroach's man."

"You said, '*My* Armando'? What does that mean?" Mac asked.

"He is…was…my only nephew. I loved him like a son. I want Cap to pay for what he did."

"The…body, we sent it to his family in San Diego. We just assumed they were his only family, I didn't know Armando was your nephew. There is no way I can even imagine the pain you must feel. I am truly sorry for your loss. Mr. Ramirez, the DEA blamed his death on the Gulf Cartel and theorized the cartel bosses were trying to claim the Florida Panhandle and your nephew was cutting into their territory. I have to ask, did you, the Sinaloa Cartel, order the hit in Gainesville… in retaliation?"

"No. You have my word, *I* did not and *I* am the only one who has the authority to make that decision," he said then cleared his throat. "I've also heard the Gulf Cartel wasn't responsible for Armando's death."

Although Mac heard him say the Gulf Cartel didn't kill his nephew, Mac didn't respond. Instead, he reached out, put his hand on the shoulder of Mexico's most dangerous drug lord, and said, "Mr. Ramirez, I am truly sorry for your loss."

"Armando was the only person in my organization I trusted. *No one* harms my family. Mr. Perkins desecrated Armando's body with one of his bombs to cover up any evidence that he killed him."

"I believe you're right but I don't know why Cap would blow up his own building with such a crude bomb. We have evidence that he had a substantial supply of military-grade C-4, a crude bomb made from fertilizer doesn't make sense. If Cap didn't kill your nephew, and one of the Gulf cartel's goons did, why would he cover it up? I doubt he cared about his marijuana operation being discovered; even a bomb of that magnitude wouldn't destroy *all* the evidence. Maybe, the cartel just made it appear Cap built the bomb, so they could deny any responsibility. I believe Cap killed your nephew *for* them and hoped there wouldn't be a body to identify if he built a large enough bomb to incinerate everything in sight."

"You may be correct, either way, it makes no difference. He must pay for what he did to Armando and the man Mr. Perkins is working for, will pay dearly for his role," El Diablo said.

"And who do you think is giving Cap his orders?"

"I know with certainty, Senator Diaz is the one who is compensating him. The Senator's father and Mr. Perkins were friends in college and fought together in Vietnam. If he thinks he can kill your General Bonner, and my Armando, without paying a price, he is mistaken. Detective McCain, I will take care of Senator Diaz; he is not your concern. I will help you find the man you keep calling 'Cap'."

"Why don't you go after him yourself?" Mac asked.

"I have an agreement with my contacts in Belize not to bring Cartel business to their country, that's where you will find him. The people that have been helping Mr. Perkins stay hidden are very important people in your government, and I'm not just talking about Senator Diaz. The woman you rescued years ago for Senator Diaz happened to be an embedded operative, not a family member. You were chosen for the mission and the Senator was following orders when he contacted you to lead the rescue mission," he said, and then handed Mac a folded piece of customized stationary.

The first thing Mac noticed was an embossed image of a devil on the note and said, "What is this, I'm referring to the numbers."

"That is where Mr. Perkins can be found. When you find him, show him no mercy if he resists. I would much prefer if you brought him to me, but I will understand if you choose to go through your government's procedures. Whatever you decide, you must act immediately. He's connected with my enemies and will disappear the moment he thinks his location is known. The day I found out where he's been hiding, I called you. I hope we are not too late; you must act quickly."

Mac unfolded the piece of paper that read:

"Pair-a-Dice"
Placencia 16 31' 6.3012"N 88 22' 3.3636"W

One call from the United States Embassy sent the Belize military and Placencia police force to the yacht anchored at the exact coordinates provided by El Diablo. After surrounding the luxury boat by water and land, Mac, along with a few agents from the Agency boarded the vessel. The cabin door was ajar and a cut-crystal *WELCOME 2 PAIR-A-DICE* sign hung on the door's handle. After searching every inch from bow to stern, it became evident the ship hadn't been occupied for awhile.

The boat's interior couldn't have been more lavishly furnished; even the built-in wine cellar didn't seem out of place. Cap had been living a life of luxury and excess while hiding from the authorities. Strewn throughout the cabin were piles of empty wine, beer, and champagne bottles with cigarette and cigar butts, floating in the remnants. Swarming Palmetto bugs and flies feasted on the scraps of food left on plates, in pizza boxes, and half-eaten to-go meals that were littering the cabin.

After an unsuccessful search of Senator Diaz' yacht, Mac cleared the piles of molded, insect infested food and ashtray bottles from the teak dining table with the sweep of his arm to make room for a stack of old newspapers.

"All of these papers date back to the day after Mr. Perkins disappeared, and they stop a few days ago, that's most likely when he abandoned ship," Mac said.

"Maybe El Diablo picked him up already," a local officer said in Spanish and brought out a couple of suppressed laughs.

"Unfortunately, he didn't leave any electronics. I doubt Mr. Perkins communicated with anyone on a computer that could be traced to his location, he may be a crazed killer but he's not stupid. We know he had to communicate with someone, if for no other reason, to get his money. It would take a lot to maintain this lifestyle, even here in Belize. The answer is in these papers, we just need to find it."

Mac wondered if the local officer who mentioned El Diablo, also warned Cap. While he contemplated the possibility, he stared at the swarm of flies landing on a pile of greasy tamale cornhusks and newspaper wrappers saturated with orange grease.

"Judging by the amount of grease on the tamale's newspaper wrappers, I'm surprised there isn't an oil slick for us to follow," Mac said.

The Captain of the Belize police force chimed in. "I have never seen newspaper used to wrap tamales at our restaurants, they are usually served in the aluminum foil to keep them warm. I can have my men check out every street vendor to see if anyone is using old newspaper as a wrapping. We may get a lead on where he might be."

That is when Mac noticed a newspaper printed in English that hadn't been used to wrap the tamales; *Northwest Florida Daily News* stood out through the grease drippings.

"I think we may have something here," Mac said and picked up several crumbled orange balls of paper. As he sifted through the entire pile of garbage, he found two other small wads of newspaper print. One article included a photo of the Destin Chamber's ribbon cutting ceremony held for T.D. Security. Even with a pumpkin-colored tint, the photo clearly showed Michelle, Mac, and Rich surrounded by community leaders at their opening. Upon closer examination, all three of them had black dots drawn on their foreheads.

The other newspaper clipping had the story Mary Perkins foiled attempt to kill General Bonner and a photo of the hero who killed her, Colonel Rebecca Fagan.

Mac pulled out the flip-phone provided for him and said to one of the agents, "I know where he's headed; I just hope I'm not too late. I've got to warn them."

After placing his call, Mac started paced while screaming into his personal phone. "Come on Michelle, answer the damn phone!"

CHAPTER 43

J ust before dawn, a dark green kayak tried to slice quietly through the mirrored water of Choctawhatchee Bay as invisible as it could be with an inexperienced person. Despite the extra care, the kayak's captain took not to hit the paddle against the sides of the fiberglass hull, an occasional thud echoed over the bay. No matter how hard he tried, the craft darted from port to starboard with each alternating stroke of the double paddle. Drenched in sweat, and with shooting pain in his back from sitting on a numb butt, the novice boatman couldn't understand why anyone would own a kayak. By the time he made it to the small beach behind T.D. Security, the pins and needles in his legs were so severe; he needed to massage them before he could walk.

Described as a computer geek in his youth, J.J. was a tech "prodigy" as an adult. When other kids were enjoying the outdoors, he buried himself in the world of computers. His only experience with a boat happened on a paddleboat in Central Park during a summer internship with the tech company that trained him to be a data broker.

He made his first millions as *the* pioneer in data gathering on consumers using the internet. Then, he developed the software for intercepting text messages and cell phone calls without leaving an imprint. At that point in his career, J.J. became a self-described "genius" and changed his goal to making his first billion dollars. The NSA wanted his software for their eavesdropping platforms and considered his expertise, a matter of national security; they took control of him and his company. At the time, his programs gave the United States an invaluable lead in the surveillance field, and made J.J. rich beyond his wildest dreams. His stature grew when he became a member on the government's *Tiger Team* who developed the government's XKEYSCORE data gathering application.

At first, J.J. resisted the government's offer. After his arrest on a trumped-up charge, he made a plea deal to show some of the government's top computer techs how a hacker could get into their systems. The ease, at which he could infiltrate any computer or network, impressed and concerned them enough to give him a grant to start his own cyber security firm. The company stayed under the watchful eyes of the government, to make sure J.J. didn't share his software with any foreign government. In a little over a year, he had a dozen offices around the world, and employed the best hackers he could find. Whenever a government computer system was hacked, the NSA contacted J.J. immediately.

To everyone's surprise, most of the hackers, were teenage "computer geeks", as brilliant as any adult programmer working for him. When he identified an infiltrating culprit, J.J. hacked his way into the perpetrator's own system, and froze their screen with a personal video message that gave them the choice of interviewing for a government job or face prosecution.

To the delight of the legal divisions at the agency, the video would disappear without leaving any digital imprint that it ever existed. Filled with visions of espionage and grandeur, J.J. portrayed a James Bond image during the interviews with the hackers. The Agency's decision makers found him laughable, somewhat delusional, but harmless.

The bayside building housing Team Destin's office had an antiquated security system on the doors and windows, but the blueprints J.J. hacked off the builder's computer, showed him a way to bypass the alarms. Once they were disabled, he removed the rooftop grate of the building's ventilation system and slid into the crawl space above T.D.'s break room. After lifting the ceiling tile closest to a support wall, J.J. dropped down undetected, and proceeded to search for the report compiled by Detective McCain.

Some of the classified documents in the report implicated several people in the government; there was one, he needed to find. Separately, they were just documents, but Mac had pieced them together properly. His report painted a picture of corruption, bribery, sabotage, treason, and murder that implicated several top politicians in Washington.

J.J. started his search in Mac's office, and rifled through a bookcase filled with books on criminal law, memoirs of the world's greatest war strategists, and countless mystery novels ranging from A. Conan Doyle's, Sherlock Holmes to James Patterson's, Alex Cross. Frustration took hold, and he swept his hand through each shelf, clearing the entire bookcase, which left an impressive pile of books on the floor.

The drab-green, military surplus filing cabinet behind Mac's desk contained only irrelevant files that J.J. tossed in the air and fell like exaggerated confetti into another pile. When he saw Mac's computer and within seconds, successfully hacked in and searched Mac's personal files until he spotted an obscure file folder labeled *FISHING PICTURES.* Buried in the dozens of fish photos, a Word document named *Flyh2o* caught his attention. When he opened it, he found the Mac's report regarding the attempted murder of General Bonner, Colonel Fagan, and her orders to investigate the sabotage of the F-22 Raptor program. While that file downloaded on his USB flash drive, he let the computer search the hard drive for the originals Mac used to compile the report.

J.J. accidentally found the documents, but not on the computer. While waiting for the compute search, he found a box under Mac's desk that contained *The Women of Destin* calendars. When he took one out, he uncovered a manila envelope with **Flyh2o** written on it. Even though he had what he came for, J.J. couldn't resist checking out a calendar. He was half-way through the months of gorgeous women from Destin, when he stopped at the month of May, his mouth hung open in disbelief. *Ms. May* who was dressed in lingerie, looked familiar, but he wasn't sure. Upon closer inspection, he realized, Ms. May and Agent Milton were the same woman.

When the download completed, J.J. put the flash drive, along with one of the calendars, in the envelope holding the classified documents. As a final precaution, he removed the hard drive from Mac's computer and ground it on the floor with his boot.

J.J. felt he was on his way to becoming an international spy now that he successfully completed his first assignment outside of the CIA's Computer Espionage Division. "Agent" J.J. snapped back to reality, when he heard the distinctive beeping of the office's alarm system on the keypad. Holding his breath, and pinned next to the door, J.J. prepared himself for a confrontation with whom he suspected was an early morning employee. The sound of water running gave him the opportunity to crack open the door of Mac's office, and see a young man, with a high and tight military haircut, making coffee in the break room. He had what he came for, and if he could find the opportunity to slip out undetected, he would. Then, he saw the man looking up at the ceiling tile he foolishly left slightly ajar, and his self-image as a cool and calm spy, disappeared. Rich never heard J.J. coming, he only heard a throat cleared, and then hit with a single fatal shot to his forehead.

J.J. stood surprised and somewhat sickened, by where he hit his target. Then he heard the low rumble of Michelle's black Hummer and watched her pull into T.D.'s designated parking space, check her appearance in the rearview mirror, and headed his way. Every step she took towards the front door made his heart pound harder. As she entered the T.D. Security's offices, J.J., tossed the calendar on the counter, peeked through the open crack in the break room door, and drew his small caliber handgun.

Michelle shouted "Good morning Rich, will you pour me a cup? I heard from Mac, he has a lead on that asshole Cap. I'll be out in a minute to fill you in."

Hearing Cap's name sent chills through J.J., but it gave him an idea, and he tiptoed his way to Michelle's office. When he looked through her partially opened door, he noticed she had changed into a classic Quantico Academy sweatshirt. He didn't care about her age, the image of her on the calendar left him regretting the missed opportunity to see her topless.

All of sudden, J.J. felt the cold steel of a gun pressed against his neck and a heard a voice whisper, "Turn slowly and go out the back door. Do not look at me, or you will die. Go somewhere that no one would look for you, make yourself invisible." J.J. felt the barrel pressed harder on his throat. "Do you understand?"

J.J., frozen with fear, nodded and slowly turned. The pressed steel rotated with him and kept him from coming face-to-face with the whisperer. As he headed towards the door, his peripheral vision allowed him to get glimpse of a nondescript stranger wearing a black hoodie and sunglasses. Nothing about the voice or partial image from the edge of his sight gave him a clue as to gender. When he heard two muffled shots, he didn't care about anything except making it out the door without the sound of a third shot.

The force of two shots to the chest, dropped Michelle immediately, and she crumbled behind her desk. Killing Rich gave J.J. an adrenaline rush, but hearing the two shots meant for the calendar girl had him swallowing repeatedly to keep from getting sick. Once outside, he shoved the envelope down the front of his pants and sprinted in a panic to his beached kayak, and then paddled furiously towards the public boat ramp next to Mid-Bay Marina.

His plan to return to his Cadillac Escalade ESV and drive straight to his safe house fell apart at the ramp. For a second time, his legs were dead weight, and he rubbed them vigorously until he could stand without falling. He wobbled up the railroad tie walkway to his vehicle and his heart started to race again, when he couldn't find it. Hyperventilating and frantic, he looked in both directions to see if there happened to be another ramp; he didn't see when he left in the predawn darkness. After sprinting back down to his kayak, J.J. set off across the bay, frothing the water with a paddle that he didn't know how to use.

Splashing across the seemingly endless span of water, left him out of breath, drenched in sweat, and his muscles fatigued, but he made it a beach house on the other side of the bay. To his dismay, he couldn't get out of the kayak. With the nose of the kayak on the beach and using the paddle as a crutch, he wiggled out and stood. Unfortunately, when he tried to steady himself, it broke, and sent him to his knees in less than a few inches of water. Even with one leg dead weight, and the other "pins and needles", he managed to hobble his way to guesthouse by driving the shattered end of the broken paddle into the sand, steadying himself before each step.

Once inside and lying on the cool tiled floor, he laughed hysterically in relief, and then shouted, "I did it! I fucking did it!" The celebration was short-lived when a heavily accented voice came from another room, "Senor Diaz?"

J.J. Diaz, lying in the pool of water that had drained from his shoes and clothes, propped himself up, and saw two men standing ready with their handguns. Before he could reply, a distinguished looking man in a suit walked in from an adjoining room.

"Who are you and what do you want?" J.J. asked.

"I am Armando's cousin, and the right hand of El Diablo. I am your worst nightmare; I want what you took from Mr. McCain's office."

J.J.'s bravado and dreams of working in espionage disappeared when he felt the pressure of cold steel on the back of his neck. Using his trembling hands, he lifted his shirt, and handed over the envelope.

"Who are you working for?" Carlos asked.

J.J. remained silent as Carlos reached into his pocket, brought out a syringe. J.J. tried to speak, but it was too late. Carlos had expertly pierced his jugular and J.J.'s eyes rolled white.

CHAPTER 44

The unmistakable low and powerful rumble of Rebecca's Porsche decelerating was the last thing Bonn wanted to hear as he sat on the stoop of his porch cradling his hand. When he saw her long slender legs swing out of her sports car, he temporarily forgot about the pain he unsuccessfully tried to hide

"Hi baby. Bonn, why are you holding your hand like that?" Rebecca's face was awash with concern, her mothering instincts were showing.

Bonn forgot to quit holding his injured hand when he said, "I think I broke my finger, it's no big deal. I'm fine."

"Every time I ask you how you're doing, you say that. Why don't you just admit you're lying?" Rebecca's irritability started to overtake her concern.

"I don't want to add to your duress."

"You don't want to add to my duress? Is that a joke? Let me see it. Oh-my-God. Yep, it's definitely broken. Let's go," she said and helped him stand. Bonn grunted and groaned for effect, which only made her laugh.

"Your poor little broken finger pales in comparison to some of the hits you've taken in the military. Quit your whining."

Bonn found breaking his bad habit more difficult than he realized when he blurted out, "I'm *fine*." If it's broken, I'll just pop it back in and tape it up."

"Damn it, you are *not*...whatever. You're going to 'pop it back in'? It isn't dislocated; it's broken. We're going to go see Susan and don't argue with me. How did this happen?"

"It happened while practicing my somersault routine on the stairs. Rebecca, Dr. Benson has better things to do than deal with a bruised finger." Bonn hoped a little levity would go a long way.

Rebecca accidently touched it to show him what she thought about his humor. "I'm sorry, did that hurt? Don't argue with me, I have her private number and if she can see you...you're going."

Bonn started waving his good hand in protest as Rebecca put her cell phone up to her ear, tapped her foot impatiently, and rolled her eyes in disgust, which made it clear, arguing with her would be futile.

Susan sat behind a rare seventeenth-century desk admiring her exquisite Tiffany desk lamp, and lost in thought. Her office was an eclectic private museum of antique furniture, various floor and desk lamps, and very expensive artwork. The Monte Blanc pen she had been using to doodle: Mrs. Mac McCain, Mrs. Susan McCain, and Susan Benson-McCain, flew across her desk when her modern, three-line, black plastic telephone rang.

Susan snatched up the receiver with the speed of a gunslinger. "Mac?"

Rebecca sensed the tension in Susan's voice. "Sorry, it's just me. Susan, is there something wrong?"

"Rebecca? You caught me thinking about...well...Mac. When I saw the light blinking for my private line, I guess I figured he telepathically knew I was thinking about him, and decided to give me a call."

"It's not a problem. I'm happy for you and Mac," Rebecca said, but he couldn't hide the underlying concern in her voice when her statement sounded more like a question.

Susan snapped back and asked, "What can I do for you Rebecca?"

"It's Bonn; he's had a little accident."

"What kind of accident? He didn't get shot again, did he?"

"No, thank God. It's nothing like that. He has a broken finger and it needs to be set. Should I bring him into the ER or take him to his G.P.'s office?"

"You want to take him to a general practitioner's office? Now, that is funny. Does he even have a G.P.? I thought he only went to a doctor if he was dying. I just finished my early morning rounds, bring him to my office and I'll take care of it. Come to the ER entrance, I'll send my new assistant to get you."

When they pulled into Emergency parking, and Rebecca found a spot right up front, she didn't feel quite as guilty about having handicap parking hanger. Bonn had teased her about the blue *Disabled* permit dangling from the mirror of a Porsche with an *automatic* transmission. The level of pain in her shoulder that radiated down to her foot would have made shifting gears difficult. When they were driving through the parking lot, he listened to her give a little grunt every time they went over a speed bump. The intense pain that plagued her daily, she shared only with Susan. Bonn never let on that he noticed her every grimace and moan at night when she rolled on her side

To gloat after pulling into handicap parking, she stared at Bonn until he asked, "What's wrong?" She smiled.

"Alright, let's do this; I've made my point," Rebecca said.

"Okay, I'll admit an automatic is exactly what you needed, and I'm sorry for teasing you about it, my bad. Rebecca, we don't need to be here. I'll be careful and it will heal on its own…" Bonn's protesting ended when he tried to open the door and bumped his finger.

To get to Susan's office they had to go through the ER and the mass of hallways that were behind what Bonn called "the Iron Curtain".

"I will never complain about military hospitals again. As veteran, with over thirty years under my belt, I can't remember having to wait more than a few minutes to be seen. This reminds me of the V.A. Center. It has been exactly nine minutes and there still isn't anyone at the front desk to see if I'm dying, just that stupid sign that says *Please Sign-in and Have a Seat.* I wouldn't mind, but my hand is throbbing and

I'm a little nauseated." While Bonn complained, Rebecca noticed his complexion had turned to the pale shade of a Yankee tourist.

"General Bonner, Colonel Fagan?" Susan's new assistant magically appeared from a door leading into a mysterious area identified by an aggressively bold sign, RESTRICTED. WAIT FOR BUZZER!

"Do you think BUZZER is a person?" Rebecca asked, pointed at the sign, and let out a little snort as they walked towards Susan's assistant.

A man wearing a swimsuit, and covered with welts from an encounter with a jellyfish, led a series of protests. "What the hell? We have been here for thirty minutes! Are they more important than us?"

The rest of the patients weren't very happy with the personalized attention the *"Colonel and General"* received and complained to each other.

The nurse escorted Bonn and Rebecca past the triage rooms and down several hallways to Dr. Benson's office in the main hospital. The antiseptic smell even had Rebecca a little nauseated, and wanting the trek to end. Gratefully, they saw Susan standing with her hands on her hips in the doorway to her office. Judging by her body language, Bonn knew, at some point, he would be hearing a lecture.

"Alright General, what have you done now?" Susan asked.

"I'm…*okay* Doc. Rebecca insisted we come here and bother you," Bonn said and watched Susan and Rebecca roll their eyes.

"You aren't 'bothering' me. I'm sure you'll survive, come with me. Rebecca, you can come and hold his hand," Susan said and led them into a private exam room adjoining her office.

Susan remained eerily quiet during a procedure that involved setting Bonn's broken finger and binding it with tape to the fingers on both sides. His disappointment was obvious when they saw his frown.

"What's wrong? Are you in pain?" Rebecca, who noticed the slightest changes in Bonn's moods, asked.

"I expected a little more than some tape; I envisioned a cast covering my hand that my friends could sign," Bonn joked. Rebecca and Susan were both aware he had been looking forward to the cast.

"There you go. Try not to injure it again while the bone is healing." Again, Susan seemed to be dismissive, an attitude out of character for her.

"Alright, I'll try not to fall down the stairs." The women's faces, made it perfectly clear, his sarcasm wasn't well received.

"Your depth perception will be off until you get all your peripheral vision back. Does that sound familiar? Didn't I already tell you something like that? Maybe your next eye surgery will help, until then, hold on to the damn railing."

Bonn didn't know why he had the feeling; he was on the receiving end of a scolding that was meant for someone else. "Yes ma'am, I'll try not to break anything else."

Rebecca smiled but Susan didn't react. Instead, she checked her cell phone for a text message or missed call.

"Are you going to tell us what's bothering you? We can see there's something on your mind," Rebecca said and held Susan's hand.

"It's Mac. Ever since he left the police department and opened his own private security firm, he acts as if he's bored. He used to complain about the never ending caseloads, I think he misses the action."

"Susan, every time Mac and I came back from a deployment we both went into a funk because we missed the action. It takes time to acclimate back into civilian life. When we retired, Mac and I were both depressed and needed to find a way to cope. I decided to accept some missions as a contractor, and Mac went to work for the police department. We missed the adrenaline rush, I'm sure he'll come around," Bonn reassured her, in spite of the fact he found it a little strange Mac hadn't confided in him.

"Rebecca is still active duty and understands what I'm talking about. She's seen the pitfalls of returning to civilian life in many of her friends and associates."

"Some of them reenlist if they're young enough or they go to work for the 'Feds'. It's sad there are way too many that find comfort in a bottle, a syringe, or by taking their lives in an attempt to end the pain." Rebecca lowered her head and slowly shook it as she relived some painful memories.

"I get what you're trying to say. I've tried to support whatever he wants to do, including the time he's spending at home, and I encourage his fishing. That is, until a few days ago." Susan frowned.

"What happened a few days ago?" Rebecca and Bonn asked simultaneously.

"He got a call around midnight and said he had to leave for a few days, maybe longer. Yesterday, I took him to the Destin airport, where he boarded a private jet with a small Mexican flag on its door. When he left, he looked…I guess I would describe it as…happy. It scared me. Mac called last night to let me know he's somewhere near Cabo, and he wouldn't discuss anything else." Susan lowered her head to shield her moistening eyes.

"He didn't say who he went to see?" Bonn asked.

"No, not exactly, Mac had a lead on a suspect he's been hunting. I asked him who could be that important, and he said, '*Just* a man, a psycho that Bonn would definitely be interested in as well'. He emphasized the word 'just', so I assumed that meant your friend Cap." Susan hesitated to see if Bonn's assessment would be the same, before she continued.

"Why does everyone keep calling him my 'friend'? Mac is off chasing Cap and he didn't say a word to me, or Rebecca? That's out of character for him. Rebecca, we need to talk with Michelle and see if she knows what Mac's doing."

"My gut tells me, he's…in danger. Can you call her now?" The possibility of getting a status report on Mac caused Susan's voice to crack.

Rebecca, always one-step ahead, already had her cell phone to her ear. "Damn it, voicemail!"

"Tell her we're on the way to Destin," Bonn said.

"Hi girlfriend…Michelle, where are you? Give me a call as soon as you get this. Bonn and I are heading over to T.D. to see if you're there. Remember to call me or text me as soon as you get this!"

"I think we need to get over to her office, now! Susan, thank you for taking care of Bonn's finger and try not to worry. If there is one person that can take care of himself, it's Mac. We'll call you as soon as we get to Michelle's. Who knows, maybe she knows, what-the-hell is going on with Mac?" Bonn said and followed Rebecca out of the office.

When they reached her Porsche, Rebecca spoke with a sense of urgency. "Bonn, I'm getting a feeling, and it's not a warm and fuzzy one. We need to hurry. I hope it's nothing but you better buckle-up."

Bonn knew not to tell a woman like Susan or Rebecca, not to over react' or to 'calm down' when they are using their intuition.

"Rebecca, the hairs on my arms tingle whenever I hear you tell me you're having a 'feeling', and they're standing straight up."

"I'm getting the same *feeling* as Susan, Mac's in danger," Rebecca said and kicked her Porsche into launch mode, pinning them back, and left billowing smoke screen over the parking lot.

The single-story building holding the offices of "Team Destin" were modest compared to most of the multi-level terra cotta colored buildings on the bay. Michelle insisted the view of the water made the high rent worth every penny. After parking next to Michelle's black military-equipped Hummer, Rebecca couldn't resist revving the engine of her Porsche to announce her arrival.

"I think you were a racecar driver in a past life. You could have just honked to announce your arrival. You know, even though the windows are smoked, and you can't see in, everyone inside can see you." Bonn regretted his attempt at sarcasm as soon as the words left his mouth.

"And your point is…?" Rebecca's response chilled the air.

"I'm sorry, I don't have a point. Why don't we go talk to Michelle?" Bonn hoped his simple apology would suffice and alleviate some of the tension they were getting from her "feeling".

Rebecca made *her* "point" with strides that propelled her several steps ahead of him. Immediately after using one hand to open the unlocked door, and keeping the other on her weapon, Rebecca called out, "Michelle? Michelle, are you here?'"

"Maybe, she's in the bathroom." Bonn found it strange the entire office was empty and a phone rang repeatedly without being answered.

"Someone called the answering service off, or that phone wouldn't still be ringing." Rebecca didn't need to say anything else and drew her gun. Bonn had already pulled out this weapon, and used the tongue depressors taped to his broken fingers, as a stabilizer for his gun. The hairs on both of their arms stood at attention when they saw the door to Mac's office wide open. Trash cans were emptied on the floor, law books and mystery novels were strewn next to the bookcase, and the walls were empty. All of the pictures, paintings, and prints were on the floor, along with shards of broken pottery.

"See if she's in the ladies room, I'll see if I can find anything else," Bonn said in a hushed voice.

Rebecca stood to the side of the bathroom door, slowly pushed the handle down, and then charged into an empty room, Bonn heard, "Clear" from the ladies bathroom. Through the open door, he saw the office that was tossed, but whoever did it, was gone. He refocused his attention to the break room. The second he opened the door, the unmistakable odor of gunpowder hit him, but the sight of a crimson and blackened collage of flesh, hair and coagulated blood on the wall, had him yelling. "Rebecca!"

Richard Smit, the brother of Ashleigh Smit, slumped against the wall with his chin resting on his chest. Sitting on the counter were two empty coffee cups, a full pot of cold coffee, and an unopened box of Krispy Kreme donuts with a set of keys on top of it.

Rebecca came running with both hands wrapped tightly around her Glock and burst through the door. As soon as she saw Rich, she wheeled and swept the office from where she had just come, making sure they weren't in the middle of an ambush.

"It's Rich. Where's Michelle?"

"I don't know. Bonn, what in the hell happened here?"

"Whoever did this either knew Rich or surprised him; his gun is still in his holster. It looks like he was making the morning coffee and brought donuts."

Rebecca used the barrel of her gun to tilt back Rich's head from the resting position on his chest and gasped when she recognized where he had been hit. "Bonn, the back of his head is gone; somebody shot him at close range with a hollow point."

"The entry wound on the forehead tells us who that 'somebody' might…wait a minute, what's this?"

Bonn had his head cocked and was looking at something on the wall above Rich's head and said, "Rebecca, there's a *Women of Destin* calendar laying here and take one guess who's picture I'm looking at."

Bonn focused on the top half of the calendar that had a picture of Michelle scantily dressed in black lingerie with her agent's badge pinned to her garter. She was holding the barrel of her service revolver to her lips, and blowing away the smoke. The caption under her pose, read, SHE AIMS TO PLEASE.

"I've seen it. That's the calendar she posed for when she left the agency, and moved to Destin. You were in the hospital, what about it?" Rebecca asked.

"She's the model for May and it's December. I doubt she turned it to *her* month for everyone to see," Bonn said.

"I know Michelle; I can guarantee she didn't put that calendar here. She told me she's a little embarrassed about it."

"Michelle could pass for a woman twenty years younger, with very few imperfections, but I don't think that's a mole on her face," Bonn said and leaned in for a closed inspection of Michelle's picture. A small black pushpin stuck out in the center of her forehead, and attached the calendar to the wall.

"Bonn, it can't be…, can it?"

"I don't know. Cap hasn't been seen since he escaped, and there hasn't been a single confirmed sighting.

"Well, I would bet he's here now. Why would he kill Rich, and where in the hell is Michelle? Do you suppose he has her.?" Rebecca asked.

"We don't know for sure it's him."

"The pin…, the bullet hole…, it's his calling card. Bonn, he has her; I can feel it."

Rebecca started to call in Rich's murder until Bonn stopped her. "Wait a second, we'll only have a couple of minutes after we call it in, swarms of cops will be here and lock it down. We need to stay focused and figure this out before any of the evidence is compromised."

"There isn't any sign of a struggle…we both know Michelle wouldn't go without a fight. I'll check out her office and see if you can find anything," Rebecca said.

He scanned the area, and then picked up a few fuzz balls of lint and a several pink strands off the floor. When he held one of the fibers up to the lights, his suspicions, confirmed.

Rebecca left Michelle's office, walked back into the break room holding a cell phone with the CIA's logo on it and saw Bonn staring at the ceiling.

"Bonn? What is it?"

"I think Rich was caught off guard," Bonn said and pointed to the ceiling. "This place has alarms on the doors but not up there, someone came in from the roof. He came down from the ceiling, there's fiberglass dust everywhere from the ceiling tile being moved. And…," Bonn picked up a clump of wet sand from the counter and pinched it between his thumb and index finger.

"And…, the shooter brought in some of the beach with him."

Bonn cautiously palmed the glass coffee pot, filled to the 12-cup level. "It's cold; he died before he had his first cup. There are two cups and judging by the four empty sugar packs, he never poured a cup for Michelle either. Since neither cup has any coffee in it, I'm going to guess Rich was waiting for it to finish brewing when he was killed. The light is off; the machine would shut off automatically after a couple of hours, which means he probably has a substantial head start on us."

Rebecca held out Michelle's phone and swiped through the histories of text messages and phone calls to see if there might be a clue.

"There's a *MISSED CALL* from someone named *BB* that she received early this morning; it's our area code and lasted for one minute. The call history shows *BB* calls her at least twice a week at the same time, 0600. This call came in at 0700."

"It sounds like a classic morning briefing call. I wonder why there's a one hour time change. We need to track down her A.I.C. and see if that's *BB*. For now, we need to figure out if Michelle is a hostage, or if she left on her own. I can't imagine her leaving her cell phone unless she's been kidnapped. Plus, why else would her Hummer still be parked in her space? The front door is unlocked and I don't think he would take the chance of anyone seeing him leave with a hostage by going out the front door. Let's check the back and see if we can find anything."

Bonn and Rebecca drew their weapons a few steps away from the rear exit, then stopped abruptly, as if they didn't want to cross an invisible line. Bonn holstered his gun, and went to a knee to inspect a red dot on the floor. "What the…?"

"Blood?" Rebecca asked.

"No, it's a fingernail," Bonn asked. "Did Michelle wear fake fingernails?"

"Michelle loved them. Although she never wore any during her entire career in law enforcement, now…, getting her nails done is a weekly event. This is a nail for the 'Pinky finger'; it must have popped-off. If I know her, she would have glued it back on until she could get it fixed at the salon. Michelle either left in a hurry or was forced out the back, otherwise, she would have picked it up," Rebecca said.

Rebecca drew her weapon again, and then leaned into the door's aluminum push bar. Before Rebecca could open the door, she heard, "Drop your weapons and put your hands up!"

The sheriff's SWAT team, armed to the hilt, came charging through the front door. To their surprise, Michelle walked in and said, "I'm a little late for our lunch date, I got here as fast as I could."

The ensuing laughter began and ended when Michelle bent over and grabbed her ribs.

"Girl, what's wrong?" Rebecca wrapped an arm around Michelle's waist to keep her from falling.

"I took two for the team. Fortunately, I had my Kevlar vest on; I have a couple of bruised ribs. You know which ones I'm talking about, don't you? The ones that *just finish healing* from getting shot by Ashleigh?" she said and held a hand against her side.

"Michelle, what the hell happened here? Rebecca and I feared the worse for you."

"When I pulled up to the office this morning, I got a call from Mac. He told me, Cap's either on his way or already here. I saw Rich's truck in the parking lot, and when I walked in, I just assumed he was making coffee, I could smell it. So, I went in my office to put my Kevlar on and change into my sweatshirt. Not more than a minute later, I turned around to someone dressed in black and wearing a stocking mask. The next thing I knew, he opened up on me."

The intensity in the room surged in a palpable wave as Michelle touched the back of her head then checked her fingers to see if there was any blood. "I guess I fell and blacked out. When I woke up and started searching for the creep that shot my ass, I found..." Michelle buried her face in her hands and fell against Rebecca.

Choking back her emotions, Michelle said, "that's... that's when I found Rich. Shit, I'm a trained agent and I've seen so many bodies in my career, I've learned to detach...I'm not supposed to cry."

Rebecca took Michelle's hands and said, "Look at me. You're human; it's okay to shed tears."

"Michelle, do you think Rich was already dead when you arrived at your offices?" Bonn asked.

"I don't know what difference that would make."

"I'm wondering if Rich was the intended target or just in the wrong place at the wrong time. Someone searched thoroughly for something in Mac's office, its possible both of you interrupted a burglary; Cap isn't a burglar, he's a killer. If it's him, why did he put up the calendar, he already used his signature shot. This doesn't make sense, someone wanted it to look like Cap did it," Bonn said and shook his head.

"Whatever Mac kept in his office, had to be so important, Rich's killer wasn't going to let anyone keep him from searching for it. We need to figure out what was worth killing for and where that bastard went before he kills someone else," Rebecca said

"I know where he went, let me explain. Rich hadn't been dead for very long when I found him and he was still bleeding out. Also, there was full pot of coffee and the room smelled of a recently fired weapon. I didn't see anyone out front so I ran out back to see what I could find. I saw the footprints of one individual leading up from the shoreline, and the same set of prints leaving from the rear door, and heading back down to the water. That's when I spotted the guy in the kayak." Michelle looked exhausted from telling the story.

"What? You saw the person who did this?"

Michelle pointed towards the bay and said, "I figured, whoever did this, came and left by water. That's when I saw the guy in a kayak splashing and zigzagging across the bay. Judging by the way he used the paddle, he had never been in a kayak. You see, a kayak has a paddle with two cupped ends, and instead of digging it deep in the water, the way you would in a canoe, you just skim it on the surface with alternating strokes. If you don't, the kayak turns way too quick and you end up doing crazy zigzags." Michelle's eyes glassed over for a moment.

"I did tell you that already? Anyway, I was saying…" Michelle shook her head to clear the cobwebs.

"Oh yeah, I *borrowed* a skiff from the marina, and by the time I got it fired up, he was almost to the other side of the bay. I made it in time, to watch him, as he went into Senator Diaz' guesthouse. Did you know an outboard motor can't be hotwired like a car?" Michelle continued to ramble.

Rebecca's mouth formed a tight circle before she asked, "What the hell are you talking about? Michelle, you're rambling."

Bonn found Michelle's behavior bizarre as well. At the risk of having to listen to another grueling story, he said, "The Senator hasn't been seen since he tried to fake his own suicide. The house has been vacant, and your zigzagging kayaker paddled there? Did you get a good look at him?"

"Bonn, its Cap. I think…I can't be sure. No, it's him. I think. The guy in the kayak was Cap's size. Oh yeah, I forgot…he had a limp. Well, I guess I didn't forget, I just told you. If I remember correctly, Cap had a limp after you shot him in the foot. Ouch, I'll bet that hurt. Why did you shoot his foot?" Michelle sucked in a deep breath and continued with her story. "Anyway, he looked like he could barely walk when he went into the guest house. Do you know how many nerve endings are on the foot? I don't either, but I'll bet there's a lot"

Rebecca and Bonn looked at each other in disbelief without answering her off-the-wall questions.

Michelle gasped another lung full of air to keep from passing out. "So, I flagged down a passing pontoon boat and used their cell phone to call the Calvary and…" She stared into a vastness that only she could see and remained silent.

Rebecca's impatience was evident as she kept saying under her breath, "And, and…,"

Bonn asked, "Michelle, did you get him?"

"Get who?"

Rebecca took Michelle by the hand and led her into the break room. "I want to show you something."

As soon as they entered the room, Michelle averted her eyes from Rich and went straight to the calendar on the wall. "Why in the hell is that thing up there?" Without thinking about preserving evidence, she reached up to rip it down, and Rebecca grabbed her arm. The hateful glare coming from Michelle heightened their concern about her mental health.

"We think Cap put it up there. I believe he meant it to be a warning for you. Look at it closely."

Michelle leaned in and examined the black push pin. "Why would he leave me a message, and then shoot me? This doesn't make sense; maybe it wasn't Cap."

"What do you mean?"

"It looked like him…, I'm not positive. I was flying across the bay with the spray hitting me in the face, and I came out of the daze I was in, it looked like Cap. Something doesn't feel right about all of this; I can't say it was definitely him," Michelle said, and then stared aimlessly into space. Slowly, her eyes rolled back, and she dropped dead weight to the floor.

CHAPTER 45

The prints lifted from Mac's office came back as J.J. Diaz III, the son of Senator Julio Diaz II, and the grandson of Julio, the man who served with Cap in Vietnam. The ballistics results found Rich and Michelle were shot by different weapons. The fact there were two shooters wasn't released to the public. Officially, the police listed J.J. as *missing;* the FBI believed he and his father were in hiding together. The kidnapping theory was "highly unlikely", and only one of the many theories tossed around. El Diablo had already left for Mexico and J.J. ended up in the capable hands of his right-hand man. Carlos had J.J. bound, gagged, and unconscious until he received further instructions.

Even though the FBI rejected the kidnapping theory, there were those that knew better. The SWAT team found footprints and sand from the deck to the foyer, where they stopped. There, a small pool of water had collected on the tiled floor, with two other sets of shoe prints, but nothing that would give them a clue to his whereabouts.

The roadblocks were unsuccessful and did nothing but back up traffic in every direction. By the time the entire dragnet was in place, J.J. Diaz was laying unconscious on a beach towel, shirtless, and with his sunglasses on. To a passer-by, he looked like any other sun-worshiping tourist or beach bum enjoying the sun, sand, and surf.

While on his way to the private jet, for his flight back to the Florida Panhandle, Mac didn't use either phone that he brought with him. He watched the black limo disappear, and then stepped up the retractable stairs where he met an extremely large flight attendant who had a hand extended. Mac gave him the burner phone provided for him when he arrived in Cabo. After the attendant crushed it with his bare hands, he held his hand out again, and took Mac's personal cell phone then removed the battery.

"Please understand 'Amigo', tracking a phone is not new. I will return your battery, when we land."

The moment they landed in Destin, the "flight attendant" gave Mac: El Diablo's card, an envelope stuffed with money, and the battery he confiscated.

"Mr. Ramirez wants to return some things that belong to you."

Mac put the card in his wallet without looking on the back of it, and immediately called Susan. She made it to the airport in record time and found him standing outside of a hanger, and pretending to be a hitchhiker.

At first, Susan kept her hands on her hips and tapped her foot on the tarmac while shaking her head at the multi-million dollar jet.

"First-class commercial isn't good enough for you? I don't know why I was worried when you didn't call and let me know you were on your way back."

"I'm sorry. It's a long story, let's get out of here," Mac said.

After an extended make-out session in the front seat, they headed back towards her house and held hands, and she kept their conversation limited to small talk. Both of them had something they wanted to say, and just as Mac was about to speak, Susan turned her Mercedes down Hospital Drive instead of continuing to her house.

"What are we doing? Did you get called in?"

"No, I have a patient I need to check on. I was going to wait until we got back to our house to tell you, it's...how did you put it, *'A long story'*? Susan made her point and parked in her designated space, Mac took her subtle message in stride. After all, she did say, *"our* house".

"Susan, why would want to wait till we got home to tell me about a patient, then change your mind and bring me along with you? What is it..., did Cap come back?"

"It's Michelle, she took a bullet. What is it with 'Team Destin'? I've treated everyone of you."

"Damn, how bad is it? I've had a bad feeling ever since I called to warn her that Cap's probably on his way back to Destin."

"You warned *her*, and I didn't get a call to warn *me*?"

"The moment I thought he might be heading back here, I called Michelle and told her to contact you. Rich was supposed to shadow you at work, the house, and everywhere you went until I got back. I just assumed… the next thing I knew, I was on the jet and they took my cell phone from me until we landed. I worried about you the entire flight and prayed they would keep you safe until I got back. Are you going to tell me, Rich hasn't been watching over you?"

"Mac, Rich is dead. I'm sorry,"

Mac remained silent as he tried to process the news.

"I never received a call from either one of them. I know it's no consolation, but Michelle told me…your call came just in time, it saved her life. After your warning, she put on her vest right when she got to her office."

"What? Someone…shot her? Is she all right?"

"She has two broken ribs, a punctured lung, and fortunately, we stopped the internal bleeding. If she keeps improving, I'm going to release her in a couple days. Trying to keep her in the hospital is like trying to keep you or Bonn here."

During the short walk from Physician Parking to the hospital entrance, Mac spotted an undercover officer sitting in a wheelchair, another in an unmarked car, and noticed there were new security cameras on the building. When Mac saw the SWAT sniper on the roof, he clipped his badge on the front of his belt and let his hand brush against the holster on his hip.

Mac stopped when they arrived at Michelle's room and said, "I want to speak with the guards, I'll join you in a minute."

When Susan entered the room, Michelle wasn't in her bed; she sat on the visitor's chair, with one hand, gingerly held over her broken ribs. Susan knew, Michelle was leaving against the surgeon's advice; *her* advice.

"Where do you think you're going? I told you if you had another good night, I would release you in the morning. Besides, I have someone with me, who wants to see you."

"Doc, I've given my statement to so many people, there isn't anyone..."

Mac walked in her room and said, "Will you talk to a member of Team Destin?"

Michelle burst into tears as she got out of her chair to embrace him. "Mac...I wouldn't be alive if you hadn't called me and told me about Cap. I immediately put on my vest, and a minute later, I took two hits. I owe you one big guy."

While Michelle hugged Mac and wept, Susan placed crossed hands over her heart and bit her bottom lip.

Michelle backed away to collect her emotions and return to her role as Agent Milton.

"Doc, what I'm getting ready to tell Mac is classified at the highest level. It's definitely safer for you *not* to know what's going on but... since you are Team Destin's personal surgeon..., you're welcome to stay. Mac, what do you think?"

Mac jumped at the chance to give his personal and professional opinion.

"Susan is brilliant, and would make a great investigator. The day Cap's wife came into the ER, she displayed uncanny observation skills and based on what she found, concluded she might have been the victim of an attempted murder, she was right. As far as I'm concerned, you can speak freely around her."

"Susan, I want to make it clear, we are dealing with killers who place no value on human life. While you're dedicated to *saving* lives, there are animals in this world that *end* lives without giving it a second thought." Michelle retraced the events from the time she arrived at her office, to hot-wiring a boat, so she could chase down a kayak that went to Senator Diaz' house.

"You are lucky to be alive. I can't believe Cap killed Rich and you chased him in a stolen boat. He's trying to kill us one at a time."

"Mac, I don't think we're the targets. Cap didn't shoot Rich, someone just made it look that way…, and the calendar on the wall was an attempt at misdirection. Why would Cap shoot Rich with his signature shot and then shoot me twice in the chest? He wouldn't. The ballistics results confirmed what I suspected, the slugs that hit me, didn't come from the same gun that killed Rich…I haven't figured out exactly who did this, but I will," Michelle said.

Mac froze in place, as he tried to process what he just heard. Susan remained silent.

"He went there looking for something specific.., your office is trashed. Whoever destroyed your office, ended up at the computer, and he must have found what he was looking for, then removed the hard drive and destroyed it. It's possible I interrupted a burglary and the shooter never had the intention of killing anyone. Why else would he be in the offices so early?"

Susan and Michelle watched the wheels still turning in Mac's mind, while he thought about it, his fingers drummed increasingly faster on the armrest of his chair.

"Here comes the strange part, it appears someone was waiting for our shooter when he went inside the Senator's guest house, I wonder if he was setup by whoever helped him plan his escape. There were three sets of large footprints on the tiled floor. It looked like the man in the kayak walked in from the bayside door and fell to the floor; he had to be exhausted from paddling across the bay. The other prints were made by walking through the wet mess brought in by the shooter. We could see drag marks from where he was laying, to the front door. He may have been dead or incapacitated; there wasn't any sign of a struggle," Michelle said with confidence.

"Whoa, so your theory is, he drops in through the roof before sunrise, kills Rich with a forehead shot and puts up the calendar to make it appear to be Cap's work? Then, he escapes in a *kayak* to Diaz' house, where he's abducted by three men who are waiting for him? Why escape in a kayak, and why the senator's guest house?"

Mac asked. "Forgive me Michelle; I know you are one of the best investigators and profilers in the Agency, but that's quite a stretch."

"If you think that's far-fetched, there was something very interesting lying on the floor, a business card with the image of a devil embossed on it."

Mac instantly knew what happened. He reached into his back pocket and took out the directions to Cap's location given to him. "Did it look like this?"

"That's it! Where did you get that?" Michelle grabbed it, and then read the information written on it."

"El Diablo gave it to me." Mac waited to see if Michelle made the connection.

"Ramirez? *The* Ramirez, gave this to you? What are these? Coordinates? Is Pair-a-Dice the name of a boat?" Michelle asked.

"You're right, they're the coordinates to a beach house Senator Diaz owns in Belize, and that's where the 'Pair-a-Dice' is docked. Unfortunately, Cap was already gone, and I didn't know if he was on his way back to Florida or not. Michelle, that's why I called to warn you, and thank God, I called when I did."

"If Cap wasn't at the senator's house, why was Ramirez there? More importantly, are you his next target?"

"I'm not in danger from Mr. Ramirez. The man is totally devastated and grieving the loss of his nephew; he wants Cap and Senator Diaz as much as we do. I believe he's paying Diaz back, and now, his sights are set on Cap," Mac said.

"What did the senator do that was so bad; Mr. Ramirez wants to get even with him?" Michelle asked.

"He's convinced; Cap is working for Senator Diaz. He also believes, Cap killed his nephew and tried to cover it up. Here is where it gets complicated, the man you saw in the kayak was Senator Diaz' son, and the grandson of... Julio Diaz, Cap's old college buddy."

"Julio? Cap and Julio served together in Vietnam," Michelle said.

"I tried to figure out why J.J. would break into our offices, there's only one thing his dad could have wanted bad enough to risk his own son's life. Michelle, did you find anything else, besides the business card?" Mac asked.

"The only thing we found was El Diablo's card."

Susan broke her silence during the improvised briefing between Mac and Michelle.

"Mac, what about the envelope you gave me? Weren't there were classified documents with your report?"

"The originals were in a box of Michelle's calendars, but I made copies of everything and scanned the entire report into my computer. I'm sure, J.J. hacked through my files and when he found them, he destroyed my hard drive."

"Well, that means J.J. had the originals, and now they are in the possession of Mr. Ramirez."

"If Ramirez has them, he can electronically send your report to anyone he wants and taking down Diaz is the least of our concerns. There will be a lot of nervous people in Washington," Mac said.

Michelle grabbed Mac's arm and had a disconcerting look on her face. "You're right, the classified reports regarding the sabotage of the F-22 program were in there; we need to call Rebecca."

"I doubt someone like him is going to care about a report on the crash of one our jets. Although, if he figures it out, there will be some very wealthy and powerful people that he could blackmail. I don't think J.J. took the time to read any of the paperwork. The only person who would know exactly what J.J. had, would be my friend from south of the border. Susan, did you give the envelope to Rebecca?"

"No, Bonn appeared well enough to handle it, so I gave him the envelope with everything in it. What he did with it, and where it is now, is anyone's guess. I wonder if that's what Cap's mother was after when she tried to kill him in his room," Susan said.

Mac stiffened at the shock of hearing what Susan just said, "Cap's mother tried to kill Bonn? Michelle, did you know about this when I called you from Cabo?"

"I didn't tell you when you called because our conversation lasted only a few seconds. You said to be careful because Cap might already be here, then you told me you couldn't talk and hung up. Mac, I need to call Rebecca, I think she might be in danger."

Michelle called Rebbeca while Mac tried to reach Bonn; both left messages. Susan decided she was out of her expertise when she heard Mac say, "Bonn, this is *Flywater, Flywater! Tell Alex, Bewaken*"

"Mac, I think it's time for me to leave and I have a feeling it is for you too. Michelle please be careful and try not to do anything that might re-injure those ribs."

The moment the door closed, Michelle said to Mac, "There is one more thing I need to tell you; I also found something else at the scene, a line drawing of a Mayan or Aztec chief."

Mac shook his head in disbelief upon hearing the description of the Aztec Indian. "I need to call Mr. Ramirez and tell him. The Indian chief drawing you described is the symbol of the Mexican Familia Astecas; they're the enforcers for the Juarez Cartel and sworn enemies of Mr. Ramirez and his Sinaloa Cartel. I wonder if they also were also at the senator's place. I don't get it; the drawing of the Astecas logo could be a warning to Ramirez from the Juarez Cartel. Give me your hand; we need to get over to Bonn's, right now!"

CHAPTER 46

The desk of Fort Benning's Commander, was covered with various cardboard boxes, crammed with his personal belongings. The custom fabricated, metal boxes on the floor contained his "spoils of war". There were priceless Iraqi artifacts, dating back to the early Mesopotamia period. During operation Iraqi Freedom, General Fagan befriended corrupt government officials who had confiscated treasures from the palaces of the disposed President of Iraq, Saddam Hussein. In exchange for some of the most prized artifacts, General Fagan ignored his orders to destroy any weapons and supplies that might fall into enemy hands when the US troops pulled out.

The ancient pieces of pottery and sculptures he traded for brought more value to his financial portfolio than his retirement and savings combined. General Fagan's initial plan to market a couple of the rarest pieces, and then retire from the army on a tropical island was on hold. Initially, he didn't want to jeopardize his divorce settlement by increasing his wealth, and now, he feared he might me implicated in Ashleigh's death. The spoils of war would have to be sold for cash; he couldn't risk selling to reputable dealers or Rebecca would have been entitled to her share of the assets in the divorce. It was time to move everything to a secure location to avoid getting caught with stolen artifacts.

General Charles Fagan made the calculated decision to deal with the two remaining problems that could tie him to Ashleigh, Cap and the senator from Florida. Cap knew about his affair with Ashleigh, and

Senator Diaz was his connection with the defense contractor who tried to sabotage the Air Force's Raptor program. If either happened, his divorce would turn ugly, and he could face criminal charges.

Following Ashleigh's demise, he didn't hear from Rebecca and feared she already discovered his secrets.

When his cell phone rang, the screen identified the caller as *Bertelli's Pizza*, the most popular pizza parlor that is in the contacts list of most cell phones on base. On the general's phone, it wasn't Bertelli's phone number; the number belonged to the phone he used to talk with Senator Diaz. Concealing phone numbers by assigning bogus names was a trick he learned on the internet, and he used a throwaway phone to call Diaz, but he never expected to receive one from him.

Charles closed his office door and answered the call in an angry hushed tone. "I told you not to call me; you have been given your orders, the only contact between us is through the appropriate channels."

"Now Charles, is that anyway to talk to the person who can make your problems go away? I'm back…and sitting on the beach drinking a brew, I think you should come join me," Senator Diaz said.

"Don't ever call me 'Charles' again. Why can't you stay dead? What do you want?"

"I'll tell you what I want; I want you to bring me the balance of what you owe me."

"I don't owe you anything until you've delivered what we've agreed upon. My patience is running out. I'm going to hang up now and don't contact me again. Your control will let me know when the job is finished; you can deal with her."

"Listen to me, I'm not one of your soldiers, she's my handler, not my boss. I will be at the Okaloosa Island pier in one hour, bring my money and you'll get what you want from me. And Charles, make sure your tackle box is full."

Satisfied his demands were going to be met, Senator Diaz slam-dunked his cell phone into the flowered beach bag. Neither the General, nor the Senator, realized their conversation had been victim to one of the NSA's eavesdropping programs. Not only did someone hear and record their entire conversation, both of them were now blips on a large screen, tracking their every move.

Oblivious to any possible surveillance, and preoccupied with the prospect of his impending windfall, Senator Diaz danced a jig and laughed at thought of an army general stuffing a bag with bundles of money, his money. To ensure he stayed incognito for his rendezvous, the senator slathered on an excessive amount of suntan lotion, whitened his nose with zinc oxide, and adjusted the sunglasses he wore under a pork-pie hat. After pulling up the knee-high black socks he wore with his sandals, Diaz took a leisurely stroll through the mass of sunburned tourists towards the pier.

As he sat in the shade under the pier and waited for his big payday, the *Hail to the Chief* ringtone began playing on his cell phone. Only one person besides General Fagan had his number and he answered, "J.J., I've been waiting for your call. I could use some good news."

"Senor Diaz, your son isn't able to speak to you right now. He is about to join Armando, that is up to you," El Diablo said in fact.

"Armando? I don't know anyone named Armando. Who the hell is this, and why do you have my son's phone?"

"Armando is the young man that you and your friend Mr. Perkins killed. You remember Cap, don't you? If you want to see your son again, you will do as I say. I have in my possession, the information your son went to great lengths to get. I must say, after seeing it, I don't blame you for wanting to get your hands on it."

"I don't know what you're talking about; I didn't have anything to do with killing anyone. You didn't answer my question; who are you?" Diaz asked.

"I am the *devil*, and I'm talking about being in possession of information that proves you contracted Mr. Perkins to kill General Bonner, proof that General Fagan used his girlfriend to try and kill his ex-wife, so she wouldn't expose the cover-up of the crash of a very expensive jet. I have the name of the contractor you are protecting. Now, do you know what I'm talking about Mr. Diaz, or do I need to continue?"

"What do you want?"

"I want you to tell me where I can find Mr. Perkins."

"I don't know where he is, and I don't care about him or any documents."

"You said, *documents*, that's interesting, I never said anything about being in possession of any documents. I said, 'I have *information*.' Do you know what I'm talking about now?"

Senator Diaz remained silent while he tried to process the implications of Mac's report falling into the wrong hands.

"You have nothing to say? I'm talking about the report your son went to great lengths to get for you. Now, *I* own the...*documents*, but they are of no concern to me. However, I know they are quite valuable. The way Detective McCain so brilliantly pieced them together in his report will be very bad for many people. I'm sure there are others, besides your government that wants this information. By others, I mean the contractor whose billion dollar contracts are in jeopardy. The only thing you are protecting is their stock, it would fall to unacceptable levels, and they can't have that happen, can they? Are you listening to me Mr. Diaz? I can only imagine the financial rewards you could receive for returning Detective McCain's report, especially the original documents."

"If you are trying to extort money, don't talk to me, talk to them. You're forgetting something, I'm dead. I'm sure whoever '*they*' are, would want to talk to you personally, they would pay whatever you ask."

"I don't need their money and the last thing I want is for the people you're working for to interfere with me and my business. I have learned it's always better to have government officials on my side. So all you have to do is tell me where I can find Mr. Perkins. If you do as I say, I will spare your son's life and you will save your career. If you refuse my offer, you *and* your son will die."

"I want to see J.J., and bring the 'information'."

"Come down the beach, towards Destin, until you spot a bright red blanket and a sombrero. Your son is waiting for you. You have one minute."

The prospect of receiving additional money from the defense contractor as a reward for getting the documents, made his decision to reveal Cap's location, an easy one. But, he also wanted to save J.J. as well as himself. Already short on time for his meeting with General Fagan, Senator Diaz removed his black socks, sandals, and trotted down the beach, then ended up in a dead run to meet with "the devil".

CHAPTER 47

Rebecca moved into Bonn's house, and leased her condo at the Ft. Benning Recreation Center. The local property management company informed her that the condo had been leased to a disabled veteran. As a bonus, he paid the first six months of the lease, in advance.

Rebecca reflected on her new home and rekindled relationship until she saw the glassy, far away reflection in Bonn's eyes. This time, when the symptoms began, Rebecca remained calm. She had become accustomed to Bonn's maladies and never considered them a deal breaker in their relationship; she wanted to be with him forever. Whenever Rebecca spotted the first sign of an oncoming seizure or a headache coming on, she recited a mental checklist: "Blinds closed, candles lit, and lights out, check. Water, meds, and patience, check." To ensure as much peace and quiet as she could, both of their phones were on silent, and as a final precaution, she cracked open the front door, and hung a sign taken from Caesar's Palace. *Quiet please! High Roller Resting.*

"Thank you Darlin', I think we caught this one before it got bad. Why don't you take a little nap, and when you get up, we'll go see how Michelle is doing."

Bonn knew he avoided another bad episode and realized Rebecca had gone through her "checklist" routine, so *she* could get some rest. He tucked his service weapon between the cushions and wondered if there would be a time when they didn't need to be armed.

When Rebecca went to their bedroom, he spoke to their new pup, which wasn't new and had grown out of the puppy stage.

"Alex, if you're going to live at this house, you have to show me what you've learned, 'Bewalkin'."

After a short time stretched out on his couch, Alex jumped to all fours and growled Bonn sat straight up when he heard a barely perceptible, ticking and tapping of fingernails on his front door.

When Bonn gave the command to guard, Alex crouched at the door with bristled back hair; silent and ready. Alex's trainer conditioned him to bite, and never bark; he would silently wait to attack.

"Rebecca, are you expecting company?" Bonn called out. Even though he knew Cap wouldn't knock, he slid his hand between the cushions and wrapped his fingers around his classic Colt 1911.

"No, it might be Michelle. I just saw a couple of missed calls from her while we were napping; I had my phone on silent."

Bonn raised a slat from the blinds and said, "It's not Michelle, its Sienna. How did she know…?"

"I don't have a clue. Except for a courtesy visit at the hospital, I haven't talked to her. It must be important or she wouldn't be here, let her in," Rebecca shouted from the bedroom, and then slid out from beneath the covers.

Bonn tucked his gun in the waistband of his lower back and opened the door. Alex let out a half-hearted growl that Bonn stopped with the snap of his fingers.

"Agent Harris, what are you doing here? Is there a problem?"

"Is that how it is now, Agent Harris? Why are you so formal?"

"Sienna, you've never been the social type in all the years I've known you. That is, unless you've changed now that you're with the agency."

"Have it your way *General*. Where's Colonel Fagan?" She asked and never took her eyes off Alex.

"Don't worry about him; he won't bother you unless I give him the command. Colonel Fagan is taking a nap. If you have a message, I'll pass it on to her when she wakes up."

When Rebecca heard Sienna refer to Bonn by rank, she yawned loud enough to be heard, then exaggerated a waking-up stretch as she stepped into the room.

"Agent Harris, I thought I was dreaming when I heard your voice. You were the last person I expected to see today. What brings you to Destin?" Rebecca intentionally left out the fact that she hadn't told anyone in the Agency, including Sienna that she had moved from her condo into Bonn's house.

"I tried to call on my way from Tyndall and it went to voicemail. We need to talk."

Rebecca noticed Sienna brushed her hair to the side before she spoke and had already seen the only missed calls on her phone were from Michelle, but she played along. "I've had my phone off while we were sleeping, when did you call?"

"I'm not sure; it was probably when I left Panama City, possibly a half-hour ago. Who knows, maybe the message disappeared; I hear a lot of people have been having that problem lately," Sienna said and grinned.

Out of nowhere, Bonn pulled his Colt and aimed it at Sienna. "Keep your hands where I can see them. I can't wait to hear you try to explain your way out of here, even though it will be a waste of time."

"Alex, Heir...Bewalkin," Bonn said, and then pointed Alex toward Sienna.

Rebecca drew her weapon while Alex crouched by Bonn's side and bared his teeth. Sensing he had been called into duty by the tone of the Bonn's voice, Alex wasn't sure exactly what he was supposed to do, besides give another menacing growl and be prepared to attack. If the look on Sienna's face was any indication; he did so, convincingly.

"You can say goodbye to your career, *Bitch*," Sienna said to Rebecca and slowly raised her hands.

"So you are the one who sent me the text when Bonn was shot...BYE BYE BITCH. At first, I thought you might have been threatening to hurt my big brother Bob, his ID on my phone is **BBB**. I was briefed on…"

Sienna shifted her stance and said, "Your career is going to be over very soon."

"You think Rebecca's career is over? That's funny; it's *your* career that's over. You're showing your hand, literally. Tell me Sienna, who at Cyber Command gave you that software you've been using to send her those magic messages?"

"Bonn, what is it?" Rebecca asked.

"It…it is her right hand."

"Are you insane? What about my right hand?" Sienna asked.

"Of course, why didn't I see that? Agent Harris, how did you lose the nail for your pinky finger?"

Sienna held out her hand, as though she was inspecting her manicure. In the instant, it took for Bonn and Rebecca to divert their eyes to the finger missing the nail, Agent Harris kicked the Glock out of Rebecca's hand and pulled her own weapon.

The ensuing standoff between Agent Harris and Bonn halted when young Alex sprang from several feet away, and clamped down on Sienna's wrist. When Alex hit her arm, Sienna fired an errant shot and Bonn reacted by blowing a hole in her chest.

"No, no, no! Alex…," Rebecca screamed then fell to her knees cradling her motionless puppy.

Michelle and Mac burst onto the gruesome scene too late. Rebecca sobbed and shook uncontrollably as she knelt with bloodied hands, and coddled Alex's lifeless body in her arms. The sight of her ex-partner Sienna, lying in a pool of blood, confirmed Michelle's suspicions, the bullet passed through Alex on its way to Sienna's heart. Local law enforcement officers, federal agents, and suits from Homeland Security streamed into Bonn's driveway at breakneck speed with their sirens screaming. Commander Bentow ordered Security Forces to surround the property from the road to the water's edge, and a swarm of micro drones flew over their house with their cameras scanning the entire area.

CHAPTER 48

T he horizon reflected orange on the slick Gulf waters and mirrored the mood of Team Destin as they gathered on Bonn and Rebecca's deck. The private memorial service commemorating Alex's heroics, and accidental death, left Bonn devastated and choking back tears. There wasn't a dry eye as he gave the same eulogy he heard too many times in his military career.

"I am proud to have served with Alex. He gave his life to save a fellow soldier."

Every person attending the service understood the emotional analogy. Alex had been accepted into the Navy's canine training program where he earned a reputation as a fierce soldier, with an excellent nose, and intelligent beyond his age.

Tears slid down Bonn's face when he placed one of his Purple Hearts on the small pine casket, and then, in perfect military form, took a precise half step back and saluted. The bullet from Bonn's gun hit Alex midair, passed through his neck, and struck Sienna; both died instantly.

The silence on the deck was deafening. Until they heard the only canine member of Team Destin, whine. Lexi walked up to a dejected Bonn, who sat with his elbows on his knees, and nudged her head under his arm. She rested her muzzle on his leg and appeared to share his pain as her woeful eyes looked up to him.

"If Lexi could talk, she would tell you her boy did what he had to do, and he did it for you." Mac's compassionate words echoed and agreed upon by everyone.

Lexi gave Bonn exactly what he needed to snap out of the funk consuming him. He lit a cigar, stretched his legs out, and blew a stream of smoke from his 'Cuban' to the heavens, then said, "Cap's been working for Sienna since the beginning; Senator Diaz is nothing but a lackey. As far as J.J. is concerned, Sienna must have had something important on the senator for J.J. to give away his software."

Michelle smiled when she heard Bonn's take on Cap and said, "You're absolutely right, Cap worked for Agent Harris *and* Senator Diaz. She's brilliant and didn't let J.J. or his father know they were both working for her. Once she made the senator aware of the report and where to find it, she let *him* ask his son for help, J.J. couldn't refuse his father."

"There was another component of the software program that J.J. didn't disclose to anyone except her. Whenever someone answered a call or read a text from her, she tracked them. Every single call, conversation, text, and voicemail sent or received on our phones was recorded on a database that could be heard in real-time too," Michelle said.

Bonn raised his hand to speak. "I remember receiving one of those messages the morning I was shot and didn't have a clue what it meant. The message, *Bye Bye Flywater*, stayed on my phone only long enough for me to read, and then, it disappeared one letter at a time. She's been locked-in on my phone, since the morning Cap shot me."

"J.J. belonged to a group of genius IT Geeks, and they communicated in one of their secret 'Dark web' chat rooms. I'm not sure why, but I have a feeling Sienna sent me a warning message. Maybe, Sienna knew Cap was going to take a fellow agent out, and regretted it. Hell, I didn't even remember getting it," Michelle said. Bonn sensed there was something she wasn't disclosing.

"She sent me one too," Rebecca said. "When I was driving like a maniac on the way to the hospital to see Bonn, she let me know he belonged to *her*, and…I shouldn't be *sad*, but I didn't know who sent it. Do you remember when you told me you dated an agent that worked with the Agency's Special Activities Division and made the stupid joke about her being SAD? I finally figured out what the word in the text meant."

Michelle held up her hand, palm facing out, as a sign to wait before anyone commented. "Guess what, Agent Harris also sent *me* a message the morning Rich was…murdered."

"Why didn't you tell us?" Bonn asked.

"That's because, I didn't see it until days later at the hospital. I went through all of the messages and calls I missed, and I saw, 1 *Unread Message AIC*, I knew immediately it was Agent Harris, it took me a second to realize the text was sent the morning of the break-in; she *never* sends text messages," Michelle said with a grin.

"I thought Mac was the only person who still doesn't know how to send one without help," Bonn said.

Mac pretended he didn't hear Bonn's remark and asked, "What's a text?"

"Okay boys; let's get back to Sienna's composing and sending electronic words between mobile, fixed, or portable devices over a phone network." Michelle trumped the "boys" and shut them down.

"You go girl, I'm impressed." Rebecca winked at Michelle who gave her a quick nod then continued.

"Here's the thing, the text message Sienna sent me didn't make sense. *Give me a call?* Why would she tell me to call her, when she could have just called me? Michelle asked. "And why didn't it go away like all of the other ones? So, I used my other phone to take a Vine video to have proof that it existed."

Bonn and Mac looked at each other then said, "Vine video."

"It's a six-second, looping video clip," Michelle deadpanned her answer and brought a little levity to what had been an exhaustive few days. She was convinced her explanation confused them even more and made it funnier.

"Anyway, no sooner had I snapped the Vine, the message disappeared all at once, instead of one letter at a time," Michelle said and waited to see if anyone understood the significance.

"Obviously, there's a glitch in J.J.'s software. We have to figure out how to use it to our advantage," Bonn said.

"I didn't delete it, I turned it over to our tech guys, and guess what... the glitch is their doing, we're already using it to our benefit," Michelle said, and held out her other phone for everyone to see the Vine video she took of the message.

"Don't forget how tech savvy I am, how about a little explanation on how the techies were able to do anything from a video?" Mac asked.

"Mac, the video was only the confirmation that their improvements on J.J.'s software were actually working. When Agent Harris..., Sienna, recruited Senator Diaz' son, she had access to the program. It was taken from Sienna and modified; she stole it for the agency without knowing it." The powers that be at Quantico, realized our country's enemies would hacking the program as soon as they heard about it," Michelle said without being condescending.

"Although his software was originally developed for cell phones, J.J. crossed platforms for it to be used by any computer as well. So, they added a viral worm that eats away at any computer or device that uses the software. Now, all we need is the phone's number to turn on its recorder or camera and take complete control of every function." Michelle was unable to hide the pride she had in her former employers.

"By the way, strictly as a precaution, I have little gift for each of you," Rebecca said as she opened up her designer backpack, and then handed everyone a new 'burner' cell phone.

"We don't know who else had J.J.'s original software program, until we find out; I believe all of the communication between us needs to be on a 'burner' phone that hasn't been corrupted. We only call and text each other with these phones. Each phone is going to have an identity that is a series of dots. Bonn, your cell will be six dots, Rebecca you have seven, Mac, eight. A call from me will show up as six asterisks."

Again, Mac's inexperience with the cyber world had him questioning the specifics of how his caller ID will show a series of dots.

"On my phone, if the person calling is in my contacts, their name comes up, if they're not, they are either UNKNOWN or PRIVATE," Mac said.

"One of the advantages of working for the Agency is having access to the latest technology. These phones are programmed to trick the phones you're calling into interpreting the phone's number as dots and asterisks, and to display them on Caller ID," Michelle said.

While Michelle enlightened her friends in Team Destin, she made sure to give them the opportunity to ask questions or give their opinions. They all had a new respect for her. Each of them nodded approvingly, their questions, answered.

"That's how Sienna knew Mac and I were on the way to warn you about her. She must have had your house under cyber surveillance for her to show up unannounced that fast. She intended to kill both of you before we got there. Thanks to poor Alex, she failed." Michelle instantly regretted her comment about Alex and was relieved when Bonn broke the awkward pause in the conversation.

"Michelle, bringing up Alex's name isn't taboo. Thanks to our brave boy, that crazy bitch won't hurt anyone else."

Rebecca took a deep breath after hearing Alex's name, then cleared her throat, and cleared up any possible confusion.

"Sienna had two phones, her agency-issued phone, which she couldn't risk being tracked by the NSA, and another one, a throw-away with the app J.J. developed. When she sent the text on her work phone, she hoped you would answer and tell her about a robbery. That would have been the confirmation that young Diaz had finished the job, and by texting you on her work phone, she could prove she wasn't there if anyone looked into her cell records. When you didn't answer, I think she freaked."

"So, when Michelle didn't call Sienna back, she went to our offices to make sure J.J. didn't need any help," Mac said.

"The parking lot's security cameras revealed a black government-issued Tahoe with nonexistent tags, making a couple of passes on the road in front of the building. She must have seen my Hummer and parked somewhere out of sight. Plus, there's video of a person wearing a hooded sweatshirt and sunglasses going into the offices shortly after I arrived. I have to believe that person to be Sienna, and when she came in and found Rich, she saw the opportunity to make it look like Cap shot him. Hanging the calendar on the wall with the push pin on my forehead had to be a misdirection to protect J.J.'s involvement."

"So, do you think Sienna shot Rich? I have a hard time believing J.J. could make a shot like the one that hit Rich?" Bonn and Rebecca nodded in agreement with Mac's assessment.

"I agree. Agent Harris is…was, trained in weapons and it would make more sense for the one in Rich's forehead to have come from her. The coroner estimates the shot came from a distance of no more than 10-feet, the exact distance from the door to the coffeemaker. As close as that seems, we all know how much skill it would take to make that shot, and it would have been a lucky one for J.J. to make, but that's exactly what happened. Rich was shot with a small, twenty-two handgun. The bullets recovered from my vest, came from a forty-five, which happens to be Agent Harris's favorite service weapon. There were two shooters, she didn't kill Rich," Michelle said.

"Sienna pulled her weapon before I shot…her," Bonn said, and then remembered he also hit Alex, so did everyone else.

"She had a problem; I don't think she knew what to do when one of her fake fingernails had come off. It's the only thing placing her at the crime scene; she had to decide whether or not to go back in and try to find it. Sienna wasn't too worried, if anyone found the nail, there wouldn't be any reason to think it belonged to her. When you pointed it out, Sienna knew, her time had come, and the rest is history." Michelle and Rebecca subconsciously looked at their own nails.

"Sienna's problem got worse. The rear door has a push bar latch that only works from the inside, which means, she would have to go around and come in through the front door to find her pinky nail. She couldn't take the risk being seen, so she left it, and hoped it wouldn't be seen as possible clue if it was found. Hell, we thought it was blood when we saw it on the floor. I never would have given it a second thought if I hadn't seen she was missing one," Bonn said.

"Well, we all agree, Sienna was brilliant and had an evil genius persona that controlled quite a few people. Does anyone else see the irony, if El Diablo had a role in bringing her down?" Bonn didn't really expect an answer.

"Sienna manipulated J.J., as well as his father, but I don't think she knew anything about Rebecca's ex-husband and his efforts to have Ashleigh eliminate her. There is one only one person who figured out what Sienna was doing, your old friend, Cap. If one of us didn't eliminate him from her plan, she would have tried to kill him herself, and do it 'in the line of duty'. I don't think she counted on Diaz working with your friend as much as he did," Michelle said.

"Why does everyone keep calling Cap, 'my old friend'? I met him in college. Back then, all I wanted to do was change the political system, Cap was already a criminal."

"Point taken, he's not anyone's friend. Agent Harris's plan began before Senator Diaz gave him the contract to kill you. Rebecca, that's where your husband…ex-husband, comes into the picture. If Sienna could figure out a way for Cap to eliminate Bonn *and* you, it would be the solution to both her problems. I believe her interest in paying you back for stealing Bonn from her affected her judgment. She didn't care about any sabotage by a Defense Contractor until she saw a way to blackmail General Fagan into do her dirty work."

"But, Charles was offered the job with the contractor before I received my orders. When I told him I had an assignment that would take me to Eglin, I didn't tell him about my mission," Rebecca said.

Michelle anticipated the timeline questions and said, "Rebecca, he knew where you were headed before you received your orders. Actually, they made the decision to send you, months in advance. Agent Harris promised to help 'Charles' get a high paying, high profile, post-retirement job with the contractor, but not if his wife was investigating the F-22's problems. You would be a conflict of interest, and they would most likely rescind their offer, that's where Ashleigh became a player in *his* plan. General Fagan…, Charles, had to convince Cap, to go along with Senator Diaz' request, before he brought in Agent Harris. You see, Cap didn't have any experience with female handlers or officers, taking orders from someone like Sienna, had to stick in his craw."

"I don't think Cap knew he was being played at the time, I guarantee he does now. When he finds out Charles worked with Sienna *and* Senator Diaz, he'll want revenge. I don't want Charles to, but his retirement was supposed to be from work, not from life," Rebecca said.

CHAPTER 49

In the middle of Team Destin's briefing by Michelle, Mac said, "I believe I know who can help us find Cap." then excused himself to get something from his car.

Team Destin looked at each other, and were speculating on who Mac thought could deliver Cap, when he walked back into Bonn's house holding up the missing Manila envelope. He lifted the flap, reached in, and retrieved a card with an embossed image of the devil on one side, and a personal handwritten message, followed by string of letters, numbers, and coordinates on the other. Before anyone could comment, Mac opened his other hand and revealed another missing component, his lost flash drive.

"El Diablo gave it to you?" Bonn asked.

Mac confirmed Bonn's deduction with an almost imperceptible nod and handed him the card. Rebecca, Michelle, and Susan huddled behind him as he read aloud:

> Mr. McCain,
> Justice always finds the way to the cowards of the world. They cannot hide. Do what is right for my Armando, so he may rest in peace.
>
> 86.118565/30439355-CAP
>
> 30.4894N/86.5422W 2RAPTOR2/Dark Web

"Mac, do you want to tell us what this means?" Bonn asked.

"The first coordinates were for an old fish camp that has been abandoned for decades, and had a dilapidated cabin hidden in the woods. The camp sat in the back of a slough off the Choctawhatchee Bay, and the only way to get to it was by boat. When we finally got there, we were prepared, for a fight to the death with Cap. Instead of finding *him* in the cabin, we found Senator Diaz and his son J.J., duct taped to chairs, with a bullet hole in the back of their heads. The envelope and flash drive were sitting on J.J.'s lap."

"Thanks to Mr. Ramirez, we at the agency have been very busy with the information in Mac's envelope and on his hard drive. We have scoured Mac's report. It is a masterpiece of detective work, and I have turned it over to the Attorney General. Our data analysts uncovered a one-of-a-kind code that J.J. had hidden behind a firewall that we normally would never have seen." Michelle said and took a deep breath before continuing.

"2RAPTOR2/Dark Web on El Diablo's card turned out to be J.J.'s password to enter an exclusive Dark Web chat room filled with some of the world's most brilliant hackers. By posing to be J.J., we were able to gain access to the room's 'vault' and identify the hackers who wrote the program used to sabotage the Raptor. It appears J.J.'s software was nothing more than misdirection. The information he and his partners had on the contractor was used in a blackmail scheme worth millions." Michelle let what she revealed sink in before continuing.

"The second coordinates, led to a heavily guarded building at Eglin that housed the mainframe computer of the defense contractor that lost the initial bid on the Raptor. The contractor used a program, designed by J.J.'s group, to corrupt the jet's core software with a sophisticated worm that made surgical attacks on the Raptor's system controls.

The virus grew exponentially as the aircrafts own computer system trained its pilots on the maneuvers required to stabilize the plane after a stall. Over time, as each pilot learned and practiced the stall maneuvers, the virus made the same sequential tactics less effective on future attempts. Once the worm fully embedded, none of the techniques previously used for the stalls were effective and the engines would shut down. They hoped the unexplained crashes would lead to the scraping of the Raptor in favor of *their* replacement, the F-35. The contractor, North American Aeronautics, wanted to claim their share of an order that would be worth a trillion dollars over 50 years. Even though I left the Agency, I'm still proud of their work."

"Michelle, there's a problem with the information they uncovered. The White House may have known about the virus and the NAA's role before Congress voted on the funding for the Raptor," Bonn said with a confidence that told both Rebecca and Mac, their friend was back, and ready to get back to work.

FULL CIRCLE

Overhead, flying at 30,000 feet, a brand new Gulfstream G450 banked hard over the Gulf on its way to El Paso, Texas. This time, the luxury jet carried the new manager of Gonzalez Landscaping, previously owned by the late Armando Gonzalez-Ramirez. His newest jet came to him as a gift from a Chinese tech mogul who wanted to show his appreciation for the 'apps' taken from J.J. Diaz after his abduction. The United States' tech experts considered the **BYE BYE** software nothing but a hybrid program, and not worth the price tag. The Chinese wanted the technology J.J. developed and used to corrupt the F-22 computers. Consequently, a bidding war ensued on the Dark Web.

The real winner was Armando Ramirez, who kept the secret tracking and communication component of the program to himself, and made calls to every rival Cartel boss in Mexico. When El Diablo heard about the Aztecas gang leaving their calling card on J.J.'s body, he realized the Juarez Cartel, not Cap, was responsible for his nephew's death. Although Cap was the first person he wanted to call, there was someone else who wanted to activate Cap's phone and its camera, even more than El Diablo, his passenger. Fortunately for "El Diablo", the SIM card and software in Cap's fancy phone was the mother of the program and untouched any Agency worm or virus.

Paula was eighty pounds lighter, stylishly dressed in a black cocktail dress that matched her new hair color, and for the first time in her life, beautiful. After recovering from her stroke, she met with the Sinaloa Cartel's finest surgeons who performed gastric bypass surgery, liposuction, and laser surgery on her excess skin.

Armando Ramirez tapped his bottle of Corona beer against her Waterford-crystal glass, filled with Diet Coke, and made a toast:

"You can take the girl out of the country, but you can't take the country out of the girl."

"Armando used to tell me he *loved* the 'country' in me." Paula could feel herself blushing and held her ice-cold glass against her neck.

"Ms. Paula, that wasn't the only thing he loved about you, and if Armando was here right now, he would ask for your hand," he said, and then handed her a cell phone.

Paula admired the rhinestone-covered cell phone, especially the pink diamonds that form the letter 'P'.

"This is the most beautiful phone I've ever seen. Thank you. Who'd thought a '*Mexicun*' like you; would help a '*Merican*' like me?"

"When we land, do us both a favor and send your husband... ex-husband, one of those special text messages. Don't worry; he has no way of knowing where you are right now, and after he reads your message, it will disappear without a trace. The man who built this phone made sure that it couldn't be tracked. Mr. Perkins number is the only number in your contacts list, but I left some photos, and all the social media apps. Once you have settled in your new life, I will give you a number that you can use to speak with me. This will be the only phone that you can use to reach me."

While looking through the photo album on J.J.'s old phone, Paula's hands started shaking. "I think I'll send him a picture I found, it's one of Carl with a buddy of his when they were in Vietnam. It'll drive him crazy."

"He will be even more loco, if he thinks General Bonner is sending it, and you will be able to see his reaction. Let me show you how."

After sharing a laugh, he took Ms. Paula hand in his, and said, "I'm sorry for the loss of your sister Sienna. I want you to know, she loved you. As you know, what she gave me is extremely valuable to me, and my business. I am able to know what my enemies have planned with a single call. I want you to know, even if your protection wasn't part of my deal with Sienna, I would have helped you. Armando told me how kind you were to him and his men from the first day he met you. He is looking down from heaven and smiling."

"Mr. Diablo, Armando was the sweetest and kindest man I've ever met. I miss him every day," Paula said, and a single tear matched the one trickling down the cheek of Mexico's most-feared drug lord.

The view from the condo at the Fort Benning Recreation Center in Destin was conducive to healing. Unfortunately, for Rebecca, the veteran renting her property would only heal physically. The new tenant, known as "Carl, Just Carl", squeezed a rubber strength ball. And, in his own twisted way, found pleasure with every twinge of pain. His mood changed the moment his cell phone chimed. *new message, M.D. Bonner.*

Printed in the United States
By Bookmasters